"It is my greatest wish, that as time goes by, the world will eventually believe that preventing war is of the greatest importance. If that day finally arrives then through cooperation and collaboration I believe we can reach out into space, finding new homes and colonize."

Signed by
Omar
Guardian for Azorka in the year 8,312 BC

Adventure *in* Adventure

AZORKA
IMMORTAL

PART II

CORRIE GILMOUR

BLUEPRINT PRESS INTERNATIONALE

ISBN
978-1-961117-57-0 (Paperback)
978-1-961117-58-7 (eBook)
978-1-961117-56-3 (Hardcover)

Table of Contents

CHAPTER ONE

March 3rd 1688
Cap Francois, Hispaniola

Sam woke up to squabbling seagulls flying overhead. He rolled out of bed, his five foot five frame landing squarely on the soles of his black buccaneer boots which he still had on. Tucked into these rolled up clod-hoppers, as Sam called them, were extremely itchy canvas pants dyed a dark brown and complimented with a wide black sash which wrapped around Sam's waist and pot belly. He rubbed perspiration from his bald crown as he walked over to the Captain's cabin window, drew back the dark drape and pushed open the window: A warm sun in the late morning was showcasing a picture perfect bright blue paradise. The palm trees swayed in the briny breeze and the beach sparkled like gold one hundred yards from where Sam's boatswain dropped anchor.

A shout coming from Leif's ship interrupted the morning silence.

"Hello! Phillip, attach your safety line while you're working up there." The cautious first mate shouted.

Leif's ship, only twenty yards away faced out to sea and Sam walked over to the opposite cabin window and flung it open, at the same time reaching down to a nearby table where his telescope rested. He put the instrument to his eye fully extended and was greeted by the wooden lion he had carved for Leif's ship. Sam raised the glass to the upper deck and sure enough his gruff looking partner in this mission was just exiting his cabin and stretching in the late morning sun. Leif's mule shaped face was always unshaven and his large gentle looking eyes always belying the scoundrel beneath. His baggy white shirt blowing in the breeze had the stains of last night's celebratory rum which he had borrowed from the Wizard. Sam checked his own white shirt and was relieved to see it free from stains. So he continued watching the morning unfold on his partner's ship, as Leif dragged his almost six foot tall and protesting body further along the upper deck. He looked up at Phillip, the ship's rigger, on the fore top sail as he took orders from the first mate below.

"Hello up there Phillip!" Randeep called out. "We'll need the main sail and main top sail done as well. Just loosen up the bindings enough that we can pull the sails free at moments notice."

Leif descended to the main deck and disappeared from Sam's view. His men, like Sam's, had received their written orders that were delivered to the quartermasters of both ships late last night. The orders instructed the men to be ready for a quick departure after this evening's mission.

Sam left his cabin and walked out onto the upper deck. He looked about the ship for his quartermaster and found him below on the main deck.

"Helmut I need a few moments of your time to discuss tonight's mission." He called down to the main deck where his quartermaster was inspecting the shroud for the main mast to be sure it was taut.

"I'll join you shortly Captain. I just have to check the other side." Helmut replied.

Sam walked back a couple yards and took a seat on a built-in bench for the starboard side of the upper deck and looked ashore at the fieldstone and wooden Tavern where they had received their intel for tonight's mission. Leif had an excellent command of the French language which granted them acceptance with the patrons of this popular Tavern. They were able to find quickly the person who could provide the information they sought.

Sam thought this afternoon would be a perfect time to make his log entry for the Wizard. The men would be busy completing their chores and he'd have the time. But first he would organize those men going to shore tonight. He had selected certain men from the crew according to their abilities and knowledge as he had yesterday for the visit to the Tavern.

Helmut was one of the four he had selected and soon the clicking of his boots on the deck announced his arrival. He was about twenty-five years of age, six foot two, and one hundred eighty pounds of trim muscle. Helmut was intelligent and one of the best quartermasters Sam has ever had.

"Sorry I took so long Captain." He said in his deep voice.

"Helmut, I want you to know I appreciate your diligence, as I'm sure every member of this crew does. I've called you to confirm my orders reached you last night and....well it looks like you've completed some of those orders." Sam paused.

"Yes sir! All those orders have been double checked by the first mate. I've notified the men that four of them will be selected for tonight's mission and those men will set their lasers on "stun" and the men remaining behind are to have their lasers set on max or "vaporize" which is what we'll do to the ships or boats of attacking pirates should we encounter that challenge." Helmut finished.

He reached into the hidden pocket of his sash and withdrew his flesh colored laser pistol which was so small that it disappeared into the palm of his hand. The laser pistol was "L" shaped with a retractable trigger built into the handle. It had a short barrel but was accurate, and could hit a target five hundred yards away.

"Which setting should I have on for tonight Captain?" Helmut brushed a lock of his blonde hair back revealing the inquiring expression in those blue eyes that Sam had seen so often. He was always anxious for life threatening adventure and action as though it was a recreation.

Sam smiled and said, "I'll have you set that on stun. Helmut, I need you with me tonight. I also wanted to see if you agreed with my selection for the other three men. You know the weakness and the strength of the crew members and I value your opinion."

"Thank you. I appreciate your confidence sir." Helmut replied.

"But first I'll review the plan for the ships while were ashore tonight. I want to leave Leif's ship with five men on and five men resting. The five men on lookout will cover sea side and our three men aboard this ship will cover their starboard side which is a significant blind spot advantageous for pirates. Tortuga Island hosts some of the most dangerous pirates in the Caribbean and like us they sail in brigantine vessel which is able to escape larger ships in shallow water ways. But unlike us they don't have laser pistols or laser cannon. They don't have a backup propulsion system secretly concealed in the stern of their ship. If a pirate ship pulls alongside Leif's ship while we're ashore, our men have been instructed to laser the pirate's cannons which will vaporize this firepower before they can sink his ship. If the pirates persist, by rowing over to board the ship or by sailing alongside to board the ship, our men will vaporize the bow of the vessel causing it to sink which will soak the pirates gun powder and whatever is already loaded in their muskets. Of course every effort will be made to spare the pirates." Sam finished.

"Would you have any questions regarding the plan for the ships?" Sam asked.

"No sir I don't have any questions. This does sound like the best plan and distribution of our men for the security of the ships." Helmut replied.

Sam nodded his head. He was satisfied that this was the best plan. Helmut's experience supervising covert operations while the Captain was absent in the past, made his opinions valid in Sam's mind.

"Now before I discuss our plan with all four of you, I want to get your opinion, so speak freely. I am selecting our "cooper", Chuck because he is burly enough to replenish our water supply, and remain as a rear-guard close to town. He'll assemble three barrels, fill them with fresh water from the Tavern's well. Chuck will roll them close to our boat, tie rope around them, and bind them securely to a raft of his own construction. If we have not returned by that time he will move two hundred yards closer to the jungle and wait. My next choice is our "rigger" Anthony. He is tall and comfortable with heights so it would be an advantage to have him staged as a sniper in a tree. His dark hair and Mediterranean dark skin will help conceal him. Chuck's dark beard and hair will do the same but his face is fair skinned so he will have to mud-up before we leave tonight. That goes double for my next choice which is our red haired and freckled doctor. Mkenzie is strong and young enough to handle the mission and wise enough to save a life in case we run into trouble." Sam finished.

Helmut thought about Sam's choices and he only had one suggestion.

"Captain, I think you've made excellent choices. I would have Mkenzie consider a dye as a more reliable way to cover his white skin. Otherwise I find your selection excellent. With your permission I will go and collect your candidates for the briefing." Helmut offered.

"Thank you Helmut. I would like you all to rest in the afternoon after the briefing. Tell the first mate to complete any of those tasks left to do by those men." Sam said.

Helmut left and in five minutes he rounded up the other three men. The briefing went smoothly even the education concerning the strange natives they would be up against tonight. The meeting concluded and the men left to catch some rest before the night time mission. Sam's freedom had arrived and he returned to his cabin to catch up yesterday's log entry.

March 2nd 1688
Entered March 3rd 1688
Captain Sam

We dropped anchor one hundred yards from shore at a sparkling beach in Cap Francois in the French colony of Saint Domingue on the north coast of Hispaniola Island. The indigenous Tanio called this island Haiti which in their ancient language translated into the land of high mountains. Hispaniola island was originally established by Spain in 1492 and at the time rumors of this island being rich in gold proved false. Years went by until maintaining Spain's declining empire was starting to deplete its resources. By 1659 the French had established themselves on the western portion of Hispaniola and their first permanent settlement was on Tortuga island where the buccaneers lived. French colonist had also settled the north coast of Hispaniola and in 1670 Bertrand d'Ogeron became the first French Governor of western Hispaniola. Cap Francois served as the capital of the French colony of Saint Domingue and by 1685 this settlement had become home for the French citizens leaving France and the campaigns of King Louis XIV.

Captain Leif suggested we go ashore that afternoon with four other crew members fluent in the French language. We should seek our information from the residents who would be enjoying a drink after the day's hard work. I was beginning to understand that Leif's judgement can sometimes be clouded. His estimation of three days sailing time to Hispaniola was way off. It was close to ten days, albeit ten perfect sailing days, before we arrived. But on this point I agreed that we should be departing quickly from an area infested with pirates. We did need information as soon as possible and the local Tavern provided us with a fortune of information from the loose lips of Pierre, a middle aged regular. He was seated at the back of the room and was relating, in a loud voice, how his sensibilities had been offended by a late night activity deep in the jungle one mile from the Tavern. Leif nudged me when we overheard Pierre's rantings.

The obese Pierre was leaning back in his chair, his tricorne hat placed on the table in front of him. Spittle flew wildly about through his black and grey beard as he barked at the other patrons in the Tavern about witchcraft and warning of the danger from late night excursions into the jungle. Last night he was lost, and had wandered into the jungle by mistake. He had stumbled into Voodoo worshippers. They were dancing around a fire while their King held up a crystal ball. He saw this spectacle about twenty yards ahead of him. Then he heard screaming and branches breaking. Someone was fleeing. Would the victim escape or die at the hands of those in pursuit? Another branch broke and that's when he heard the fatal shriek, which was suddenly cut off. The hunters had caught their prey. Pierre was still frozen in place until he heard the deep and mysterious chanting of natives who seemed to be creeping closer. He turned and ran tripping over rocks and branches as he went. He arrived back to the safety of his room in the upper floor of this fieldstone and wooden Tavern.

The patrons in the Tavern enjoyed a good jug of rum and a good story but they weren't overly enthusiastic with Pierre's experience. Some of the patrons accused him of imagining the experience and others said he was making up the story to be entertaining. The second suggestion caused the patrons of the Tavern to roar with laughter.

However, Leif sat down beside Pierre and pointed towards a free bamboo crafted chair I could use to join them. Introductions were made and Leif immediately launched into his own story. He was looking for his missing nephew who had an interest in the customs of the local natives. Could he give us an idea as to where he thought this chanting occurred in the jungle? Pierre did and we thanked him while getting up and leaving the Tavern for our ships. We walked back down to the beach, got in our small boat and our crewman took their place at the oars. It was a quiet evening and we made our way across the still water to Leif's ship where we would formulate a plan for the next night's excursion into the jungle. Leif had said that good luck has already struck twice. Monsieur Lobau's suggestion we start our search at Cap Francois and Pierre who has pointed us in the direction of the jungle natives. Pierre had seen the top of the crystal skull that night and mistook it for a crystal ball. The thief would have given the crystal skull to the voodoo worshippers knowing they would never sell it or give it up. The voodoo King would guard the crystal skull believing it would give him power and be able to contact the deities the tribe worshipped.

We made our plan in the comfort of Leif's ship that night and celebrated our good fortunes until four in the morning with a few drinks of rum which Leif had managed to squirrel away from the beginning of our journey. Most likely he borrowed this rum from the Wizard who may not be aware of it missing. Our quest for the crystal skull would begin tonight at sunset.

(Log Entry complete)

***

A dark blue ocean gave way to sparkling streaks of red and gold as a blood red sun spilled its treasure over the distant horizon. A long beaked dolphin broke the still surface giving a shrill greeting to Sam and Leif. Its call echoed in the small cove. Soon a spotted dolphin joined the disappointed orator who had decided this party of six were unsociable and both dived for the depths below. Four crewmen, specially selected for this mission, used all their strength for every pull on the oar. Sam looked on impressed with their effort while Leif looked behind at the Empire's ship, its hazel color made invisible by the evening shadows. However the lion's head on Leif's ship, anchored twenty yards apart from the Empire's ship, had managed to catch the last of the setting sun. Its luminous countenance looked across at the party of six like a sentinel and Leif imagined it was wishing them more luck for the night's mission.

Sam looked ahead and spotted a heavy growth of ferns between two melocactus trees. The wind picked up a little and the swaying trees seemed to be nodding their approval.

"Men, we're about fifty yards from shore. I need you to land us about thirty degrees to my right between the two cactus trees where we can conceal this boat in the undergrowth." Sam whispered.

"Aye aye, sir." The four crewmen whispered in unison.

They reached shore and all six men grabbed their sides of the boat and practically ran it into a heavy growth of ferns that would conceal it. Just above their heads a palm crow and white necked crow flew out of the trees calling out angrily for the disturbance.

"This looks like the path mentioned by Pierre." Leif spoke quietly. "Talk about ridiculous luck."

"If my French is as good as yours Leif, a marker for the property will be up ahead by about two hundred yards at which point it's only another hundred yards to the jungle entrance." Sam whispered.

"That's what Pierre said alright but we have a stealthy half mile hike into the jungle to be where he was when he heard the chanting." Leif returned.

Leif was right about being stealthy. It was a must for the mission to be successful. Sam had arranged for footwear that would be suitable for the jungle so that approaching a target could be done with the least amount of noise. Sam had selected leather moccasins as the least likely footwear to cause a branch to crack.

Sam was also confident about their self defense. There were five laser pistols between them. He had one because the final approach would be Leif and himself. The four crewmen had laser pistols and three of them would remain hidden in the jungle. Should a chase ensue and Sam gives the signal, the other crewmen will laser the angry natives. Sam had told his men to do so out of Leif's "eyeshot". All lasers were set on low so that no one got killed. The natives would be unconscious for two hours and those who got away would be traumatized enough by witnessing what took place that further pursuit of these thieves would not be considered. Leif would be too busy running to notice the take down by laser and would chalk up his successful escape to luck anyways. The laser pistols that fit into the palm of your hand were silent but shot a visible ray that was purple in color and this would spook the angry natives.

"Well let's get going, Sam." Leif said.

Leif was a little impatient and perhaps nervous. He realized that the next four hours were going to be full of action. He also knew that if the two ships were spotted by buccaneer's that they'd have another fight on their hands.

Sam looked back at the small town by the beach just in time to see Chuck walking towards the Tavern with a bundle of barrels he would re-assemble close to the well.

"Let's get moving." Sam addressed the remaining men and whispered as loud as he dared.

Leif led the way so Sam walked behind him while Helmut held back fifty yards with Anthony and Mkenzie following him. The path led to the jungle entrance, which was recognizable from the heavy growth and sudden abundance of trees. Sam and Leif had reached the entrance about one hundred yards past the property marker just as Pierre had said. A Hispaniola parrot flew across their path and startled them. Inside the jungle it was quiet except for the occasional bird call or flapping of wings. Palm trees continued for a short walk then gave way to a mangrove forest and a thick growth of ferns and large plants. A narrow stream was splashing over rocks as it made its winding way through the forest. Macaya and spotted frogs sat close by in the refreshing spray of the stream while a black and brown colored python slithered closer to its late night snack. The deeper into the jungle the party of five went the darker it seemed to get. A few Hispaniola pines joined with the mangrove trees as they penetrated deeper and that's when they heard the chanting. All five men froze in their tracks. Helmut and the other men were only ten yards behind now, anticipating orders for their covert dispersion in the forest.

"There's the chanting that frightened Pierre." Leif whispered, while he looked around the jungle for native sentries.

He looked back at the men in their dark clothing, moccasins and muddy faces. They were curious he thought, but not anxious or frightened. Since sailing with this crew Leif had to admit he found them kind of strange. He had expected some roughness, stories of dangerous encounters and at least a couple of bottles of smuggled rum onboard. None of that was the case with these men. They were obedient and polite to the point where Leif had to wonder what they would do if they encountered real rough and ready pirates. One night he had over heard six of his crewmen comparing what they called the outside world to their own society. They had no understanding of treasure hunting or acquiring more wealth. Why didn't the outside world just provide people with an equal share of the necessities? There would be no more wars or killing. The social interaction from helping your neighbor with their basic needs could be rewarding. Leif couldn't believe what he heard but kept it to himself.

"Alright Anthony, you have your choice of trees. I need you to take your position." Sam whispered.

Anthony nodded his head in understanding and walked to his left where he had spotted the perfect Hispaniola pine for his purpose. He began climbing the tree until he reached a perch that would conceal him and give him a good view of the path below.

"Mkenzie, Helmut. I need one of you on each side of this path. We'll proceed for another hundred yards, and then you two take your positions ten yards away from the path. Mkenzie you can cover the left side and Helmut the right. When you see us running like blazes back down the path, you know what to do once Leif and I pass you. Any questions?" Sam finished.

There were no questions. Both men followed Sam a further hundred yards and then took up their positions. Helmut and Mkenzie removed their laser pistols from their sash and waited as Sam and Leif walked further down the path towards the eerie sounds of the natives chanting.

Sam and Leif were aware of the clouds above occasionally blocking the light from the moon. The extra darkness was a welcome advantage. They crept closer through the jungle. Their moccasins helped them navigate the jungle path without snapping branches. They could feel every stick and bump on the path while wearing them. The chanting which had taken on a hypnotic droning sound sent chills down Leif's back. But despite his natural revulsion for the ceremony, Leif had come for his treasure which was the recovery of the Wizard's crystal skull and he planned on being successful with this endeavor.

The undergrowth on the path was developing a little bit of a spring for each one of Sam's and Leif's steps as though encouraging them onward. This accumulation of sturdy branches and moss resulting in springy undergrowth offered Leif an advantage when a sentry for the voodoo worshippers suddenly and silently popped up to challenge the men. The sentry's white markings and glyphs looked eerie on his ebony skin. His almost seven foot height towered over Leif.

"Leif, watch out!" Sam uttered in as low a voice as could be afforded for the situation.

Leif had already used the natural spring in the undergrowth and his instincts for a quick kill by jumping forward and upward by about three feet so that he could bring the hilt of his sword down hard on the sentry's head. The sentry crumbled to one side of the path buried in the undergrowth of the jungle, and without missing a beat Leif carried on forward.

"I can see the flicker of flames from a fire and the chanting is getting louder." Sam whispered.

Both men crept forward on the path slowly and cautiously while looking for more sentries on either side of the jungle. Leif could see the jumping shadows from the voodoo dancers moving around the fire and flickering against the tree trunks of the circular clearing. Sam and Leif were about fifty feet away from the clearing when they decided to move off the path and five yards into the jungle on opposite sides of the path. Sam found cover behind a fallen tree and Leif found cover behind a boulder. They watched as Taino natives and African slaves danced around the large fire in the center of the clearing. The African slaves had been fortunate enough to escape from their slave masters and the Taino natives had a history of being worked to death in the silver mines. Leif wondered if they were trying to conjure a curse against those who had made their lives so miserable. The dancers perspiring and naked chests and arms were painted over in voodoo glyphs and symbols covered most of the dancer's faces giving them a ghostly appearance. Sam also thought they might be cursing their former slave drivers which he would be glad about. Slavery was going to be stopped once the Empire controlled the world.

"Danbala, Ogouferay, Lenba, Danbala, Ogouferay, Lenba" they chanted.

Leif knew that they would be invoking the names of the "LWA" which were the spirits that the natives believe in and worship. These were the "Dahomeyan" spirits from Benin in West Africa. Perhaps the curse would reach the shores of those horrible countries that had approved using slaves for the sake of commerce. Leif felt that slavery was a profound evil against humanity.

Suddenly the chanting stopped, the dancing stopped and the scene ahead seemed frozen. This shook Leif and Sam from their wandering thoughts. At the clearing's edge furthest away from Sam and Leif, there was movement in the jungle. Soon a procession of four natives carrying a bamboo stretcher appeared. A wooden chest and a captive were tied securely to it. The four natives walked across the clearing past the fire and motionless dancers then stopped in front of a large obese man, who sat on a wooden throne fifteen yards away from the dancers who were watching the ritual unfold. This King wore a crown on his head made of gold and holding seven peacock feathers colorfully arranged in a half moon formation. His naked upper body was decorated in white symbols which were similar to the dancers who were slowly moving around the fire, their arms and hands tracing invisible arcs in the air. The King raised his arm, a signal to the four natives in front of him and they placed the stretcher down in front of him. Bowing in obedience to the King they left and took up positions with the slowly moving natives and began tracing invisible arcs in the air with their arms and hands.

A young and attractive Queen sat ten feet to the left of the King on her own wooden throne. She wore a cloth band over her head that had thirteen colorful feathers attached at the back that rose high above her head. She watched as the King walked over to the chest on the stretcher and lowered his considerable bulk to lift it. The Queen wore a bright orange dress that covered her entire body except her shoulders and arms which were covered in white voodoo symbols. She rose from her throne and her dress touched the flattened ground in front of her. The king brought the chest over and set it down in front of her. The Queen bent. down and removed the lid from the chest then reached in and pulled out a large python that had been covered in a white powder. The Queen held the snake close and allowed it to lick her face with its slimy forked tongue. She believed this would help her gain the power from the snake. She walked over to the captive on the stretcher and held the snake up in the air and yelled some thing in a strange foreign language. The dancers moving around the fire responded by moving faster,their arms mimicking the movements of a snake. The King dragged the captive off the stretcher and set her down in the trampled grass of the clearing while the Queen set the python close by to eventually feed on the captive.

Sam had seen that the captive was a young lady wearing a green dress and with long bright red hair falling half way down her back. Her hands were tied in front of her and her ankles were bound tightly with rope. The snake, for the moment was motionless but only two yards from her feet.

Sam looked around for Leif and was relieved to see that he had slipped over beside him.

"We have to rescue that poor lady before the snake gets to her." He whispered to Leif who nodded his head in agreement.

The Queen walked over to the King and grasped both of his hands in order to transfer the snake's power which was another requirement of the ritual. The King and Queen returned to their thrones. The King reached under his throne and pulled out a green colored crystal skull. The King stood up and held the crystal skull over his head. Sam watched and was amazed when the crystal skull began to glow. He could see what looked like red inclusions deep within the crystal. Those red lines, each of different thickness, ran from the forehead to the jaw in random directions. It was a haunting suggestion of blood running down the face of this work of art and it was highlighted more as the skull began to glow brighter. The crystal skull suddenly shot out two powerful beams of light from its eyes and illuminated the natives dancing around the fire. The natives stopped dancing and uttered, in unison, low moans of amazement at this supernatural feat.

An idea struck Sam but he had to distract Leif for one minute in order to make it work.

"Leif! What was that sound behind us!" He whispered.

Leif drew his sword, and moved in the direction Sam was suggesting in a cautious crouch. Leif had moved away by five feet.

Sam was ten yards from the King, the dancers fifteen yards from the King, and fifteen yards behind the dancers was the edge of the clearing where the procession had emerged. But the edge of the clearing was beginning to get busy with more painted natives anxious to see the spectacle. So Sam put his plan into action. Standing up he drew his laser and fired at the dancers who collapsed beside the fire. The laser was effective from this distance and able to render unconscious two dancers for every shot fired. This additional spectacle caused the crowd of painted natives at the edge of the clearing to flee in terror. The King still holding the crystal skull high over his head was frozen in shock and so was the beautiful voodoo Queen. Sam used this to his advantage and ran the ten yards as fast as he could.

"Leifl Forget that! Come grab the girll" Sam shouted. This startled the King who began to search for the source of this voice.

Leif turned around just in time to see Sam go flying through the air. He had used a fallen tree to spring into the air and he tackled the overweight King. The King fell flat on his back and Sam landed on the King's stomach which cushioned his landing. While the King was recovering from the air being knocked out of his lungs, Sam immediately got up and retrieved the crystal skull which lay a short distance from where the King had dropped it.

"I'm on my way!" Leif shouted.

Leif put himself into high gear and he came crashing into the clearing; bushes and branches snapping under his feet. In one heroic scoop he had hefted the captive over his shoulder and was racing back into the jungle. Sam followed him at full speed with the crystal skull tucked under his arm.

The Queen had struggled out of her shock and began shouting for the fleeing natives to return. She shouted out, in a foreign language, that this was a trick to steal the skull and that there was nothing to fear. In a few moments there was movement around the opposite edge of the clearing then the natives burst forward running and yelling war chants as they passed their Queen.

Up ahead on the jungle's path Leif had passed Mkenzie and Helmut. Sweat ran down his face and he drew in as much breath as he could while carrying the five foot two captive who must have weighed just over one hundred pounds. Helmut was surprised to see how physically fit Leif was. Sam with his not so well distributed weight was close behind and gave the signal. Helmut and Mkenzie shot at the pursuing natives, dropping ten of them onto the jungle's leaf carpeted floor as they wandered into the purple beam from their laser pistols. The remaining natives decided this spectacle was a display of witchcraft and turning back they fled in fear to tell this tale to their Queen.

But Sam and Leif were not free from danger yet. Sam heard crashing on both sides of the jungle and knew that a couple of brave and foolish natives had made a different decision. He looked to his right in time to see a native pull back the string on his bow and let fly a wickedly sharp arrow in the direction of Leif.

Remarkably the arrow found its target striking Leif in the back of his right leg in the middle of his calf. He hollered and fell dropping the captive harmlessly into a fern bush to cushion the fall.

"Yeow! Leif complained. He reached around and broke the arrow so all that remained in his leg was the arrow's head which would have to be carefully removed. The rescued captive was sitting up when Leif turned to check on her.

"Give me your sword. I can free my legs and help you." She said.

Leif thought her voice was melodious like a singer, and considering the dangerous situation, he was surprised she was so calm. He struggled to free his sword and passed it to her.

Behind them Anthony had caught the second native firing at him from above in the tree. Sam stood guard for more approaching natives while Anthony climbed down from his perch. There were no more wild eyed natives so both men returned to the jungle path and walked up to join Leif and the captive.

"What's your name dear lady?" Leif asked as he cut the ropes from her wrist. "Gerta Ludwig." She replied.

"I'm Leif Andersson. I'm travelling with these men on a mission. How did you find yourself the captive of voodoo worshippers?" He asked.

Before Gerta could answer, Sam, Anthony, Helmut and Mkenzie arrived.

"We better get back to the ship. Helmut help Leif with some support." Sam said. Helmut walked over to Leif as he struggled to stand.

"Put your arm around my shoulder and take all the weight off your right leg. We're going to try a brisk walk for the remaining four hundred yards." Helmut instructed.

Leif did as he said and soon they were hobbling down the jungle path. Gerta, Sam and the three men followed. Twenty minutes passed in silence until they reached the jungles exit. Chuck came running up unexpectedly and almost out of breath. He addressed Sam.

"Sir! We have a problem! Pirates have attacked and sunk Leif's ship!" Chuck said.

Sam turned to Leif.

"I'm going to run ahead to see what's going on. Make your way to the concealed boat and be careful with that injured leg. As a precaution I'm going to send Mkenzie with you and Gerta. If I'm not there by the time you get there, set out in the boat and get back to the Empire's ship and wait! Helmut, Anthony and Chuck follow me!" Sam finished.

Sam led the three men jogging in the direction of the Tavern where they had received their intel for this mission. They soon disappeared from sight in the cover of darkness thanks partly to swift moving clouds which were hiding the moon. Mkenzie and Leif got into position with Leif wrapping his arm over Mkenzie's shoulder for support. They set out in the direction of the hidden boat by retracing their steps along the path. Gerta followed close behind occasionally looking around as though she expected the natives to come back and chase them.

Leif was beginning to think that all his faith in luck had gone out the window. His ship was sinking and he had been mutilated by a voodoo natives arrow. However, they did recover the crystal skull and now all they had to do was sail back to the Wizard, who was anxiously awaiting their return.

"How are you doing Gerta?" Leif asked. He found he couldn't turn around to speak to her.

"I'm doing alright now that I'm free from those natives and certain death. Thank you for rescuing me. How far is it to the boat?" Gerta asked.

"We should be about fifty yards away by now. I recognize a few of these patches of wild flowers and a row of palm trees up ahead." Leif answered.

In another ten minutes they walked off the path and arrived at the spot where they had hidden the small boat. Gerta and Mkenzie took up position on their sides of the boat and dragged it out of the heavy growth of ferns and bushes between the two melocactus trees and down to the beach. Chuck had three water barrels rigged to a small raft of eight branches tied together waiting to be towed behind the boat when it left.

Leif looked out to sea and saw the continuing chaos had been illuminated by a fire burning on the bow of his ship.

The bow of the ship was now in the air as the stern took on more ocean water through a hole four feet in diameter just below the upper deck's port window opposite Leif's hand carved lion. While Leif watched his hand carved lion drown, he noticed that the attacking pirate ship, now holding steady forty yards away from his ship was filling up its lifeboats with blood thirsty pirates. They were dressed in an array of different clothing, most likely stolen from those ships which they raided. Beneath their scarfs wrapped around their heads and the different hats they wore, was an immoral criminal who would kill for any reason, especially treasure. This rag-bag band of marauding maniacs dressed in dirty shirts and torn jackets carried knives in their teeth and their musket pistols were tucked into their sash. The two lifeboats were filled with four pirates each and a torch was burning held by the leading pirate in the bow. They began rowing over to attack the Empires ship. Leif knew he had a little time before the pirates reached the ship but he was suddenly very anxious about getting onboard and defending against the attack.

Leif turned around in the dark and saw that Mkenzie had already tied the homemade raft's rope to the boat's hook.

"I can help us get there quicker by rowing. Leif didn't wait for an affirmative from the doctor. Let me get in first and take up position." Leif shouted over the boisterous noise from the pirates.

He settled himself close to the bow and took up the oars while Gerta sat in the middle and Mkenzie pushed off the raft with one week's supply of fresh drinking water, then hopped into the stern of the boat and began rowing. Leif and Mkenzie put all their strength into the oars. Fortunately the raft was sea worthy and did not slow them down. About half way across to the Empire's ship, Leif noticed that Gerta had removed an item from inside her dress pocket. The unusual item was black and in a shape of a half moon. Gerta put the item to her lips and began blowing into it.

"What's that in your hand, Gerta?" Leif asked.

"I think I can provide us with some help." She answered in a smooth and calm voice which was so unusual for this desperate occasion that it startled Leif.

This brief conversation caught the attention of Mkenzie who quickly turned around and noticed that the half-moon device now resting in Gerta's lap had several holes drilled in it. Gerta was beginning to spook Mkenzie. He thought she was suffering from shock. He went back to rowing and in another five minutes they made it to the Empire's ship, on starboard side and climbed up and onto the main deck. The crew unloaded the fresh water and hoisted up the lifeboat.

Sam, Anthony, Helmut and Chuck we're already aboard thanks to having borrowed a small row boat from the Tavern's rear dock that Sam had noticed yesterday.

"It's a relief to see you folks made it." Sam said.

"We've got the fresh water on board. Thank you for a perfectly crafted raft, Chuck." Leif said with a slight hint of exhaustion in his voice.

Sam could see Leif was still in some pain from his injury. He did make a brave show of hiding his discomfort.

"Mkenzie take Leif up to the Captains quarters and dig that arrow out. I've got some whisky in the cooler you can use to clean the wound and numb the pain for Leif." Sam said.

"Those are blood thirsty pirates you're up against. You need my help." Leif protested.

"You're no good to us dead or infected. All the men from your ship are here, no one injured, so we have enough man power for eight pirates. Get up there and get fixed up." Sam said raising his voice a little for emphasis.

Leif gave in to Sam's common sense and let Mkenzie lead him up the stairs to the upper deck and the Captain's quarters. But he stopped at the top of the stairs.

"Where is the crystal skull?" Leif called down to Sam.

"It's safe in my cabin. Now concentrate on getting yourself fixed up." Sam replied.

Sam turned around to see how Gerta was doing. For some odd reason she was staring up into the night sky. Probably unloading some stress he thought.

"Gerta you are safe and sound which we are all happy about. Is there anything I can suggest like a meal? When was the last time you ate? Sam asked.

"Thank you, but I would like to remain on deck and be of some help against the attacking pirates." Gerta answered.

This got a respectful laugh from a few of the men and others clapped applauding her bravery.

"I've been discussing a plan with the men and we're going to act now. But you remain seated here on the starboard side of the ship." Sam said.

The crew had drawn their lasers now set on maximum to cause the most damage to the pirate's invading lifeboats. Sam shouted out his command to Helmut who was below deck and ready to fire the laser cannon. The laser cannon silently sent out a purple colored beam of destruction which shone brightly on the stern of the pirate ship sixty yards away and burned a hole ten feet in circumference. The damage to the pirate ship would allow enough ocean water in to sink the ship in twenty minutes. The bow of that ill-fated pirate ship rose up in the air as if to protest the outcome. The pirates in the lifeboats watched in stunned amazement at this display of what they believed to be supernatural firepower, but it did not shake their resolve. They were not frightened off and did not react to the frantic shouts heard across the water from the crew of the sinking pirate ship.

Sam turned around to check on Gerta. Her blue eyes seemed to light up as she gazed up at the evening sky. Sam followed her gaze to see what she was looking at.

In a few seconds a spectacle appeared in the night sky, while the screeching pirates below made their approach. He saw a mysterious ring of fire. Something black and large flew through the burning circle and into the cover of the night's clouds. The burning circle suddenly vanished. Sam trained his gaze on the peculiar dark shadow moving about within the blue and black clouds. He saw what looked like a large tail slicing through the night clouds. It moved left to right erratically and finally appeared as a monstrous scaly tail which rose up ominously out of the clouds. In a sudden blur of movement, the creature exited the clouds and hovered above the conflagration below. Both of its fifteen-foot-long powerful black leathery wings looked similar to those of a bat. Of all the creatures Sam had seen recently, this one had the most unusual features. On the top of the creature's head, amphibious fins, like a mockery of hair stood up in different directions. The head must have been three feet long, similar to a velociraptor in shape, with two tusks or horns where the missing nostrils should be. Its jaws ran further back and widened behind the tusks. The color of the creature was black or navy blue; Sam couldn't tell because it was nighttime. Scales covered its eighteen- foot-long torso, powerful legs and arms. The creature's muscular legs must have been six feet in length and it's arms four feet. They were joined with four sharp claws on large feet and hands.

Gerta stood up, put her half-moon flute to her mouth and a series of sounds, only the creature could hear, drifted upwards. This must have been a precise communication only Gerta and the creature could understand, because the creature folded up its wings and descended head first at lightning speed towards the unscrupulous pirates. The pirates dived over board just as the creature pulled its body back up and smashed into the small boat with its powerful legs and feet. The boat was smashed into small pieces. Fortunately all the pirates survived but their muskets and gun powder were soaked and therefore useless to them. The smart pirates decided to swim to shore hoping the creature would not chase them. The other marauders in the second boat, not so gifted with common sense, continued rowing towards the Empire's ship. The creature was hovering twenty feet above the ocean, watching the second boat and realizing there was only one cure for the pirate's defiance, it climbed high into the night sky until it was no longer visible. Those stubborn pirates stood up in the boat. The torch held by the leading pirate spread its light and Sam could see the pirates were preparing to shoot the creature when it dived down to attack them. The pirates looked up into the sky, with muskets held high above their heads, waiting for the attack and confident they would destroy the flying menace.

Sam's crew were mesmerized by the spectacle and had already holstered the laser pistols in their sash.

"Gerta! Do you have control of this powerful creature?" Sam shouted. He wanted to be sure it would not attack the Empire's ship next.

Gerta smiled back at him, she seemed truly happy to see the creature or enjoyed seeing the pirates suffer; Sam wasn't sure which.

"Yes and don't worry my friend! It can sense you're on the side of good. Mother Nature gave the creature remarkable mental abilities. I believe it is somehow discerning, and able to read the thoughts of humans." Gerta answered.

"Is that a guarantee it won't attack my ship?" Sam asked.

"We've been together a long time and consider each other family. I will provide for some of its needs and the creature will protect me. The creature will not attack your ship with me on it, or any of your crew. The creature is intelligent and will understand you are friends or allies in a difficult situation." Gerta answered She looked back up into the sky just in time to see the creature exiting the clouds and flying full speed head down and arms extended towards the waiting pirates. The pirates fired their muskets. Black smoke from the musket's barrels filled the night sky but Sam could swear he saw four holes appear on one of the creature's wings. Miraculously that black wing healed and the creature caught up with one of the pirates grabbing him with powerful four foot long arms. The protesting pirate squirmed and howled until two of four fingers with six inch claws clamped over his mouth. The other two fingers cradled the top of the pirates head removing his battered tricorne hat which fell into the ocean below. The struggling pirate was flown to shore and dumped in some bushes close to the beach. The creature returned to the Empire's ship and hovered close to the port side railing. It stared down at Gerta sitting on the bench.

Gerta got up from the bench and walked over to the creature as the crew and Sam backed away to give her room by the port side railing.

"I remember I promised you an African vacation. Well we're close enough now! Let's go on that vacation!" Gerta called out to the creature.

Gerta brushed her hands along her creased green dress and raised her arms up in the air. The creature reached down and using its powerful arms and hands, gently raised Gerta up until she was sitting just below its nine-foot-long neck.

"Sam! We will see you in five days with some provisions like fresh fruit!" Gerta yelled down to the ship.

"Will you be sailing north or south?" She asked.

"We will be sailing north for the Azores." Sam yelled back. He didn't want to mention the Empire's island yet.

"If you catch up with us in five days we should be half way there." Sam shouted. "Then I will pick up your route in five days' time." Gerta shouted back.

Sam watched the creature turn and rise up into the night sky, its leathery black wings a blur of motion. The men on board pulled the sails free and made the necessary preparations to sail.

Before disappearing into a cluster of dark clouds, Gerta looked down at the Empire's ship now as small as her thumb from this height. She had to be sure they were far enough out of sight that the men below couldn't see her creature open the portal.

Gerta didn't know that Sam had already seen the portal and wasn't aware that the crew, minus Leif, had seen their share of supernatural sights.

Gerta ran her hand along the creature's neck and this signal let the creature know they were far enough out of sight that it could begin their covert exit. The creature opened up the portal. This mental ability was still a mystery to Gerta. An electrified circle, with lightning swirling around its ninety-foot circumference, materialized in the dark blue clouds ahead. A strange humming noise and burning smell issued from the portal. The burning smell caused Gerta's nostrils to pucker as they flew through the portal into total darkness and silence. It was as though they had entered a tunnel it was so quiet. In another sixty seconds they exited the portal and arrived on the south coast of Africa. The night time sounds of birds and other wildlife rose up to Gerta and her creature. The sky was calm and only a few clouds were floating by occasionally covering the light of the moon.

It was now four hours before sunrise, so Gerta and her creature decided to stop in Cape Town and sleep under a row of palm trees on the beach which blocked out the light from the moon and offered shade in the morning. Her creature folded up its wings behind its back and walked upright over to a comfortable bank of sand under a palm tree and lay down. It stretched out to its full length of twenty-seven feet and slept peacefully.

Gerta was in the habit of concealing the creature in the least populated areas to avoid confrontation by a community. She had already been accused of witchcraft and there was a reward out for her capture.

Gerta wasn't tired enough to sleep. She stopped about ten feet away from her friend and sat down on a beached log replaying the events of the last nine months in her mind.

Gerta's family had left the Black Forest region of Germany on a tip from her father's cousin. They left the comfortable log cabin they had made for the prosperity in the new colonies of America. It was not a difficult move. Gerta was the only child and at the time she was only eight years old when she settled into a small community in Massachusetts. She had already mastered the English language and was able to help her family in matters of importance requiring translation. While attending school in the community of Dedham, Gerta was popular with those classmates who were not jealous of an honor student. She made several friends and after school in the heat of the summer she would invite them out on her canoe for a cool ride on the water.

The Algonquians called Dedham "Tiot" which means land surrounded by water, and on a hot day Gerta was grateful for the refreshing paddle in her canoe.

Gerta led a happy life in Dedham until reaching twenty years of age and that's when things changed. The trouble started when she decided to take a short cut home from Dedham's General Store where she worked. She cut through the woods which were a private area for the needs of the local natives. She was just taking a short cut so couldn't see that she was causing anyone harm. If Gerta had taken the usual circuitous route home, a well-travelled path from town to the small village where she lived, things would have turned out different.

Gerta made her way through the thick forest and had just about reached her cut off which would return her to the path home, when she heard a shrill cry echoing through the forest. She stopped and decided to investigate thinking this might be a small animal that was caught in a trap; maybe she could rescue it. As she moved closer to the shrieking cry, she noticed six natives huddled around a boulder just twenty feet away from her. Gerta found some cover behind another boulder and continued to watch the natives. They had their bows drawn ready to shoot the animal being hunted. Gerta wanted to see what poor misfortunate creature had wandered into the sights of their bows. She moved silently through the forest until she could see the creature they had wounded. Gerta was in shock and amazement when she saw the twenty-seven foot reptilian-like creature standing up in the middle of a stream that ran through the forest. How did this lizard become so over grown she wondered then she noticed there were two fish attached to tusks which were situated on the end of the creature's snout. The creature had fifteen foot long black leathery wings, much like those of a bat, and those wings had been pierced with the native's arrows. The creature shrieked in pain and the sound echoed around the forest. It sounded more like a plea begging its tormentors to stop. The natives had a different idea as they came out from behind the boulder to finish it off. The creature watched the natives leave the shelter of the boulder and could see the malevolent intent in their eyes, so it lowered its nine foot long scaly neck and opened its mouth. A loud booming sound poured out past its razor sharp teeth. The sound had a physical force and the natives were caught up in it. Nearby trees and branches were bending backwards and rocks twigs and other debris from the forest floor blew into the faces of the natives. The natives were sent tumbling backwards through the forest; their bows still clutched in their hands were broken. They regained their balance once the sound had stopped. Bewildered by the attack, they looked back at the creature, but fear intervened and the natives ran for their lives tripping over rocks and branches as they went. With the battle won the creature raised its head and looked directly at Gerta who had stood up to watch this spectacle. The large reptilian whined softly. This touched Gerta's heart and her sympathy for the creature propelled her forward. She walked right up to the stream and walked in until she was knee-deep and looking directly into the dark orange eyes of the pain stricken creature.

"Let me help you." Gerta said out loud as though the creature could understand her.

She raised her arm slowly and pointed to the arrow close to the creature's body on its right wing. Gerta reached behind the wing until she could feel the arrow's head, then she broke the shaft and the arrow's head fell into the stream. She pulled the arrow out from the other side where the feathered end was and the puncture wound in the wing immediately closed up healing instantaneously right before her eyes. Gerta was amazed at the healing ability of the creature. Unfortunately so was a watcher nearby who had happened to hear the unusual wailing from the creature and took a chance as Gerta did, by trespassing to investigate.

Arthur Jenkins had been a rival school mate and jealous of Gerta's studious abilities. The best he could manage for himself by the time age twenty came around was a blacksmith's helper and apprentice. He had wanted to be a lawmaker, but lacked the intellect for the job. Now he thought the chance had arrived to redeem him. Arty, as the townsfolk called him, would report this to the local authorities. Gerta was obviously involved with witchcraft and should be burned at the stake. She had bewitched the dangerous creature effectively enough to approach it. He would help remove this threat from the community and earn the right to be a lawman. But first he must contact those natives who witnessed the demon that Gerta was helping. That was going to be his story. This would be accomplished through Arty's good rapport with the native community. He set out on his new mission just as Gerta was removing the last arrow from the creature's left wing.

Arty's accusation of witchcraft stuck, as planned, when the town council heard the testimony of the natives experience, through a translator at a special town meeting two days later. As it turned out, one of the fleeing natives had briefly turned around to see if the creature was chasing them and instead he had seen Gerta standing in the stream with the creature. He had testified that a young woman with red hair, wearing a white and yellow striped dress seemed to be talking to the creature. That had been the convincing story which caused the town meeting to conclude. The town's governing officials appointed a group of men to arrest Gerta.

Fortunately Gerta's employer had got wind of the proceedings, and knowing what an incorrigible person Arty was, he refused to believe that Gerta was involved with black magic. He told Gerta about the accusation and gave her the rest of the day off to organize her escape. Gerta used this time to explain to her family that she'd been falsely accused of witchcraft and that she was sorry for the trouble this would bring her family. Her father's English cousin, who had secured a carpenter job for him in Dedham, could do the same in a community twenty miles south. The family would change their last name and Gerta could visit them after one year. By that time memory of Gerta's escape would be foggy in the minds of the New England townsfolk. Gerta thanked her family and fled into the forest where her creature was waiting. The creature gently raised her up onto its back and they escaped from Dedham that late afternoon flying south and eventually stopping in Peru, where they spent several enjoyable months until arriving in Hispaniola.

Gerta looked over at her friend sleeping peacefully and decided that she had enough reminiscence for one night. She walked over to a nearby palm tree and found a soft patch of vegetation to lie down on. Soon Gerta was fast asleep dreaming about the pyramids in Egypt and the exotic fruit that they would feast on while enjoying a brief vacation.

Back on the Empire's ship the men had dropped sail and left Cap Francois as soon as Gerta had disappeared in the clouds on the back of her creature. Leif had hobbled out of his cabin ten minutes after this, followed by a perspiring doctor Mkenzie. It was a difficult surgery but he saved Leif from permanent damage. Leif's first question was how the pirates were able to sink his ship.

"The nights roaming clouds had cancelled the light of the moon long enough for a ship, which had all its lamps extinguished, to sneak closer and fire its cannon." Randeep answered.

"You got rid of the pirates? Leif asked with open mouthed incredulity.

Leif made his way slowly to the port side and looked over the railing where he could see the splinters from the shattered lifeboat. The other lifeboat, from where the arrogant pirate had been scooped up by the creature, was still intact but empty. The other three terrified pirates had made it to shore. All that remained of the pirate's brigantine was a mast sticking up in the water that hadn't quite sunk yet.

"We fired our cannon and the shot took out their ship by blasting a hole in the stern." Sam said.

"How did you bust up that lifeboat?" Leif asked. He pointed to the remaining pieces of the lifeboat floating fifteen feet away from the Empire's ship. The other abandoned lifeboat was making its way out to sea and would soon disappear into the darkness of the night.

"Chuck helped us with that. He raised the rear of the heavy cannon chassis. Chuck is one very strong person and he muscled that cannon into place for a close shot." Sam uttered this falsehood with great pride and conviction in his voice.

That seemed to settle Leif. They had luck on their side for both of those situations. What else could defeat trained killers but their own bad luck? It was a lucky shot from this distance and one incredibly strong crewman able to lift the cannon into place for a devastating bullseye. That saved the crew and ship of the Empire.

Leif gave the main deck a quick glance then looked around the upper deck quickly.

"Where's Gerta? Is she still aboard the ship? Is she sleeping somewhere? Leif asked.

"She decided to return the small boat I borrowed from the Tavern. Gerta said she could make other arrangements now that she was out of the clutches of the voodoo worshippers. She asked me to thank you for rescuing her. She told me that the voodoo Queen thought she was a powerful witch. The voodoo natives actually believe in a transfer of her power by sacrificing her to the snake." Sam lied again.

"Where are we keeping that creepy crystal skull? How did... how did light blast out of its crystal eyes?" Leif asked, still in disbelief about what he had witnessed. Sam was afraid that Leif might have caught this but he had an explanation.

"The Wizard's crystal skull is safe under lock and key in my cabin. Those beams of light that you saw pouring out of the skulls eyes is a design feature. It is so expertly crafted that it can catch the light from the moon, store it, and then release it. What you didn't see is when those beams stopped pouring out because it had released all of the stored light." Sam answered. He was proud of this creative falsehood. If the truth be known he didn't have a clue how it shot out those beams of light but the Wizard would know.

Sam felt he had to change the subject in order to be free of Leif's barrage of questions.

"Is there still some rum left in that bottle? (Maybe this would be a tempting distraction) Sam asked.

"There's about a half bottle left. Come to think of it we should celebrate our successful mission." Leif answered.

Sam thanked his lucky stars for his partner's sudden thirst. He would need some time to think about how he was going to explain Gerta's creature when she arrives back in five days. Sam's men had seen the Wizard's creatures before, but Leif will be the only one on board surprised or worse shocked.

Leif hopped forward and held on to Sam for support and they both hobbled their way into the Captain's cabin for another late night celebratory toast to success. Back in Cape Town that beautiful beach was providing much needed peace and quiet for an exhausted rider and creature. Gerta was dreaming of that day when her new friend had presented her with the black half-moon flute she used for communication. They spent hours together in Peru on a beach drawing diagrams in the sand as the creature pointed to the corresponding hole on the flute. The creature's drawings were surprisingly good. It drew a picture of Gerta with her arms up in the air to represent "needing help" and then pointed to the second hole on the flute.

Gerta was an accused witch on the run without a home. She didn't know that Sam and the Wizard would alter her destiny. Gerta slid back to the anxiety of the unknown and tossed and turned until reaching a dreamless and sound two hours of rest.

Chapter Two

That night's drifting clusters of dark clouds travelled northwards arriving in Azorka by morning. Azorkans and Zapatsaurs were beginning their day in dim light from a sky clouded over with the grey and dark blue patch-work of angry clouds. It looked as though Azorka would get some spring rain today which may cool down a comfortable sixty-five-degree day.

On Zapatsaur mountain four Zapatsaurs had gathered together at the fifteen-foot entrance to the Elders cave. They were waiting for one elder so that they would have proper quorum for a very important meeting. The Elder's cave did not have living quarters but was reserved for discussions and decisions affecting the entire population of Zapatsaurs. Today the weather would be the last thing on the minds of the four elders.

Two of the elders shuffled about impatiently, moving deeper into the tunnel. The other two elders waited at the entrance occasionally looking outside for the arrival of the fifth elder. After another five minutes they were able to announce the arrival as the fifth elder flew down from the cave one hundred feet above. The fifth elder's wings folded behind it's back, it stood upright and followed the other four Zapatsaurs. The procession of elders walked down the tunnel at a thirty-degree angle in silence. The tunnel's laser cut rounded walls and ceiling formed a half-moon shaped corridor with crystal torches attached to the rounded walls every twenty yards. The floor was perfectly flat and the ceiling provided just enough head room for the Zapatsaurs.

The first elder was supreme leader for the Zapatsaur population. Number one already had a prepared agenda but was nervously wondering what the Wizard was planning. Surely he would attempt to rescue the Dragon Queen. Will this meeting help prepare for that eventuality?

The procession came to the turn in the tunnel then arrived at the half-moon shaped conference room with its comfortable bench and large wooden tables polished and clean. The five Zapatsaurs took their seats and the first elder began the telepathic discussion.

"The Azorkans think of us as intelligent animals. They are constructing an alphabet so that we can communicate better. They are not aware of the fact that our adolescent Zapatsaurs receive an education while visiting their domed schools. The lesson learned is circulated to the rest of the young Zapatsaurs daily and unlike the human memory, cannot be forgotten. Our IQ levels are three times greater than humans. We must continue the pretense that we are intelligent animals for the next two-hundred and fifty years. We will learn their alphabet, while our scholars and astronomers keep a look out for human progress and the big event. That's why we were sent here as settlers five thousand years ago; to establish a relationship and allow for human development to occur naturally without any outside interference. Are there any questions or does anyone have anything to add?" The first elder asked. Silence followed so the first elder continued.

"The Wizard has broken the law and murdered two of our loved ones. He has become a significant threat along with Amy and the Dragon Queen, so this trio can now be considered outside interference. The negative influence from the Wizard's desire to control is going to cause the Azorkans to become militarily proficient which may affect their spiritual development." The first elder paused. There were no further contributions to this theory and no questions so the first elder continued.

"As good fortune would have it, the Dragon Queen has been captured and imprisoned. We have an opportunity to confirm her DNA. Our medical scientists believe it will be from the Dheginian Star System and will confirm or deny this fact at the inner city laboratory one hundred miles below us. If it turns out to be Dheginian then we will prepare with counter measures to deal with her should she escape. Some of our military experts have suggested a copper net." The first elder paused.

The first elder continued, hoping for ideas the other elders may have on the threat of the Dragon Queen. If the Dragon Queen turned out to be a maturing Dheginian the challenges to contain her will be great.

"The Dheginian Star System is greatly feared throughout the universe. We could have their powerful mental capabilities to deal with if they decided to invade earth. The planets inhabitants from this system have no respect for life." The first elder said.

The fifth elder was Minister of Defense and decided to join the telepathic discussion.

"I have been giving the matter a great deal of thought. First of all, a copper arrow and copper net as well as other invented deterrents are being constructed within the inner city labs and shops. They will be made available shortly. The arrow and bow will be much larger than what the Azorkans use and will be operational for three fingers." The fifth elder paused. There were no comments or questions.

"My second idea is somewhat more complex. I should have consulted with the Minister of Health before this presentation."

"The Dragon Queen went through substantial biological change ten thousand years ago when she agreed to the Wizard's experiment. Sections of her brain opened up and became active that were dormant before the operation. These sections served her new arms and wings and other previously dormant regions of her brain began to serve the extra network of nerves and muscles for her legs and feet. Would it be possible to humanely shut down some of those areas of her brain?" The fifth elder asked the Minister of Health.

The third elder was the Minister of Health and was ready with a response.

"I'm glad your consulting with me. It sounds like a brilliant theory that is worthy of further exploration. I'll do the research and arrange a meeting with you when I have the results."

"Presently I would suggest that we take notes on the Azorkans treatment of the Dragon Queen. The observations should be recorded with the notes on human development. My guess is that they will treat her humanely and that would be the positive development we hope for from the Azorkans." The third elder paused again, then continued after realizing there were no questions.

"I am also concerned about the Dragon Queen's immortality. The Dheginian Star System does host a variety of life and those blessed with immortality have mental capabilities that are always maturing. We must keep her under observation as much as the situation permits. She could acquire incredibly powerful mental abilities and become more of a threat to Zapatsaurs and humans. Perhaps stress from her imprisonment would trigger this or maybe it will happen in the near future. We can't afford to overlook any possibility."

The fourth elder, Minister of Human and Zapatsaur Affairs, decided to join the telepathic conversation.

"I thank the Health Minister for suggestions concerning the Dragon Queen. Those recorded notes will be kept within the inner city. We need more intelligence to be prepared for the big event. Right now I would request a review of the Dheginian and Yetz Star Systems.

The second elder was Minister of Science and offered to do the review.

"The nearest life supporting planets in the Dheginian Star System are forty-six light years from Earth. The Dheginian humanoid is ten feet tall, covered in black scales with powerful mental abilities enabling him to freeze his opponents in combat and teleport. The leathery winged creature he rides in the sky on is twenty-seven feet in length, covered in black scales and uses its incredible strength and sound waves in combat. Both creature and rider are telepathically linked and equally intelligent. The creature reads the minds of most lifeforms in the universe warning of hostile intent. They explore the universe in disc-shaped star ships stealing resources from planets and enslaving the population." "Eleven thousand years ago we travelled to the Yetz Star System, twenty-five light years away, in our star ships, navigating worm holes and portals to shorten the journey. We were welcomed on Yetz-an, the ninth planet from a sun twice as large as ours and separated from planets ten, eleven, and twelve by an asteroid belt. After planet twelve, a much larger asteroid belt orbits around the sun and all twelve planets. The climate is colder on planets ten and eleven but livable, unlike the twelfth planet where life is non-existent. The hotter climates of planets one to eight were uninhabitable, but Yetz-an is beautiful with a climate similar to our planet and four seasons. It is ten times larger than Earth supporting a population of five billion on continents surrounded by oceans that are teeming with life. Wildlife is abundant and the land is peppered with beautiful forests and crops." The second elder paused again, this time to see if there were any questions. "Our explorers were told, during there six-month stay on Yetz-an, that those, members of the population who were in opposition to the established law were banished to planet ten. The rogue elements were teaming up with the Dheginians and invading other planets to steal resources, which was strictly forbidden."

"The Yetz have powerful mental abilities but their telepathy is not advanced enough to reliably communicate with other life forms, although the Wizard may have found away to bio-engineer a solution with his creations. They can influence the actions of some life forms and humans by telepathically sending suggestions, but they can't mind read to confirm message received.

"As you all know the Yetz are signatories of an agreement with a collaborative of other civilizations in the universe that had agreed to let earth mature on its own without alien interference. We expressed our gratitude and pledged our cooperation with the "Alliance of Peaceful Worlds." However, the Wizard and Amy escaped the notice of the "Alliance" Amy concealed her identity with make- up and contacts, appearing as the petite brown-eyed diplomat for the Empire. The reclusive Wizard seldom appeared in public. Some Azorkans believed his gray skin was a rare reaction to sunlight and that his immortality came from his experiments, mentioning the Dragon Queen's immortality as an example."

Recent events caused Mitch to search records left by previous Guardians. He believes that Amy, in the past, has appeared as diplomat for the Empire using different names and even wearing a hair piece as a disguise. However, she slipped up with the previous guardian and he remarked that Amy looked thirty years old even after his fifty-year reign. This led Mitch to investigate and he now believes that Amy and the Wizard are aliens. Amy was not subjected to experiments granting immortality and two people are unlikely to have gray skin and the same reaction to sunlight. Mitch will share his suspicions with family and his closest commanders only. We believe that the Wizards closest commanders keep the secret of their true origins. Two weeks ago, our team launched a daring mission to spy on Amy, confirming that they could not read her mind and that they saw her applying flesh colored make-up in the castles courtyard in the morning."

"The Dragon Queens mind cannot be read although we can somehow detect her presence when she is a couple hundred yards from us. We suspect the Dragon Queen's DNA will have a Dheginian signature which would explain why we can't read her mind and would incriminate the Wizard as a Yetz rebel.

"The Dheginian humanoid's cognitive and telepathic powers are greater than the Yetz's. They are quite physically powerful as well. The face is horrifying with its protruding lower jaw filled with six inch long razor sharp teeth, and they have an unusually large cranium and occipital bone. They are covered entirely in black reptilian scales. Their upper body muscle mass is slim but powerful and the lower part of their bodies, like the Dragon Queen, is massive and powerful. Their hands have four fingers with six inch claws, and their feet, like the Dragon Queen, have three reptilian toes with long and lethal looking claws.

"The Dheginian Star System is out of bounds because of some war thousands of years in the past which did not result in a peace treaty. Yetz-an forbids sharing technology with those inhabited planets in the Dheginian star system. They are still considered enemies. We believe that the rebel Yetz's trade technology with the Dheginian's from planet twelve. But it is difficult to confirm because of planet twelve's distance from Yetz-an." The second elder decided to pause. There were no questions so the Minister of Science continued.

"It is rumored that fifteen-thousand years ago, thirteen crystal skulls representing planets and their humanoid occupants from neighboring star systems were crafted on earth. The Wizard was the craftsman and he alone knows what planets and persons of importance they are named after. We believe that the Wizard used Dheginian technology to produce the skulls. During the war, ten thousand years ago, they were stolen by an unknown thief while the Wizard was preoccupied with fighting the Azorkan's. We believe the crystal skulls were taken to Peru in South America. The Mayan legends mention the crystal skulls and claim that one day the thirteen skulls will come together to save the world from a catastrophe. Our military experts and scientist are suspicious of the Wizard's urgency to recover the crystal skulls and believe that even individually a crystal skull could be a dangerous addition to the Wizard's arsenal of tricks." The second elder finished.

The first elder thanked the Minister of Science then summarized the meeting.

"If the Dragon Queen's sample is void of Dheginian influence, we can consider the possibility of the Wizard arriving on Earth by accident, perhaps crashing his star ship, now beyond repair, and unable to transmit a call for help. He kept his and Amy's true origins secret to avoid suspicion and blended in with our society as a benevolent influence for the Empire. But this doesn't explain the very detailed crystal skulls, like the one we've seen through Heather's eyes, that could only have been accomplished with Dheginian technology. If our scientists discover Dheginian influence this would suggest that the Wizard was from planet ten or eleven and was trading technology with one of the most ferocious and dangerous species in the Universe on planet twelve." The first elder finished.

The fourth elder decided to join the telepathic conversation.

"If I'm understanding our intel correctly, we don't know what threat the crystal skulls represent to our terrestrial home here on planet earth, or the human and Zapatsaur population."

"That is correct. If the findings support Dheginian influence, then we have to formulate a plan around the worst case scenario which would be the Wizard communicating with the Dheginian Star System for help. Perhaps amongst the thirteen crystal skulls is one that will allow communication or send out a beacon for help. Maybe when all thirteen are assembled, the Wizard will engage in more malevolent acts using this power. That's why a task force will be assigned to spy and report; learn anything and everything about these crystal skulls. This team will be secretly hidden on the enemy island and will listen for the conversations between Amy, the Wizard, senior commanders and observe their actions. It will be a dangerous assignment because of the creatures the Wizard may produce or still have for sentry duty. For this mission we will rely upon military deterrents as mentioned by the Minister of Defense to protect our team." The first elder finished.

The fifth elder, the Minister of Defense, joined the conversation again.

"We will have the ten by ten-foot copper net available shortly. It will be thrown over the attacking adversary, and will be effective regardless of sensitivity to copper. The net will fold up neatly into a holster on a belt and worn by the defending Zapatsaur. The copper bow and arrow should be ready in ten days, at which time I shall return here and wait by the entrance to the inner city to receive four samples for testing."

"Thank you Minister of Defense." The first elder said. "I think we can conclude this meeting and arrange for two very important covert operations."

"For the operation concerning the Dragon Queen's saliva and blood samples, I will ask the Minister of Health to organize the necessary and specially selected participants for surreptitiously acquiring the samples for our doctors and scientists. The Minister of Health will coordinate with the Minister of Defense on findings for the humane blocking of the Dragon Queen's brain functions. When this research is complete we will meet to discuss the implementation of this process."

"I will also ask the Minister of Defense to select and organize a group for the covert spying on the enemy island. When information is discovered about the crystal skulls, the group will be reporting back immediately."

"The Minister of Human and Zapatsaur Affairs will be available for any extra assistance required by both covert operations which will be concealed from human knowledge."

"As usual a (telepathic) report of today's discussions is available for our population." The first elder finished.

The Zapatsaurs got up from their comfortable seats and were about to leave but stopped and listened as news of Sally and General Zen arriving on their Zapatsaurs broke through the telepathic chatter on Zapatsaur mountain.

The first elder reminded everyone that the pictorial alphabet lesson will take place, on the opposite peak, directly across from the Elder's cave, at the Public Assembly cave. This cave was used for public assembly and entertainment. There were no living quarters. Several large auditorium sized rooms had been cut and shaped by laser. In some cases comfortable furniture had been installed by Azorkan craftsmen. The first room in the complex would easily accommodate the lessons for the pictorial alphabet. A group of six by six-foot sandboxes equipped with wooden pointers to draw with were organized and ready.

The five governing Zapatsaurs left the half-moon shaped conference room and walked out into the corridor. They retraced their steps, walking around the bend in the tunnel where the secret entrance to the inner city was concealed, and walked up the thirty degree angled tunnel to the entrance. They all paused at the entrance and looked northward in the sky where General Zen and Sally were still small specs in the sky. The Zapatsaurs left the Elders cave one by one to the remainder of the day's duties. The Minister of Human and Zapatsaur Affairs flew the short one hundred yards across the way to the Public Assembly cave to witness and record the first pictorial alphabet lesson.

Sally was only half a mile away from the four peaks of Zapatsaur Mountain. The General Zen was to her right, flying forty yards away and dressed in dark brown pants and a heavy black sweater that Indie had made for him. He looked lost in thought or nervous about the success of the pictorial alphabet they had designed together.

The sky was like a sheet of grey silk and a strange mist had begun to accumulate on Azorka's east coast. Sally looked at a small ship in the ocean which looked like it was heading north for Portugal. From this height it was no larger than her finger nail. The four serrated peaks of Zapatsaur Mountain loomed closer and occasionally pierced the clouds rolling past. Sally was glad she decided to wear a large wool poncho over her gray shirt and pants. The poncho was green, but she was happy to trade the color clash for the warmth it provided.

Sally looked to her right at a pre-occupied General Zen, gazing ahead and gliding at a comfortable thirty miles per hour beside her. The General's emerald green speckled Zapatsaur moved its wings up and down carrying him and its fourteen foot muscular body with little effort. The Zapatsaur was an intelligent animal and a mysterious animal. That was the General's thoughts on the subject and he seldom elaborated; probably because so little was known about them.

Although rolling mist drifted by, sometimes in folds which seemed to cling to the mountain tops, Sally's view of the countryside was spectacular. The old growth forest, they flew over earlier in the flight, had been replaced by a variety of colorful trees grouped into small forests and rocky fields. They were flying one hundred feet above the tree tops and closing in on Zapatsaur Mountain. Her Zapatsaur's scales were warm on this moist day but its red specs and the emerald green specs of the General's Zapatsaur no longer glistened with the absence of sunlight. Sally looked down as the last of the tree tops disappeared and the two hundred yard long rocky field that ran up to the entrance of Zapatsaur Mountain came into view.

The General Zen shook himself free of his daydream and looked at Sally flying beside him. Pointing downwards with his right hand he signalled for their landing. They would land in the narrow one hundred yard rock valley between the Elder's cave and the Public Assembly cave, then proceed towards room one already set up for the Zapatsaurs first lesson.

A green canvas back pack was strapped to the General's back, which contained some of the specially cut stencils they would use for the pictorial alphabet. Stencils would help advance the communication time and learning process. It was Indie, General Zen's wife that gave them both the idea of using stencils. She argued that the stencil would remind the Zapatsaur what it represented and how it could be used for other communications. The Zapatsaur could easily press the stencil in the sandbox, leaving an impression then finish the communication with the pointer. Each stencil was a comfortable handful for the Zapatsaur at eight to twelve inches in size and would be placed in a small bag attached to a rope which could be worn by the Zapatsaur.

After changing to a south westerly direction and another ten minutes the two Zapatsaurs landed. Sally jumped down in front of the Public Assembly cave and Zen joined her. Their two Zapatsaurs folded back their wings and walked upright behind them then down the half-moon shaped tunnel. The laser smooth walls held a large crystal lamp every twenty yards which provided more light than the crystal torch in the Elder's cave. The tunnel was also slightly larger. The width was sixteen feet and the ceiling was twenty-three feet in height. It angled downwards at twenty-five degrees and after fifty yards of walking they came to room one on the right side of the tunnel.

The group of four walked into a large rectangular room with square walls and ceiling. It was sixty feet long by thirty feet wide and well illuminated by six large crystal lamps which hung from a thirty foot high ceiling. In front of General Zen and Sally were thirty-eight Zapatsaurs standing patiently in front of a sand box with a pointer stuck in the sand. General Zen and Sally's Zapatsaurs joined in, filling the remaining two vacant spots.

The General Zen was the first to introduce the daily lesson. Sally had agreed to take notes on the lesson so that they could later evaluate and maybe improve. She would also be distributing the stencils by dropping the forty sets of stencils made up and attached to a small rope over each of the pointers in the sandbox. "Good morning, my friends and students." General Zen's voice echoed in the large room. The forty Zapatsaurs moved their heads up and down in a silent greeting.

"First of all I'm going to arrange my stencils at the front here against the wall so everyone can see. I'm going to explain what each stencil can communicate and the various combinations they can be included in for other communications." The General finished.

Sally watched Zen place the stencils against the wall behind him. His muscular six 'foot frame and dark brown hair framing a face free of wrinkles certainly helped make him look sharp and young, but Sally knew he didn't sleep well last night and that he was tired. She decided that this would be a good time to place the forty rings of stencils over each pointer in the sandboxes. Sally picked up the box containing the stencils and started walking from sandbox to sandbox placing the stencils, arranged on a short rope, over the wooden pointers. By the time Zen had finished arranging his stencils at the front of the room Sally only had two more sandboxes to equip.

Zen smiled appreciatively at Sally, thankful for an organized assistant. Sally smiled back then gave Zen a quick nod of her head, as she placed the last ring of stencils, signaling that she had finished and joined him at the front of the room.

Sally looked around the large auditorium that had been cut out by laser almost five thousand years ago. There was still some evidence of the Great Flood but most of the water marks had faded. Sally remembered her father telling her that ancient Azorka believed that they had escaped the Great Flood by going down into the inner earth below the world's oceans for forty days. They had meditated to lower their heart rate and were able to survive a compromised version of breathable air. However, when the biblical account for the Great Flood was discovered, new questions arose and the suggestion that they were off planet for a period of thirteen months. But who arranged this temporary exodus?

Sally wondered how to enrich the lives of the Zapatsaurs. Maybe after the pictorial alphabet had been mastered they could communicate their needs better. Would they appreciate more decorative surroundings? The crystal lamps that hung from the ceiling and in the hallway were utilitarian but not stylish. What kind of furnishings would they select or would this be important to them. Sally wanted to do more for the Zapatsaurs to enhance their lives.

Unknown to Sally was the presence of the Minister of Human and Zapatsaur Affairs, who had made a mental note of her kind thoughts which would be entered under the heading of "Human Development" in the records stored below in the inner city. Sally's spiritual development would probably exceed the expectations of the Zapatsaur population. She truly loved her neighbors and was considerate of their needs and feelings. Unfortunately she was also carrying the burden of guilt for the loss of two Zapatsaurs who were trying to rescue their baby from the clutches of the Dragon Queen and the Wizard's creature.

The Minister of Human and Zapatsaur Affairs would also record the Generals feelings. Zen was suffering from the same guilt and had feelings of inadequacy for not being able to prevent the kidnap of the Zapatsaur's baby. The General was also preoccupied with thoughts concerning Heather's wellbeing. Heather's eyes had begun to change color and she was waking up late at night screaming from unusual nightmares. The doctors had said the nightmares would go away with the passage of time, but they could not explain her eyes changing color from hazel to dark blue. They would monitor Heather's eyesight weekly. The General knew that Sally accepted the doctor's explanation for the nightmares as did other family members. However, Heather had not told anyone about the unusual things she had been seeing in her nightmares. Only the Zapatsaurs were aware of these thoughts and right now the entire population of Zapatsaurs were more concerned for Heather than her family because they knew what Heather was seeing.

Chapter Three

He slammed the reception room door which led to his upstairs office. The Wizard began leaping up the stairs two at a time and his gray cone-shaped hat almost flew off his head. His tiny four foot frame was exhausted by the time he reached the top. The Wizard was anxiety riddled but keeping up a passable pretense of calm and organized. He was a calm companion at a pleasant breakfast with Amy, making small talk and keeping the conversation positive. Amy had stared back across the table with her penetrating dark blue eyes knowing that he was fuming mad about the kidnap of the Dragon Queen. However, he had a plan to rescue the Dragon Queen. The Wizard had adjusted his formula and created another creature which was still incubating in the lab. He had asked Amy to keep an eye on the creature's development. He believed this creature might stay alive longer and still have the necessary enhanced intelligence to help him in a secret mission to free the Dragon Queen. The Azorkan's had caused him to rush the process he would have spent more time perfecting.

The Wizard reached his office door, flung it open, rushed inside and slammed the door behind him. He went to his window and closed the dark drapes on a damp and gray day. Walking over to the bookshelf, he reached up to where the dark blue crystal skull sat on the second shelf between two of his favourite books and grabbed it holding it steady between his sweaty palms. He carried the crystal skull over to his desk and set it down so that it would face him while he sat in his recliner.

The Wizard had lost precious hours of sleep last night after discovering the crystal and metal helmet he had Heather wear for his experiments was set for the mind of a Yetz and not a human like it should have been. He had been too hasty, too emotional after Heather's kidnapping and didn't check the settings. He could only guess at what might happen to Heather as a result of this mistake. Heather had been blasted with more energy necessary to release the blockages in her brain for collective consciousness. Would this also unlock other cerebral blockages? Would Heather become a danger to herself and others?

On those days that the Wizard was conducting his experiment with Heather, the instruments were reading normal for cerebration. The instruments should have registered abnormal participant with the setting for Yetz. He should have double checked! The Wizard decided to stop himself from further musings, realizing he had given in to his emotions.

He looked around his office at the beautiful European needle point chairs, comfortable couch and his desk crafted from the most beautiful and figurative wood then decided to get up and lock the door. He returned to his desk and leaned forward in his recliner, gazing deeply into the eyes of the crystal skull. The Wizard had a strong aversion for this mental procedure, but he just had to know what was going on with Heather. After about five minutes of staring deep into the eyes of the crystal skull it seemed to come to life. Thin jagged white lines, like lightning bolts, flashed wildly from within the skull and its dark blue color became a lighter shade. Connecting with the Wizard's dark eyes brought this ancient creation of artificial intelligence back to life and it gazed back at him, deep into its creators mind. The wide-eyed and now mesmerized Wizard could feel a familiar tingling sensation and knew that the crystal skull was probing his mind.

The office was silent and after a further ten minutes the Wizard could feel his release. He felt himself slowly floating out of his body, rising up out of his motionless head with his arms at his side as though his ethereal head arms and chest had to squeeze through a narrow doorway. What looked like a trail of white smoke where his legs and feet should be followed. The Wizard looked at his astral body. He could see through himself yet his arms, chest, hands and fingers were defined by black lines. This outline of half his body was attached to a trail of smoke the approximate thickness and length of his legs. It would fluctuate trailing downwards as the Wizard rose to his office ceiling and assuming a kneeling shape when he stopped to look at his motionless body still staring into the eyes of the pulsing crystal skull.

Thousands of years ago when the Wizard had been dealing with the Dheginians, they had told him that when he had finished crafting the dark blue crystal skull that he would be able to leave his body after a short meditation with the skull. He would be invisible to the world and would not be able to move objects by physical means. He would still have his mental ability and be able to persuade his subject through suggestion but he would not be able to communicate using his voice. He could travel at incredible speed without discomfort from weather or friction and pass through solid objects at will. The Dheginians also warned him that if the crystal skull was removed from its place in front of his frozen body while he was out of his body that he would be trapped in this state forever. The Wizard had locked his office door so he felt secure enough to carry on with his investigations.

The Wizard moved down from the ceiling of his office and over to the window with its dark drapes drawn. He hesitated for a moment then moved through the wall beside the window and outside into a gray day with light rainfall. He couldn't feel the dampness or rainfall which was beneficial considering the speed he would reach while searching for Heather. The Wizard hovered in front of the castle wall momentarily while he prioritized his search. He held out his outlined arms and hands in a flying position in front of him and took off at an incredible speed heading northwards in the direction of Azorka. He was travelling so fast that the Empire's landscape of fields, small forests and palm trees on the north beach appeared to blend together; their colors smearing and distorting like an indefinable pastel painting. The ocean below from one hundred feet above, looked like a dull blue blanket and in the next couple of seconds he was approaching Zapatşaur Mountain, what the Azorkans call Village "C". The Wizard slowed down to thirty miles per hour for his approach and touched down on the entrance to the Elder's cave. He paused for a moment and looked around at the bone white mountain peaks and below to the one hundred yard wide valley floor. There was no activity and it was so quiet he knew he'd be able to hear a pin drop. The Wizard moved inside and traveled down the angled tunnel till he came to the half-moon shaped conference room, where this morning's meeting was held. The entire cave was empty, silent and void of any activity. Where had all the Zapatsaurs gone? If a Zapatsaur was here, the Wizard wouldn't be able to read its thoughts. The Wizard and Amy would have to apply, with some effort, a mental shield when in the presence of Zapatsaurs to conceal their presence. If the Wizard removed his mental shield now the Zapatsaurs would pour out of their caves and pandemonium would ensue ruining his plan.

The Wizard travelled past the conference room to the lowest levels, where rooms had been built for special committee meetings, to confirm that the entire Elder's cave was empty. Frustrated, he raced upwards and shot out of the Elder's cave into the open fast as a shot fired from a pirate's musket. He hovered above the valley dreading the possibility of having to check every cave on the mountain in order to find Heather with her Zapatsaur. The Wizard decided on checking all the large meeting facilities first, so he flew above the one hundred yard valley below and entered the Public Assembly cave across the way. He might have searched longer for public meeting areas if it wasn't for the Dragon Queen's partial intel and reconnaissance of Zapatsaur Mountain. The Wizard raced inside the cave and paused ten feet into the tunnel when he thought he heard the faint echo of voices. below. He descended slowly in the tunnel until he came to room one where the voices were coming from. The Wizard looked inside to find the General Zen and Sally standing at the front of the large room facing forty Zapatsaurs standing beside six foot square sandboxes. It looked as though they were conducting a lesson in front of this assembly. The Wizard found this interesting so he decided to float up to the ceiling where he'd have a bird's eye view. Maybe Sally or Zen would mention Heather's whereabouts.

"Now I need each of you to take the circle and the long narrow rectangle stencils and make an impression in the sandbox." The General Zen said. His voice echoed off the walls and ceiling in this auditorium sized room.

"Placing the circle at the top of the long rectangle will communicate a tree. The circle is used for the top branches and leaves and the long rectangle would be the supporting trunk. To illustrate the time of day, use the circle again if it is daytime and use the half-moon stencil for night. If it is an island that the tree sits on use the half-moon stencil again as the land. If it is a continent use the long rectangle stencil below the tree. If the location is high in the mountains use the triangle stencil and place it beside the tree to indicate this." The General finished.

It was Sally's turn to speak so the General reached for his canteen to take a sip of water, relieving a parched throat and dry mouth.

"So we are building a picture in order to provide a more precise communication." Sally began. The Wizard thought Sally's portrayal of a teacher was quite good despite the fact she was so carelessly dressed in a green poncho and gray pants and shirt.

"Now to add you to this communication use this stencil." Sally held up a stencil cut in the shape of a letter "" and kept it held high till she fellt every Zapatsaur had a chance to study it.

"If there are more Zapatsaurs or humans that you need to add to your communication then use this stencil." Sally held up a stencil cut in the shape of a W. It was Sally's idea to add a few letters representing language. She thought this would help advance the Zapatsaurs more quickly towards written communication in the future.

"Add the letter "I" to your communication and it could read, "I am on land in the daytime." Or, using the letter "W" it could read," We are on land in the mountains at night." Depending on the circumstances, you may find this a more precise method of communicating with your rider." Sally suggested.

The Wizard was entertained but growing impatient waiting for Zen or Sally to casually mention Heather in conversation. He couldn't read the minds of humans or Zapatsaurs but he had the mental ability to provoke a desired result. The Wizard concentrated on Zen. He looked down from the ceiling and into Zen's eyes. He sent the thought directly into Zen's mind, "Where is Heather today?" and he continued to repeat the question. Finally Zen blurted out, "Where is Heather today?"

Sally turned around from her inspection of the first sandbox and saw the puzzled look on Zen's face. They had both waved good bye to Heather before they left the Guardians castle and flew south for their lesson with the Zapatsaurs.

"I don't know why I said that." Zen mumbled.

Sally was beginning to think Zen was too preoccupied for his own good, and she was beginning to worry. However the Zapatsaurs were moving their heads around the room as though they were frantically searching for something. They seemed to be more suspicious than worried about the General's outburst. They continued their searching looking a little panic stricken from the frustration of not finding whatever they were looking for.

The Wizard saw that they were aware of his presence and realized his mistake. The Zapatsaurs were constantly probing the minds of Sally and Zen especially during the lesson. They had heard his subliminal messaging loud and clear. Fortunately for the Wizard it was too early in the learning curve for the new alphabet, to communicate this.

The Wizard picked a spot on the opposite wall and shot forward head first with lightning speed. He went through the wall five feet above the laser smooth floor and emerged in the now empty hallway on the other side. The Wizard moved forward in the hall standing upright on his smoky trail. He casually travelled upwards in the twenty five degree angled hallway while thinking about the failure of his attempt to gain information. Maybe Zen was too startled from the Wizard's message to react the way the Wizard had expected. He continued to blame himself for the waste of time, until he left the Public Assembly cave at which point he shot forward in the direction of the Guardians castle. The ground, two hundred feet below, became a blur of colors and when it changed to a blur of solid green the Wizard knew he was approaching the castle. It was a quick trip which had taken a grand total of five seconds. The peculiar looking castle, a bright white concrete, and marble architectural wonder, loomed closer. The Wizard came to a sudden stop at the hand carved front door. He marvelled at the workmanship that had gone into producing the front entrance. It was such intricate and artistic work for a mere carpenter. Before floating through the front door, he looked behind him and saw that two Zapatsaurs were feeding in the front lawn garden. The Zapatsaurs were not aware of his presence and he would make sure he didn't make the same mistake twice. The Wizard would have to hope that Heather was home or that her parents would bring up her whereabouts in conversation. The household must be in an uproar over her new problems.

The Wizard passed through the hand carved front door and into the castle hallway with its shining white marble floor and where decorative frescoes tapestry and beautiful paintings adorn the hallway walls. He stopped to admire the enormous living room capable of comfortably seating fifty guests. The couches and chairs were huge. The luxuriously upholstered furniture could easily accommodate the tallest guest in the kingdom. Furniture color ranged from rich blue stripes to bright red paisleys. The coffee table was a dark mahogany and some of the wooden chairs featured hand carved Zapatsaurs on their backs, with a comfortable dark green upholstered seat.

The Wizard overheard some conversation coming from the kitchen so he abandoned his casual examination of the décor and started floating down the marble hallway towards the kitchen entrance. He stopped at the entrance and looked in on a dimly lit room, the skylight no longer effective on such a gray day. The castle's King and Queen were dressed for a damp day. Tamara was comfortable in brown pants and a brown knit sweater that Indie had made for her. Mitch was dressed in a green sweater and brown pants. They were both seated at the marble kitchen table, a popular meeting place for family conversation. Tamara faced Mitch across the table with a cup of warm tea cradled between shaky hands. Mitch reached into his pants pocket, pulled out a console and turned on the room's crystal chandelier above them. Soft light poured down from eight crystals fashioned into candles and mounted on a wooden wheel.

Enough light was now available for Mitch to see the effects of anxiety in Tamara's red and haunted eyes.

"The doctor said that recurrent nightmares suggest that Heather is suffering from post-traumatic stress disorder." Tamara said.

She had her dark brown hair held in a pony-tail. This unobstructed view of her somber expression and wrinkled eyes, gave the Wizard an idea of how serious Heather's condition was affecting her family. Tamara was showing signs of losing sleep. The Wizard floated over closer, deciding to join them at the table. He sat his invisible form down beside Mitch.

"What has the doctor recommended?" Mitch asked calmly.

He was maintaining his composure and was like a wall of strength for Tamara to lean on.

"He is suggesting that we modify Heather's diet to promote good health for her neurotransmitters and for relaxation. He'll do another blood test in two weeks. The doctor would like Heather to exercise three hours before going to bed and he has asked us to record what we consider unusual behavior and any details of the nightmares she is having." Tamara finished.

"What did the doctor say about Heather's eyes changing color?" Mitch asked.

"He has never seen anything like it before and he is suggesting that it is a reaction from the Wizard's experiment. As for what it could mean for her future eye health he couldn't speculate, but when he tested Heather's eye sight it had improved significantly. He'll want to test her eyes in two weeks' time as well." Tamara said. "It sounds like the doctor is approaching the problem with good common sense. The dietary enhancements he is suggesting should be a boost for Heather's health and might help with her recurring nightmares." What new foods should we go shopping for this afternoon?" Mitch asked.

"The doctor recommends an increase in the amount of fish Heather consumes. He said that a small piece of salmon every day around lunch time would be the best routine. Next on the list was passion flower and lemon balm tea. He wants Heather to include one drop of oil from each of these in her tea and consume at least three cups per day. This will help her deal with anxiety and any insomnia that may occur as a result of her condition. In order to promote relaxation he recommended one cup of black or green tea before bed. Heather should also have leaves from the gingko tree made into a soup or tea in order to kill any free radicals that may be circulating throughout her system from her stay with the Wizard. This precaution the doctor said is necessary insurance." Tamara finished. The weather outside did nothing to raise optimistic thoughts. Mitch and Tamara sat for a couple of minutes while the Wizard, sitting beside Mitch at the marble table, watched them wrestle with their mental agony. Mitch was first to break the silence.

"You know sometimes anxiety can lead to physical problems like lack of energy or stomach upset and a weakened immune system. Heather is perfectly healthy and does not demonstrate a lack of energy or motivation. She carries out her work for Azorka's agriculture just as energetically as before and maintains a positive outlook as though nothing is bothering her. I think there may be a good chance Heather's experience with the Wizard will fade away into insignificance with the passage of time." Mitch said.

"Except for her late night screaming which wakes the household, Heather appears perfectly normal." Tamara admitted.

A smile broke across Mitch's hardened features and his moustache and goatee seemed to stretch appreciatively with his optimistic expression. He stood up; his seven foot muscular frame cast a shadow over the Wizard's place at the table. The Wizard was enjoying the privileges of his invisibility but getting anxious about gaining the information he needed.

"Why don't we go shopping now and get those dietary ingredients. The trip to the store will help us get rid of some of these emotional cobwebs. By the time we get back, Heather will have returned from her test flight with Lana and Sally will be back from Zapatsaur Mountain." Mitch suggested.

Mitch was hoping his optimism was infectious and that Tamara would stand up and exit the kitchen with him. Fortunately, Tamara did exactly that after stretching up on her toes to give him a kiss in return for being her husband and a fortress of support she could count on.

"Where are Heather and Lana testing the new flying machine?" Mitch asked. He stopped just before they reached the kitchen entrance.

"There testing the craft over Africa where it's unlikely they'll be visible to travellers from the outside world. The terrain offers perfect testing grounds for the crafts low altitude manoeuverability. They will also be testing the stability of the craft at top speed and maximum altitude." Tamara finished.

Mitch smiled down at Tamara. She was sounding more like her natural self.

"Heather is enjoying being part of Azorka's future, thanks to the efforts of the Aryans. I'm sure her experience today will be rewarding and I look forward to her stories tonight." He said.

They both left the kitchen hand in hand and smiling having found a small stream of happiness to ride upon for the afternoon.

The Wizard left the kitchen smiling as well, having found the information he so badly wanted without forcing the effort and spooking the Zapatsaurs. He approached the front door after Tamara and Mitch had departed for village A in the valley just below the castle. The Wizard drifted through the front door and re- appeared outside. He took one last curious look at this, he thought, bizarre looking castle. It wasn't the typical block or fieldstone construction so common throughout the world. This castle had long white walls, of concrete and marble without any visible sign of expansion joints. The windows were recessed and the castle rose straight up at the front and was angled downwards at forty-five degrees at the back. From a distance it was hidden from the world by the remainder of the old growth forest that managed to live on top of the hill as well as the valley below where the other two villages were. The top of the castle was only partly exposed from a distance looking like half of an arrow pointing into the sky and assumed by many to be a bone white mountain peak.

The Wizard rose two hundred feet above the castle and decided on assuming a flying position. He held his outlined arms stretched out in front of him and took off with incredible speed in a southerly direction towards Africa, his smoky trail, where his legs should be, rigid and straight behind him. Once again the Wizard was travelling so fast that the various landscapes on Azorka and the Empire's island blurred together in a confusion of color. The Wizard marvelled about the advantages of his transformed state. It was advantageous because he couldn't feel the air friction or temperature of the climate. But it was a disadvantage because he couldn't move physical objects. The Wizard reached what looked like a long blanket of dark blue, the ocean two hundred feet below and increased his speed. In five seconds he had reached the west coast of Africa, so he slowed down and searched the sky for Lana's flying craft. It was almost a clear blue sky with the occasional tufty cirrus cloud floating by. The sun shone down on the jungle below.

Another brief moment passed and the Wizard caught a twinkle of light in the distance. What would cause a reflection at this altitude? The Wizard thought for sure this would be the flying machine and he moved forward at a cautious two hundred miles per hour to investigate. In another thirty seconds the Wizard saw a familiar sight he had not seen for ten thousand years. He pulled up beside a silver tear-drop shaped flying machine that was about fifteen feet long, and ten feet wide at the front for the cockpit where Lana and Heather were seated. The craft at the rear was three feet wide where a battery was secured in its own compartment two feet long and below the center of the craft was the propulsion system. The craft inside was designed to transport four people, having two green upholstered seats in the rear and two in the front where the ladies sat strapped in between a throttle that Lana had her left hand on.

The Wizard decided to join the ladies. The entire top half of the craft was covered in glass and a barely detectible seam at the front just one foot behind the ladies was the hinge work for the pilot's pop-up exit. The Wizard slid through the metal and glass, his invisible form taking up a kneeling position on the seat behind Lana. He leaned forward to look at Heather's eyes and saw that they were a dark blue and identical to Amy's eyes. Lana leaned forward to look at a temperature gauge, illuminated in a green glow. The speedometer read two hundred miles per hour, a reasonable cruising speed for this craft, and the temperature gauge was reading average.

"It's not showing any sign of overheating and we've been doing two hundred miles per hour for the last three hours." Lana said.

Lana pushed the throttle forward another notch. The craft silently increased in speed and the gauge read two hundred seventy five miles per hour. The Wizard could not hear a whining of a motor or the rush of air over the craft. It was precisely crafted to a perfection and silent, with the exception of Heather's voice.

"Were you saying that the propulsion system works like a merry-go-round, using centrifugal force and centripetal force?" She asked.

Lana smiled and tucked a lock of her blonde hair under her dark brown head band while she thought about her answer. While an uncomfortable silence followed the Wizard noticed that both ladies were dressed in identical outfits of white robes over white shirts and pants with white slip on shoes. He wondered if this was a coincidence or Heather's new condition unconsciously directing her to dress like Lana would be that morning.

"Air flows through rotating inlets into a chamber designed with a twisting configuration, the air molecules compress in size as they approach the center of the chamber then return to their original size as they leave the chamber. This system results in energy strong enough to allow the craft to defy gravity and fly." Lana finally answered.

Lana saw that Heather looked a little confused.

"Heather, I wish I knew more about it. I'm the pilot chosen for my natural flying skills, but I can give you a rough description. The battery in the rear compartment starts the motor. Air enters into a specially designed disc shaped inner chamber which directs the air molecules towards the center of the chamber. The air molecules decrease in size with the effect of centripetal force and as they make their journey through the inner chamber a vortex of powerful energy is created from the swirling air. When the air molecules exit the chamber, they regain their original size due to centrifugal force. Air is rotated into a twisting form of oscillation and a build up of energy results which causes levitation. The build up of energy also recharges the battery.

The craft's glass is unbreakable and the metal is extra durable and able to withstand a crash at two hundred miles per hour. It is a marvel for a flying craft and it is weaponized with laser cannon. It even has its own atmospheric chamber should we be travelling the full eight hundred miles per hour and venture to close to space." Lana finished sounding a little out of breath.

"I thank you Lana!" Heather looked over at her friend and smiled.

Lana's beautiful blue eyes with her unique square pupils picked up Heather's reflection and she saw her dark eyes in that reflection.

"Do you think I look ugly with my new eye color?" she asked.

"Of course not Heather! This is just the result of a peculiar experiment with the Wizard. You said your eye sight was quite a bit better. Maybe we should all be grateful for your rescue and the unexpected enhancement of your eye sight. Good eye sight is a gift and I'm sure Ted would agree with me that your eyes look as beautiful as before." Lana reassured her, then continued.

"What I can't understand is your sudden interest in the technical operation of this craft." Lana said.

The Wizard took note of this statement as it indicated a personality shift, and after all, besides being aware of her determination and strong character, he didn't really know that much about Heather.

"Come to think of it, I don't know why I'm interested either. I'm usually satisfied with simply recording readings for you and being a sort of copilot to help you." Heather answered.

Heather thought about this and her thin brown eyebrow arched upwards, almost mimicking a question mark.

"It feels like an itch in my brain for more knowledge." Heather rationalized.

Lana was silent while Heather looked down on the colorful and beautiful African landscape. She didn't realize that she was gazing further ahead than what would be considered normal.

"Look! Lana down there below to your right!" Heather shouted excitedly.

Lana looked to her right but didn't see what Heather was seeing. They were travelling faster than two hundred miles per hour. It took a couple of seconds. before Lana saw what Heather was referring to and she brought the craft to a stop and hovered directly over the trouble spot.

They had flown five hundred feet above a Congo rain forest with mahogany, teak, and the great moabi trees which towered over the forest with a crown of leaves and branches. The herbaceous plants like begonia and dark red flowering impatiens spilled out from the forest tree line onto a field of long golden grass where a wounded okapi and two of her young were surrounded by three leopards. Heather could see that the mother okapi had suffered a wound to its rear leg, although Lana could not see those details.

The outside world was not aware of the existence of okapis in the seventeenth century. The okapi is an elusive herbivore with black and white stripes on its hindquarters and legs like a zebra. They have reddish colored bodies and white faces that look similar to that of a giraffe. The adult okapi is about five feet tall and the native pygmies refer to it as a horse.

"Those leopards are going to attack the okapis!" Heather shouted.

Lana was considering whether or not she should use the flying craft to scare off the leopards or the laser cannon, when a bright round electrified circle of what looked like lightning appeared beside the flying craft about fifty yards to Lana's right. The electrified circle hung there in the blue sky for a few seconds then Gerta and her creature flew through and the circle disappeared behind them. Heather and Lana were stunned into silence by what they saw. The creature hovered in mid-air for a moment while a surprised Gerta looked at the futuristic tear-drop shaped flying machine with wide eyed astonishment. The creature was concentrating on the animals below and didn't seem to be aware of the flying machine. Suddenly it dived to the ground below, with Gerta leaning forward to compensate for the steep and sudden descent. The creature landed smoothly, and Gerta straightened her posture but remained seated hanging on tight to the creature's neck. The creature had landed in front of the advancing leopards and those predators growled out loudly their displeasure at this unwelcome arrival. The creature responded by lowering its scaly neck and opening its large jaws revealing two rows of razor sharp teeth, and growling back. The three leopards growled again, this time a warning for the creature not to interfere. The creature answered by opening its mouth a little wider and releasing a deafening booming sound. The tremendous force of the sonic vibrations sent the leopards tumbling backwards along with the debris of sticks and stones hidden in the tall golden grass. The three shaken leopards regained their footing and they raced back into the dark safety of the jungle terrified of this strange reptilian creature. Gerta had remained seated on the creatures back and now that these dangerous predators had gone she got down and walked over to the injured okapi. The mother okapi. was at first shy, shuffling about nervously, but when Gerta spoke softly to her she settled down. Gerta saw the shallow wound on the mother okapis leg from one of the leopard's claws. It was bleeding but it wasn't a life threatening wound, so Gerta ripped off a strip of her dress from the hem and gently wrapped it around the okapis leg, securing it in a knot to hold in place. At least this will stop the bleeding and help prevent infection she thought.

Gerta's creature approached the okapis after she had completed her doctoring. To Gerta's surprise the okapi's family were not afraid of the creature and the two younger okapis walked over to greet the reptilian as a gesture of appreciation for their rescue. The mother okapi gave a faint whistle or bleat and soon her two young joined her. The creature watched the departing okapi's family walking in an easterly direction towards a stream to satisfy their thirst. Then the creature looked back towards the jungle to see if any more predators were lurking about but all seemed quiet. It was now satisfied that the okapis were safe.

Gerta returned her attention to the strange flying craft above, which had remained hovering in the same position watching the drama unfold below. Who were those strange ladies she saw inside the craft? What kind of craft could defy gravity and hold its position in mid-air without falling to earth? Was this a work of witchcraft? If so would they be a threat to herself and the creature?

Gerta's creature walked upright, its large black wings folded neatly behind its back, and stood beside Gerta gazing up at the craft. It uttered a low growl, what Gerta had come to recognize as a cautionary growl. The creature was uncertain of the threat the flying craft and its occupants presented, but something about the flying craft and its occupants was unsettling. Gerta's creature was very protective and intuitive. It was only one hour ago that the creature had uttered the same low growl when Gerta had reached for a light orange colored ackee from a tree on the West African coast. The creature thought it was a dangerous food. Gerta moved on searching for more familiar food and settled for a banana instead. Gerta had almost become familiar with all of her creatures expressions. Heather and Lana had been amazed by the dramatic events below. They sat still in the hovering flying craft peering down in silence at a creature that was twice the size of a Zapatsaur, furnished with dangerous looking tusks and a red-haired lady that was the rider. The ladies had watched the creature rescue the cornered okapis with some kind of invisible force that had flowed out of its mouth with a booming sound and sent the leopards tumbling backwards. The red-haired rider had torn a strip off her dress to patch the wound for the mother okapi. All this had taken place in less than five minutes.

The Wizard was equally amazed, although Heather and Lana were not aware of his presence, he felt sure that the creature knew he was aboard. That was because the Wizard recognized the immortal Dheginian creature that often carried a Dheginian warrior during the conflict with Yetz-an. The Dheginian warrior and creature were telepathically linked. The rider could send instructions using telepathy and the creature could confirm those instructions telepathically. The creature would often be used in space explorations to find and identify hostile animal life on alien worlds using its powerful telepathy to pick up on those animal's intentions. The Wizard knew the creature's telepathic powers will have "sniffed him out" by now. But what was this creature doing here, so far away from home?

Heather was the first to break the silence.

"Did you see how that creature got rid of the leopards?" She asked.

"I'm not sure what happened, but when the creature opened its mouth and that low booming sound came out the leopards were hit with a powerful invisible force that sent them tumbling backwards. It must have knocked the wind out of them because they fled back into the jungle." Lana answered.

"Do you recognize the red-haired rider or the creature?" Heather asked.

"I don't recognize her or the creature." Lana answered.

"Look! The creature is gazing up at us with its wings spread out on the grass. The lady is climbing up and seating herself on the creature's back! There flying up here! Heather shouted.

Gerta and her creature flew up to meet the occupants of the flying craft. Gerta was still discovering her creature's various behaviors and she had a feeling that the creature's curiosity was the driving force compelling it to investigate. She knew that it somehow picked up her thoughts, which would have told the creature that she didn't mind the investigation as she was curious herself.

The creature made its ascent at about sixty degrees with Gerta hugging tight to its lower neck. It didn't take long for the creature to reach the craft, five-hundred feet above. It levelled off and hovered in place beside the flying craft. The creature's large head drew closer to the cockpit and it looked at Lana. But when it raised its head to look at Heather the creature uttered the same low growl it had below. Gerta could see that there was something about Heather the creature found disconcerting. Then the creature looked at a green upholstered seat behind Lana and whined. Its complaining cry of frustration caught Gerta's attention and she wondered what had caused this expression.

The Wizard decided to test his telepathy with the creature in an attempt to settle it down. The Wizard looked directly at the creature's eyes and sent his message. "There is no threat here and no need to be alarmed. I'm a friend in astral form. I cannot appear before you. Can you understand me?"

The creature's head happily bobbed up and down in appreciation and relief from this revelation. The Wizard took this to mean yes and now he was really excited because not only could he communicate with the creature but the creature understood the English language. The creature had been around long enough and exposed to the outside world that it had learned the language. This also suggested that the creature had witnessed some of the horrors of this war-like planet and would become a willing ally in the Wizard's plan for world domination. While the Wizard was admiring the creature's tusks, which he felt gave it a sense of true majesty, the creature's left tusk grazed Lana's craft just below the glass. Heather felt the jolt and looked over at Lana who had been surprised by the sudden appearance of the creature and its rider. The creature's mishap shook her from a trance like state.

"Hey! I think it's time to get out of here!" Lana shouted as she reached down and grasped the throttle. Using her right hand Lana turned a small round control mounted on the silver dashboard in front of her. A half-moon shaped instrument beside it lit up in a dazzling green revealing the various angles the craft may safely travel and its current position. Below this gauge, a panel dropped down automatically and a small handle bar rose slowly for Lana to grip in her right hand. The small handle bar was the steering wheel for the craft. It allowed the pilot to control the crafts upwards and downwards direction as well as turning left or right.

"I don't know what kind of damage those tusks can do but I'm not hanging around to find out!" Lana yelled out her anxiety.

The craft shot forward with incredible acceleration and down at a swift descent of sixty degrees. Lana had spotted a small grouping of trees two hundred yards ahead and aimed the craft downwards to enter it. This was welcome cover from the creature who would not be able to follow them in with its enormous wing span.

Heather's stomach was just beginning to recover from the craft's swift descent when Lana brought it to a standstill at what she believed was the entrance to a small forest and looked up through the glass to see if the creature was following. The creature wasn't finished its investigation and wanted to communicate more with the Wizard. It matched Lana's sharp angle of descent, causing Gerta to lean forward and hang on with her arms wrapped tightly around her creature's neck.

The creature had recognized the invisible Wizard as a Yetz. The creature regarded him as a like-minded ally who may be able to help navigate this planet and contact its home world so it could return.

The creature was approaching fast so Lana entered the forest and accelerated to thirty miles per hour, slowly moving around trees and bushes in a north-easterly direction. Lana brought the craft to a stand-still after a couple of minutes and looked behind her to confirm that the creature wasn't following.

Heather was the first to speak after regaining her composure.

"Do you think we've lost them?"

"I don' know but I'm going to open the cockpit and get some fresh air." Lana said.

They were hovering twenty feet above the forest's natural path. Monkey vines hung down from every other tree. The forest's floor was colored green, red, orange and yellow from various flowers and plants of different sizes. There was a chorus of sound from the wildlife especially various species of birds perched in the branches above. A large African gray parrot startled Lana as it suddenly appeared within arm's reach flying frantically across the forest.

Lana looked up into the trees to see a small group of chimpanzees swinging on the vines in the same westerly direction the parrot was headed towards. Maybe the crafts sudden appearance startled the forest's wildlife. She looked over at Heather who was gratefully breathing in the fresh cool air of the forest and wiping perspiration from her face using the sleeve of her robe. Lana could hear a waterfall in the distance and as she gazed in an easterly direction she could see that the forest sloped downwards. Perhaps it was a much larger forest than she originally thought.

Lana removed her headband and shook her head from side to side. She ran her fingers through her shoulder length blonde hair.

"I don't see any sign of the creature or its rider." Lana said.

Heather turned around, looking through the Wizard's astral body, and saw the bushy mane of a lion leading a lioness and her two cubs across the forest path heading in a westerly direction. There was no sign of the creature behind them. Heather reached behind her head and ran her fingers through her brown hair which had stuck to her neck. Like Lana she shook her head from side to side a couple of times to free up her damp hair.

"I think we may have lost them." Heather said.

The Wizard knew better. He was looking all around the forest and upwards through the trees for the creature. The Wizard was sure the creature would find a way into the forest because he knew the creature wanted to continue communicating with him. The Wizard began to compose a quick and concise telepathic message which would direct the creature to the Empire's island. He would be a perfect host and Amy could help the red-haired rider with a loan of clothing and a warm bath followed with something to eat. The Wizard remembered the Atlantic salmon he had in the freezer and thought this would be the most palatable for the creature.

While the flying craft and its occupants, both visible and invisible, held steady in position, Gerta and her creature had flown away from the forest entrance and hovered in place above the flying craft. Looking down through a tiny opening in the tree tops, the creature listened to Lana and read the Wizard's thoughts. It moved over in an easterly direction until it found a group of trees that it preferred to hover over. They had shifted from their original position by about fifty yards in an easterly direction. The creature held this position but Gerta noticed it was slowly drawing its wings closer to its body forming a sharper curvature and lowering its neck so that the head faced the tree tops. The creature held this position for about five minutes. Gerta was wondering what the creature was planning to do. The creature reached up slowly with its powerful arms and hands, grasping Gerta's waist gently but firmly.

"Heather! Listen! Do you hear anything?" Lana asked.

"No! The entire forest has gone silent. I can't even hear one bird! This is kind of scary! I think you should stop stretching your six foot frame and sit back down." Heather whispered.

"Lana, shut the door quick!" Heather suddenly shouted.

Like an answer provided to confirm Heather's sudden premonition, the creature let out its booming call and the tree tops spread wide, straining from the sonic vibrations, Gerta and her creature floated down through the space provided by the spreading tree tops. The creature's wings were pulled in tight and reminded Gerta of an umbrella. Those large wings slowed the rate of descent and they both landed gently on the forest floor. The creature released its secure hold on Gerta and held out its hands, palms upward and pointing at the flying craft fifty yards away in a pleading gesture.

Lana was glad she had taken her friends advice, but like Heather she was frozen in shock by the creature's tactic. She continued gazing at the creature and its rider fifty yards east of the craft, wondering what would happen next. Lana understood why the wildlife was moving in a westerly direction. All those animals were just as terrified of the reptilian as she was.

The creature remained hunched down and motionless with Gerta on its back. It looked across at the empty space the invisible Wizard was occupying. The dim light of the forest had caused the creatures reptilian pupils to dilate and its yellow eyes were like lamps in the shade of the surrounding trees.

The Wizard had moved his astral body closer to the glass of the craft and was straining to connect with those strange eyes. He noticed that the red-haired rider was looking confused but otherwise bravely handling the surprising chain of events. Unfortunately, Dheginian creatures and humans do not have a telepathic link. The rider or creature would have devised a form of communication that was probably dependent upon illustrations or symbols. But that was'a useless way of communicating when sudden action was necessary. The rider would have to trust her safety to the creature's judgement. She was courageous, silent and stared ahead without any expression of fear or anxiety. The rider must be familiar with the creature's independent personality and instincts.

In the next second both creature and rider disappeared into thin air with Lana, Heather and the Wizard watching. The ladies were wide eyed wondering what to expect next, but the Wizard was jumping up and down with excitement because he knew what the creature was up to.

Gerta prepared herself for what would feel like the longest second in darkness. Gerta would never understand how she could perceive so much in one second of time. Suddenly the forest disappeared and Gerta was in a dark and silent place. She could feel her legs on the creature's scales but she couldn't move them. The creature was also frozen still. A bright pin-prick of light appeared about fifty yards away. This light grew into a familiar circle of electrified light which Gerta immediately recognized as the same circle or portal the creature would fly through when leaving or arriving at a destination. It was approaching rapidly, lightning swirling around it's twenty-foot circumference. The portal did not make a humming noise like the portal Gerta was familiar with. It silently passed over and under Gerta and the creature, but without leaving a burning smell as the portal used for travelling greater distances would. When the second had passed, Gerta and her creature were one foot away from the glass of the flying craft. Gerta could move her body again and the forest had reappeared.

Lana was shocked by the creature's sudden arrival and jerked her head away from the window so fast she almost hit Heather sitting beside her. Heather's dark blue eyes were wide with astonishment and she was wondering how they could get away from this persistent menace. What did it want?

The Wizard's black lined but invisible smile was ear to ear and he immediately sent a telepathic request for the creature to meet him at the Empire's island. The creature was looking through the glass behind Lana where the Wizard's astral body was seated. It was nodding its head up and down, acknowledging the Wizard's invitation, but before the Wizard could give the creature directions to the Empire's island, the flying craft took off.

Lana finally shook herself free from shock and swung into action. She reached down for the handlebar and thrust the flying craft's throttle backwards so hard that the craft catapulted away from the creature and Gerta at such a rapid speed that they almost crashed into a tree. Lana regained control twenty yards away from the creature and returned the craft to the forest path. She maneuvered the craft into position heading back to the forest's entrance and open field beyond.

Heather turned around in her seat and saw that the creature had retracted its wings and was charging towards them on foot. Gerta was hanging on tightly with her head down to avoid the lower branches of the forest. The creature chased the craft at what must have been forty miles per hour, and Heather could see that it was steadily gaining on them. The forest floor, twenty feet below the flying craft, shook with every footfall from the creature.

Lana paid careful attention to navigating the flying craft as quickly as possible out of the forest and away from the creature. She didn't want her anxiety causing a mishap. She was wondering about the creature's actions. Back in the forest the creature might have considered more aggressive action by landing two of its huge feet on the upper glass of the flying craft. However, it seemed as though something else had won its intrigue and determination. While these perplexing thoughts helped to add perspiration already building on Lana's brow, so did the creatures massive movements and crashing footfalls behind her. The creature was moving so fast that Lana could see the green dress of the red-haired rider rippling from the rush of air.

Gerta raised her head from the wind breaking shelter of the creature's neck and saw that they were only twenty yards from the flood of light at the forest entrance. Just before her eyes glassed over from the sting of rushing air, she saw the flying craft exit. It gained altitude quickly and disappeared from her view. In the next ten of the creature's accelerating footfalls they reached the forest entrance. The creature extended its wings and sprung up into a clear late morning sky. Its powerful wings moved up and down rapidly and it chased the flying craft rising in the sky, three hundred yards ahead.

The Wizard was thinking about leaving the flying craft. He had learned enough of Heather's condition and the new flying craft to declare his covert mission a success. Heather was still growing into her new heightened senses. Her good eye sight, intellectual curiosity and enhanced intuition didn't add up to being a threat. to the Empire.

He would leave the flying craft and give his new friends directions to his castle.

The craft had levelled off at one thousand feet. Lana could see the creature coming on fast with its arms stretched wide, as though it planned to grasp the body of the flying craft. A green flash from the dashboard caught her attention and her hopes of escape sank. It was the warning for the automatic purging process that was a safety feature built into the motor. The craft would gradually slow down then stop and hover while the process cleared the motor of an accumulation of dust and dirt.

"We must have picked up some dust when the creature came through the trees and landed in the forest." Lana said while pointing at the dashboard gauge. Heather turned in her seat and saw the pursuing duo behind them. She saw the rage and frustration in the creature's expressions. The eyes, now focused on the object of its anger, were like orange and black burning lamps. The creature's fingers were flexing and stretching those large lethal claws in preparation for the attack. That huge wingspan and those leathery black wings were a blur of activity. Its ferocious determination and abilities were narrowing the gap between them. The red-haired rider had her head down and somehow, Heather didn't think she had much say in the pursuit.

"Well I hope it will purge fast!" Heather yelled.

The creature was only one hundred feet away when the Wizard passed through metal and glass, leaving the flying craft to fly down for a meeting in mid-air. Heather and Lana's heartbeats slowed down a little as they were relieved to see that the beastly creature had cut off its attack. The object of their torment was hovering in place below them. It's long black leathery neck and hideous head with those tusks were moving up and down as though addressing an invisible visitor. The red-haired rider was silent, her eyes fixed on the flying craft above.

"That's twice now! This creature could have physically tackled the flying craft in the forest and it was within striking range just now when all of a sudden it broke off the attack. What was causing it to stop?" Lana shouted, releasing some of her tension and anxiety.

"I don't know but we're lucky it broke off the attack." Heather said with relief.

Lana was trying to understand the creature's motivation for chasing them. If she knew why the pursuit was taking place maybe she could find a solution for the problem.

"While we were hiding in the forest, this creature could have physically tackled the flying craft. Instead it did the fast forward trick to gaze through the window at the empty seat behind me." Lana said.

"I don't think we'll figure out this creature's reasoning behind the chase any time soon. Maybe Mitch can offer some insight concerning the creature's origins. There could even be info on this kind of an adversary in the Azorkan historical pyramid. However, when the purge is done we should head back to Azorka and report our incident." Heather finished.

"I think that would be a great ideal I see that the purge is almost done." Lana said with relief.

"After all this drama today, we should treat ourselves to some relaxation and good food. How about joining me and my family at the castle for dinner tonight?" Heather suggested.

"That is an even better idea considering Tamara's delicious dinner recipes. I accept your invitation, dear friend! Lana said.

The purging process had reached its completion and in another five minutes Lana pushed the throttle forward for Azorka. Heather and Lana were back in Azorka within the hour and all ready to relax after a very heart throbbing test flight.

Meanwhile, the Wizard had reached the creature and red-haired rider one hundred feet below. There mid-air meeting was nine-hundred feet above the picturesque Congo rain forest and golden fields bustling with a variety of wildlife. The Wizard was successfully communicating directions back to the Empire's island while the creature nodded its acknowledgement. The red-haired rider hugged the back of the creature's neck. She was expressionless but patiently waiting for the conclusion of her creature's investigation.

Looking into the creature's eyes, the Wizard sent a mental picture of his castle and where he wanted the creature to land. He couldn't telepathically converse but he could send images and instructions.

The creature received the image and saw the large outside court where the Wizard wanted it to land.

"Now my astral form can travel there in about forty seconds. I know you can teleport and probably be there in a couple of minutes, so I'll wait in the courtyard for both of you. We'll get some food into both of you while my men enclose the courtyard for your shelter and furnish it for your comfort. Amy will be delighted to meet both of you." The Wizard sent telepathically.

The Wizard sent an image of Amy. The creature recognized her as a Yetz and moved its head up and down in acknowledgement.

The meeting reached its conclusion, so the Wizard departed, his astral body accelerating to an incredible speed. In forty-five seconds he touched down in his castle's courtyard to wait for Gerta and the creature. It wasn't long before the electrified portal appeared directly over his castle. Gerta and the creature flew through then down to meet their host.

Heather and Lana were looking forward to dinner and an evening of relaxation.. They had many questions on their minds and hoped that Mitch could answer them. He might have some suggestions for defending against the creature's aggression. Both ladies felt certain they would meet the creature again. This time they would be ready for action.

Chapter Four

Heather was walking slowly, shrouded in a ghostly gray mist. She was wondering where she was and what she was doing. The ground crunched under her bare feet and her long white night gown was dragging along the ground occasionally snagging on a stick or sharp stone along the moonlit path. As the mist drifted from her view she saw bright red clouds appear. The sky was almost black yet these drifting clouds, were strangely bright, illuminated by some invisible energy. The path took Heather up a hill where nature had placed three lonely trees on a cliff. The tree to the right of the path, closest to the cliff's edge, still had green leaves which were moving in slow motion from a gentle night wind. As Heather walked towards the tree, she noticed some movement beneath its drooping branches. It was General Zen's wife Indie who walked out from the shadows. She was dressed in a long white robe with a blue collar and held a silver colored crystal skull at waist level. Indie silently stood there facing Heather; her eyes were haunted, wide and unblinking. Slowly Indie's lips began to move but her speech was not audible. She was looking through Heather and talking to someone behind her. Heather looked around to see who Indie was speaking to but all she saw was more mist drifting across the path. She turned back and Indie was still speaking silently to this invisible individual. A movement out of the corner of Heather's eye caught her attention. Behind Indie a dark figure was moving through the strange red clouds. Like a large black menace it moved from one cloud to the next by some unseen propulsion which defied gravity and came closer to the cliff. Heather sensed danger from this peculiar figure and as it drew closer she could see it was almost man-like in appearance. It jumped down from its position in the sky and landed on the top of the furthest pine tree in front of Heather. This strange visitor had an unusually large head with an extended cranium and occipital bone. The legs and feet closely resembled those of the Dragon Queen except they were black in color. The upper body was thin and spindly but the hands with four long fingers had lethal looking sharp claws. It jumped again; it's monstrously large three digit feet found a branch to perch on at the top of the tree behind Indie.

The grotesque looking black figure moved its upper body down so that it could see Indie below. Heather saw the monster's reptilian dark orange eyes looking at Indie so she shouted out her friend's name to alert her to the danger above. Her voice echoed, bouncing around the landscape but Indie didn't hear the warning. Indie seemed hypnotized and continued to move her lips in slow motion addressing that unknown someone that Heather could not see. The monster jumped down from the tree and landed three feet behind Indie. It was easily ten feet tall and covered entirely in black scales of different shape and size. The monster's mouth was horrific with a protruding lower jaw filled with razor sharp teeth. It was creeping closer to Indie. Heather was certain the monster was going to harm her friend. She let out a blood curdling scream, releasing built up frustration and fear, in a futile effort to save Indie.

Suddenly the bedroom light was turned on Heather woke up in a pool of sweat and sat up in her bed. Perspiration ran down her forehead and her mouth was still wide open from screaming. Tamara stood there by the bedroom door, her hand still resting on the light switch. Heather looked up to the ceiling at the white light fixture crafted in the shape of a sea shell, and held up her left hand to shield her eyes from the glare.

Tamara saw the torment in her daughter's eyes which were dark and wide with fear.

"You had another nightmare. I thought that would happen after your frightening experience in Africa. Tell me what were you dreaming about before you forget." Tamara said.

Heather was slowly waking up. However, she shook her head from side to side letting Tamara know that the fragments of horror from her dream were dissipating too fast for her to relate.

"I'm sorry mother but I can't recall what the nightmare was about. The sky was dark and I remember strange red clouds. I was walking somewhere in this sweat- soaked night gown I'm wearing. That's all I remember." Heather finished.

Tamara felt that she should try to keep Heather awake for a while. She didn't want her to go back to sleep and revisit the same nightmare. Maybe with a short break from sleep the images from the dream would flush out from her memory.

"Let's grab a hot chocolate in the kitchen. You're not going to go back to sleep right away." Tamara suggested.

"I think that would be a great idea, mother." Heather agreed.

She quickly changed out of her nightgown and put on a yellow robe similar to the one Tamara was wearing and walked out into the hall where her mom was waiting. The second floor hallway was seventy feet long but she could still hear Mitch snoring in his sleep fifty feet away. She wondered how Sally across the hall from Mitch and Lana in the guest bedroom close by could sleep through that noise.

Tamara and Heather walked down the hallway to the stairs. Like the rest of the castle the hallway was a work of art with walls of mahogany wainscot and decorative white marble. The hallway lights were gold-speckled twelve-inch-wide crystal shells mounted on the marble every twenty feet and they shone down on a rich red teak floor complimented with one of Indie's specially crafted carpets which ran down the hallway and the gold gilded staircase.

Tamara and Heather drank hot chocolate in the kitchen at about the same time the Wizard was pouring tea for Gerta and Amy in the courtyard of his castle. The creature was comfortably resting in a hammock the Wizards men had constructed from the spare sails Sam had kept for ship building. Over head the courtyard had received a make due roof of tarps strung together to shelter the creature from the elements.

As soon as Gerta and the creature had set down in the courtyard, the Wizard had raced upstairs to his locked office. He passed through the door, rose above his frozen body and entered it through the same astral opening on top of his head. He began to feel the circulation in his limbs. When the last part of his astral body, his head, had entered he stopped gazing at the crystal skull. The crystal skull immediately stopped its pulsing of thin white lightning-like lines and returned to its original darker blue color. The Wizard got up, unlocked the office door and ran back down the stairs to meet Gerta and the creature in the courtyard. He had his men assemble a living area for the creature including the table and chairs in the courtyard which is where they sat together at this late hour.

"Gerta, why did you decide to visit Africa?" The Wizard asked.

Gerta had borrowed some of Amy's clothing and she sat comfortably at the table in a yellow cashmere sweater which complimented her red hair and skin color. The Wizard thought a glowing outdoor fireplace gave her skin a little extra color. Brown tweed cargo pants and slouch boots made up the rest of her outfit. Amy was dressed in her white robe and sat across from Gerta. She listened quietly to the Wizard and Gerta while twirling a lock of her long grey hair between her fingers.

"I had been telling my friend about the different wildlife and food we could enjoy in Africa. I know the creature is interested in other animals and an exotic diet of fruit and fish. We deserved a little holiday and variety after our experience in Haiti." Gerta answered.

"So tell me where it all went wrong in Haiti." The Wizard asked.

"We were getting tired of Peru and decided to leave for Haiti and do a little exploring. Landing on a mountain, maybe five miles from where the voodoo worshippers were going to sacrifice me to the python, we found a cave and stopped just outside the entrance. The creature communicated with me by using a stick to draw in the dirt and said it would leave me for a short while to see if it could find a tunnel below, then pointed to my half-moon shaped flute suggesting I use this if I had an emergency it could help me with. I wanted my friend to have the freedom of exploration without me if it thought this was necessary. I agreed and the creature disappeared into the cave. Then shortly after the voodoo worshippers jumped out from their hiding spot and took me captive binding my hands behind my back and placed me on a cot which two natives used to carry me back to their camp. I couldn't call for help because my hands were tied and the flute was in the pocket of my green dress. I believe that they thought I was a powerful witch that commanded a ferocious flying creature. They wanted to feed me to the python so there could be a transfer of my power to the snake and then to the Voodoo Queen. I watched them throw white powder on this huge snake. It had a sedating effect on the animal because it stopped struggling. Later that night the Voodoo Queen was able to reach into the basket and pull its head out and hold it close to her face without fear of the snake biting her. I gather she was instructing the snake to eat me with her weird chants. I thought that as soon as the tranquillizing effects of the powder wore off, the snake would consume me." Gerta finished.

The Wizard sat at the head of the table and faced Amy on his left and Gerta to his right. He took off his gray cone-shaped hat and scratched the top of his head, as though that might help him absorb all he had just heard of Gerta's story. The creature was searching for tunnels or a tunnel complex deep in the earth. What countries, was the creature expecting a tunnel system in Haiti to connect with? Why was the perceived tunnel system so important to the creature? How deep in the earth would this tunnel be that the creature would abandon Gerta while it explored? This last question led the Wizard to believe that the oxygen supply would be so limited that Gerta might not survive the exploration. The Wizard was relaxed and comfortable, dressed in his usual gray suit, but now he felt a curious mental nudge that was demanding his attention. He would ask the creature about its explorations when Gerta and Amy have retired for the evening.

Gerta was carrying on with her story while Amy listened attentively. "That's when Sam and Leif showed up and rescued me." Gerta continued.

"Sam and Leif rescued you!" The Wizard shouted.

The Wizard's eyes flew wide open and he had shouted so loud it startled the creature who had been reclining comfortably in the thirty-foot long hammock. "Those are my men and there on a mission to recover one of my crystal skulls which was stolen from me many years ago." The Wizard said. He was still surprised that Gerta had been rescued by his men in Haiti.

Gerta carried on with her story telling the Wizard and Amy about the crystal skull which Sam and Leif had recovered from the Voodoo worshippers. She mentioned the beams of light pouring out from the crystal skull's crafted eyes. Gerta noticed the Wizard's eyebrows arching upwards in surprise at this revelation and wondered about the significance of the crystal skull's performance. She told the Wizard and Amy about the struggle with the pirates and the loss of Leif's ship. When she let them know that Leif and Sam as well as every member of the crew was safe, she saw the relief and gratitude towards the creature and Gerta for their help, on both of their expressions. Gerta told them that she had promised to meet Leif and Sam in another three days.

While Gerta had been telling the story, the creature had been making its own inquiries by the most powerful mental telepathy currently on the planet. It saw that the Wizard was creating another creature and that it had been moved to the same facility as the previous creature had occupied. The creature probed the Wizard's and Amy's memories and saw both the excitement and disappointment from this experiment. The Wizard had made this creature more intelligent using some of the bodily fluids taken from the kidnapped baby Zapatsaur. Unfortunately, something in this process was responsible for the created creature's short life span or complete break-down of its immunity system. The creature probed the Wizard's knowledge concerning the Zapatsaurs and was amazed that this creature could also read the minds of humans. The Wizard could not read the minds of humans and it could not read the mind of a Dheginian creature or warrior. However, the Zapatsaur seemed to display a unique intelligence and telepathic ability. The creature would put up a mental shield if ever in the presence of a Zapatsaur.

The creature stopped probing the Wizard's mind while it thought of a possible solution to keeping the new creature, being created by the Wizard, alive longer. If the Wizard was experimenting, what would he have to lose if the creature made an offering towards his endeavor.

"I hope the doctor did a thorough job of Leif's wound." Amy said. Her concern for Leif's well-being was sincerely displayed in her facial expression.

During the conversation, the creature had crept forward and removed a saucer from the table without anyone noticing. The creature was only eight feet away from the table. It only had to move forward a few feet to accomplish this. The ladies missed this; the Wizard saw its stealth. He kept his eyes focused on Gerta when the creature reached for the saucer. Then he looked over at the creature while Gerta reassured Amy that Leif's wound had been well looked after.

The creature looked over at the Wizard, knowing he was watching and nodded his head slightly hoping the Wizard would inquire when the ladies had retired from the courtyard. Amy's eyes were glued to Gerta after her amazing story and Gerta seemed far away still recalling her brief nightmare in Haiti. Both of the ladies looked tired.

"I want to welcome you both to the Empire, your new home!" The Wizard said enthusiastically.

"I am very grateful, sir. What can I do to earn my citizenship in the Empire?" Gerta asked.

Gerta had always wanted to contribute to her country; to pull her own weight and not be a burden to those around her.

"Don't worry about contributing. You'll do that naturally as each challenging situation unfolds. For now, please enjoy the fellowship of our society and educate yourself with our struggle against Azorka. Acquaint yourself with the history of our two civilizations and how we differ. But above all other considerations I want you to relax and let time mend the trauma and turbulence in your life this year. We'll build a home for both you and the creature close by to my castle." The Wizard finished.

"I am getting tired, so I think I'll retire and get some sleep. I have fixed up a bed just inside the reception room for you Gerta." Amy said.

"I am going to take advantage of that right now." Gerta said.

They both said good night to the Wizard and got up from the table to leave the outside courtyard for some well-deserved rest. Gerta's story, earlier in the day about her experience in Massachusetts, was another drama that had exhausted Amy.

Gerta was the last to leave, saying good night as she closed the door. The Wizard turned back to face the creature and saw that it had left its hammock and was holding a stick over a patch of dirt and drawing. The courtyard was not fully tiled. The Wizard had made a patio of large grey marble slabs for the outdoor oak table and wall mounted fireplace which had died down to smoldering embers. The Wizard got up from his comfortably upholstered gold chair and stepped down from the marble patio. He walked over to the creature to see what was drawn. The creature paused from drawing and raised its head as the Wizard approached. Its dark orange eyes sparkled in the remaining light from the fireplace. The Wizard froze in his tracks when he saw what the creature had drawn.

"I didn't want anyone to know that I could write in your language; especially Gerta who would have too many questions that I wouldn't want to answer." The creature had scrawled this in the dirt but the Wizard could still read it.

The Wizard believed Gerta would ask the creature where it had come from and why it was here. He understood the creature's dilemma. There are too many misunderstandings that crop up when your audience can't grasp certain concepts. Both the rebel Yetz and the Dheginian Star System with eleven inhabited planets of various Dheginian races, believed in managing a planets resources for future trade within the universe. The Yetz were extraordinary scientists and the Dheginians had extraordinary talents including military skills. Together they would find the technology that will be used to control the earth's population.

The Wizard was still surprised that the creature could write in his language. He moved around the patch of dirt that the creature was using like a blackboard and took up a position beside the creature while it wrote a new message.

"I'll tell you why I took the saucer. I decided to offer you some of my blood, as an experimental option for your creature's development. I don't know what the outcome would be but I believe this option is a chance to help increase the life span of your new creature."

The message was hurriedly scrawled in the dirt but it was still legible. The Wizard realized this creature had read a great deal of his thoughts both past and present. He thought about the creature's offer. What would the result be if he introduced the bodily fluid from an immortal? He had introduced the bodily fluid from a Zapatsaur to produce greater intelligence and this had produced the desired result. However, the Zapatsaur lived the same amount of years as a human being. The Wizard didn't believe the additional introduction of blood from a Dheginian creature would jeopardize his experiment.

"I am grateful for your help and accept your offer." The Wizard said.

The creature moved back over to its resting place and reached underneath the hammock where the saucer was hidden. Picking up a sharp rock the creature made a slice on its right palm and immediately a flow of its golden colored blood fell into the saucer. When the surface of the saucer was filled with blood, the creature removed the sharp rock from its palm and immediately the wound closed up and healed. Half a tea cup of its bodily fluid had been captured.

"I'm going inside to the kitchen where I can get a pocket size beaker and cork that blood. We can visit my creature tonight in its incubation chamber so that I can add the fluid to the intravenous connection I use to feed it while it sleeps." The Wizard said.

The Wizard entered the castle while the creature reached up to the canvas covering the courtyard and untied the two sheets opening them wide enough in the center to fly through. Then it returned to the patch of dirt and brushed out its last message just in case Gerta came back out into the courtyard.

The Wizard returned closing the door behind him and saw the moonlight pouring into the courtyard and onto the creature who was facing him. He took the saucer from the creature and carefully poured the blood from the saucer into the small beaker, corked it and placed it in the pocket of his gray jacket. The creature made a fist with its left hand and withdrew one digit, pointing at the Wizard to climb onto its back. The creature was practically lying down to accommodate the limited reach of the Wizard's four-foot frame. The Wizard pulled down his gray cone-shaped hat and climbed up using some of the creature's larger scales as a foothold. The creature extended its wings and they rose into the night.

At three hundred feet above the castle the creature paused and they hovered for about thirty seconds. The Wizard suspected the creature was probing his mind again; this time for directions to the old ruby mine now converted to a laboratory for his experiments. He had found a comfortable sitting position at the bottom of the creature's neck and he looked down at his castle which looked no larger than a shoebox from this height. It was a clear night and the moon was a natural spot light for the peaceful scene below. The ocean was calm and there was no wind but in the distance the Wizard heard a lonely cry from one of his new wolf-like creatures created to patrol the island at night.

The creature stopped hovering after a couple of minutes and flew west at a leisurely pace enjoying the sights of the Empire's island. It looked down with amazement at the concealed domed homes submerged slightly below ground level where they would be hidden from the wandering telescope of the intrepid mariners. The creature had read the Wizard's mind and knew exactly where the laboratory was located. It even knew that the Wizard had moved an incubation chamber from the lower levels of this new facility into the cage where this creature's short lived predecessor had stayed.

The Wizard looked out from the shelter of the creature's neck and saw that they were approaching the west beach. The ocean on this side of the island was still and with the help of moonlight on a clear night, it almost looked like a sheet of glass. The creature began to angle downwards preparing to land on the beach ahead. In another minute they touched down on the cool sands of the beach five feet away from the large fifteen by fifteen foot wooden door which was partially concealed from sight by the bushes of the beach's natural embankment it had been built into.

The Wizard waited until the creature had lowered its body then hopped off and walked over to the massive door. He opened the smaller four by three foot hinged entrance built into the door and walked inside. The Wizard walked over to the large metal wheel mounted on the stone wall and turned it clockwise. The large wooden door squeaked in protest and the connecting chains rattled above but with a few more rotations of the wheel he had opened a space wide enough for the creature to walk through. The creature folded its wings and walked upright through the opening. The short landing and thirty stone steps leading down to the new creature's cage were illuminated by under-powered crystal lamps mounted on the walls. The Wizard made a mental note to get these re- charged and decided to leave the large door open. The opening would provide some extra light.

The Wizard's shadow marched down the stairs in the dim light and the creature followed occasionally ducking down to avoid injury from the rocky ceiling. They approached the cage at the bottom of the stone steps. Much better lighting had been afforded for the operating area and larger crystal lanterns were mounted on stands around the incubation chamber, which was a vat of chemical mixtures in which the Wizard's sleeping creature was submerged. The Wizard opened the cage door and walked up to see his new creature. A special motorized device circulated the mixture of liquids within the twenty by ten foot gray metal vat, and it bubbled loud enough to drown out the creatures shuffling footsteps as it took up a position beside the Wizard. A large bright red reptilian was laying on its right side in a fetal position, with leathery black wings folded neatly on its back. It had two horns that pointed downward at the back of its head with jaws and teeth similar to a wolf. The legs and arms were similar in proportion like the Zapatsaurs were but it was at least a couple feet taller. The hands and feet were outfitted with three long and lethal looking claws.

The Wizard moved over to the bottle for the intravenous feed mounted on a stand close to where the creatures head was resting. A small flexible tube, trailed down from the bottle and into an opening cut into the side of the vat. The other end fed into the creature's mouth where it was securely wrapped into place. Every three hours a timer on a nearby monitor would send the signal for a small measure of food to be released into the creature. The Wizard was glad that half the formula inside the bottle was gone because he required the additional space for the Dheginian creature's blood. He removed the cap from the top of the bottle and poured in the golden blood. He stirred it in to the remaining food solution he had formulated for the creature's nutrition until it turned gold in color. The Wizard recapped the bottle and checked the copper wire that attached to it tracing it back to the monitor to be sure the connections were secure. The three foot wide two foot tall monitor was on a nearby stand and the gauges were lit up in a bright yellow. The Wizard reached out and turning a small half-moon dial on the monitor, he changed the feed time on the monitor to every four hours. He believed the creature's enzymes would utilize the additional nutrition more effectively.

While the Wizard continued with his checks, the creature made a mental note of the laboratory. This set up would be a perfect nursery or maternity ward on its home planet. It was warm inside the cage and well away from the daily distractions of the surface. Outside the cage, the walls in the large oval space had been cut smooth with laser tools. The ceiling was sufficiently high enough in this section of the laboratory to be left in its natural condition. The Wizard's shadow danced about on the wall as he moved from one monitor to the other recording readings on papyrus paper attached to a clipboard. In another five minutes the Wizard had completed his various tasks and they both exited the cage with the creature leading the way up the stone steps.

Once outside the Wizard mounted the Dheginian creature to fly back to his castle. As they both ascended into the silent night, the Wizard thought about the possibilities for his new creature. He wondered if it would live longer and if it would have special abilities from feeding on Dheginian blood.

***

Back in Azorka, Heather had just fallen back to sleep after her late night hot chocolate with Tamara. However she had fallen back into her previous nightmare and found herself walking uphill along that same moon lit path surrounded by a milky fog. The strange luminous red clouds drifted past the two pine trees and the leaves of the tree where Indie had walked out of the shadows. Another figure stood where Indie had been, dressed in a dark gray cowl that touched the ground. The hood of the cowl concealed the identity of the silent and motionless stranger. Heather's curiosity was a powerful persuasion for her to investigate, and she moved forward cautiously. Somehow she remembered the sharp rock which had snagged her nightgown. Heather veered off the path to avoid it. Her bare feet landed on a soft mound of moss that had grown beside the path. As she approached, a bolt of lightning flashed out of the blood red sky and struck the top of the mysterious figure's hood.

Instantly the cowl was transformed into a bright glowing silver color as though brought to life by the lightning. The cowl was still radiant when Heather stopped in front of it and peered inside the hood to learn the identity of this individual. She was not prepared for the shock she got when instead of a head with a friendly face to greet her; she saw empty black space with stars and a sun with orbiting planets of a different solar system surrounded by a large asteroid belt inside the hood. Heather suppressed the urge to scream. She bravely waited to see if the strange figure would communicate with her and wondered if there was a purpose to this dream.

There was an uncomfortable thirty seconds of silence then finally the cowled figure spoke to Heather.

"Heather. Do you see that rock to your left?" It asked in a deep male voice which echoed around the dreamscape.

Heather looked to her left about three feet away where a small boulder about the size of a footstool was nestled in a patch of grass.

Heather turned back and answered the figure.

"Yes I see the boulder." Heather replied. Her trepidation had left her and been replaced by curiosity.

"Raise your arms and using your index finger in each hand, point them at the boulder." The mysterious figure said.

Heather turned to face the boulder and raised her arms with both index fingers pointing at this two hundred-pound rock. To her surprise, a bright white border appeared around the boulder.

"Do you see a white border around the boulder?" The figure asked.

"What is it? Did I cause this to happen?" Heather asked.

She was getting used to the idea that her senses had been altered or made more powerful by the Wizard's experiment. Heather wanted to know if she was becoming super-human. Maybe this strange individual, obviously a man judging by the deep voice, could offer her an explanation.

"For now, during the early stages of developing your ability, think of the border as an energy field to assist you when manipulating objects with your mind. Now will or command the boulder to rise three feet and hang motionless in mid-air." The figure instructed in his deep voice that eerily echoed around Heather.

Heather was still facing the boulder and its dazzling white border. She concentrated and silently commanded the boulder to rise three feet above the earth and hang in mid-air motionless. She was amazed when the boulder rose obeying her will, and hanging motionless in mid-air. Her eyes opened wider as if to confirm that this was really happening. She could manipulate the mass of an object with her mind. Heather was beginning to understand what an advantage this would be in combat.

However, the mysterious figure, although he couldn't read her thoughts, was quick to respond, warning Heather about a restriction affecting this ability.

"There is one draw-back that you have to remember and that is to keep your subject outlined in the power of the white border which your mind automatically creates, you have to be able to see your subject at all times. For example, if you decided to banish a dangerous creature upwards into the frozen waste-land of outer space, where a lack of gravity would prevent its return, the creature would come tumbling back down a minute or more after you lost sight of it. If the creature entered a bank of dark clouds, your view would be obstructed and the creature may fall to quickly back to earth before you could apply the border." "Heather you have acquired these abilities thanks to a careless mistake the Wizard made before the experiment began. He had failed to check his settings before the experiment began. The setting was for a Yetz, what the outside world will eventually call an ET.

As a result, you have had a larger dose of energy go through you than what is appropriate for a human being. You've experienced the removal of several genetically engineered blocks in your brain. Scientists on my world have been perplexed for many years about humans. They believe the limited abilities of the human race is deliberate because they often resort to violence. Your new abilities may help save your world from chaos and destruction. which will be present in three hundred years." The mysterious figure finished. Before Heather had a chance to ask another question she saw that the red luminous clouds were parting behind the figure, actually ripping apart with beams of bright light shining down on her between the ragged rips in the sky. The strange figure began rippling and wavering as though his substance had become liquid.

"I must leave you now." He said. "Remember threeee...hundreddd..... yearssssss."

The rip in the dreamscape had reached the top of the cliff. It was tearing the leaves of the tree behind the rippling and shimmering mysterious stranger. The tearing had reached the trunk of the tree ripping it in half and as it fell apart crashing to the ground the mysterious stranger disappeared from sight. Heather watched helplessly as the tear advanced towards her. Bright beams of light shot out of the earth from the widening tear as it approached. Automatically Heather held up both her hands to shield her eyes from the discomfort and before the destructive tear arrived she sat up in bed. Her hands were still held above her eyes, a shield now for a bright morning sun. It was going to be a beautiful day in Azorka, she thought.

Heather searched her conscious mind and sure enough the dream was intact. Vivid details from this experience challenged her to investigate. The strange word "Yetz" stood out and she made a mental note to ask Mitch if he knew the meaning. The last sentence the mysterious stranger had uttered, rang in her mind like an alarm bell. She would explore this message and its possible meaning privately.

Outside her room, Lana, Sally and Mitch were making their way down the long hall together. Tamara had called them down for breakfast. The mouthwatering scent of a freshly cooked meal made its way up the gold gilded staircase to the hallway above. The hungry trio ran down the staircase on the way to the kitchen, laughing and joking as they went. The extra noise and excitement was enough to jolt Heather from the comfort of her bed. She rolled out, got dressed and confidently pranced down the stairs to join them. Heather had made up her mind to keep the details of her most recent dream secret. When she could be alone, Heather intended to test her new ability in the real world.

Just as Mitch enjoyed a plate full of maple syrup drenched pancakes from one of Tamara's special recipe's, the Wizard downed a mouthful of Amy's specially barbequed pheasant and scrambled eggs. Gerta's breakfast was delicious; she hadn't enjoyed a home cooked breakfast like this for a long time. The Dheginian creature enjoyed a breakfast of salmon filets and dried seaweed dipped in sesame seed oil.

The Wizard looked up at the blue sky through the opening in the canvas the creature had left in place from last night's secret excursion. It was a warm sixty- five degrees and not a cloud in the sky, so they had decided to dine with the Dheginian creature in the courtyard. This would be a perfect day to relax. The Wizard would complete some minor chores and record last night's readings from the monitors used for his new creature's development.

The Dheginian creature was looking forward to more casual outside exploration of their new home and was considering taking Gerta along later on in the day. For now, Amy and Gerta would walk around the grounds after a tour of the castle. They ate in silence while the Dheginian creature looked into the Wizard's mind. The Dragon Queen was resting on the surface of the Wizard's conscious mind and if the Dheginian creature had vocal chords it would have screamed out its surprise. Did the Wizard know that his captured friend closely resembled one of the fiercest and feared of the Dheginian races? The creature saw her predicament, and became extremely anxious to rescue her; help which would be welcomed by the Wizard. This would take some teleportation and some mind reading, but it could be accomplished by mid-day.

Not far from Amy's mouthwatering breakfast, deep in a cavern, one very curious reptilian eye opened and glowed a bright emerald green. Another champion for the Empire was born this morning.

Chapter Five

From a distance, Azorka looked like a green crown for creation with its old growth forest clustered together sheltering buildings and Azorkans below. The late morning sunlight twinkled in the dark orange eyes of the Dheginian creature flying above the tree tops. The creature had seen a few Zapatsaurs flying about the village. Their eventual arrival above the tree tops was anticipated and the creature was able to teleport out of the range of their sight until they returned to their destination below. The creature had also raised a mental shield so that the Zapatsaurs couldn't read its mind. This precaution had been in place for over forty minutes and the creature was satisfied this was sufficient defense against early discovery.

After arriving at village E, close to the south west coast of Azorka, the creature had found a large tree and climbed down waiting for an Azorkan below who was thinking about the medical center in the village. After reading the mind of an Azorkan on his way to the medical center and suffering from a sprained foot, the creature got his directions and was able to teleport two hundred yards west of its position onto a large branch about one-hundred and forty feet above the dome shaped medical center. When a doctor left the center for a breath of fresh air, the creature learned that the Dragon Queen had been moved by General Zen to village B where he lived with his wife Indie. The Dragon Queen was moved for more testing and amputation of her two extra arms which attached to her white leathery wings. The creature left village E and teleported above the tree line until arriving at village B.

After a brief search, the creature found a tree that would support its weight. It began climbing down. The tree was also ideal for concealing the twenty-seven foot body which the creature wrapped around the tree trunk. When the creature was one hundred feet above a fieldstone covered rectangular medical center it stopped. There were two guards posted at the east side entrance and the west side entrance. The creature read their minds learning that the medical center was one level with an operating room in the middle of the center and patients rooms on both sides running down to the last room in the wing which was a laboratory.

After about forty minutes, a doctor walked outside of the center and the creature was able to read from his mind that the operation was to be performed this afternoon in another two hours. The surgeon had exited the east side of the complex where Ming was on guard for any attempt by the Wizard to rescue the Dragon Queen and walked down to the west side of the center where Seiji was on guard for the same reason.

"Good morning Seiji." The doctor said with a wide smile. He brushed back a lock of his black hair and adjusted his glasses.

"Good morning doctor. No sign of the Wizard or any kind of problems here. Should be a calm afternoon for your operation." Seiji said.

Seiji's family had come from Japan to Azorka a thousand years ago about the same time Ming's family had left China. They were both masters in martial arts and frequently taught young soldiers what they needed to defend themselves in combat. Seiji had long black hair tied by silver rope at the back, and a long black mustache which almost reached his chin. He was dressed in a traditional white jacket which was specially made with extra room in the shoulders and arms for fighting. Long baggy white trousers were tucked into durable black boots. Ming was bald and had no facial hair on what some would describe as a long face. He was dressed in a similar fashion, albeit the styling was suited to his ancient homeland. They both carried their traditional swords, for defense from the Wizard's creatures. Ming had a slight advantage as he was about one foot taller than Mitch and part of that one tenth of the population in Azorka who were seven to ten feet tall. Seiji was about six feet tall, two feet shorter than Ming.

The doctor had walked on in silence after his greeting and the creature was able to read from his mind that the Dragon Queen was unconscious and would remain so for the next six hours. The creature was also able to get a visual of the inside of the medical center and operating room, which would help speed up the rescue process. Discovery would occur so the creature had to teleport out and up through the trees with the Dragon Queen in its arms. Once above the tree line the creature could conjure the ninety-foot ring of energy and be back on the Empire's island in a matter of seconds.

The creature looked down from its perch in the tree one hundred feet above the center. The Dheginian creature had avoided the Zapatsaurs with superior mental powers, but it would continue to exercise caution. There were four Zapatsaurs below outside the medical center on the east side feeding in a nearby garden. Humans could not read minds nor could the Yetz. However, the Yetz can send thoughts or compelling suggestions at any lifeform they encounter, thereby influencing the actions of the lifeform. That is how the Wizard got caught yesterday because the Zapatsaurs are constantly in touch with the minds of their riders. But the Dheginian creature could read the minds of those riders, providing they were within view, without the Zapatsaurs being aware, which had proven true with Ming and Seiji. So long as the creature didn't send a thought, which would be like speaking out loud, the Zapatsaurs wouldn't be aware of the intrusion. However soon after the rescue attempt was discovered the creature would have to deal with possibly four powerful foes as well as the humans depending on how events unfolded. This had to be a lightning quick rescue. The creature could teleport on to the wooden roof below on the west side which would be out of view of the Zapatsaurs, but the sunroof for the operating room would probably not open and the glass was impact resistant. The best course of action would be to teleport in front of Seiji, knock him unconscious and rush the entrance that looked wide enough to accommodate its bulk. Then race down the hall to the operating rooms double doors, enter and scoop up the

Dragon Queen. The creature would return to the west side entrance and teleport outside where a beam of sunlight indicated a break in the tree line above.

The creature looked down at the many branches, loaded with leaves, that would prevent teleporting. The creature could not teleport through an object. The only solution was to climb down the tree trunk till it had a clear path for teleporting. The creature often wished it had the same teleporting capability as a Dheginian warrior who could teleport through objects. Making matters more frustrating was Seiji's peripheral view. He was looking in a direction which would easily allow him to see movement above, so the creature had to wait till the time was right.

While the creature waited for an opportunity to clear twenty feet worth of lower branches, Heather and Tamara were in the doctor's office three doors down from the operating room in the east wing.

The doctor was a stout man of fifty-five with a bald head that captured the glare of the crystal powered light above as he sat comfortably at his oak desk. Doctor Fritz adjusted his round gold-framed spectacles that rested on his pudgy cheeks, and brushing a spot on his white lab coat, he reclined back in his high back leather crafted chair. He looked at Tamara and Heather sitting in front of him, both dressed in green robe and pants, looking a little anxious. Tamara had done the best she could with make-up to hide the fact that she had gone without sleep last night. Her hair was done up smartly in a ponytail and her "bubbly" tone of voice hid her exhaustion. But it was Heather who was failing at covering up her anxiety. The doctor watched his patient and wondered if she would divulge all of her disturbing dream. She might skip an important detail, so he would have to question her carefully.

Tamara was the first to speak, while Heather sat silently beside her.

"Last night Heather woke up screaming around three thirty in the morning. I went in to her room, turned on the light and immediately asked her to recall her dream. She didn't remember much, only that the sky was dark and filled with strange red clouds. She was wearing her night gown and walking in an unfamiliar place. We had hot chocolate in the kitchen then returned to bed forty minutes later. After that Heather didn't experience any more dreams. She came down to breakfast with the family this morning like nothing happened last night to dampen her good spirit. She was the same old Heather, bold confident and fearless." Tamara finished.

The doctor sat forward and reaching for a pen and papyrus note pad, he prepared to record Heather's statements.

"Dear ladies, I appreciate you reporting this incident so that I can examine some possibilities. Heather would you say that you sensed a message in your dream, but just can't remember it?" The doctor asked in a deep voice that resonated around the white walls of the office.

"I think you might be right doctor. It's unsettling that I can't remember." Heather replied.

Heather wanted to satisfy Tamara's concern for her mental health so she had agreed to see the doctor. She felt it was important to keep secret the memory of her second dream. So she didn't mention that she later remembered snagging her night gown on a rock. The second dream was instructive and unlike her first dream she remembered all the details. Heather was going to confirm whether or not she did have this new ability later when she'll be alone. If she does have telekinesis ability, then she will demonstrate this to her familly. She knew her family was concerned for her because of all the changes she was going through. A proper presentation of her new ability would at least show them that she was sane and able to handle the shock of new abilities.

***

In the laboratory for "Zapatsaur Medicine and Research", on the west side of the medical center, a fifth Zapatsaur was quietly checking the shelves for samples of the Dragon Queen's blood. Occasionally, it would look through the glass and a short way down the hall where Seiji was guarding the entrance. It did not want to get discovered in the lab. Leaving the Zapatsaur section of the medical center would be natural but not rummaging around in the laboratory. Finally the Zapatsaur found what it was looking for and tucked it into a leather pouch it was wearing around its neck which contained the stencils for communicating. The Zapatsaur left the laboratory and made its way down the hall.

Seiji was becoming bored and weary from his guard duty. It was a beautiful day and he preferred the idea of fishing during such good weather. But duties must be shared by all. Fortunately his replacement was only one hour away.

Seiji heard some shuffling steps behind him and turned to see a Zapatsaur through the glass of the door about to leave the center. The Zapatsaur on the other side of the glass raised its scaly arms and three digit hands pushing the double doors wide enough to allow it to exit.

"It's a beautiful day for flying!" Seiji said with a smile.

The Zapatsaur responded by nodding its long scaly neck up and down then stepped past Seiji and was airborne heading back to Zapatsaur Mountain. A small part of the Zapatsaur community's mission had been accomplished.

That was the distraction that the Dheginian creature had been hoping for. It made good use of this time by climbing down below the obstructing branches. The creature was in place by the time the departing Zapatsaur took to the sky. Its dark body blended in with the trees and the Zapatsaur flew past the Dheginian creature unaware of its presence. The creature held its position for five minutes more in the hope that the fifth Zapatsaur had flown far enough away that it wouldn't hear the commotion that was about to begin. Having four Zapatsaurs to evade was enough to deal with.

Then the creature prepared to teleport. Suddenly the scene below disappeared and the creature was motionless in a tunnel of darkness and silence. A pin prick of light appeared on the right side of the tunnel from fifty yards away, at approximately forty-five degrees to the creature's position. The creature was frozen but could see the light below and it estimated that the light would be just a couple of feet in front of Seiji's position. The light grew in size until it was that familiar circle of electrified light. It approached the creature rapidly and passed silently over and under the creature. When the second had passed the scene below reappeared with the creature standing two feet away from Seiji. Before

Seiji could draw his sword in defense, the creature reached out with its huge four digit hand and hit Seiji in the head, sending him flying through the air. Seiji landed on the ground six feet away bruised and unconscious.

The creature pushed ahead nearly taking the double doors off their hinges as it crashed through the entrance. It was a narrow fit but the Dheginian creature had about eighteen inches of clearance on both sides of the doors and the corridor beyond. The creature barrelled down the hall at a reckless pace. Its tail smashed the laboratory glass and set off the ringing of a deafening alarm. The creature didn't care; it was in a race to rescue the Dragon Queen and was approaching the operating room on its right.

Tamara and Heather were finishing up with their doctors appointment just before the alarm bell began to ring.

The doctor and his colleagues were astonished by some of the changes Heather was going through. They all agreed that Heather's condition was evolving and for that reason and the fact that the changes were physically beneficial, minus the nightmares, they were reluctant to prescribe beyond a customized diet to ease the anxiety caused by the nightmares. The doctor would refrain from commenting on the alarming colors in Heather's latest nightmare.

The doctor said, "Dear ladies I will need your assistance before I draw any conclusions about these nightmares. Heather I've asked your parents to keep an accurate diary of your dreams and now I would like you to do the same. Keep a daily record and record in it whether or not you dreamed and as many details about the dream as possible." He instructed. He watched Heather for signs of anxiety through his thick glasses. Heather was nodding her head up and down, silently acknowledging his request.

"It will be interesting to see how this information recorded by you and your parents compare." The doctor said.

Tamara was the first to stand up.

"I thank you doctor for your help and...." Tamara started to say before she was interrupted by the loud ringing of an alarm from the west end of the medical center.

Heather got up and ran out of the office. She rushed past the receptionist and heard Tamara shouting behind her.

"Heather! Where are you going?" Tamara yelled.

Tamara realized she would have to chase after heroically motivated Heather. She heard the slamming of the doctor's office door which launched her into action. Tamara raced out of the office and into the hallway. To her right she saw Heather running full speed down the hall towards the corridor doors. Behind these doors and six feet to Heather's left were the double doors which led into the operating room.

Tamara looked at the door to Doctor Fritz's office. The proper protocol for an alarm bell was to remain in the room and let security handle the situation. Doctor Fritz had been his calm and logical self during the appointment and Tamara believed he would deter anyone behind this door from entering the hallway. Convinced that the room's occupants were not going to complicate matters by entering the hallway, Tamara set off after Heather. She had turned around in time to see the last of Heather's green robe disappear as the doors up ahead swung shut. Tamara ran down the gleaming white tiled hall at a frantic pace.

Heather was shocked when she saw the same monster that had chased her and Lana in the jungle, carrying the Dragon Queen. That notorious foe of Azorka looked like a small rag doll in the arms of a twenty-seven foot reptilian. The creature's massive tail slid along the white floor tiles and was last to leave the operating room allowing the doors to swing closed. The creature raced back down the hall heading for the exit. The weight of its heavy footfalls shook the hallway.

Heather knew she had to try and stop it. She decided to try her new talent. Heather would find out if the dream's message would come true in the real world. Twenty feet ahead and hanging on the right side of the hallway wall was an orange fire extinguisher. Heather raised both her arms and hands, pointed them at the fire extinguisher and concentrated. To her delight the white border, that only Heather could see, instantly surrounded the fire extinguisher. Heather concentrated on willing it to move and the fire extinguisher broke its strap which held it in a shallow recess in the wall. The orange fire extinguisher was airborne now and hanging still. Heather moved her arms and pointed with her long fingers at the Dheginian creature's muscular right arm where the Dragon Queen's legs and feet hung limply. She willed the thirty pound fire extinguisher to fly through the hallway at an incredible speed and it struck her target. The creature's right arm was temporarily paralysed with the force of the thirty pound fire extinguisher and it dropped the Dragon Queen's large green legs and feet. The sound of the fire extinguisher rolling on the floor tiles and crashing into the exit door echoed down the hall. The creature stopped just ten feet from the exit and turned its long neck around until the head was looking directly at Heather.

Heather would not be intimidated. She defiantly raised her arms and with her long fingers, pointed them at the Dragon Queen's lower body, encircling it with as much of the white border as would be allowable. Heather willed a powerful force to pull the Dragon Queen free, but the creature held the Dragon Queen tightly. She looked around the hallway to see if there was another object to throw at the creature. Unfortunately, the hallway was tidy and empty with the exception of the orange fire extinguisher, which lay on the floor against the right side wall two feet from the exit doors. She would have to use the fire extinguisher again or find another way to stop the creature from escaping with the Dragon Queen.

Heather returned her attention to what she believed was an agent of the Wizard. It looked to be twice the size of a Zapatsaur and very muscular. Was this creation, the Wizard's new version of an intelligent creature, able to organize and execute the rescue of the Dragon Queen without any assistance? She looked up at the black scaly head of the Dheginian creature as it moved slowly from side to side like a reptile about to strike. The head was at least the size of the boulder she had caused to levitate in her dream. The top of the creature's head was crowned with what looked like rows of tiny fins and two nine inch long tusks were positioned above its jaws. Dark orange almond shaped eyes looked down at her and Heather thought she saw anger in those hideous orbs. The elliptical pupils were constricted and looking like thin black swords of hatred.

Before she could decide on a course of action, the creature opened its mouth revealing two rows of six-inch long razor sharp teeth. Heather was sure it was going to strike her with those lethal looking jaws. To her surprise, a booming blast of sound shot out from that hideous mouth. It was such a powerful force that it lifted Heather off her feet and sent her flying through the air and into Tamara six feet behind her. Heather's flying body sent Tamara backwards a couple of feet as she lost her footing and crashed onto her back. They both lay on the white tiles of the hallway floor with their green robes in disarray and looking like a couple of crumpled leaves. The creature was a further thirty feet down the hall; ten feet away from escaping.

Tamara had arrived in the west side hallway and watched the scene in front of her in frozen amazement. She had watched Heather pointing at a fire extinguisher twenty-feet away which broke its anchoring strap and moved forward about one foot in mid-air, hanging there motionless. Heather pointed her long fingers at the creature and the thirty pound fire extinguisher flew down the hall at an incredible speed and hit this monster in the right shoulder which caused it to drop the Dragon Queen. Heather seemed to command the fire extinguisher to become a projectile which stopped the creature from getting away. But before Tamara could wonder further about what she had seen, the creature fired back at Heather with ear shattering sonic vibrations. The booming sound waves echoed throughout the hallway and sent Heather flying through the air and crashing into Tamara knocking the wind out of her.

Heather had taken the force of the sonic vibration in the chest and had the wind knocked out of her as well.

"Mom! Are you all right?" Heather gasped.

"I'm I'm getting my...my breath back back slowly." Tamara managed to answer.

The creature was satisfied that its adversary was out of action, so it moved towards the exit cautiously, believing that by now the Zapatsaurs would be waiting outside and will have learned the specifics of the intruder through reading Heather's mind. They'll know a creature twice their size was rescuing the Dragon Queen and that it uses sonic vibrations as a deterrent or weapon against those who challenge it. But they don't know about the teleporting yet. They will organize their positions by spreading out so that they can take a run at their target and overwhelm any defensive tactics by out numbering the intruder. However this strategy worked in favor of the Dheginian creature. There would be a central track not covered and a clear shot at teleporting out of this area of conflict.

The creature approached the exit and moved its head forward to gaze out the small square window in the exit door. Outside the four Zapatsaurs waited.

The Zapatsaurs had arranged there formation side by side but with a distance of twenty feet between them. The first two Zapatsaurs were only fifteen feet from the door. What the creature didn't like was the position the other two Zapatsaurs occupied. They were only twenty-five feet away from the beam of sunlight which marked the opening at the tree top level and position for the second teleport. The creature would teleport to this spot, only eighty feet away, then directly upwards just beyond the tree tops by about fifty feet where it could open its wings. It would have to be fast. A Zapatsaur could probably cover twenty-five feet in three seconds.

Outside the medical center's west entrance doors, on the creature's right side, Seiji was receiving help from Ming who had run quickly to the west side entrance where the four Zapatsaurs were already waiting for the intruder to emerge. Almost half of Seiji's face had bruised a deep purple color and he was stumbling around, barely able to walk from the concussion. Ming and Seiji were on the medical centers lawn close to a picnic table which Seiji could lean against while he tried to remain standing. They were twelve feet from the entrance doors.

The creature moved back three feet from the doors. It had recovered the use of its right arm. The creature's immortal body had repaired the damage swiftly. The Dheginian creature picked up the Dragon Queen's legs and feet, holding them securely then lowered its neck and opened its mouth. Out of that horrible mouth issued a sonic boom much more powerful than what Heather had experienced and with a force strong enough to take both double doors off their hinges. One of the double doors hit Seiji's Zapatsaur, who was to the right of the creature, and it fell to the ground. Ming's Zapatsaur was able to dodge the other door and it crashed into some bushes behind it. Tamara and Heather's Zapatsaurs were positioned further out from the entrance. Heather's Zapatsaur decided to move in and help Seiji's fallen Zapatsaur which was already struggling to get to its feet. The Dheginian creature was satisfied that the injuries to Seiji and one Zapatsaur was enough to thwart any plan to rush forward and attack. The calamity had also caused one Zapatsaur to move in from its position. The creature would only have to deal with one Zapatsaur. It decided to teleport past them in a sitting position so that it was ready quicker to make the final leap upwards into the bright blue open sky.

The creature moved out from the now door less west entrance, on to the cement porch and sat down with its tail coiled behind. In this upright position the creature's neck, chest and Dragon Queen cradled in its arms were exposed to the enemy. It prepared to teleport before danger arrived. However, just before teleporting away, Ming who had snuck up on the creature's right side, brought his ancestral sword down swiftly on the creature's tail cutting off six inches of the creature's flesh. The creature let out a high pitch growl of pain but did not give in to the temptation to retaliate with a sonic blast and started to teleport. The Dheginian creature's superior ability of concentration had pin-pointed the target directly under that beam of sunlight. In another second the creature was motionless in that silent tunnel only it could see and looking at the small point of light which rose from the target area. Inside the tunnel one second could feel like ten which suggested that outside the tunnel Ming would be frozen in time and not able to strike a second time. The circle of electrified light, which would also be invisible to any on-lookers, had grown to a twenty foot circumference as it approached the creature. It passed over and under the creature disappearing behind just before the door less entrance.

Tamara's Zapatsaur had begun moving in towards the medical center and was now forty feet from the beam of sunlight the creature would arrive under. When the creature disappeared into thin air, a shock wave of amazement temporarily froze the observers. But Tamara's Zapatsaur detected a presence from behind, turned and got hit with a loud blast of the creature's sonic vibrations that echoed loudly around the small community sheltered in the old growth forest. Tamara's Zapatsaur was sent tumbling backwards. Dust flew up around the Zapatsaur and it came to a stop a further twenty feet away from the creature and the Dragon Queen. Tamara's Zapatsaur was a little bruised but determined, and it immediately got up and charged forward in an attempt to tackle the creature.

The Dheginian creature looked up through the top of the trees to open sky then the tunnel reappeared and the creature with the Dragon Queen clutched securely in its arms were motionless in darkness and silence, unable to hear the commotion of alarms and shouts coming from the medical center. The light appeared in the dark tunnel and moved down to the creature from the targeted area in the open sky above, growing larger as it approached. In another moment the electrified circle of energy, now twenty feet in circumference, fell over the creature and the Dragon Queen disappearing into the ground beneath. The tunnel suddenly vanished and the creature with the Dragon Queen in its arms, appeared in the open sky fifty feet above the tree tops. The creature was still in a sitting position and they were beginning to fall. With lightning speed those black leathery wings spread out and they regained altitude twenty feet above the tree tops.

The creature was flying at a leisurely pace in a southerly direction back to the Empire's island. It was about to conjure that circle of energy that was ninety feet in circumference with electrical charges moving in a counter clock direction. This version of long distance teleporting would be visible to any onlooker but it would instantly transport the creature and Dragon Queen back into the courtyard of the Wizard's castle. The coordinates telepathically sent to the electrified circle from the creature, were derived from alien values and mathematics of the Dheginian Star System. However, before the creature began, a small spec above the tree tops in the distance caught its eye. The spec grew rapidly in size as it approached and the creature saw that it was a Zapatsaur; probably the fifth Zapatsaur the creature had hoped would be far enough away before the rescue of the Dragon Queen began. The Zapatsaur came to a stop and hovered in place when it saw the creature with the unconscious Dragon Queen in its arms. The creature came to a stop fifty feet away from the Zapatsaur and hovered in place. The creature knew that the Zapatsaurs telepathic range is fifty miles and hadn't considered this to be a problem so long as it could block out any attempt by the Zapatsaur to probe its own mind. But now the creature understood the combat advantage for this benevolent race of reptilians. They could communicate and organize without a visual presence through their own unique psychic ether. This Zapatsaur must have tuned in on the emergency situation at the medical center as broadcast by the other four Zapatsaurs and turned back to see if it could help.

While the creature hovered in place it concentrated on trying to read the Zapatsaurs mind. To the creature's surprise it couldn't read the mind of the Zapatsaur and considered the possibility that this reptilian could raise its own mental barrier keeping out those capable of mental probing. On the other hand if the Zapatsaur could read the mind of a Dheginian creature it would surely turn around when the Dheginian creature conjured the circle of energy to teleport out. The creature conjured the circle of energy thirty feet behind the Zapatsaur and saw that the Zapatsaur didn't turn around to look or was oblivious to its presence. It would be safe to assume that the mental block for Dheginian creatures was sufficient defense against mental probing from a Zapatsaur.

The creature stopped hovering and flew towards the Zapatsaur. The Zapatsaur remained in place but prepared for what it assumed would be an assault by extending its arms and clenched fists outward. The creature flew past the expressionless Zapatsaur just out of its reach, while the Zapatsaur looked on, confused but now curious. The Zapatsaur turned its neck and head in time to see the creature and unconscious Dragon Queen fly into the center of a circle of lightning and disappear from sight. The Zapatsaur watched as the remaining five feet of the creature's tail vanished and moments later the electrified circle was no longer visible. This would be difficult to explain to the elders but the Zapatsaur decided to deal with that later. So, the brave Zapatsaur stopped hovering and began flying in the direction of the village medical center, preparing itself for the probable chaos below.

Chapter Six

When the alarm bell rang out at the medical center, General Zen had been home for a day off from work and duty. He had enjoyed the leisure time and relaxation with his wife Indie and they had both enjoyed Indie's gourmet late morning breakfast.

The unexpected excitement started after breakfast when Indie decided to carry on with some of her cleaning duties after finishing the morning dishes. She had completed her cleaning quickly by going from room to room with her homemade dusting wand. She was just about finished her cleaning duties when she reached the short hallway between the kitchen and living room. The walls of this short hallway were decorated with her latest cloth patterns and Indian art. Indie had also included a family heirloom she had placed on a gilded table which complimented the glossy gold tiles of the floor. The heirloom was a globe of the world from the distant past, before the great flood and included Lemuria and Mu with other ancient civilizations. As always, Indie was admiring its artistic beauty while dusting when she lost her footing on the slippery floor and fell onto the table knocking the globe to the floor.

Zen was ten feet away in their red carpeted living room, dressed in a casual green shirt and brown pants comfortably seated in his favorite recliner. He was reading a medical report concerning the Dragon Queen. The investigation had uncovered a second brain located behind the Dragon Queen's human brain at the back of her skull. The second brain was connected to the human brain and was only about one-third of the size. It also connected to a series of nerves thought to be operational for her wings and extra two arms which powered her high speed flight. The medical scan had revealed activity in regions of the Dragon Queen's human brain that were thought to be dormant. Although a before and after scan couldn't be provided for comparison, the report suggested that most humans don't have activity in the regions of the brain that the Dragon Queen's scan revealed. The report went on to state that today's scheduled operation to remove her wings and two extra arms may lead to new revelations. Possibly a new hypothesis for the restoration to human form of the lower half of her body. This was based on the belief that they would find some indication that the second brain also connected to the reptilian lower half of her body. This much the author of the report admitted was an optimistic assumption and based on the operation being a success.

The paper gave the name of the physicians responsible for explaining the psychological impact of the operation to the Dragon Queen and how she might possibly combat those feelings of loss or mutilation on her way to becoming human again. Sadly, the Dragon Queen seemed uncooperative. She had remained silent and unwilling to share her feelings with the doctors.

Zen had read just about to the end of the report when he heard a crash behind him. He turned to see Indie sitting on the floor, her red paisley dress spread out beneath her and her hands on the globe which had separated a little at the top from its short drop from the table. He got up from his recliner throwing the paper down on the table next to it and hurried out to Indie to see if she was alright. "Indie! I heard a crash. Are you hurt?" The General asked.

Indie got up from the floor, brushed dust off from her dress and looked up at Zen.

"I'm not hurt Zen. I was rushing to finish my cleaning so that I could relax with you in the living room when I slipped on my freshly waxed floor and fell knocking the globe onto the floor." Indie said with a note of disappointment in her voice.

"Now it has come apart and I will have to think of a way to repair it." She continued.

Zen stepped into the hall and crouched down to examine the separated seam which ran around the globe. He picked it up and noticed something rattling around inside. The globe had always seemed a little heavy considering the papyrus material it had been crafted from and Zen had always assumed it was solid. He was curious about what was inside. Zen pulled at the separated seam near the southern pole of the globe and the ancient family heirloom came apart a further six inches which was just wide enough for Zen to look inside the globe. "Be careful not to break it Zen." Indie said anxiously.

Zen looked up at Indie with an expression of disbelief. He could see part of an object inside the globe which reflected some of the light from the open dome of their home. Indie had opened all the roof shutters which neatly recessed into the round walls of their home. Their roof was a gigantic skylight and the smooth surface of the object glittered with the late morning sun.

"There's something inside the globe Indie!" Zen said excitedly. "I'll have to open the globe to get it out." He finished.

Indie didn't reply but moved closer to Zen and crouching down she looked inside the family heirloom to see what this mystery artist had installed inside the globe two thousand years ago. She saw the smooth surface of the object which looked to be silver in color and a couple of hooks protruding from the inner walls of the globe which must have held it securely in place all these years.

"Do you think that we can put this back together again if I pull it apart and take out what's inside?" Indie asked.

"I can get some adhesive that will seal the papyrus without destroying the globe. I can also secure it with a couple of small screws, one on each end, so that it will permanently hold together even if dropped again." Zen replied.

He examined the globe. It was a beautiful work of art colored blue for the oceans with green and tan for the continents, and islands. The lettering looked like an ancient form of calligraphy. The globe would fit back together again easily enough and Zen had an adhesive in mind that would not have a caustic reaction when applied to the seams of the papyrus. The two screws, one at the north pole and one at the south pole which would prevent it from falling apart again, could be filed down and painted.

This was enough assurance for Indie. She carefully pulled the globe apart and pulled out the peculiar object. When she saw what was inside the globe Indie thought she would faint. She took a deep breath and put a silver crystal skull, crafted to represent a human skull, down on the floor in front of her wide- eyed husband.

"I think we may have found one of the Wizard's missing crystal skulls." He whispered.

"What should we do with our discovery?" Indie asked. There was a note of incredulity in her voice. She just about couldn't believe what they had stumbled upon.

"We need to be sure that it's authentic and not an imitation of what your ancestor acquired from thousands of years ago after the crystal skulls were stolen." Zen replied. "I think we should take it over to the Guardians castle and see what Mitch makes of it."

Indie agreed with Zen. This was an amazing discovery and they should try to confirm whether or not this really was the stolen crystal skull from the Wizard's collection. She looked at Zen as he got up from his kneeling position on the floor. Before Zen could remark further, the alarm bell for the medical center began to howl and echo throughout the village. Zen froze for a moment. How many more surprises, he wondered, did today have for them.

"What will be next! Indie I've got to find out what's wrong at the medical center!" He shouted.

"Go ahead Zen! I'll place this in our bedroom out of sight from any visitors until you get back." She said. Indie reached up and gave Zen a quick kiss on the cheek. Zen returned her kiss with a quick peck on her cheek, then raced down the hall, past the kitchen and outside where his Zapatsaur was waiting to fly him to the medical center.

Back at the medical center, Ming had left Seiji briefly to go inside the west side laboratory and turn off the alarm. Heather and Tamara had recovered and walked out through the damaged west entrance to see if anyone had been injured by the invading creature. They spotted Seiji leaning on the picnic table for support and ran over to him.

"Seiji! Are you alright?" Heather shouted.

"I'm alright for now but Ming suggested I wait and get checked over by a doctor when things settle down. He thinks I may have suffered a serious concussion and I do feel a little dizzy right now." Seiji replied.

Tamara looked around at the Zapatsaurs and the arriving security team. Seiji's and Tamara's Zapatsaur were caught up in the fury of the monster's escape but had escaped serious injury. Ming's Zapatsaur stood still and expressionless and was closest to the damaged entrance. This Zapatsaur had been clever enough to pocket the severed section of the creature's tail in its stencil pouch worn around its neck when no one was looking.

"That is a hideous bruise on your face Seiji. I think Ming is right about seeing a doctor. I'll help you in now. Just lean on me and will find a doctor to examine you." Heather said.

Heather hurried over to Seiji and putting her arm around him she helped him back into the medical center. Tamara remained outside and waited for the security team. Two minutes later and three security men came running up the path to meet Tamara. They were dressed in black military jackets and pants complete with body armour and trauma pads sewn into their uniforms. The dark-haired leader of the team stopped and gave Tamara a quick salute.

"We heard the alarm bells ringing so I assembled a team to come down and investigate, Tamara. Can you fill me in on what happened here?" He asked.

Tamara looked past him to the rest of the team arriving on Zapatsaurs. Those five soldiers were dressed in gray and sky blue camouflage with the same body armor and trauma pads sewn into their water resistant uniforms. The uniforms blended with their Zapatsaurs and weren't as obvious to an on-looker well in flight. Tamara watched them dismount and stand beside their Zapatsaurs, waiting for further instruction.

"Captain Jeff, it is good to see you, but I'm afraid the intruder has escaped. Heather chased it down the west side hall inside the medical center but it was too powerful for us to stop. We both suffered some minor injury and by the time we recovered it had already disappeared from the entrance which it tore the doors from with what we are calling sonic vibrations." Tamara said. She took a deep breath realizing she was still suffering from the ordeal.

Captain Jeff took a couple seconds to survey the scene. He would ask about the sonic vibrations later.

"Is there anyone outside that can fill in the details of what happened or how the creature escaped?" Captain Jeff asked.

"Yes. I believe that Ming was outside when the creature made its escape. Heather and I were recovering from the creature's sonic vibrations which sent Heather flying into me and knocked the wind out of my lungs. We heard the same booming sonic vibrations again when the creature knocked the doors off their hinges and by the time I looked down the hall to see what had happened the creature had vanished. Both Seiji and Ming were outside at the time so they could tell you more about the creature's disappearance." Tamara finished.

Well Captain Jeff was writing this information down, Tamara saw another Zapatsaur, without a rider, flying in and landing in front of the Zapatsaurs which had been caught up in the conflict. The four Zapatsaurs were lined up close to the damaged west entrance and the fifth Zapatsaur landed in front of them with its back to Tamara and Captain Jeff. Tamara watched while the fifth Zapatsaur shuffled closer to Ming's Zapatsaur. She couldn't see Ming's Zapatsaur handing off the severed section of the intruding creature's tail. She assumed this was just an offer of help from the fifth Zapatsaur. It was probably told that help was not needed so it turned and left the village, flying back up through the same tree tops the creature had cleared to make its escape. This didn't seem unusual to Tamara. Captain Jeff looked up at Tamara after he finished recording her statements.

"There are four Zapatsaurs here involved in the conflict. Could you tell me who the riders are?" He asked.

"Heather and I are the riders for the two Zapatsaurs furthest from the entrance. Seiji and Ming are the riders for the other two Zapatsaurs they are standing beside. Ming's Zapatsaur, closest to us, was not injured. Seiji's Zapatsaur standing beside it has recovered from being hit by the flying door. My Zapatsaur, furthest from you, took a direct hit from the creature's sonic vibrations and fortunately recovered. Heather's Zapatsaur was not injured." Tamara replied.

Captain Jeff went back to his writing recording everything Tamara had said. Tamara heard footsteps behind her and turned to see Ming returning from turning off the laboratory alarm. Behind Ming the other two members of the security team that Captain Jeff commanded were leaving from checking the inside of the center.

Both of the security men were dressed in the same black uniform their leader wore. Peter, the tall blonde security member closest to Ming called out to Captain Jeff.

"All clear Captain. No one injured inside. They remained in their rooms while the conflict played out." He shouted.

"That's good to hear. Thank you Peter." Captain Jeff replied.

"Ming could I speak with you for a moment?" Captain Jeff asked.

Ming was standing a couple of feet from the ruined entrance and looking for something on the ground. He looked up and addressed the Captain.

"Yes Captain. I'll be glad to fill you in on what I saw happen." Ming answered.

While Ming told Captain Jeff about the creature's escape as seen from outside the medical center, Zen's Zapatsaur was already flying through the village as fast as it dared, seventy-five feet above the ground. It flew past the "Pyramid for Advanced Education". The pyramid's capstone, called a pyramidion, was eye level with General Zen who was looking down below at the crowd of students leaving and entering the school's main entrance. He wondered if the History department had records dating back ten thousand years to the war, that would also include information on the crystal skulls. The historians of the day would have recorded the crystal skulls as just one more dangerous weapon in the Wizard's quiver. But the intel of the day would have recorded anything they might have learned about the crystal skulls. Zen had studied the legend and was always concerned that the assembly of all the thirteen crystal skulls in one area together might produce the disastrous power the Wizard sought. If Indie's ancestor had somehow acquired one of those skulls, then the incomplete assembly should counter that threat provided they were able to keep it away from the Wizard.

Zen looked up ahead, saw that they were approaching the medical center and a larger than usual gathering of people and Zapatsaurs at the west end. Zen could see five Zapatsaurs with security team riders standing side by side and further up the walk four more Zapatsaurs were standing side by side just outside of the west entrance. Tamara was standing and talking with the Captain of the security team and Ming, who was Zen's personal trainer for martial arts, was moving his hands up and down while he was talking with the Captain.

Zen landed close to the Zapatsaurs with the security team, dismounted and carried on up the walk for twenty yards stopping just behind the Captain.

"I heard the alarm bell so decided to investigate. What happened that caused the alarm to ring?" Zen asked.

"We're under control now General but the intruder has left with the unconscious Dragon Queen in its arms. We believe this is another of the Wizard's intelligent creatures and it caused the laboratory alarm to go off when it smashed that rooms glass on its way to rescue the Dragon Queen in the operating room. Ming has described the creatures escape and it has led me to believe that this creature has the power of teleportation. The creature is also capable of sending powerful sonic vibrations from its mouth which caused the damage to the west entrance." Captain Jeff finished.

Zen looked over at Tamara and Ming who were finished recounting the shocking events that had taken place.

"How are you two doing after all this trauma?" He asked.

Both Tamara and Ming were facing the General. Tamara gave a thumbs up sign with her hand and quick smile to indicate she was alright.

"General Zen it's good to see you again! It has been a long time since we have worked out together." Ming answered warmly and with a thinly veiled note of excitement.

Zen looked up at his eight-foot tall friend. Ming looked like his confident self, alert and he had escaped injury unlike Seiji who was still being examined by the doctor. His black handled ceremonial sword hung by his side in its sheath attached to his waist by a white cloth belt. Like Seiji he was dressed in a white jacket that had been modified with trauma pads on the elbows and shoulders worn over baggy white pants which tucked into black boots with specialized treads for rugged terrain.

"You escaped injury Ming. I'm glad of that. Can you describe the Wizard's creature?" Zen asked.

"Yes General, I can give you a fairly accurate description of what must be one of the Wizard's new creations. But I did better than just escaping injury. I managed to cut about six inches of the creature's tail off before it disappeared into thin air and re-appeared a second later eighty feet away under that beam of sunlight over there." Ming answered.

Ming pointed behind Zen and the General turned to look at the position he was referring to. Zen recognized this as being the preferred exit for the Zapatsaurs. He turned back and nodded his head in response to Ming then looked over at Tamara.

"Tamara, can I assume that you escaped serious injury?" Zen asked.

"Thank you General for asking. I'm fine and so is Heather. It would be best if Heather explains what she encountered and experienced from this monster. She got ahead of me when the alarm rang and by the time I caught up to her in the hallway this monster had hit her with its devastating sonic vibrations. She was hit in the chest with those powerful sonic vibrations and sent flying into me six feet behind her. We both struggled to get our breath back and by the time we did the creature had disappeared." Tamara answered.

She looked at Zen and knew he was absorbing everything mentioned by her and Ming. Zen was calm and expressionless, the way he always appeared when he committed details of an event to his excellent memory.

"General I should return to the medical center and see how Heather and Seiji are doing." Tamara said. "In another half hour I'm expecting Mitch and Sally to arrive. They had planned to meet us here after Heather's appointment."

"That's perfect Tamara because I need to speak to Mitch about a military matter." Zen said. He realized he was stretching the truth a little but didn't want to reveal the existence of the crystal skull until he'd spoken with Mitch.

Zen watched Tamara turn and walk back inside the medical center.

He noticed Captain Jeff's men moving the damaged doors closer to the west entrance which Peter was examining. The tall blonde security team member was uncomfortably hunched down wondering if the hinges for the two doors could be bent back into place in order to temporarily repair the entrance.

Captain Jeff turned to the General and gave a quick salute.

"If I could be excused General, I'll let my security team and their Zapatsaurs return to base until I can work out a security watch for above the tree tops this evening just in case the creature returns. Although I believe a return of the Wizard's forces unlikely I wouldn't feel comfortable without a watch to alert us." Captain Jeff said.

"That's a good precaution Captain. Let me know when you have worked out the details." Zen replied. He saluted Captain Jeff who turned and marched down the walk to the camouflaged security team waiting beside their Zapatsaurs. The Captain described the incident and discussed possible strategies with the team.

Zen turned to Ming who was anxious to share the details of the creature and his thoughts on combating this new threat.

"General, let me start by asking you to imagine a Zapatsaur that is one third larger than the largest Zapatsaur we are aware of, black in color with two large ten inch tusks seeming to grow from its upper jaw. The creature is able to teleport a short distance of eighty feet reappearing and attacking those nearby with sonic vibrations released from its mouth. It would appear as though the Wizard has made a design change and substituted fire breathing for sonic vibrations. The creature has a four digit hand so it may have better dexterity and ability to use a weapon than a Zapatsaur. I did not see the wing span for the creature as they remained folded while it carried out the escape. But before it teleported the eighty feet to a spot where it could teleport directly upwards, I cut off six inches of its tail with my sword and it hollered in pain." Ming finished.

"It would be a fair fight if three Zapatsaurs could challenge one of these creatures. I wonder if the Wizard is producing more than one of these creatures." Zen said.

"That is a possibility to frightening to consider. Can you imagine the difficulty we'd have fighting off two of these monsters?" Ming answered.

"I think that what we didn't see, the creature's ability to enter Azorka without being detected and the creature's strategy for rescuing the Dragon Queen, is the most difficult challenge we face if we hope to prevent future attacks." Ming suggested.

"I would agree with that Ming and of course it will be up to us to find out how this was accomplished. This may mean that we will have to continue our covert surveillance of the Wizard's island." Zen said.

"Yes I believe that we need to launch a mission to the Empire's island in order to learn more and I would consider two important questions. Did the creature have knowledge of the Dragon Queen's new location and if so how was it able to precisely locate the Dragon Queen when she was unconscious? It suggests to me that the creature has the ability to read our minds or that the Dragon Queen has a way to contact a creature that we had no previous knowledge of after killing off the Wizard's creatures when we rescued Heather and captured the Dragon Queen. For now, what I'm suggesting for Captain Jeff to consider is posting sentries closer to the southern portion of our island, with additional sentries watching Zapatsaur Mountain. In the near future, I think it is possible that the Wizard may be interested in replenishing his supply of Zapats aur fluids he took from the kidnapped baby Zapatsaur. At least this way we can prepare for an attack." Ming finished.

"Thank you for your ideas, Ming. I believe you have some excellent suggestions for Captain Jeff to consider and I will be sure to share these with the Captain." Zen said.

"If you haven't any further questions General, I'd like to see how Seiji is doing." Ming said.

"You've answered all the questions I might have had except one. What happened to the six inches of the creature's tail you chopped off?" Zen asked.

"I guess it got lost during the creature's escape. Seiji's Zapatsaur was hit in the head by the door that was ripped off its hinges and Tamara's Zapatsaur was sent tumbling from the creature's powerful sonic vibrations." Ming offered.

"It is a mystery to me as to why the creature felt it necessary to attack Tamara's Zapatsaur. Is there some delay time before teleporting?" Ming wondered.

The General made a point to remember this last thought that Ming offered. Perhaps there was a way to prevent the creature from teleporting.

Ming gave a quick salute and turned towards the medical center. The General returned the salute and turned in the opposite direction to speak with Captain Jeff about Ming's ideas for security.

On Zapatsaur Mountain, the fifth Zapatsaur was landing in the small valley in front of the Elder's cave. It waited a brief moment after announcing its arrival waiting for permission to enter the cave and meet with two elders. The second elder, the Minister of Science and the fifth elder the Minister of Defense were waiting in the half-moon shaped conference room. They gave permission to the fifth Zapatsaur to meet with them. The Minister of Defense was anxiously waiting for this Zapatsaur's account of the creature's teleportation. The supreme leader was made aware of the meeting and was telepathically listening in from the comfort of its own cave.

The Zapatsaur flew up to the entrance of the Elder's cave and made its way down the tunnel until it arrived at the half-moon shaped conference room. It sat down and faced elder two and elder five seated at the table.

The Zapatsaur reached into its pouch and removed the creature's severed tail and the vile of the Dragon Queen's blood and placed it on the table for the elders to see. The Minister of Science reached for the tail, picked it up and looked at it then set it back down for the Minister of Defense to examine.

"We are glad your back safe and sound after your encounter with this mysterious creature." The second elder said telepathically.

"We all received the telepathic image of you hovering in place and preparing for a physical battle with the creature." The fifth elder said.

"We saw the creature disappearing into what looked like a ring of energy or lightning. Was there a sound that accompanied this appearance of the ring and disappearance of the creature?" The second elder asked.

"There was no sound or I would have turned to see the ring when it appeared. When the creature flew past me and disappeared into the ring there was no sound when the ring disappeared." The Zapatsaur answered.

The fifth elder, the Minister of Defense, reached down beside him and pulled out a couple of items and set them down on the table in front of the Zapatsaur. The two items looked like small ten inch wooden spindles with three grooves carved into them to make a pistol grip for Zapatsaurs. At the top of the wooden pistol grip was a crystal which would release the laser beam. The bottom of the wooden pistol grip was hollowed out to hold the energy source which was a three-inch-long rounded crystal fully charged. It could be recharged by removing it from its housing and placing it in direct sunlight for three hours.

"These are laser pistols for our two Zapatsaurs on the Empire's island. They are gathering as much intel as possible to find out about the Wizard's future plans. They may be faced with real danger and I'm glad I went to the trouble of collecting them from the inner city earlier this week after today's incident." The fifth elder said.

The Zapatsaur picked one up and saw that it was a secure fit in its hand.

"I want you to deliver these to our team on the Wizard's island tomorrow. You are to do so in the late morning when it will be unlikely for the Wizard's creatures to be patrolling because of the stinging rays of the sun. Contact them telepathically when you are only fifty miles from the island. They will direct you to a satisfactory meeting spot, most likely on the island's north shore where the palm trees are, then leave their hiding spot to collect the weapons." The fifth elder instructed. "Keep your telepathic conversation brief as there is a possibility that this creature may be able to read the minds of Zapatsaurs. Until we have confirmed this about our new adversary we will take this precaution." The second elder said.

The Zapatsaur watched the fifth elder take the severed tail and vial of blood and tuck it into its pouch.

"I'll be heading back down to the inner city tonight and in the morning I'll deliver the tail section and the Dragon Queens blood for testing to confirm that both have originated from the Dheginian Star System. During our visit on Yetz-an, nothing was mentioned about the creatures in this star system being able to teleport. The fifth elder said.

The Zapatsaur took the two laser pistols and placed them in its pouch then stood up and gave both elders a quick salute. The Zapatsaur turned and left the half- moon shaped conference room to return to its own personal cave where it could rest up for the morning mission to the Empire's island.

Before the elders made their exit and attended to other duties, the Minister of Science decided to share the latest intel from the medical center, with the Minister of Defense.

"Tamara and Heather's Zapatsaurs had been reading the thoughts of their riders and discovered that Heather appeared to have the ability to move objects with her mind. This ability is called telekinesis, the ability to move objects by nonphysical means. Perhaps Heather's condition is evolving beyond her enhanced human senses. I thought you might find this interesting." The second elder finished.

"That could be very advantageous in a combat situation!" The fifth elder said. "But have there been any physical consequences from this new ability, like headaches?"

"It may be too early to tell. However, the community is monitoring this new development so we'll know soon enough if there are complications that accompany this new ability." The second elder answered. "Tamara's thoughts are on her daughter and she is very concerned. As you know she believes for every action there is a reaction." The second elder said.

The meeting was over for the two elder Zapatsaurs. The Minister of Science left the cave with a busy mind, calculating a variety of scenarios in combat and the advantages of telekinesis. The Minister of Defense decided to leave for the inner city earlier and accessed the secret entrance within the Elder's cave. This elder was leaving with an anxious mind wondering how to defend against teleportation and hoped it would find the answer in the inner city's research center.

The victorious creature had returned to the castle's courtyard and to a hero's welcome. When the Wizard saw the unconscious Dragon Queen cradled in those muscular scaly arms he shouted out his appreciation so loud that it brought both Amy and Gerta outside to see what all the excitement was about.

Amy had come racing out from the reception room with Gerta following close behind. Lunch was over and the ladies were clearing off the dishes from the table. Amy hadn't bothered to put her brown eyed contacts in that late morning when the household finally woke up. The Wizard and Amy had decided to tell Gerta about their home planet and immortality. This was not a shock to Gerta, as they had suspected. Gerta had already befriended a creature with remarkable abilities and intelligence. She had already been accused of witchcraft by a hopeless world and the Wizard wanted her to know that from now on she wouldn't have to be afraid of those narrow minded people. Gerta will live securely with the Empire and a ruler with superior technology that will be able to defeat those who would challenge his people.

Gerta would learn more about the Empire's technology and objectives gradually from her ruling neighbors.

Gerta walked out into the beams of sunlight that were pouring through the opening of the make do roof for the courtyard. The sun highlighted her red hair giving it a fiery appearance. She was wearing a green blouse with beige pants tucked into black boots provided by Amy from her vast collection of stylish clothing. It was a convenient coincidence that Amy and Gerta wore the same shoe size. Amy, was dressed in a freshly washed gray robe and gray slacks with gray shoes. She stood on the outdoor marble patio while Gerta approached her special friend.

Gerta rushed over to greet the creature, delighted to see her friend again and raising her hand to its neck she gave the creature an affectionate pat as it lowered its large scaly head to greet her. Gerta knew that her friend would smile if it could, but she didn't know how right she was, for the creature was truly happy with the result of its late morning struggles.

The unconscious Dragon Queen lay on the creature's hammock behind it and she gasped when she saw Maria. Fortunately, Amy and the Wizard had gone into a detailed description of the Dragon Queen so Gerta was prepared for this sight. Maria is how everyone on the island referred to her. The Dragon Queen was the hateful title given by the Azorkans. Gerta was aware that Maria had suffered the unintended results from an experiment that had gone wrong and deformed the lower half of her body. The positive outcome was Maria's super strength, ability to fly and immortality.

Gerta realized for all that she had imagined from the Wizard's briefing, she was still shocked at that sight of Maria's green skin. She thought that Maria was quite beautiful although the lower part of her body she found repulsive. Gerta had vowed to treat Maria with great respect and even seek to learn what ever Maria was willing to teach her in preparation for combat against Azorka.

Amy stepped off the patio walking up to Gerta, her dark blue eyes lighting up at the sight of this happy moment. They had all been worried about the creature's sudden disappearance earlier in the morning.

"Do you think our friend is hungry Gerta?" Amy smiled as Gerta turned to answer her.

"I think you could be right about that Amy. Do you have some of that salmon from last night left over?" Gerta asked.

Gerta saw that in the light of the courtyard, Amy's beautiful gray skin was almost luminous and her gray hair sparkled in the sunlight. Her dark blue eyes were alive with excitement and Gerta was glad that she would never have to hide her true appearance from her again.

"I still have a couple pounds of salmon left over in the fridge. I'll warm it up in the oven for five minutes then bring it out for our hungry friend." Amy answered.

Amy turned to leave and prepare a special snack for the creature but before she got to the castle's outside door, which led down the hall to the reception room and kitchen Gerta called out.

"Do you want some help with the preparations? I can help you get things ready for a quick snack or after lunch dessert. Would you like that?" Gerta asked.

Amy turned her head, glancing over at Gerta and thought about her proposal for a second. Then her features lit up when she remembered the honey glazed donuts she had in the fridge just freshly made.

"That would be great Gerta. We can try some donuts I just made for our dessert." Amy answered.

Gerta turned back to address the creature and gave it a quick pat on the neck. "I'll be right back with some salmon for your lunch." She said, smiling up at the creature.

Gerta turned and followed Amy back into the castle. Their happy voices could still be heard echoing down the hall on the way to the reception room and kitchen.

The Wizard was silent, lost in his thoughts and comfortably seated on the patio in a fresh gray suit he had put on that morning. He'd tipped his cone hat back a little on his head in order to scratch a particularly itchy spot on his head. He ran his fingers through his gray hair back and forth till a small snow storm of dandruff fell in front of his eyes. He had been quietly thinking about the Dragon Queen and all the annoying medical testing that she may have gone through during her time in captivity.

The creature watched the ladies leave the courtyard then got up from its sitting position and walked down to its favorite patch of dirt. It began scrawling a message in the dirt with a stick for the Wizard to read. The Wizard got out of his chair and walked down ten yards to see what the creature had written. There in the small patch of dirt the creature had scrawled as legibly as possible, a new message.

"We have to tell Gerta and Amy that I can communicate in writing. I didn't think Gerta would be so accepting of Alien life. I must admit I'm relieved and hoping that you can help me communicate my story."

The Wizard looked up at those large dark orange eyes and imagined that they were burning with anxiety and anticipation. He smiled reassuringly at the creature and nodded his head.

"We'll tell Gerta and Amy after we've had a chance to prepare your story. I'll ask Amy to walk Gerta down to the plot of land, not far from here, that we have selected for the construction of your new home. That will give us a reasonable amount of time to record your story. I'll have Amy read the story when they return." The Wizard said.

The Wizardthought he heard the ladies in the hallway again.

"I think the ladies are returning with our snacks. We should get back to our original positions." He said.

The Wizard hurried over to his comfortable chair on the patio and at the same time the creature moved beside the hammock where the unconscious Dragon Queen lay.

Gerta was the first through the door carrying a silver platter of honey donuts, which she placed on the table. Amy was next carrying a bucket of warmed up salmon fillets which she placed in front of the creature. She looked up at the creature and smiled then took her place at the table with the Wizard and Gerta. The donuts were passed around while the creature snacked on salmon in the warmth of the sunlight which was now streaming down onto the hammock and lighting up half of the Dragon Queen peacefully sleeping. For the next couple of minutes all that could be heard was the smacking of happy mouths enjoying honey coated donuts and salmon fillets. Then Gerta decided to break the silence. "How long do you think Maria will be unconscious?" She asked, looking at the Wizard for a reply.

"We can't be sure about that or why the Azorkan doctors wanted her unconscious for such a long time. Perhaps they had planned a major operation and our friend rescued her before they could carry out what would probably be a cruel mutilation." The Wizard answered.

At this suggestion, Gerta bristled with hatred for those who had captured Maria. She was beginning to suspect that they had planned to amputate her reptilian legs and feet or her wings which would guarantee the loss of Maria's mobility and threat to Azorka.

"Those hideous Azorkan people! I am starting to loath that society." Gerta barked. Amy raised one of her beautiful gray eyebrows in surprise at this outburst which seemed out of character for Gerta who was usually soft spoken. Gerta's beautiful melodious voice was raised several octaves expressing her unexpected emotion. "They like to set their own standards and morals but are so uncompromising that they risk the wellbeing of this planet which we find out of control." Amy offered.

"We just have to be on guard for their intrusions and motivations." Amy finished with her reassuring expression directed at Gerta to calm her.

"I will be watching out for their intrusions." Gerta said. Her beautiful voice was back in calmer tone.

"We've been watching out for them for countless years and that will continue until we have subdued them or recruited them to our cause. I have a couple of creatures that patrol the perimeter of the village and our castle late at night." The Wizard said.

"Will your creatures recognize me as a resident of the Empire?" Gerta asked with a slight tremor in her voice.

"Don't worry I will train them to recognize both you and this beautiful Dheginian creature." The Wizard said with confidence.

"Dheginian creature?" Gerta asked.

"Yes. Our friend is from the Dheginian Star System. I recognized this when I saw the two of you teleport in the jungle." The Wizard answered.

"Do you mean the creatures way of shrinking distance? Gerta asked.

"Yes. The Dheginian creatures' have this ability; another form of teleporting. That was the brief description by the riders. Some of the thirteen plants in this star system are involved with mining and sharing resources throughout the universe. To locate new resources the riders and creatures work together. So, we may learn the fate of the creature's rider when I find a way to communicate with your friend." The Wizard finished.

The Yetz's limited telepathic abilities still allowed the Wizard to send a silent message to Amy. He couldn't read her mind to confirm that she received the message, so he always looked at her and relied on her to nod her head as confirmation.

He sent his silent message. "Take Gerta out to the land we will develop for her home with the creature. I need time to communicate with the creature."

Amy moved her head in acknowledgement. "Gerta lets go outside after our snack. It's a beautiful day and I want to show you the land we'll use to build your new home. The view is spectacular!"

Gerta perked up a little and a happy smile washed over her expression. This would be exciting and she was already beginning to imagine how she would furnish her new home. The reality of having a home and belonging again; not having to run from the witch hunters, gave her a burst of energy.

"That would be great!" Gerta excitedly replied.

"I'll stay and keep an eye out for Maria's awakening." The Wizard said.

The creature was quietly reading their minds while digesting a full pale of the salmon fillets which tasted like a rare delicacy compared to the make do diet well travelling with Gerta over the past months. There was one detail that had been front and center in the Wizards mind and that was the crystal skull recovered by Leif and Sam, now on their way home. They would have to talk about this.

Amy stood up at the table unaware that a ring of honey around her petite mouth had become a comical touch added to her youthful features.

"I'm ready to go!" Amy announced.

The ring of honey around her mouth glistened in the sunlight and reminded Gerta of a goatee. This thought caused her to burst out laughing.

"What is so funny?" Amy asked.

"You've got an artist's goatee made of honey!" The Wizard answered.

Amy smiled, rolled her dark blue eyes in acknowledgement and wiped around her mouth with a cloth napkin until all the honey was removed.

"Now I'm ready." She looked over at the Wizard. "We'll be out for about two hours. Then we'll come back and do a little cleaning up and prepare dinner for tonight." Amy said.

The Wizard waited until the ladies had left then went into the castle to retrieve his papyrus note pad from the laboratory. By the time he returned to the courtyard the creature had just finished the first message to be recorded.

The Wizard and the creature spent a busy afternoon scrawling in the dirt and recording in the papyrus note pad all the details of the Dheginian Star System and the creatures story. It was close to two hours before they had finished.

After returning to the patio and his comfortable chair, the Wizard noticed that the Dragon Queen had rolled over on the hammock and now faced the outer wall of the courtyard. The Wizard thought it wouldn't be long before she woke up and felt certain she wasn't in any pain as he hadn't heard any groaning sounds that would have accompanied her movement. She lay there in the shadows with a peaceful expression on her green face.

The Wizard set down his afternoon notes at Amy's place at the table. The creature took up a resting position in front of the hammock, curling the tail beneath its twenty-seven-foot body and facing the patio. The Wizard took his place at the table after turning on the outdoor crystal lamps. They had been recharging in the sun all day. Now their powerful light chased away late afternoon shadows from the patio while the sun slowly set in the west.

After another twenty minutes, the ladies return to the castle was announced by Gerta's boisterous laughter echoing down the hall on their way back out to the courtyard. Amy was the first out the door and she noticed the note pad at her place on the table. She gave a quick wink to the Wizard then sat down at her place. Gerta entered with a slight spring in her walk, energized by the excursion and plans for her new home. She smiled at the Wizard and took her seat at the table.

"I can't thank you enough for your generosity! Both of you have been very kind and I know my friend will love the room I have planned in our new home." Gerta said excitedly.

"What's this note pad about?" Amy asked, pretending not to know.

"That dear ladies, is our friends story and I'm sure you will find it as fascinating as I did. While travelling with Gerta for the past months, communication was restrained somewhat until the right time to tell all arrived. Some answers to specific questions could have had shocking results during this time. When Amy and I explained our origins and goals the creature realized you would accept that your friend was an alien in this world. It is hoped that you will forgive the creature about not telling you it could read and write in English." The Wizard said. Gerta got up from her chair and walked over to the creature. It looked down at her with its large orange eyes, which were a little moist she thought.

"I understand that you didn't want to take a chance on frightening me. I'm more open minded than you might expect. We will always be friends." Gerta said softly. The Wizard carried on. "So I have recorded all that was scrawled into the patch of dirt at the back of the courtyard and I'm hoping that Amy will be so kind as to read this story out loud."

"That I will be happy to do!" Amy said with enthusiasm.

She picked up the note pad in front of her, flipped it open, took a deep breath, brushed back a lock of her shiny gray hair and began.

"Gerta by now you know that Amy and the Wizard come from the Yetz Star System, twenty-five light years from earth. They were on Yetz-an, the ninth planet which is ten times larger than earth and orbiting a sun twice as large as earth's sun. Planets one (closest to their sun) to eight do not support life but planets ten and eleven do. The last planet in this star system is the twelfth and it is barren and frozen like your south pole here on earth. It is on this planet that Amy and the Wizard would trade technology with our scientific committees. This was strictly forbidden on Yetz-an and when they found out what Amy and the Wizard were doing, they were banished to planet ten which is just outside the asteroid belt that orbits around planets one to nine and the sun. Planets ten, eleven and twelve are closed in by a second, even larger asteroid belt which also orbits around the sun and all twelve planets."

"I come from the Dheginian Star System which is forty-six light years from Earth. This is a binary star system with a yellow star that is half the size of your Earth's sun and a red star that is two thirds the size of Earth's sun. Thirteen circumbinary planets, about the size of Venus, orbit around both stars. In summer we orbit close to the red star and in winter we orbit a greater distance away from the yellow star."

"My planet is referred to as planet six in the Dheginian Empire and the Dheginian creatures and their riders are the only ruling intelligent life on a planet with tropical temperatures, jungles, rain forests and lakes. The majority of wildlife is reptilian, with some amphibious species and there's an abundance of fish in our lakes and oceans. We are great builders and the planet has many cities."

Planet thirteen is home to an intelligent Dheginian reptilian with green scales and white wings like Maria but unlike Maria. they are vicious, uncontrollable, and uncivilized. They stand ten to twelve feet tall like our black scaled riders and have a similar head which features a large or elongated cranium, protruding lower jaw, two small nostrils on a nose barely visible, with large malevolent almond shaped orange eyes. We do not include them in our explorations but have always been waiting for them to evolve, hoping that someday we could count them as a military asset. The remaining planets in our system are homes for intelligent reptilian life and together we form an Empire which is dedicated to creating planet to planet trade and commerce through the exploitation of the resources of the universe. The Wizard and Amy are allies in this endeavor and we helped them acquire technology to produce the crystal skulls and provided a variety of DNA from different life in our star system including the Dheginian reptilians on planet thirteen which Maria received."

"After the Wizard had been on earth for close to forty thousand years we left on a mission to learn of his progress. Our scientific committees arranged for the expedition. They only had vague details about the Wizard's mission from long ago and unfortunately the Wizard did not communicate back to the Dheginian Star System. He had crash landed his disc close to earth's Middle East area and his communication equipment was destroyed. Our scientific committees wanted to know if the Wizard had found valuable resources on this planet and if he had been successful producing an intelligent hybrid from the DNA solutions we provided."

"We left on an exploration disc half a mile in circumference, which was average size for a group of twelve Dheginian creatures and their riders. The disc could travel close to the speed of light and was able to navigate worm holes in space to shorten the journey.

"We made the trip to earth in three months which still gave me time to familiarize myself with details of the mission and information about your planet gathered from previous missions in the past. Dheginian creatures and their riders are immortals of equal intelligence, so I memorized information about your planet's geography, weather and wildlife. But I spent most of my time reading about the Wizard's hypothesis for a human-Dheginian hybrid which he proposed to our scientific committee."

"When I saw Maria I considered this experiment a success, especially for her. Maria is now immortal, with incredible strength and has the freedom of flight. However, our scientific committee would have preferred her to be ten feet tall with slimmer legs, hips, and feet.

Our scientists believed that a hybrid with a slimmer lower half would be able to fly faster yet still have enough power in the legs to jump fifty feet in the air for combat situations requiring this maneuver." "The upper half of Maria's body remained mostly human. She wasn't entirely covered with green scales like the Dheginians on planet thirteen or our black scaled riders and she had a human head. Her skin color changed to green and like the Dheginians on planet thirteen, she had white wings attached to two powerful arms growing out of her back. Maria had the power of speech and would have been able to communicate terms of surrender for some of our adversaries that were not telepathic. But our scientists would have been disappointed that she could not teleport, shield her thoughts from adversaries like the Zapatsaurs, or read the minds of other lifeforms."

"When I read the mind of the Wizard and saw Maria's predicament, I was fearful for her and compelled to rescue her. I had picked up bits and pieces of information from those ignorant doctors who worked at both locations where she was kept and I felt that if I didn't rescue her soon they would mutilate her. Maria was also proof of the Wizard's intentions to help our scientific committee. I felt sure our scientists would invest more energy into the hybrid experiments of the future which would provide the Dheginian Star System with a significant combatant for future missions."

"The Dheginian Star System suffered several military distractions, battling opponents from other star systems, that prevented us from visiting your planet to check on the Wizard's progress and catalogue of your planets resources. After defeating a three-star system's military force which was only four light years away from earth, the pathway to your planet was finally clear and our mission was launched."

"It was twelve thousand years ago that we crash landed while trying to land at the South Pole during a blinding snowstorm. Half the crew were killed; the ship destroyed beyond repair, and our food and medicine was lost. As you know, the South Pole is an ice covered and barren land. Some of the survivors experienced serious injuries after the crash into a snow covered mountain and we moved them to the remaining shelter that our ship could provide. We required fresh water, food and warmer shelter in order to recover from our injuries. Except for a few bruises and a mild concussion my rider was in reasonable shape but still couldn't teleport. My ability to teleport was shaky and for longer distances, possibly dangerous or I would have teleported us one by one to New Holland, which was enjoying a summer season in November. This would have to wait for when I recovered from the trauma of the crash."

"My rider hopped on my back and we exited the ship into blinding snow to explore the area in short leaps for shelter and possibly water. After a couple of hours of freezing temperatures, I teleported five miles away from the ship to a distant mountain range. To my delight we saw a cave up ahead and landed at the entrance. My rider jumped down and entered the cave with me following close behind. Stalactites hung down from the cave's roof like large icicles and further on the cave's forty-foot width and thirty-foot tall ceiling narrowed to twenty feet in width and fifteen feet in height. We moved deeper into the cave and it angled downward at about forty-five degrees. I noticed that the walls and ceiling were smooth as though the surface was cut by the laser tool of some unknown civilization. My rider was thinking the same thoughts. The walk down the shaft was slow going in the darkness and it wasn't until we had descended about two miles that we saw a dim light from some unknown source below illuminating the exit.

"With the light shining into the tunnel we were able to move allong quicker and arrived at the exit in ten minutes. Our next challenge was to climb down fifty feet of a rocky face to the ground below. It looked like a paradise with lush green grass growing around scaly tree ferns called cyathea, black tree ferns, and dicksonia antarktiko tree ferns which were bushy and twelve feet across. There were gingko trees close by that were surrounded by bright red heliconias which attracted hummingbirds. Various insects were buzzing around large pitcher plants of the nepenthes genus and mosses grew on rocks surrounded by puzzle grass called equisetum which was a member of vascular plants that reproduce by spores instead of seeds. The land framed a peaceful fresh water lake that carried off into the distance where the bright light of an unknown source lit up the horizon. Above us rocky walls ran upward for at least two hundred feet then disappeared into darkness. The air smelled fresh, and the temperature felt like a warm seventy degrees. Large fish, at least three feet in length, were jumping up out of the water to catch those flies resting on the surface and I watched a gold and green fish dive back into the water with a large fly clasped in its jaws. The fish, insects and plants were, from what I had studied, planetary irregularities. The fish and insects were too large and some of the plants were mostly extinct. However, this was a welcome sign for our survival. It appeared to be daylight two miles beneath the ice but it was a dim daylight and my rider lit a laser torch and placed it on a rock close to the rock face where we had climbed down from the exit. We moved down to the lake's shore where we soothed our parched throats with the most delicious fresh water and filled a canteen my rider had brought along. I noticed that there wasn't any wildlife. There were no scavengers or predators. The paradise was eerily quiet. Not even the sound of a chirping bird or the flutter of its feathers in flight could be heard."

"My rider was leading our walk down the sandy beach and we had moved along for about five minutes when suddenly my rider stopped sensing movement up ahead. I moved up beside my rider and focused my eyes on three indistinguishable forms lying motionless between two boulders on the sand. We decided to investigate and cautiously moved down the beach side by side until we had covered seventy-five yards of the distance between us and those mysterious forms lying in the sand. Again we sensed movement and stopped but by the time we focused our eyes in the dim light all was still. When my rider was only twenty feet away I received a telepathic message suggesting that they were unconscious Dheginian riders, three of them, possibly in distress. Empathy replaced fear and we abandoned caution moving forward quickly. At about ten feet away I looked and to my surprise they appeared to be three unconscious Dheginian riders lying in a fetal position facing the lake. My next thought was to call out to them telepathically and try to wake them and communicate. Where did they come from? Were they stranded here from a previous mission? Those fins you refer to on top of my head are actually a cranial accessory that helps enhance my telepathic ability with other life forms and it has never failed me. But this time I couldn't get a response from these unconscious riders. The Dheginian creatures were a great asset for scientific exploration because we could read the minds of other life forms advising our riders of their peaceful or violent intentions. I felt certain these Dheginian riders were dead so I sent my rider back this suggestion. My rider moved closer to see if this could be confirmed. In the next minute, as my rider approached, now just five feet away, the Dheginian rider in the middle moved its head and a large green eye with a horizontal pupil regarded my rider with malevolent intent. The shape unraveled shifting into a multi-limbed cephalopod horror which reared upward from its position, towering over my rider. It moved forward on four of its long tentacles and its head grew larger revealing its hideous beak which yawned wide revealing two threatening rows of needle teeth. My rider was frozen to the spot in a state of shock. A tentacle with two rows of disc shaped suckers lashed out at my rider in an attempt to wrap around those powerful scaly black legs. My rider jumped up out of the way and the tentacle missed hitting a nearby rock which sizzled and smoked upon contact. I looked at the gigantic cephalopod, its massive bulk was the size of a grizzly bear and it was three feet taller than my rider. I saw that the tentacle that had missed my rider had two long rows of disc shaped suckers beneath the tentacle that ran the entire fourteen-foot length. Some of the suckers had a fleshy tube which poked out from the disc and was dripping what must have been an extremely corrosive natural acid. I understood why the rock smoked and melted. I also think it possible that the same natural acid had created the smooth shaft we descended down. By this time the other two forms had changed into similar horrors. All three were a dull green color and they advanced threateningly towards us. Their heads were four feet wide and five feet long with two bulging light green eyes and black horizontal pupils. My rider, hopped on my back and sent me a telepathic message to fly away from them. I jumped twenty feet into the air and spread my black leathery wings but before we could escape two tentacles lashed out from the horror in the middle and dragged my rider off my back. My rider struggled against the tentacles with those deceptively strong thin arms and clutched the tentacle with powerful four digit hands which ended in three inch claws. But another tentacle lashed around his shoulders and my rider's arms were rendered useless as the monster raised my rider up in the air opened its horrible mouth and bit down hard on my rider's head. I heard the telepathic scream and anguish before death brought silence. The remainder of my rider's body fell, headless onto the beach. I didn't wait any longer but did a short distance teleport to the burning torch we left on the rock below the exit shaft. Amazingly enough, all three cephalopod monsters pursued me and closed the distance between in a matter of seconds. They were jumping up into the air on those horrific tentacles and covering twenty feet of distance with every leap. They were within fifty feet of me when I teleported up the shaft to the ice cold cave above. I thought that climbing up the narrow shaft might slow them down so I took a minute to regain my breath and composure. The frigid temperature of the cave chased away the last of my warmth and I decided to teleport back to the ship in order to report the loss of my rider. We are immortal and self-healers but should the head be removed from the body there is no way to heal or continue living. The remaining crew just needed a reasonable environment and water to continue their recovery. I couldn't teleport long distances or use my sonic vibrations because of my minor injuries. We all needed time to heal before leaving. Fortunately, I had brought back some water in a canteen which my rider had strapped around my neck." "In a matter of a few minutes I arrived back at the entrance to the ship. I moved past the command center for our pilots located in the middle of the disc where three riders, their dead bodies impaled or shattered, were covered in snow. There was nothing there or anywhere else on the ship that could be salvaged and used to assist our survival. I moved to the area of the ship where our survivors were huddled together against the harshness of the cold."

"To my absolute distress I was greeted with an unexpected shock. The remaining survivors were all dead. Most of them, riders and Dheginian creatures, had their heads removed and lay motionless on the metallic floor of the ship. Some of the headless rider's bodies were partially melted by acid around the neck area and I knew what murdering horror had destroyed them."

"I was horrified but also fearful and wasted no time exiting the ship and teleporting in a different direction in short one mile bursts until I found a different cave twenty miles away and without an entrance downward to a strange world within a world below the ice. I carried on like this for a couple of days. Having the canteen of water helped me survive. I had fully recovered in one week and was ready to leave the South Pole using my long distance teleportation. Teleportation, technically speaking, is arriving at "B" destination from start destination "A" without having travelled the distance in-between. This is precisely what the Dheginian rider does when teleporting. I claim to be using a different more restricted version of the same and as you know the ninety-foot circle of energy locates a planetary worm hole which shrinks travel time."

"I had spent some time thinking about the tragedy at the South Pole. My strength was fully recovered and I could use my sonic vibrations if it became necessary to defend myself against deadly life forms. My rider had not been able to freeze the motor functions of the cephalopods because of a concussion, but I doubted it would have worked against these horrors anyways. They were clever shape- shifters and did a perfect job of imitating a Dheginian rider. For me, this was my first experience failing to read the mind of a lifeform. My second experience occurred today with a Zapatsaur and that worried me."

"I left for New Holland as I originally planned. I knew I'd be welcomed by the indigenous community as there were accounts of our visits recorded by previous missions to earth. The indigenous community knew that we came from the stars and gave a warm welcome to our Dheginian creatures and their riders, showering us with gifts and good food."

"It was a little unsteady but I was able to conjure the ninety-foot circle of energy on my second try and be on New Holland's south coast within two minutes. I was welcomed by the indigenous community and given food and water. I was a celebrity among them, having come from the stars, and I helped them with some of their needs, catching fish in some of those areas where the waters were full of life that threatened them but had no effect on me. After my fishing for the community,

I relaxed by watching the kangaroo, one of my favorite marsupials, gather food and carry their young in their natural pouch. My shelter was a well- constructed hut inside their village, close to a patch of dirt where I was able to communicate in their language in the same fashion I communicate with you. After two weeks I was fully healed and recovered from my tragic ordeal at the South Pole."

"While I was recovering, I had the opportunity to meet one of their young Shaman apprentices who had acquired a special talent as a result of a freak accident. He told me that a meteorite had crashed into a field close to their village and that he went out on his own, to investigate without consulting the elders. The ground was burnt and still warm around the meteorite. He accidentally tripped on a stick while walking around its eighty-foot circumference and banged his fore head. He pointed to the three-inch long scar just above his eyebrows and I examined it while he told me that since that day he has been able to move physical objects by willing them to move. He gave me a demonstration and I was amazed. I saw another demonstration of this ability today during the rescue. Heather, one of Azorka's guardians, has acquired this ability you call telekinesis and that worries me. Heather has a super ability that not even the Yetz or Dheginians have and this makes our struggle against Azorka in the future more difficult."

"I was busy during those twelve thousand years. I was looking for the Wizard, not realizing I had flown several times over his island that is hidden by an ancient hologram program that projects more ocean and causes both Azorka and the Empire's island to disappear. I also spent a great deal of time exploring caves and underground tunnels in an attempt to locate more of the dangerous cephalopods I ran into at the South Pole. My self-confidence was restored now that I had my sonic vibrations working again to defend myself and I knew that the laboratory was still intact on the crashed disc. If I could capture one and study it, I would be able to formulate a genetic poison that it would carry back to its own kind. I could start the chain of genocide which would eliminate these creatures from your planet."

"Today I have to allocate this duty to a later date so that we can gain control of this planet. It has become a priority to locate the Wizard's stolen crystal skulls. They can help us with our mission. Unfortunately, they are dangerous in the wrong hands. The Wizard and I should leave immediately to recover the crystal skull that Leif and Sam are bringing back. We can consult the Wizard's notes in order to identify it when we return. It may even be necessary to leave the Empire for a period of time while we produce a solution for locating the remaining eleven skulls. In this event it might be best if Amy assumes the leadership role and duties of the Wizard. This would include raising the Wizard's new creature and a covert surveillance of Azorka to check on Heather's progress or evolution of special abilities. It has occurred to me that these unexpected side effects Heather experiences may eventually suggest there could be benefits for Gerta should she subject herself to the same experiment. The telekinesis may prove a problem unless the Empire has a champion with the same ability."

"This is my story and suggestions to remedy future challenges in our preparation for control of the planet."

Amy finished reading the creature's story and looked over at the Wizard, with an expression of amazement causing her beautiful dark eyes to grow wider. She was surprised by some of the stories revelations.

"Did you know that our allies had visited and established a relationship with the aboriginal people in New Holland so far back in the past?" Amy asked.

"I was as surprised as you, although I chalked up the reticence to the limited time I could spend with our allies. We had to hide from Yetz-an spy-drones and had agreed to keep our meetings brief in order to avoid detection on planet twelve." The Wizard answered.

"That makes sense come to think of it. Discovery could have sparked an incident between our star systems and the agreed upon truce felt shaky enough." Amy said.

"The creature has read your mind on the latest expedition to this land and re- naming of "Terra Australis" to "New Holland" by the Dutch." Amy said.

"The old name from the second century was changed forty-four years ago. I don't think that the creature is surprised about our interest in the area and the aboriginal people. We have been keeping a close watch on the indigenous people and their medicines which may be helpful in the future for our own society. The aboriginal people of this area have incredibly good human eye sight, perhaps the best in the world and were monitoring their diet as well. They also have ancient knowledge about the stars provided by other visitors in their past as well as the Dheginians. This became common knowledge in the ancient world and there is a record of an Egyptian King visiting them although the King suffered a snake bite upon his arrival and died on New Hollands south coast where he is buried." The Wizard finished.

"I'm surprised the creature's mission encountered what sounds like "Katabatic winds" and a snow storm. I think this is bad luck, because this is an occurrence at the South Pole which is rare. That dry and cold climate has an average snowfall of only six inches per year." Amy said.

Gerta had been quietly thinking to herself while the Wizard and Amy had their conversation. She was excited about the direction the creature had mapped out for control of the planet and interested in spying on the Azorkans.

Gerta looked up at Amy and the Wizard from her kneeling position beside the creature. They were both waiting for her comments and impressions from the creature's story.

"I am delighted with everything I have heard and ready to go to work for the Empire!" Gerta yelled with joy.

The Wizard and Amy smiled, truly pleased with their new friend's enthusiasm and energy. But they didn't realize the difficulties the future would offer.

Chapter Seven

The medical center had returned to normal operation one hour after the laboratory intruder warning had been shut off. Tamara and Heather had left with Seiji after the doctor had finished his examination and made sure he was well enough to ride his Zapatsaur home. He assured the ladies that his dizziness, lightheadedness, and nausea had subsided enough to fly home. Ming had concluded his shift when his replacement showed up to guard the east entrance and said he would follow Seiji home to be sure he arrived safely. Seiji also promised Heather that he would follow the doctor's advice and take the next couple of days off from his normal duties. As soon as Seiji had left, Heather turned to Tamara with an urgent expression on her face. She thought Tamara had seen her move the fire extinguisher with her mind and wanted to discuss this.

"I'm sure you saw me move the fire extinguisher. Please don't mention this to anyone yet" Heather whispered.

Tamara looked into Heather's dark eyes; relieved to see her daughter's control.

"I will leave disclosure to you. It's obvious that you are able to deal with the trauma of this new ability. I was a little shocked but did my best to hide it. I thought this was a new side effect from the Wizard's experiment.

I was thinking of inviting everyone over for dinner tonight so that we can all deal with the tragedy of today together. Maybe this would be a good time to tell those who you are closest to about your new ability." Tamara suggested.

"That would be great Mom. However, I don't want to tell Ted about this yet." Heather replied.

Heather would need more time to consider the effects of her transition on her romantic relationship. She could become number one target for her adversaries and inadvertently cause danger for Ted.

Tamara didn't know why she wanted to exclude Ted but refrained from commenting. She was more concerned with flying out to Lana's village to invite her to dinner when she saw both Sally and Lana arriving.

"Hello Mom!" Sally called down.

She was descending slowly on her Zapatsaur through the same entrance that the intruding creature had escaped through. Above her, Lana was following in the flying craft she had tested in Africa with Heather. The flying craft silently moved lower past the trees of the forest and into the dim light of the village below. Lana was four feet above the village street and eighty feet away from the medical center ahead. Lana moved the flying craft forward until she was only twenty feet away from the picnic table where Tamara and Heather were seated. The village street's overhead crystal flood lights mounted on forty-foot tall wooden poles automatically came on with the setting of the sun. Lana popped open the pilot's hatch and jumped down to the lawn. Heather had her back to her and was watching the last of the repairmen who had fixed the west entrance doors leave for the day. He brushed his black hair out of his eyes and hefted a tool box on a strap placing it on his right shoulder for easy carrying. He gave Heather a quick wave, which she returned and walked towards the east entrance where his Zapatsaur was waiting. Tamara looked up from the picnic table and saw Lana in a navy blue blouse and pants which tucked into black boots. She had changed her head band for one that was black and tied her long blonde hair into a ponytail. "Hello everybody! Lana said cheerfully. "Heather how did it go today?" She asked. Lana was inquiring about the doctor's appointment that everyone had hoped would help Heather deal with the nightmares she was having. She was not aware of the commotion that had taken place at the medical center earlier. The sullen expression on Tamara's face told her something was not right. Heather turned around to answer Lana and with some effort gave her a smile. Lana noticed that Heather was perspiring, her green robe and pants were scuffed up and wrinkled. Heather's shoulder length brown hair hung down in wet strings framing a pale complexion.

"We've been in a battle here for the last hour and a half. The Dragon Queen has been taken away by a horrific creature acting alone. We haven't confirmed the Wizard's involvement but suspect that he created an intelligent creature, one third larger than a Zapatsaur, to rescue the Dragon Queen. It was a very destructive intrusion that left Seiji injured and two of the Zapatsaurs were roughed up." Heather said in a voice that communicated frustration and exhaustion.

Before Lana could respond, Tamara changed the subject of conversation.

"We'd like you to join us for dinner, and of course an overnight stay so that you won't have to fly home in the dark." Tamara said in a perky voice that hid her exhaustion.

Lana thought Tamara looked a little pale, but her hair was neatly tucked behind her in a ponytail and her green robe and pants didn't look as scuffed up and wrinkled as Heather's outfit was. Lana caught the hint Tamara was sending and decided not to probe any further about the calamity at the medical center.

"That is very kind of you Tamara and I'd love to join you. I have three more empty seats in my flying craft. Would you two like a lift home? Your Zapatsaurs are probably tired and would like to return to their mountain home." Lana offered.

Lana was not a rider with a Zapatsaur. The Zapatsaurs chose their riders and some Zapatsaurs preferred not to have a rider. But like all Azorkans Lana always tried to help or provide for the Zapatsaur population.

"That is a wonderful idea!" Tamara said. "As you know they were challenged by this beast and would probably appreciate some rest."

Something Tamara had just said was ringing an alarm in Lana's mind. She wanted to resist the question, but couldn't.

"Heather! Is this the same monster that chased us in Africa? "Lana asked.

"It is the same one unless there are two." Heather answered. "The creature teleported like the one we had to run from and it blasted me with its booming sonic vibrations that it used on the leopards in Africa."

Before Lana could ask another question Sally was making her way up the walk and like Lana she hadn't heard about the incident. She was brightly dressed in a yellow jacket worn over a white blouse with white pants tucked into yellow boots. Sally gave a quick hello to Mitch and General Zen who were talking quietly as she passed them on the walk. Zen had an expression of concern on his practically wrinkle free face, and Mitch was frowning. She wondered what they were discussing.

"How is everybody on this beautiful day?" Sally merrily asked.

Sally was about five feet away from the ladies at the picnic table. Three more serious expressions were gazing up at her.

"What's wrong or what went wrong?" Sally asked.

"You better sit down Sally, it's quite a story!" Lana answered. Lana pointed to an empty space beside her at the table and Sally sat down to listen.

While Sally learned about the trouble at the medical center, General Zen had just finished telling Mitch about the details he received from Captain Jeff, who had left earlier returning to security headquarters. Mitch had clothed his seven foot frame with a heavy waist length brown jacket over black pants. He was perspiring heavily, mostly from the anxiety of the bad news. He looked down and unbuttoned the winter jacket.

Zen looked up at him and said: "There is something else I need to discuss with you."

Zen told Mitch about finding the crystal skull inside of Indie's family heirloom, the globe of the old world. Zen described it and asked if there would be any way that they could confirm that it was genuine and not a copy. Was there any information on the Wizard's crystal skulls?

This new development for Mitch helped distract his anger and frustration at having lost the Dragon Queen after all the hard work of capturing her. It helped him with his anger towards the Wizard who launched a reckless rescue effort that roughed up his family. He snickered at the thought of General Zen having something that the Wizard is desperate to recover.

"I'll be honest with you Zen, not enough is known about the Wizard's crystal skulls. He crafted them here on earth before we were aware of him being a rebel, so there was no gathering of intel. We don't know who stole his collection but somehow the Mayans had access to them or some of them because they claim when all the crystal skulls are assembled that they will speak the secrets of the universe. With some research we might learn more about the dangers of the Wizard's property. The Wizard and Amy always lead reclusive lives and it took some time before we realized they were immortal. In my opinion the Wizard looks about mid-forties and Amy in her thirties. We finally confirmed they must be alien but kept it quiet. The technology he used to craft the skulls must also be alien which will make confirmation more difficult." Mitch finished.

"We've all had a difficult day. Why don't you and Indie join us for dinner at the castle tonight. It would be a relaxing night and you both can stay in one of the spare bedrooms tonight. It will give us time to read over the records past guardians have left behind. Maybe there is something from that era in Azorka's history on the crystal skulls that I have overlooked." Mitch said.

"That is very kind of you, Mitch and I'm sure Indie would like to come along. We have both agreed to release the crystal skull to you knowing that it would be safe in the castle." General Zen replied.

"It will be secure in the libraries lead-lined safe I have built into the wall. We have to be sure it won't be a danger to anyone by accidentally triggering some unknown mechanism that was built into it." Mitch said.

Zen agreed and they both walked up the sidewalk to greet the four ladies sitting quietly at the picnic table. Sally was facing the building sitting across from Tamara and beside Lana. Heather sat beside Lana quietly thinking about how to tell everyone about her new talent and admitting to Tamara that she hid details of her last dream from the doctor she had just had an appointment with. Tamara saw the two men walking towards the picnic table.

"I wondered when you two would join us." Tamara said Sally heard the echo of their boots on the sidewalk and turned to face them.

"Hello Dad. I guess by now you've heard we had a surprise visit from one of the Wizard's creatures that rescued the Dragon Queen. At least that is the assumption. I feel frustration and anger after all the trouble we went through to capture her." Sally said.

"We'll catch her again Sally." Mitch said with a reassuring tone. He was disguising his anger and frustration.

Tamara looked up at Mitch and knew he was looking at Heather's green robe noticing it was wrinkled and dirty from the fight with the creature.

"We're you two injured from your fight with this monster?" Mitch asked. He wanted them to realize he cared a great deal even though he knew they weren't seriously injured.

"No injuries Dad. Just a little shaken and frustrated at having lost the Dragon Queen." Heather replied.

Tamara stood up and walked over to Mitch. Mitch reached down and gave her a hug and quick kiss.

"We were lucky we didn't receive any injuries today. You wouldn't believe what this monster looked like. It was much larger than a Zapatsaur and used sonic vibrations which poured out of its vicious looking jaws with a booming sound, to attack Heather. The trauma has passed and I thought I would invite everyone back to the castle for dinner so we can end the day on a happier note. Zen why don't you and Indie join us." Tamara said.

"Thank you Tamara. We'd love to join you." Zen answered. He didn't bother mentioning that Mitch had already invited them.

Lana looked up at Mitch and Zen. "I've offered the ladies a ride over in my flying craft. We can go to your home and pick up Indie on the way." Lana suggested. "That will be great Lana. I have to fly back home and get something so I'll see you there." Zen said.

Zen turned and walked towards the street where his Zapatsaur was waiting. Sally watched him fly out of the area then turned to Mitch knowing how disappointed he was with the day's events.

"Let's put this day behind us and enjoy a great dinner and evening together. I'll fly home with you." Sally said.

"Great idea Sally. I'll get ahead of everyone and chop up some wood for the family room fireplace which will make for a cozy atmosphere after dinner." Mitch said.

Mitch leaned down and gave Tamara a parting kiss on the cheek then joined Sally as she made her way down the walk to her Zapatsaur. He jogged over to the east garden where his Zapatsaur had enjoyed an afternoon snack in the garden.

After Mitch and Sally had left, the ladies got up from the picnic table and walked over to Lana's tear-drop shaped flying craft. Heather looked at the exterior and thought the silver color had taken on a matt finish.

"Is it my imagination or was this flying craft painted again using a flat silver paint?" Heather asked.

"Our technicians decided it would be best if the exterior had a flat finish so that it would not attract attention. I told everyone of our encounter with the creature in Africa and the lady with red hair. They were worried about the creature chasing me and decided to add a small crystal powered engine at the back just below the battery. If I accelerate to the maximum speed and enter space to escape from the creature, I will have the option of staying in space until I figure it's safe to return to Earth's atmosphere. Before this modification, the flying craft would automatically angle downwards and return to the atmosphere if it sensed the absence of air molecules. As you know the earth's atmosphere is divided into five layers. The flying craft returned, passing through the exosphere, thermosphere, mesosphere and levelled off in the stratosphere or descended further into the troposphere if I decided to land. The technicians also suggested I use the laser cannon if the situation becomes life threatening." Lana explained.

The ladies hopped up over the three-foot deep metal nose of the flying craft and entered one by one with Tamara sitting behind Lana and Heather sitting beside Lana in the front. They fastened their seat belts attached to the green seats. Lana flipped on five of the toggle switches for the crafts operation and looked at the readings for each on the screens mounted into the control panel. When she confirmed the craft was ready for flying she took hold of the throttle and the flying craft rose up off the medical centers lawn and headed for the village street. They flew forty feet above the street at a leisurely pace of thirty miles per hour until they reached a cluster of domed homes at the edge of the village. This was General Zen's neighborhood and the village street narrowed to a ten-foot path that ran past each home. The neighborhood was well concealed with trees and bushes and just about every home was landscaped. As they flew over they saw some of General Zen's neighbors were outside enjoying the last of a beautiful day. The home at the end of the development, with the best view of the ocean, belonged to Indie and Zen.

The ladies looked down at Zen's Zapatsaur resting in the hammock the General had repaired after the Dragon Queen had torn it in order to demonstrate that she could slip past neighborhood watch. Suddenly the Zapatsaur got up and stood ready to leave. Zen opened the front door and walked out carrying a back pack which he quickly put on then jumped up on his Zapatsaur. He saw the flying craft hovering thirty feet above his front yard and gave the ladies a quick wave as he flew out in the direction of the castle.

Lana slowly descended until they sat on the General's freshly cut lawn. Indie opened the front door and ran towards the flying craft carrying a small bag filled with samples of her latest clothing designs for Tamara and the ladies. Heather helped her up, gave her the front seat beside Lana and moved to the back buckling herself into the seat beside Tamara. The flying craft rose into the sky until it was above the old growth forest that hid the village below.

"It was such a perfect day today! Look at that sunset!" Lana shouted.

The sun had set in the west leaving the sky in shades of yellow and red. There wasn't a cloud in the sky and the ocean was calm. It could be a quiet night without any wind. Lana was looking forward to the spring season.

Lana looked down at the instrument panel and saw that they were one-thousand feet above Azorka. She looked over at Indie who was gazing out the window at the view.

"There's the castle up ahead!" Lana called out. She was enjoying playing the host and wanted to give her friends a thrill so she dropped the nose of the flying craft by sixty degrees and accelerated to three-hundred miles per hour in the direction of the castle which looked like a small white triangle surrounded by trees in the distance. The castle seemed to rush up at them and Lana could hear Indie gasp from the thrill of the ride.

In the backseat Heather had put her control console for the castle and locator Ted had installed last month, on the floor. Her Zapatsaur had the belt at home in the cave back at Zapatsaur mountain and would not hesitate to use it should. Heather disappear unexplainably and out of its telepathic distance of fifty miles. She nudged Tamara and pointed at her console on the flying craft's floor three feet away. A bright white border, that only Heather could see, enveloped the console and it rose up into Heather's hand in front of a wide-eyed Tamara sitting beside her. Heather was practicing but also wanted Tamara to witness her new ability again. Perhaps this would help Tamara suggest the most appropriate demonstration for everyone after dinner tonight.

"Here we are friends!" Lana shouted. She looked over at Indie and could see that she enjoyed the ride in her flying craft. Indie smiled and thanked her for the experience and began unbuckling her seat belt as Lana popped open the glass hatch above them.

Lana had landed on the front lawn beside the garden where three Zapatsaurs were enjoying a late afternoon snack. Sally opened the hand-carved ten foot front door to the castle and they made their way down the long hall to the kitchen.

"Mitch and Zen are upstairs in the library." Sally said. Mitch had finished chopping the wood for the fireplace which would help create a cozy atmosphere for everyone to relax in after dinner. He had worked out all his frustration and anger before Zen arrived.

Tamara made the most delicious dinner of pheasant and grouse with fresh spinach and potatoes covered in gravy made from a special recipe. Dessert was the richest chocolate cake Mitch had ever tasted and this creation drew just as many compliments as the main course.

After dessert they all retired to the family room where Mitch had a fire already burning in their fieldstone fireplace. Tamara sat down with Mitch in a high-backed love seat while Sally and Heather sat down together on an upholstered ottoman for two across from them. General Zen and Indie pulled up another love seat to the edge of the coffee table and faced the fireplace. Mitch reached over to his right and grabbed the fireplace poker to rearrange some of the logs in the fireplace. They were quiet for the moment and enjoying the relaxing atmosphere.

Lana was the last to join them. She had been in the kitchen washing down that last fork-full of Tamara's chocolate cake with some milk. Lana pulled up a chair from the corner of the room and placed it beside Sally so she could be close to the warmth of the fireplace.

Heather waited until she was settled then decided she would tell everyone that Azorka has a new secret weapon. She had seen the disappointment of having lost the Dragon Queen break through the happy expressions that Zen and Mitch had adopted to hide their true feelings. Her announcement might re-direct their thinking towards the positive outcome from all the changes that she was going through.

Heather took out her console from a pocket on the white robe she had changed into and set it down in the middle of the coffee table. Then Heather broke the silence.

"I'm not the best when it comes to public speaking, but I do have to inform my family and closest friends about a new ability I discovered today. This ability may turn out to be a considerable asset for Azorka. Today, when I was trying to stop the monster from taking the Dragon

Queen out of the medical center, I applied a suggestion from one of those strange dreams I've been having. The suggestion was that I possess the power of telekinesis. I can manipulate objects with my mind; cause them to move or freeze." Heather finished.

Heather was watching the surprised expressions on everyone's face. Before anyone could speak, Heather surrounded the console on the table with that bright white border that only she could see and raised it two feet in the air. This display received the gasps of surprise she had expected.

"Tamara saw me throw a fire extinguisher at the creature so hard that it temporarily disabled the creature's shoulder and it dropped the Dragon Queen's legs and feet. Before I could pull the Dragon Queen free, the creature blasted me with those sonic vibrations you've heard us speak of and sent me flying through the air into Tamara behind me. We were gasping for breath but I managed to look up and see that the creature had made a miraculous recovery from the shoulder injury I had caused. The creature picked up the Dragon Queen then used the sonic vibrations again to destroy the west entrance doors and escape.

Mitch looked at Tamara fidgeting nervously in the loveseat beside him.

"Mitch, we thought this would be the best way to break the news. Heather wanted everyone to relax and enjoy dinner before revealing this." Tamara said in an apologetic tone.

Mitch squeezed her hand gently to let her know he understood. Tamara wanted him to relax most of all after the shocking news of the day. Mitch and Zen would somehow feel responsible for the loss of the Dragon Queen.

"Heather that's incredible!" Sally shouted. Sally was excited about this new development.

Heather was thankful for this positive reaction and continued her story.

"I have to confess that this is one dream I remember vividly and one dream that I held back from the doctor today. I didn't have time, until this encounter with the creature, to test what my dream revealed I could do." Heather explained.

For the next ten minutes Heather went over the details of her dream including the strange cowled figure and bizarre setting for the dream. Everyone listened carefully and when Heather had finished there was something that she had said that resonated with Indie.

"The setting for the dream sounds like a place I go to meditate and relax which is only one hundred yards from our home." Indie said quietly.

She was surprised by some of the details of the dream but fearful of the symbolism associated with the dark sky and red clouds. Was this dream warning of a bloody conflict in the future?

"Have I ever been there with you?" Heather asked.

"No one except Zen has ever walked up there with me." Indie replied.

"Heather what else can you manipulate with your mind? Is there a certain weight you can't move?" Zen asked.

"I'm learning as I go Zen. To answer your question, I don't know." Heather said. Lana had been listening quietly but with Zen's question she thought of a way to test Heather's ability. "How about trying to raise my flying craft? She asked.

"That's fine with me. I'd be happy to try." Heather answered.

The rest of the group got up and followed Lana and Heather who were already rushing down the hall to the front door. It was a star-filled sky and a comfortable fifty-two degrees with no wind. The Zapatsaurs had flown back to their mountain home a couple of hours ago and the front yard was dark and quiet. The light that shone out from the open front door, which slid into its recess, caught the right side of Lana's flying craft. Heather and Lana were standing together on the front porch. Zen and Mitch walked over to stand beside them while Sally, Indie and Tamara watched from the open front door.

Heather concentrated and in the next ten seconds the flying craft rose two feet in the air while her friends and family watched, frozen in their own amazement. She was delighted with the outcome from this challenge. It proved that she could raise an object as heavy as one-thousand pounds. This convinced her that she could handle the weight of the creature. Satisfied with this experiment. Heather gently lowered the flying craft back onto the ground. The party returned to their comfortable seats in the family room.

The disclosure had the positive outcome that Heather was hoping for. Heather's family and friends were more confident of her psychological health because of her careful and considerate presentation of the new ability. More importantly they were beginning to believe that this would be a military asset for Azorka.

The evening party continued until eleven at night thanks to Tamara's delicious hot chocolate and some homemade marshmallows that were roasted over the fireplace. The evening gathering had helped absorb the shock of the day's events and had instilled a certain amount of confidence in the future after Heather's demonstration of her new ability. Tamara and Mitch knew that their children would someday take over as guardians for Azorka. Any advantage that their children could acquire against the Wizard's forces would be welcomed. With this in mind they were both grateful for Heather's new ability. General Zen was beginning to consider the combat advantages that Heather's ability presented and was seeing the struggle against the Empire in a more positive light. Indie was cautiously optimistic about Heather's future but still unsettled about Heather's dreams. Zen and Indie had kept secret the discovery of the crystal skull which had been locked in a safe built into the wall of the castle library. By eleven pm Heather and Sally had gone to bed, but unlike the other exhausted members of the gathering, they began to dream.

Heather was tense and beginning to perspire as she opened her eyes in a dark dream world. She was surrounded by the stars and heavenly bodies of the universe and every now and then she could see a shooting star flash in front of her. Heather looked down at her feet and saw that she was standing on a clear sheet of glass which permitted a view of more stars below her. Her reflection in the glass showed her dressed in a tight fitting dark green suit that was tucked into black boots that felt unnaturally comfortable. Both pants and jacket were joined together and there were several buttons centered on the jacket that ran down to the waist of the outfit. Heather moved and stretched her arms and legs without any restriction from the garment. She began to look around to see if she was alone and that is when she spotted Sally behind her looking confused and a little anxious, dressed in the same outfit.

"Hey Sally!" Heather called. Her voice echoed somehow which was a mysterious effect considering there were no visible walls.

"Heather! Where are we? Is this the same dream world you've been visiting?" Sally asked. Her voice echoed just as Heather's had. However, discovering Heather in her dream seemed to calm her down.

"Why are we dressed in these green suits?" Sally asked. Her voice was calmer but it still echoed eerily.

Heather was about to say she was just as baffled and filled with uncertainty as Sally, when she heard her name being called.

"H-E-A-T-H-E-R!" The unknown speaker shouted.

Sally and Heather froze on the sheet of glass as the mysterious voice echoed around them. It was the same deep male voice Heather had heard in the dream that she could remember which helped her discover her new ability: telekinesis. She relaxed a little, then turned around to face Sally.

"This voice is no threat to us Sally. If anything the owner of this voice is a friend." Heather said. Her voice echoed around the invisible perimeters of the square sheet of glass they were standing on.

A shooting star flashed by up ahead. It's tail of light showed it traveling downwards at a forty-degree angle and Heather looked through the glass until it disappeared below her.

Sally felt confident enough to move forward and stand beside Heather. She was still testing the elasticity of the action shoulders and legs for her dark green suit. She was beginning to suspect that this was a combat suit. But before Sally could think further about her peculiar experience in Heather's dream, an object materialized out of thin air, fifty yards away, in front of them. Sally looked behind her and did a quick and rough calculation, concluding that this must be a seventy-five-yard-long see through sheet of glass that they were standing on. The object began moving towards them and as it advanced the floor behind it disappeared. It was within twenty-five yards of them when finally, Sally could see that it was a see through glass table.

The four legs of the table were translucent but crafted to resemble winged angels. Each leg of the table had a lion's paw resting on the floor, then the leg curved out and upwards to imitate the chest of the winged angel with a beautifully carved head and wings supporting the transparent table top above. The clear table top featured a second see through level, stylishly made with thick borders that rose six inches above the lower level on tubular glass legs and was the resting place for a clear glass globe of the earth.

"If you ladies have finished looking at this table then we can get down to business." The unknown speaker said. A deep male voice echoed around them again.

The area behind the desk shimmered and when this stopped the gray-cowled figure from Heather's previous dream materialized. Inside the cowl, the sun and nine planets of the Yetz Star System replaced the speakers face. The speaker turned around and faced the blackness of the universe. He pulled off his cowl revealing light gray hair that reached mid-way down his gray neck. The Yetz Star System appeared above and behind the glass desk, much larger now showing the tenth, eleventh, and twelfth planet closed in by the second larger asteroid belt. The speaker turned around facing Heather and Sally with a youthful clean-shaven gray face of a Yetz. He didn't look much older than thirty and Heather thought he was attractive looking although he was only five-feet tall.

"Behind me is my home star system and I live on the ninth planet." He said in his deep voice. Strangely his voice no longer echoed.

"My planet's name is Yetz-an and the other eleven planets that orbit our sun are not named. The Wizard was banished with Amy, when we convicted them of being rebels, to planet ten where the weather and landscape are not entirely pleasant but livable." The Yetz speaker continued.

"We decided to watch the activities of the Wizard and Amy when we suspected their collusion with the Dheginian Star System. We had concluded our war with this star system, although we had not signed a peace treaty. It was Yetz-an law that forbid trading technology with the war-like Dheginians. We found out that the rebellious Wizard and Amy were trading technology with our enemy. They had planned to control and enslave the earth's population in order to extract its resources which they could trade with other planets in an alliance that they were planning with the Dheginians. In order to defend your planet, we launched a satellite equipped with a weapon and controlled by artificial intelligence. When the Wizard and Amy arrived in their disc shaped interplanetary ship, the satellite automatically shot them down over the middle east region of your planet. Unfortunately, most of the equipment and formulas survived and so did Amy and the Wizard. Fortunately, the incident was able to destroy their communication equipment so they couldn't communicate with the Dheginians for help. They walked away from a ship that couldn't be repaired and arrived in Azorka." The Yetz speaker finished.

"The Wizard has been the enemy of Azorka ever since our war ten thousand years ago. That is when we learned of his betrayal against us. Do you believe, as we do, that a planets population should evolve by choice and not by force?" Sally asked. She noticed that her voice no longer echoed.

"We share that belief with Azorka. We are meeting now under what you might consider to be dream like circumstances. But it is actually technology from our satellite that has made this possible. To introduce this technology to you could be dangerous if it was misused. The Egyptian rulers called this out of body experience the travels of their Ka. It is a technology induced out of body experience that you are having in order for us to communicate and plan against the enemy." The Yetz speaker explained.

"The Dheginian Star System is forty-six light years away from earth and the Yetz Star System is twenty-five light years from earth. Dheginians can travel faster than the speed of light, which many had thought would be impossible. However, when it comes to the needs of their military it seems anything is possible for them to obtain. They are a formidable adversary and will be difficult to defeat. It is hoped that you three ladies will be able to defeat them, with our help."

"This meeting between us is necessary now because we have a two hour window of opportunity in which to operate tomorrow morning. We will need to have Lana as a member of our team that is if she will agree to help us. If so we will have three super guardians with super abilities to protect Earth.

"Events unfolding in Azorka are sent back to Yetz-an where our scientists can process the data thanks to our satellite surveillance. The Wizard's technology has led our scientists to believe that the crystal and metal helmet that Heather wore during his experiment and the machine that received the images from her mind and displayed them on a screen, is responsible for causing the blockages in Heather's mind to dissolve. Our scientists have a theory that the blockages are a genetic design. Possibly they will naturally disappear with the evolution of man and that could take thousands of years. They do not believe there will be a negative effect from your enhancement, Heather." The Yetz speaker finished. "Sally will you agree to the experiment?" The Yetz speaker asked.

"Absolutely! I would want to help Heather defend Azorka!" Sally answered excitedly.

"You mentioned Lana. Why isn't she here now?" Heather asked. Her voice no longer echoed and like Sally, she was relieved the effect was gone.

"I'm sure you can see the physical similarities of the Yetz humanoid and earth's humans. Except for our gray skin and dark eyes we are similar. We consider ourselves to be your cousins. The Aryans are hard to tell apart from earth's humans with the exception of those rare few that are born with the eyes that Lana has. The Aryans home world was on a collision path with another planet when they were rescued and brought to earth two hundred thousand years ago thanks to the efforts of a race of giants who rescued them. Your population was not aware of this closely guarded secret that is kept to prevent future prejudice from the outside world. I will depend on both of you to keep this secret and not discuss with Lana because even she doesn't know. Agreed?" The Yetz speaker asked.

"Agreed!" Heather and Sally shouted in unison.

"I understand that Mitch informed you both that Amy is a Yetz. She has dark eyes that are hidden behind those brown contact lenses and youthful gray skin that she covers over in make-up for a human flesh tone." The Yetz speaker said.

"Dad mentioned it after the rescue. We were both a little surprised and had thought she was just the Wizard's housekeeper." Sally answered.

"She is very intelligent and crafty so beware of her in the future. Right now she is tutoring the lady with red hair that was the rider for the Dheginian creature that chased you in Africa." The Yetz speaker said.

"That was a Dheginian creature and not one of the Wizard's creations?" Heather asked.

"That is correct and tomorrow morning the Wizard will ride this Dheginian creature out to sea in order to retrieve the crystal skull his men are bringing back to him. The creature is extremely intelligent and as you have seen can access those invisible worm holes around your planet to travel swiftly. The creature calls it teleporting. This is a time sensitive two hour operation because of this fact. Amy will be with the red haired lady twenty minutes away, feeding and spending time with the creature that the Wizard has created, and then they will return to the castle." The Yetz speaker explained.

"The Wizard has recovered another crystal skull. Will we be in any danger from the power of this skull?" Sally asked.

"We have to rely on our surveillance for that answer. We don't know enough about the crystal skulls." The Yetz speaker answered.

"For now, I need to bring Lana aboard. I have revealed the secret of the Aryans so that you will watch her carefully because we don't know how the Wizard's machine will react on an Aryan. Our scientists claim that the Aryan's are human. Our scientist say, the dying red-dwarf star in their star system did not provide enough energy or light. It is a theory that the Aryans therefore required rectangular pupils to make up for this. Most of their new generation have natural human pupils. Evolution and the thousands of years adapting to your much brighter sun, may be responsible for this." The Yetz speaker explained.

Heather was looking closer at him and noticed his youthful healthy looking gray hair ran into a "widow's peak" in the middle of his forehead. Heather loved reading about the English people and their strange ways. The English folk lore for the formation of a "V" from the hairline in the middle of the forehead indicated long life. Heather got her thoughts back on track and focused her attention on the discussion.

"Astral travel is not a natural ability for humans, the Yetz or Dheginians. That is why various technologies have to be used to produce this state for other intelligent life forms in the universe. I am going to call on the help of the satellite once again which will result with Lana appearing beside you in the same special suit you're wearing now. Lana is in the bedroom down the hall in your castle sleeping just as comfortably as the both of you are. It will be her astral body that stands beside you in the next sixty seconds" The Yetz speaker finished.

He paused to see if there was a question coming. Fortunately, the ladies were a quick study and somewhat understood his over simplified explanations.

"My name would be difficult for anyone on Earth to pronounce, so I will go by the name of "Lee" for you ladies. The Yetz speaker said.

"I will quickly explain to you the advantages of the combat suits you'll wear in the future. Your transition will be responsible for your immortality, a fact I hinted about last time I met with Heather at Indie's favorite outdoor area for meditation during Heather's dream. Now it is three-hundred years into the future that we will experience our first battle. You will appreciate these advantages." Lee said.

The dreamscape was silent for the next thirty seconds, then Lana appeared beside Heather and Sally, in the same green suit and wide-eyed with surprise. Heather had never heard Lana scream before but she might have if Sally hadn't gently touched her arm to let her know everything was alright. Lana met Lee and he caught her up with what he had told Heather and Sally. Then Lee went on to show them the Dheginian Star System and explained about the life on those circumbinary planets and the challenges they would have in the future war.

Lee did not explain anything about the Zapatsaurs even though he remembered their visit from eleven-thousand years ago and the months that they were guests on Yetz-an. This would be something the Zapatsaurs had a responsibility to disclose and they would be waiting for the right time to reveal this to the Azorkans.

Lee told them that Egyptian rulers from thousands of years ago were aliens who used astral travel to learn the military secrets of their enemies which helped them to govern and conquer. They wore a small statue of themselves around their neck while they were governing. The alien rulers, masquerading as humans, had arrived from a star system four light years away from Earth, and had a natural ability for astral travel. This was a huge advantage against the enemy and strictly forbidden interference with the natural development of Earth's population.

To hide this crime, the alien ruler told their subjects that the "Ka" would survive the death of the body and protect the body from tomb invaders. Various curses were written on the walls of the tomb in order to frighten away grave robbers and the curious. It was hoped that this deception would prevent future grave robbers and explorers from discovering that the ruler was an alien from another star system. It was forbidden, by galactic treaty, to interfere with the natural development of Earth's people.

Lee told the three ladies of his plan to use the Wizard's machine in the morning. Lana and Sally would become immortal from one-hour exposure inside the Wizard's helmet with the setting on" Yetz" which would use up most of the two hours Lee figured for their window of opportunity. When they were finished their covert mission, the two ladies would go through the gradual changes that Heather went through over the course of a couple weeks. They wouldn't dream like Heather, but all three ladies could meet with Lee as they did this evening, if there was an emergency, by leaving a note in Heather's room on the dresser top.

Lee stressed that he had only parted with a very small amount of information and that their complete education on all matters concerning the known universe would be quite extensive.

"What would determine an emergency meeting?" Lana asked. Lana was excited as Sally was about becoming immortal and she wanted to be prepared for the future.

"The unexpected hostility. There's an alien craft on its way to earth now. This happens frequently and we monitor this. Always be on your guard." Lee answered Mitch and Tamara went to bed that night with restless thoughts. They had been worried about Heather's evolving condition and the unknown consequences. Now she had entered the front lines of danger. Her new abilities were pole-vaulting her into Azorka's most powerful answer to future threats the Empire presented. Tamara and Mitch had a feeling that some trouble was about to start within the next twenty-four hours, but decided to dismiss the thought as paranoid thinking. Unfortunately, they were wrong.

Chapter Eight

It was a beautiful day. The ocean sparkled like a thousand blue sapphire jewels. The sky was a rich blue color with some wandering puffy white clouds that occasionally blocked out the sun. Sam estimated that they had sailed a good distance yesterday. He had turned on the secret motor in the stern after the wind died down while Leif slept through the night in the Captain's cabin. This reduced the time it would take to return to the Empire's island. The wind had died down a little over night but it was still strong enough to fill the sails of the Empire's ship this morning. The ship gently bobbed up and down with the waves of the ocean and the briny air felt warm. Sam was about to sit down and relax on the main deck and enjoy the moment when he heard the Captain's cabin door slam shut above him.

"Leif! Are you awake enough to join me on this beautiful day for a little conversation?" Sam yelled out. The wind and waves were just loud enough to make yelling necessary.

"Why not come up here Sam! My leg is healing well but it takes a little longer in the morning before it's strong enough to walk around on!" Leif yelled.

Sam looked up at Anthony, his rigger, on the main mast and saw that he was wearing his safety strap while working to unfurl the sail. Falling from a slippery spar was a common hazard the rigger had to protect himself from. Anthony was over six feet tall with a good reach but he was slim. His black hair and dark skin reminded Sam of a Greek sailor he had known a few years ago.

"I'll be right up Leif!" Sam barked.

Sam was dressed in dark brown pants that tucked into a squeaky pair of brown leather boots. Leif heard every footfall as he walked to the end of the main deck and climbed the landing steps to the upper deck. Sam was clean shaven and dressed in a white shirt which was tucked into a large black belt that almost hid his pot belly. His short brown-gray hair ran a circle around a perfectly round head and left Sam with a bald crown which he was running his hand over now.

"It's windy up here!" Sam complained.

He looked over at Leif who had found a comfortable seat on the starboard side of the ship. He sat there in a stained orange shirt and black pants that went well with the black stubble of an unshaven face.

"Well I guess it is. That is also a welcome gift for the travel-weary. We'll get home much sooner!" Leif barked.

Leif had been thinking about drinking the better part of a bottle of the Wizard's best rum when he got back to the island. The only thing that had been soothing Leif's boredom on the journey home was dreaming about his reward and the vacation he would take.

Sam was going to unload his prepared speech, which he had fumbled with for the last forty-eight hours and offer Leif citizenship in the Empire. He walked confidently across the upper deck and sat beside Leif on the bench. He had been struggling for the last two days on how to best explain or disclose the unbelievable facts which were associated with the Empire.

"Leif, the Wizard wanted me to offer you citizenship in the Empire and a roof over your head you can call your own. What do you think of the Wizard's offer?" Sam asked.

Leif's early morning red eyes looked over at Sam and slowly a smile formed on his long face.

"I accept!" Leif shouted with joy. He knew he had to stay hidden from European society and liked everything the Empire's island provided.

"That's great to hear Leif. Now there are some facts about our Empire that you need to understand. First of all the Empire is an advanced civilization and for that reason we have been hiding some of our technology from you while we accessed your compatibility with our society. The Wizard believes that you will embrace our philosophy and mission. That is the need to control the outside world before it causes tragedy to occur in the future. You've been fighting against an unfair and unjust society that will boldly take life and force slavery. Your skill as a thief was the only weapon you could use against this evil. It has paid off for you and the Empire." Sam said.

Leif was surprised to hear advanced technology was being hidden from him.

"Tell me about this advanced technology that you have hidden from me." He said. A short silence worked into a minute while Sam thought of a good example. All that could be heard was the creaking of the ship and the waves of the ocean. Then Sam decided to remove his laser pistol from an inside pocket cut into the black belt. Leif looked confused as Sam showed him an "L" shaped flesh colored object small enough to fit into the palm of his hand.

"Is that the advanced technology you refer to Sam?" Leif asked.

"This is a laser pistol. You may not have noticed, but some of the natives that were chasing us back in the jungle were put to sleep when my men shot them with this while it was on the minimum setting." Sam said.

Sam instructed Leif on how to change the setting from minimum to maximum and where the trigger was. Sam handed the small pistol to Leif. Leif took the pistol, which just about disappeared in the palm of his hand then stood up from the bench and walked over to the portside rail. He raised the small laser pistol pointed it into the ocean and pulled the trigger. Leif jumped backwards when he felt the power of the laser beam in his hand. A purple colored laser beam hit the the ocean leaving a small trail of steam on the surface. Leif turned around and smiled at Sam watching from the bench.

"I was running ahead of you with Gerta slung over my shoulder so I missed the magic show." Leif said sarcastically.

"Anthony was hiding up in a tree ready to take out the natives from a distance while Helmut and Mkenzie had taken positions beside the path. When the natives began their chase these three men shot them. The natives would be unconscious for two hours or more while we escaped." Sam explained.

"With this kind of fire power for protection, I will be eager for our next assignment." Leif said. He was still smiling just thinking how much easier life had become.

Sam watched Leif hobble back to the bench. Before he reached the bench he suddenly stopped and massaged his injured calf muscle on his right leg. Leif hopped the rest of the way to the bench using his good leg. He plopped down beside Sam, exhaled his nauseous early morning breath, and returned his laser pistol.

"Leg still bothering you? I'll have Mkenzie look at it tonight to be sure it's not infected." Sam offered.

"Sure that would be a wise precaution. It's painful every morning. Once I start moving around the leg begins to feel a little better. I'll be happy to see our red- haired and freckled physician just to make sure and to thank him again for his good doctoring." Leif replied.

"The laser pistol you just fired is powered by crystal. Inside the handle are two specially cut crystals; one you never remove located above the handle in the barrel and one you remove and set in the sunlight for recharging." Sam instructed.

Sam removed the tubular cut crystal from the bottom of the handle and set it in the sunlight while Leif watched.

"The Empire and the enemy both have laser technology. Azorka's laser technology is more advanced than ours because of more advanced cutting tools but we are in the process of redesigning our equipment and will eventually produce a more powerful weapon." Sam said.

"I do need you to understand that the Wizard and Amy are the Empire's rulers and that Maria is supreme military commander. The Wizard will eventually Introduce you to Maria. The Wizard and Amy brought to us advanced technology from a distant world in another star system thousands of years ago. They are immortal beings and have been our guardians for thousands of years. The general population is slowly receiving disclosure about this. You will become the Empire's expert on the outside world so you need to know everything we can share with you. If the Wizard departs on a long mission Amy becomes the ruling guardian. Maria will instruct you and me on military requirements and plans should that become necessary when the Wizard is absent." Sam continued.

Leif was looking directly at Sam, wide eyed with the expression of disbelief written across his face.

"I know this is a lot for you to digest all at once, Leif. The Wizard and Amy come from an advanced world and they are using this technology to help the planet and someday take over the world before it destroys itself from war. They are also scientists capable of creating creatures to perform necessary tasks like protecting the island from intruders at night while the population sleeps." Sam said.

"You're asking me to believe that the Wizard has created life?" Leif asked.

"I knew this speech of mine wasn't going to be easy." Sam heaved a deep sigh of frustration.

"Let me give you my best explanation. You've always wondered who made the maps of the world which we have shown you. Their accuracy is impeccable as you have experienced yourself in the short time that you have been with us. This was the work of the Sumerians of Mesopotamia, an advanced race from the stars who had access to flying machines. They used a complicated form of mathematics called spherical trigonometry and other elaborate mathematical calculations. The Wizard tells us it was a massive global scale project performed thousands of years ago before he arrived. It shows a south pole with no ice and the islands of our Empire that ran south close to Hispaniola. We used these maps to escape the devastation of the great flood and found a tropical paradise three miles below the land mass of the south pole where we could survive for five months while the waters receded. There were massive photosynthesizing plants which maintained the oxygen levels while we were underground and an abundance of fish from the fresh water lake where we made camp." Sam explained.

Leif was still listening but the features had relaxed on his face as he came to accept the incredible.

"The Wizard had retained one very powerful telescope after the war with Azorka. A war which had caused us to lose a great chunk of our technology. He had been keeping an eye on the asteroid activity and meteor showers outside the planet which had started to come close enough to hitting the planet. It was time to seek shelter and we later found out that the asteroid which had hit earth struck an isthmus which existed between the Apennine Mountains of Europe and the Atlas Mountains of Africa. A huge chunk of land collapsed and sank to the ocean. We lost our islands to the south of us and all that was left of our Empire is what you see today. We remapped those changes." Sam finished.

Leif had a strong interest in science and read books on the subject whenever he could get his hands on them. He learned to speak French, German and Spanish from reading books and was a self-taught sort of an individual. Sam's story had made sense to him. But he was still struggling with the Wizard's creation of life. "Your knowledge is impressive Sam and I'd like to know more about the ancient world. You said the Wizard created creatures, but all the time I've been on the island I haven't seen any roaming about. I would have seen one by now as I some time take in an evening stroll. I was also returning from shipbuilding at night." He said.

"The Wizard's creatures were penned up in various locations around the island then released at night to guard the island against covert intrusions by Azorka. Azorka is always spying on the Empire wanting to know of the latest technological achievements by the Empire. For some reason the Wizard's creatures could not withstand sunlight so they performed there watch at night when most of the island population was asleep. It's true that some of the population prefer to avoid direct sunlight. They spend a majority of their time underground, so it is difficult for their eyes to make the adjustment. The Wizard made special glasses for those members of our population who need to come above ground for their duties, but this could not be done for his creatures as they lacked the necessary intelligence to accept this modification. The Wizard was also careful about releasing those creatures in pens that were close to you. He had to wait until you were occupied before releasing them. Sam answered.

He waited while Leif thought this over. Leif had lost his expression of bewilderment and didn't have a question so he continued.

"Gerta is due to visit us within the next thirty-six hours. I want to apologize for my earlier lies concerning this lady. While you were getting your leg doctored that night, I happened to look over at Gerta and noticed that she had withdrawn a half-moon shaped object from a pocket in her green dress. She put it up to her lips and blew into it as though it were a flute. I assumed that this was more like a whistle than a flute when I saw what must have been a thirty foot long black creature with leathery black wings above us in those dark blue clouds. It had two long tusks that grew above its upper jaw with powerful arms and legs and it came swooping down on the attacking pirates. We were about to fire upon the pirates with our laser pistols leaving them unconscious in their boats, but the creature decided to smash those boats. The pirates were thrown overboard and had to swim to shore. A few obstinate pirates fired upon the creature but this had no effect. The creature picked them up screaming and dropped them on shore uninjured then returned to our ship where it hovered by the rail waiting for Gerta. She said her goodbye to us promising to see us again in about five days' time then climbed onto the back of her creature and disappeared into the night." Sam finished.

Leif digested the story and the look of disbelief had returned to his expression. He couldn't believe this five foot two helpless girl he had rescued from the voodoo worshippers had saved the day then flown away on the back of a dragon like creature. It somehow seemed more incredible then Sam's story concerning the Wizard's creatures.

"You're telling me this story so I won't be surprised when they show up." Leif offered.

Without answering Leif's question Sam stood up and walked down towards the stairs to the main deck. He saw his blonde haired quartermaster, Helmut on the main deck helping Chuck move a water barrel filled with fish into place for Gerta's creature.

"Helmut! When you've got a spare moment could you come up here for a couple of minutes?" Sam called down.

"Be right there Sam!" Helmut answered. He finished moving the barrel into place and brushed off some dirt on his light blue pants.

"Thanks for the help Helmut." Chuck said. He had picked up some dirt from the barrel and he brushed off his black pants and scratched his dark beard.

"It was my pleasure to help you Chuck." Helmut answered.

Helmut took the steps two at a time and reached the upper deck where Sam and Leif were seated on the bench. Sam got up and invited Helmut to sit down in his place.

"You can welcome Leif as our fellow citizen and new expert on the affairs of the outside world. Would you tell our good friend Leif about Gerta's creature? I've been explaining to Leif about our laser pistols, the Empire as an advanced civilization and now I've come to the difficult part. If Leif listens to the story from both of us he'll be more inclined to believe." Sam said.

"It will be my pleasure Sam: Congratulations on your appointment and citizenship Leif!" Helmut said.

Helmut turned towards Leif and shook his hand. Leif was noticing how sharp Helmut looked in a clean yellow shirt which was neatly tucked into his wide black belt.

"We have to keep our advanced technology secret from the world, otherwise we would be overwhelmed with invaders trying to acquire our secrets for war or personal gain. Azorka and the Empire have agreements in place to keep this secrecy and our location from the outside world. We have an advanced motor in the rear of this ship which can move this vessel when the wind dies down. We have a hazel colored ship so that the military ships for the governments of the world will recognize us as a harmless merchant ship. However, nothing could be further from the truth as this one ship could sink a fleet of attacking pirate ships from a great distance and away from the range of their cannons." Helmut said.

"I'm impressed with the advanced motor you've got if it will help us get home quicker." Leif said.

"It will at that. In fact, we were using it all last night. I'll check our position for you later." Helmut said.

"But let me continue to explain those things which will seem incredible to you. I'm sure you have heard legends of dragons in the orient and in the new world there are legends of an extremely large bird that the indigenous people call the thunderbird. You have heard stories of giant squid attacking ships by wrapping their tentacles around the deck and sinking the ship. The stories can be exaggerated but sometimes the stories are true. The Empire has studied some of these unusual creatures in the past. Tomorrow you will have a chance to meet Gerta's friend and you will think it resembles a dragon. The truth is that we don't know very much about the creature or Gerta. We are in the dark about their relationship. But we accept the reality of the creature's existence. We have noticed that the creature is intelligent and respectful of life. It did not kill the attacking pirates nor did it hurt us but waited patiently for Gerta to climb onto its back that night. The creature somehow knows we are fighting for those values it shares with us. It must have perceived the pirate's willingness to take life." Helmut explained.

Leif was letting everything Helmut was telling him sink in and adopting a wait and see approach to Gerta's creature. Leif respected Helmut as he did all the men of both crews.

"Well I look forward to meeting Gerta again." Leif said.

Helmut looked relieved to hear that. At least Leif has heard the story from two of his companions on this mission. Helmut looked up at Sam, waiting to see if there was something he wanted to add to the story.

"Thanks Helmut. I think that will be enough information for Leif to absorb for now." Sam said.

Helmut got up from the bench and walked toward the stairs descending to the main deck where Anthony was standing now looking up at the sail he had just unfurled.

Sam sat back down beside Leif who was still absorbing the details of both stories.

"Would you like some breakfast Leif? I'll go down to the kitchen below and cook up some bacon and eggs for us. Do you feel like a little solid food to wash down all this information?" Sam asked.

"That would be greatly appreciated right now Sam. It would help chase away those butterflies I seem to have in my stomach right now." Leif answered.

Sam got up, his boots squeaking on the way to the stairs, and went below to the main deck kitchen to cook their breakfast. He remembered the eight loaves of bread the crew had bought before they left Hispaniola and his mouth was beginning to water at the thought of how good breakfast was going to taste.

Leif had stretched his legs out on the empty seat beside him and was relaxing, enjoying the warmth of the sun. He was so comfortable that he would have drifted off to sleep if it hadn't been for an unusual crackling sound above him which caused him to open his eyes.

Leif bolted upright, the pain in his injured leg momentarily leaving his conscious thought. He was sitting up straight on the bench and focusing on a thirty foot flying horror that had just appeared out of nowhere, fifty feet above him. Those long black leathery wings were flapping hard enough to maintain its position with the ship. Leif saw the creature's tusks and thought about what he'd been told about Gerta's creature. He didn't see Gerta, but the happy expression of the Wizard greeted him when he poked his head out to look down at the ship below. "Hello Leif! I'm up here!" The Wizard called down.

The Wizard saw the look of amazement and shock on Leif's face and hoped that Sam had revealed those amazing details that would be so difficult for an outsider to accept.

Sam's and Helmut's stories had helped relieve some of the horror Leif felt staring up at this black scaled monstrosity, its sharp tusks shining in the sunlight. It turned its head and looked down at Leif with those eerie looking dark orange eyes. The Wizard was comfortably seated on its back and had the happy expression of a child who had just got off a ride at the fair. Leif found his jubilant countenance reassuring.

"Your mission was a success! You have my crystal skull!" The Wizard shouted down. He laughed out loud at Leif who looked surprised to hear that the Wizard had learned of their mission.

"Welcome to the Empire Leif! You are all going to enjoy the next two months of holiday and be paid very generously when you return to the island. I'm extremely happy with your successful mission." The Wizard shouted down.

"Thank you Wizard!" Leif shouted back. Leif's smile of joy looked back up at the Wizard as he remembered the reward.

"Where is Sam?" The Wizard asked.

At that moment Sam walked out from the main deck kitchen and looked up at the Wizard on Gerta's creature. He had put on a cooking apron while preparing their breakfast and the Wizard thought his appearance would have been greeted by howls of laughter by any ship full of pirates.

Sam was as surprised to see the Wizard on the back of Gerta's creature as Leif was. He assumed that the Wizard had already met Gerta and wondered where she was now.

"Welcome Wizard we are happy to see you. Is Gerta with you?" Sam asked.

"She is safe and back on the island with Amy." The Wizard answered.

"Sam I'm going to need you to pull back the lines for the main sail and give us an area of twenty-seven feet long and fifteen feet wide, clear of all objects and obstructions." The Wizard shouted down.

The creature had told the Wizard about a natural restraint on its short distance teleporting that would automatically cancel the appearance of the circle of light if an object was on the path between departure point A and arrival point B. The Wizard knew that teleporting would be the easiest way to arrive on the main deck of the ship.

Sam, Helmut, Anthony and Chuck began removing barrels, ropes, and other objects that were within the specified space the Wizard said should be free of obstruction. After five minutes, twenty-seven feet of the thirty-two-foot-wide deck was clear for the creature's length and a comfortable width of fifteen feet had been cleared from the upper deck ladder outwards. Then the men took up their positions on both sides of the thick spar for the main sail and pulled back the main sail lines until they were behind the fifteen-foot width the Wizard had requested.

The Wizard was satisfied with the cleared space on deck. The creature only required one second to teleport onto the ship. It flew out from its place beside the ship to change its flight position. The creature returned facing the ship twenty feet ahead of the clearing made by the men. By the time the creature's teleport commenced, the lead of twenty feet calculated by the creature from the forward speed of the ship lined up perfectly for the one second teleport.

The Wizard had experienced the sensations from the long distance teleporting but this was something different. Suddenly the daylight, the ship, crew and everything around him disappeared. All that he could see in the darkness was the creature and himself and a small circle of light ahead of them. He couldn't move and noticed that the creature was also motionless. Although this experience only took one second of time, the Wizard felt that thirty seconds had gone by after the circle of light, which grew in circumference, had passed over and under the creature and himself. Daylight, the ship and crew suddenly appeared and the Wizard, seated on the back of the creature, was on the main deck of the ship. They were occupying the cleared space on the deck which was beside the kitchen Sam had been cooking in ten minutes earlier. The creature was beginning to salivate from the odor of Sam's breakfast.

Helmut, Anthony, Chuck and even Sam had the look of shock written all over their faces. Leif, who was standing by the stairs on the upper deck, was wondering how much more incredible is the reality in his world going to become.

"Now that's what I call a magic show!" Leif yelled. He had finally crossed the threshold of disbelief into the land of seeing is believing and therefore accepting.

Helmut and Chuck moved the barrel of fish closer to the creature and removed the lid. The creature dug in and pulled out a couple of fillets, enjoying a delicious brunch. Leif remained on the upper deck, sitting down on the top stair while the men below huddled closer to the creature to hear the Wizard tell about all the recent events and the stories for Gerta and the creature.

***

While a couple of hours' worth of storytelling began on the ship, Lana Heather and Sally were exiting one of those puffy white clouds the day had to offer in Lana's flying craft and entering a much larger cloud that followed. Heather was in the front seat with Lana and Sally was securely buckled into the seat behind Lana. Sally and Heather had decided to wear all gray robes and pants with their black boots. Lana was dressed in her all navy blue outfit adding a dark blue robe for warmth.

Lana had thought it would be best to gain the highest altitude above the view of the sentries and closer to the majority of clouds which would help conceal their approach to the island. Sally had suggested that the Wizard would take the precaution of posting sentries in case Azorka decided to launch a mission to recapture the Dragon Queen.

In addition to the new crystal powered motor that was designed to power the craft through space, the Aryan technicians had installed heat seeking equipment so that Lana would know her adversaries location ahead of time. She reached forward and flicked a switch on the dashboard activating the device. A round screen on the dashboard, directly in front of Heather, lit up with a green color. That morning Lana, Heather and Sally showed up for breakfast at the exact same time. This was a detail they worked out while they were still in their technologically induced astral state and it was confirmation of the dream they shared. Secrecy had been agreed upon. During breakfast Mitch and Tamara were told that they would be test running the flying craft with one additional passenger. The ladies would leave shortly after breakfast then return in the afternoon.

The indicator for a heat signal began to sound its finding with a low pitched beep every five seconds. The sentry appeared on the screen as a black figure in a sitting position. The sentry was on the first cliff of the island's northern approach, concealed by the surrounding trees, and bushes. He was scanning the area ahead and out to sea in order to provide the Empire with a warning for any indication of a covert military operation by the enemy.

"If that was the creature up ahead more than half the screen would be filled in. This must be the sentry. If you look below the circle, a small rectangle appears with a read out of how far away the sentry is from our craft. Could you tell me the distance Heather?" Lana asked.

"Five hundred yards ahead of us." Heather answered.

"We are flying a couple thousand feet above the sentry but I don't want to take any chances. I need to be sure we have another five hundred yards of cloud to ride with." Lana called out.

Lana looked above and ahead through the glass cover. It was a good thing the technicians gave her craft the flat silver paint touch up. Lana was feeling more confident about moving the craft around without being spotted.

"I'm going to take us up and see if there's a cloud above that will help conceal our approach. I want to bring the craft down behind the Wizard's castle out of the eye shot of that sentry." Lana explained.

Heather and Sally sat silently trusting Lana's judgement. They had worked out a plan on the way over in the craft while Lana listened. Heather remembered a chair in the Wizard's office that would be perfect for jamming the office door. She would lock the office door as soon as they gained entry but that wouldn't do if the person on the other side had a key. She would use this extra measure to be certain they wouldn't be caught. A castle guard wanting to enter the Wizard's office would make enough noise that it would serve as a warning. Heather could use her ability to hold the door or even the guard while the other two ladies escaped into the flying craft. Heather thought it was best to prepare for the worst case scenario.

Lana had been piloting the craft slowly at twenty miles per hour on her approach to the island with the small handle bar and throttle. The handle bar gripped in her right hand would adjust the angle of the crafts ascent or descent and of course the throttle in her left hand would increase and decrease the speed at which the craft travelled. The half-moon shaped gauge illuminated in green on the right hand side of the dashboard gave her the angle her craft was travelling on. Lana pulled back on the small six inch handle which fit neatly into her hand and the craft's nose rose up on a sixty-degree angle. Sally felt her safety belt hugging her shoulders and waist firmly in the rear green seat. She looked down through the craft's glass at a clearing in the clouds. Below the northern section of the Empire's island almost looked barren with brown and green grass growing around several clusters of rocks and boulders. Before Sally could see more of the landscape heavier cloud surrounded the craft blocking her view. They had reached the top of the cloud and the craft's glass poked through till they could see blue sky above. Lana saw a large gray cloud ahead that would be sufficient to cover the five hundred yards of distance she required to stay hidden from the sentry. She pushed the handle bar forward so that the craft angled down by thirty degrees as it entered the cloud then she pulled back on the handle till the craft was level. In another minute Heather could see by the round heat seeking gauge that they had flown past the sentry with only two hundred more yards to cover before they were in the clear.

In the back seat Sally was thinking about the plan she had discussed with Heather on the way over. They would pull up to the Wizard's office window which faced north west and was situated on the west side of the castle, and hover locked in place. This window for the Wizard's office was on the top right corner of the building beside another window of identical size and construction on the second floor. The Wizard's office window faced out towards that part of the ocean that sailors in the past had found hazardous to navigate. The rocky part of Azorka which had sunk to the ocean during the war, still protruded upwards just below the ocean in various places threatening to gouge the bottom of passing ships.

Heather will use her new ability to unlock the left half of the office window which is large enough for her to crawl through. Lana will follow, take a seat inside the office and put the helmet on while she waits for

Heather's next instruction. I will wait outside in the flying craft, which is locked in place on hover, and watch for unexpected observers who might sound an alarm. When Lana is finished her one- hour session then Lana will return to the craft and I will crawl through the office window to begin my one-hour session. When my session is complete we leave without leaving a trace of our intrusion. We don't want the Wizard to realize that his invention is capable of producing immortals.

Sally's train of thought was broken by Lana's announcement.

"We're here. Lana called out. "I'm going to lower the craft into that cloud ahead which will give us another one-hundred feet of cover. Then I'll drop slowly, halfway along the east side cliff. The view for the sentry will be blocked thanks to the extension of the west side cliff. We have to go the long way around which means darting across the front of the castle where we are fortunate to have cover from the trees growing there. When we've crossed the front, we will have the cover of the west side cliff which will conceal our approach until we are facing the Wizard's office on the second floor of the top west corner of the castle. We will make a quick scan of the backyard to be sure were not being watched then fly across and around the top west corner to the Wizard's window." Lana explained."

Heather looked at Lana's blue eyes with those rectangular pupils. Her eyes were piercing and wide with excitement. Heather could feel Lana's self-confidence bubbling over. Lana also had additional assurance. Her best friend sitting beside her could manipulate objects with her mind which would keep them from harm. "That sounds like an excellent plan." Sally said. "I'm glad we set out early. Lee told us where the sun's position would be on my sundial. Heather's hour glass shows that we left early and according to Dad's European clock we left thirty minutes early. The sun's position for leaving on time would be ten on his large, thirty- three-year-old clock." Sally finished.

"I agree with Sally on both points." Heather said.

They reached the lower cloud and Lana dropped the flying craft into it and continued descending until they exited the cloud only ten feet from the top of the east cliff's edge. Lana thanked her lucky stars for the dark cloud temporarily blocking out the sun while the craft was briefly in view. Lana dropped the craft down slowly behind the cliff and continued the descent until she was only five feet off the ground facing the east side of the castle. Lana continued around the cliffs at a slow speed until they were facing the Wizard's office on the second floor. The backyard was empty and silent. She moved the craft across the backyard over Amy's vegetable garden, past bushes and trees. Lana flew the craft up to the Wizard's office and around the corner to the window that faced north west. She stopped the craft four inches from the window and locked the craft in position so that it would not move out of place while hovering. Lana opened the flying craft's front hatch and waited for Heather. The front hatch opened on the passenger side and was angled slightly towards the left so it was almost positioned perfectly.

Heather was right beside the left side window with a dark brown wooden sash bar separating the four panes of glass. The sill and the head jamb with both side jambs were also a dark brown wood. She looked inside at the half-moon window latch. It was crafted with a thumb sized handle which was used to release the lock position. A white border that only Heather could see appeared around the device and the thumb sized handle moved downwards until it was resting on the inside ledge and the half-moon piece of metal attached to it rose up out of its groove. Heather reached out and pulled open the window which was three feet wide and four feet long. She decided that there was enough space to crawl through so Heather left the right side window closed and pulled open the golden colored floor length drapes to make her entrance. Heather swung her left leg out of the flying craft and thrust it through the open window touching down on the red carpet of the office floor. She carefully and quietly maneuvered the rest of her body through the window.

The Wizard's office smelled musty and looked neglected. Heather ran her finger over the edge of the Wizard's dark brown desk and left a small track clear of the dust which fell to the carpet below. The light pouring in from the open window brought enough light to the dingy office for her to carry out the preparations for Lana's session. Heather walked to the end of the office and picked up the red, gold and green

European needle point chair which rested against the back wall. She moved it to the office door which she checked to be sure it was locked and placed it under the door knob. The room was filled with shelves of books and scrawls, mounted on dark mahogany paneled walls. A European styled couch, richly upholstered in green with gold gilded arms and legs was arranged in the room across from the Wizard's desk. The comfortable loveseat that Heather had used during her experiments with the Wizard was still facing the Wizard's desk.

The ten-inch-tall by twelve-inch wide metal framed screen which provided the imagery for the experiment, rested on the end of the desk. The helmet was not visible anywhere in the office so Heather walked around the desk and began opening its drawers hoping to find it. She breathed a sigh of relief when she found the metal and crystal helmet inside a lower drawer. Heather plucked it out by the leather straps and held it up for a quick examination. The Wizard said that a photonic crystal transferred the information into the screen where it was assimilated and rearranged into images. The crystal was so similar in color to the metal used on the helmet that it was invisible to the eye. She would watch to see if it would light up during the experiment.

Heather placed the helmet on the loveseat and walked back over to the open window. She whispered to Lana to come in the office. Lana double-checked the controls and gauges on the flying craft, making sure that it was locked in its hovering position then slid across the green front seat until she was close enough to crawl through the window. Lana had longer arms and legs than Sally and Heather but she managed to get through the window gracefully and quietly. Heather waved her over to the loveseat in front of the desk. Lana sat down examining the eloquently upholstered loveseat with its sloping back and ornamental gold gilded channels, plant-scrolls and floral designs which ran around the top of the back.

"This is the helmet you wear." Heather whispered.

Lana looked up at the peculiar helmet with its polished metal and leather straps, while Heather checked to see that the setting was still on "Yetz".

"The Wizard didn't change the setting so we're ready to go." Heather whispered. Lana nodded her head then reached up to take the helmet from Heather. She placed it on her head and secured the straps under her chin. She was amazed how comfortable and weightless it felt.

"How is this going to transfer information? There's no cord or wire to the screen." Lana asked in a low whisper.

"There's a photonic crystal, at least that's what the Wizard calls it, that sends information from the front of the helmet to the screens receiver built in at the back of the screen. I watch the results assembled into images on the other side from the desks chair." Heather whispered her explanation.

Heather reached down into the pocket of her gray robe and pulled out a diamond shaped crystal, the size of her thumb, attached to a silver chain. She held the diamond shaped crystal up for Lana to see then gently swung it back and forth on its silver chain.

"Concentrate on this crystal and listen to my voice and do as I say." Heather whispered.

Lana whispered that she was ready.

"Now I want you to relax and count backwards quietly from one hundred." Heather whispered.

Lana began counting backwards.

"Ninety-nine, ninety-eight, ninety-seven," Lana counted out quietly.

She looked at the crystal that swung back and forth in front of her and continued to count down as Heather had instructed. It was around the count of fifty, forty- nine, forty-eight, that Heather began to notice her voice was transforming into a monotone. Lana was ready for her next instruction. Her one-hour session would begin.

"Now Lana you will be going back in time to a happy family gathering that you had enjoyed ten years ago during the summer. You won't speak any longer once you have arrived. You will sit quietly with your family in the park by the beach in your village for fifty-nine minutes. The sun will be out and it is a beautiful day. Your family is relaxing in the sun and playing games on the beach. They are laughing and joking but there is no need for you to speak. After fifty-nine minutes you will stand up and wave goodbye to your family without speaking. In another sixty seconds you will wake up in this office fully refreshed and ready to leave immediately returning to the flying craft." Heather instructed.

Heather was amazed at how quickly Lana was hypnotized. She remembered Lee telling them, while they were in their astral state, that he suspected the Wizard's helmet induced a state of relaxation that would cause the most nervous participant to be susceptible to hypnosis. Usually, individuals in a state of high anxiety would be difficult to hypnotize. Those participants would find it difficult to focus. Considering the stress level of this mission Heather had to agree with Lee.

Lee had gone on to say that he would like to acquire the helmet in order to examine it and learn more about it. But for now it must be left in place after the ladies had finished the process so that the Wizard wouldn't discover its potential. Heather had thought to steal or destroy it after using it today. However, Lee warned this could reveal its importance considering the Wizard was aware of Heather's changes and abilities. It was possible the Wizard could produce another. If the Wizard found out his helmet could produce an army of enhanced human immortals, they could have a very difficult time stopping the Wizard from conquering the world. It would be best to let the Wizard continue thinking that Heather's condition was just a fluke result from her participation.

Heather pocketed her crystal and walked around the Wizard's desk. She sat down in his comfortable chair and looked at the screen where Lana appeared, ten years younger with a long golden pony tail holding her hair in place. Lana sat peacefully on a chair beside her mother on the beach while other family members were swimming in the ocean. Her father was calling out to her younger brother playing with the other children on the beach. Seven families had gathered on this beautiful sunny day in June and most of them had spread their blankets fifty yards from the beach on the freshly cut grass of the park.

Heather got up again and walked over to the open window. She looked over at Sally sitting patiently in the back seat and gave her a thumbs up hand signal to let her know all was going well. Heather gave the outside yard a quick scan to confirm they were alone then walked back to watch the screen. She noticed a quick flash of light coming from the front of the helmet and walked around to where Lana was sitting on the loveseat. The flash came again but this time she could see the three-inch square photonic crystal light up on the helmet. This flashing from the photonic crystal was at irregular intervals and Heather could only wonder why the helmet performed like this.

Heather returned to the Wizard's comfortable chair, put her feet up on his desk and continued watching the screen. Lana had closed her eyes and was relaxing in the sun. Her father was playing with the children on the beach. Heather checked her portable timer, a gift from Ted, which counted time in minutes. Lana had another forty-five minutes left in her session. How would she know when fifty- nine minutes had gone by and it was time to stand up and wave goodbye to her family? Azorkans and Aryans used seconds, minutes and hours to tell time just like the outside world. They also used the sun dial and the hourglass. Lee had told them not to worry about this and assured them that the hypnotized mind would wake up on time. Heather would check this using her timer which was on a rope she put around her neck.

Back on the Empire's ship the Wizard had just finished his first talk which was the creature's story. The men had listened in suspense and were amazed at the creature's abilities and fascinated with the Dheginian Star System.

The Wizard reached into the pocket of his gray jacket and pulled out a bottle of his best rum.

"Leif, I brought this along for you." He said, smiling as he held it up for Leif. "This rum is brewed in the New Colony. Better tasting than the Caribbean rum.". Leif got up from the top step of the upper deck and hobbled across the upper deck until he was facing the Wizard. He leaned over the upper deck rail and gave the Wizard his best smile to show his appreciation then practically snatched the bottle with lightning speed from the Wizard's hand. Leif stood straight up and held the bottle up to read the label. The label read, "Brewed and bottled in Boston, Massachusetts. Guaranteed to satisfy! It went on to boast about the quality of the beverage. Leif thought that the English were drinking French Brandy. Maybe the King had ordered rum for his naval commanders. Leif almost felt like he should tell the Wizard about the nasty rumors concerning this monarch and his close relationship with France. Too much controversy about some of this King's policies and the possibility of his pregnant wife delivering an heir to the throne were threatening the stability of his reign. Leif figured England's monarchy would experience a period of instability in another three months. He'd tell the Wizard about this later.

"Thank you! Thank you Wizard! You don't...well maybe you do know how much I appreciate this gift. Let me assure you, I will be enjoying carrying out my new responsibilities for the Empire!" Leif yelled over the wind.

"You're welcome my friend! It was a last minute decision I made with Sam before you both sailed for Haiti, to invite you to become a citizen of the Empire. If you were willing to risk your life for the Empire and successfully carried out your mission, we definitely wanted to reward you with a new home and beginning." The Wizard shouted up to Leif.

Leif stood motionless and was blushing with the praise. He wasn't used to so much positive reinforcement. Normally at the end of a mission he was running off with the loot and his adversaries were cursing him promising to bring him to justice for having the audacity to steal from there King or Queen.

"I hope you will forgive us for hiding so many of the Empire's secrets from you. The smaller creatures I had created for sentry duty were kept in the lower tunnels whenever you were around. My larger creatures were confined to their pens until I knew that you were far enough away that I could release them without you seeing them. You will also meet Maria our supreme military commander. She has ten thousand years of military experience and she is exceptionally brilliant. Amy has gray skin and dark eyes like me and she will no longer be hiding her appearance with make-up and contact lenses. Our technology is far in advance of the outside world and you will be given an in depth introduction to its advantages." The Wizard yelled up to Leif.

Leif had heard the incredible again, but then why not, he thought to himself. He'd eventually become comfortable with his new reality.

"I thank you again, kind Sir. I will only have one short drink of this rum then save the rest for tonight and all of our crew who made this mission successful." Leif shouted back.

Leif received a quick clap and cheer of appreciation from the men. He uncorked the bottle took a quick drink then recorked it and handed it down to Sam at the bottom of the upper deck steps for safe keeping.

The Wizard was happy to hear that Leif welcomed his new duties in the Empire. His consideration for the crew and appreciation of their efforts during the mission meant enough to him that he was willing to share his favorite alcoholic beverage just to toast their success. Leif was also leaping forward into a new reality with an open mind and welcomed the advantages the Empire's advanced technology had to offer.

For now, something else was on the Wizard's mind. A special reunion with a long lost item he greatly cherished.

"Sam, could you bring me the crystal skull you recovered." The Wizard asked. The wind had momentarily died down. The Wizard's voice was easier to hear and Sam wouldn't have to shout to be heard.

Sam got up from his comfortable kneeling position in front of the creature and walked over to the upper deck steps.

"I'll be right back Wizard." He said.

Sam hurried up the steps with Leif's bottle of English rum clutched in his left hand. Inside the Captain's quarters, Sam had remembered that he locked the skull in a cabinet as a precaution against mistakes that could be made, and a turbulent journey home which they had not experienced so far. Sam unlocked the cabinet where the crystal skull was kept, withdrew it and placed the bottle of rum inside. He left the cabinet unlocked and securely clutching the crystal skull by its jaw in his left hand he walked out of the room. Outside in the sunlight he could see the jade-green crystal skull clearly but not the red lines he had seen come to life running down the face of the skull when all that mysterious light was pouring out of its eyes. Sam still remembered that haunting vision he had in the jungle before snatching it from the over-weight voodoo King.

Sam hurried down to the main deck, walking past Leif comfortably seated to one side of the top step. He walked back over to the creature and the Wizard who were relaxing in the warmth of the sunlight and handed the crystal skull up to the Wizard comfortably seated on the creature's back.

The Wizard took the green crystal skull and cradled it lovingly in his arms like a newborn baby.

"Thank you Sam. It is beautiful and I am glad to have it back." The Wizard said. Leif thought he could see the Wizard's eyes becoming moist with emotion. "Thank you everyone! All of you!" The Wizard said as he addressed the crew. His voice seemed to trail off at a lower volume while he was momentarily lost in thought. Then he perked up and addressed the crew. The next story would be Gerta's story and of course it would explain to the men how the Wizard knew of the mission's success before he arrived on the ship.

"Gerta explained to me that she did not get a chance to meet all of the men; not even thank Leif for rescuing her because she decided to leave quickly. She knew that Sam and the crew should leave immediately before more pirates arrived to challenge them." The Wizard hollered over the wind.

The wind had returned with a vengeance to challenge even the sharpest hearing. "Today we celebrate two new citizens of the Empire; Leif and Gerta. For those of you who didn't get a chance to meet Gerta, you will recognize her as a lady with beautiful red hair standing about two inches taller than Amy who she is with now back on the island. Her story is a fascinating one which will introduce you to a very strong and resourceful lady independent from the outside world because of an accusation of witchcraft." The Wizard shouted.

All of the men rushed back from their duties and found comfortable seats to hear the story. The helm had been secured and the wheel was locked in place with the rudder in a north-south position. The ocean was providing waves of a reasonable size for the ship and the wind was manageable. For the next hour the men would hear Gerta's story and with the reasonable expectation that the ship would continue sailing ahead unhindered thanks to their improvised version of automatic pilot.

The Wizard looked around and saw that the men had settled in for his tale. Leif was back on the upper deck's step comfortably seated and Sam was crouching down on one knee to his right two feet from the creature's comfortable position on the deck. The wind picked up again but that didn't dampen the Wizard's determination to yell out the story if necessary.

"It was in Africa, of all places, that I first encountered Gerta riding on the back of this beautiful creature you see in front of you now. I of course travelled there as some Wizard's do and in a manner I will keep secret from you, as some Wizard's do." The Wizard yelled. He gave the men a quick smirk and continued.

"I was amazed when I saw the creature chasing off leopards in the Congo and Gerta helping with the rescue of an injured okapi and her young that had been the intended victims. This young lady was very brave and....

The Wizard launched into his story just five minutes before Lana would wake up from her session. After Lana had returned to the flying craft then Sally would begin her session and that only left one hour before the conclusion of a daring mission.

Tamara had remained at home and was walking throughout the castle tidying and dusting while lost in thought thinking about Heather's condition. She wondered how her daughter was handling the traumatic changes she was going through. Is it possible that Heather was hiding something from everyone so that her friends and family wouldn't worry about her?

Indie was outside relaxing on a comfortable chair on the castle patio. She was enjoying the warmth of the sun while thinking about recent events. Mitch and Zen had gone into village "B" to research the crystal skulls at the University Library in the Pyramid of Knowledge. Indie was grateful for the help Mitch offered with this mystery but now her greatest concern was Heather's dream. The colors in Heathers dream rang the alarm bells in her mind and sparked a suspicion that Heather was hiding something and another dream was yet to be revealed. Indie was a deep thinker and possessed and extremely high IQ. Maybe this is why she was not a rider. Perhaps the Zapatsaurs perceived complications with the mental connection of the rider and the Zapatsaur, because of her deep thinking.

The Zapatsaur population was almost in a state of shock having learned of a Yetz-an satellite in space surveilling the struggle below and for thousands of years without them knowing. The Zapatsaurs welcomed the help and appreciated Lee's diligence and tact. Lee would leave it up to the Zapatsaur population to reveal themselves to the Azorkans when they felt the time had arrived. He understood the special relationship they had enjoyed for the last five thousand years and their telepathy which monitored the needs of the rider almost constantly.

Lee must have understood that the Zapatsaurs would find out about the daring mission. The elder Zapatsaurs had sent out a communications team that would telepathically contact the intelligence team from fifty miles off the Empire's shore. The early morning mission would instruct the two Zapatsaurs hiding on the Empire's island gathering intelligence, to assist the ladies on their mission in anyway necessary without them becoming aware of the Zapatsaur presence. The communications team delivered the order from the elders and both Zapatsaurs set out an hour before Lana's flying craft arrived, hiding in the trees above the cliffs close to where the sentries were posted. The sentry closest to the north-west side of the castle couldn't see Lana's machine but after twenty minutes of the ladies' arrival he moved from his post and began walking in their direction for some unknown reason. The Zapatsaur closest to this sentry shot him with the laser pistol set on minimum. The sentry would wake up in two hours and report that he had been shot by an unknown intruder. Maybe a covert mission from Azorka had been launched to re-capture the Dragon Queen. It was just as possible that the sentry would not report the incident fearing that it would raise suspicions concerning his own abilities.

Sally was patiently waiting her turn for the session. She looked through the crafts glass at a beautiful sunny day and scanned the cliffs for sentries and those casually walking about who might be looking in their direction. Thankfully all was clear on the nearest cliff and no one walked about below them.

Sally relaxed and returned to her thoughts. She was not going to let Heather shoulder all the responsibility for protecting Azorka. Lana and Sally would be right beside her, with equal powers, to fight against the enemy.

Inside the office Heather still had her feet up on the Wizard's desk. She was sure it was about time for Lana to wake up from her session, so she pulled off the timer she had placed around her neck and set it on the desk. The timer was round and crafted from metal with a silver cover. Heather pressed the release button for the silver cover and it popped open on its hinge. Numbers were arranged on the inside face of the timer from one to twelve and the silver dial was only four minutes away from twelve which would mark one hour of time. She had started the timer two minutes after the session began so Lana would wake up in two minutes.

Heather had passed the hour with Lana by checking outside every now and then to be sure they were alone and that there were no onlookers. She would look over at Sally sitting in the back seat and Sally would give her the thumbs up signal to let her know that all was clear from her view. Heather would return to the Wizard's comfortable desk chair, put her feet up on his desk and watch the screen. During this time she had used her ability to remove books from the Wizard's many built in shelves. She would put the book back then she would try moving two books at the same time with each hand and found to her delight that each of her hands could be used to move two objects at the same time. Heather decided to remove the crystal skull. In the dim light she could see the white border surrounding the skull as it left its place on the shelf beside the scroll and book. Slowly the crystal skull moved across the room in mid-air, five feet above the European styled red carpet with its fancy floral patterns, until it settled on the dusty surface of the desk. Heather couldn't resist the temptation to touch it, but when she did the crystal skull glowed brightly in a lighter shade of blue. Heather was alarmed by the way it lit up the office and instantly withdrew her hand. The crystal skull stopped glowing and returned to its original darker blue color. Heather was disappointed and wondered if this was some kind of an alarm or warning. She remembered the Wizard had handled this without it lighting up with a bright glow. Heather decided to let the thought go.

The screen in front of Heather suddenly shut off and she looked over to see Lana pulling off the helmet. Heather checked her timer then closed its round silver cover and placed it back around her neck allowing it to hang down in front of her. Lee had been correct about her waking up on time although he didn't offer an explanation. Lana must have a subconscious timer that was enhanced to a state of perfection by the helmet. Heather regarded the helmet as a super booster for hypnosis.

Lana set the helmet down on the loveseat and looked over at Heather who was now standing up behind the desk.

"How do you feel Lana?" She whispered.

"I feel refreshed. I have to get back to the craft. I need to check the temperature gauge." Lana whispered back.

Heather walked over to the open window and waved at Sally to get ready to move into the office. Lana appeared at her side and she moved back while Lana slowly and gracefully placed her right leg out the window to re-enter the flying craft. Heather waited until Lana had entered into the flying craft, then she decided to check the helmet Lana left on the loveseat to make sure the setting hadn't been accidentally moved from the Yetz position when Lana removed it. Heather also checked the carpet to be sure that there weren't any loose blue threads that had fallen from Lana's outfit which would give away their intrusion.

Lana checked the temperature gauge inside the craft. Hovering to long in one position could invite overheating for the flying craft. She breathed a sigh of relief when she saw the needle on the gauge at twenty-five percent which assured her that the flying craft would only be halfway to the redline for overheating by the time they left the castle. Lana squeezed by Sally and took over the back seat to watch for the unexpected observer below and above on the cliffs who might raise the alarm. In case they were discovered, then hopefully Heather could catch this person using her ability before the alarm sounded for the castle guards. However, on a day of mostly sunlight, it would be more likely the light sensitive population would choose to stay indoors.

Sally made it inside the Wizard's office and saw Heather standing by the loveseat with the helmet in her right hand. Her left hand's forefinger was up to her lips and her dark eyes wide, locked on her in a dramatic request for quiet. Heather waved Sally over and pointed at the loveseat so Sally would take her seat immediately. "Put the helmet on and do up the straps so that it fits comfortably on your head." Heather whispered. She gave Sally a confident smile for assurance and to help her relax.

Sally followed those instructions while Heather dug around in her robe pocket and pulled out the diamond shaped crystal. She held the crystal up for Sally to see then gently swung it back and forth on its silver chain.

"Concentrate on this crystal and listen to my voice and do as I say." Heather whispered.

"Now I want you to relax and count backwards quietly from one hundred." Heather whispered.

Sally began counting backwards.

"Ninety-nine, ninety-eight, ninety-seven.." Sally counted out quietly.

Heather noticed that it was around the count of fifty-one, fifty, forty-nine that Sally's voice had slowed to a monotone, as Lana's had, indicating that Sally was now ready for her next instruction. She was mentally susceptible and would be more easily influenced by suggestion.

"Now Sally you will be going back thirteen years to that happy time you had with Mom and Dad on that fishing trip off the Spanish Coast. You came home from that trip to tell me about the big sword-fish you had caught. You will be fishing and the sword-fish will take your bait. You will quietly and silently reel in your catch which will take fifty-eight more minutes to land. After this you will leave this experience by closing your eyes for two seconds, then opening them to find you have returned to the office. You will remove the helmet, stand up and leave the office through the window into the flying craft." Heather instructed.

Sally nodded her head up and down then looked straight ahead, her eyes fixed on some distant subject that only she could see.

Heather returned to the Wizard's desk, put her feet up and watched the screen. Sally was only eleven and a half and about three inches shorter in height but with the same medium length hair style both sisters wore currently. Sally's hair was naturally straight like Heather's but a lighter brown color. Parted in the middle, it ran down her neck and just touched her shoulders. She was smiling and holding on to her fishing rod on the gray fishing boat Mitch enjoyed sailing the ocean in.

They were off the coast of Spain on a sunny day in June, just after school had recessed for the summer months. Mitch and Tamara were at the helm watching Sally fish. Sally had studied hard and received praise and recognition for her high grades and as a reward Mitch and Tamara had promised her a weekend fishing trip, at that time Sally's favourite activity. It was in the next thirty seconds that Heather saw the surprised expression on Sally's face as the sword-fish took the bait and dived with fishing line running out wildly on Sally's reel. Mitch called down with some advice and wished her luck while Tamara smiled with the joy of a mother watching their child's happy moments.

Heather began to day dream, remembering that she had asked Mitch why he liked the gray fishing boat. Mitch had let her in on a secret. The boat, suitable for six passengers, was equipped with a laser cannon, secretly hidden below and there was a crystal powered engine for the small fishing vessel that could be turned on in case of an emergency. The boat would be able to reach thirty miles per hour thanks to the solar energy stored in the crystal which caused the engine to turn an underwater propeller mounted in the stern of the ship.

Heather settled in for the sixty minutes. She was watching for the unexpected trauma within Sally's experience which would throw the results, making it necessary to wake Sally and re-hypnotize her. Sally was to have sixty minutes of a blissful experience. However, negative trauma was unlikely to happen. Sally had assured her ahead of time that she had selected the perfect experience for the session.

***

The Wizard was close to finishing his story about Gerta. The crew were enjoying the tales of all those challenges Gerta had gone through over the course of the many months she had been with the creature. They were anxious to meet her and welcome her to the Empire. They could tell by the Wizard's story that he was quite impressed with her character.

"The voodoo worshippers had captured Gerta, tied her up so she couldn't escape and were about to feed her to a python. That is when Gerta told us about the Voodoo King taking out the crystal skull and holding it over his head while beams of light poured out of the skulls crystal eyes. The dancers were illuminated from the light, parts of the clearing where the ceremony was taking place and the night clouds above." The Wizard explained dramatically.

Sam had a look of confusion on his face as though remembering a detail that had been overlooked.

"Excuse me Wizard for interrupting, but the beams of light emanating from the skulls eyes were so powerful that I was sure they penetrated through and beyond the night clouds." Sam explained.

"Do you mean that the beam of light looked similar to a laser beam except that it was white in color?" The Wizard asked.

"That would describe it Wizard." Sam said.

The Wizard stopped to catch his breath. He looked up at a fluffy white cloud rolling by against the rich blue late morning sky. The cloud looked like a white Wizard with a pointed hat like his. The Wizard reached up and felt his hat. He was beginning to perspire sitting in the sun for so long and decided to remove it. He ran his hand through his hair removing a ring of his own perspiration where the hat had been, then he put his gray pointed hat back on his head.

A minute of silence had passed. The wind had died down a little but was filling the sails above. The ship was stable, moving straight ahead and still unattended while the men listened to the Wizard's story. The Wizard continued with his story.

"That's when Sam came running out of the jungle to tackle the Voodoo King." The Wizard said.

There was about twenty minutes of story left to tell but the Wizard was also thinking about his notes on the crystal skulls he had in his office back in the castle. He did need to check his notes on this crystal skull.

The creature was enjoying the company of the crew and the relaxation in the sun on a beautiful day. The crew had warmed up quickly to the creature. Their respect and understanding for the creature had been confirmed by reading their minds. The companionship had grown from the creature's perseverance which the crew respected and their likeminded goals for the control of this planet. This new relationship reminded the creature of the companionship it had shared with the riders back home.

The creature longed to be home in its own star system. The large cities the riders and Dheginian creatures had built, offered a variety of entertainments like the sports played in the gigantic oval coliseum, which was designed to seat thousands of riders and their creatures as spectators. The forests of the home planet have trees twice the size of earth's trees and refreshing streams run through the forest where the creature can fish. The leaves on some of the trees of the coastal plains are about the size of a pirate's flag. The enormous dark brown trunk and branches are covered in large orange leaves in the summer time. These trees have often accompanied the subject matter of many artists, usually riders, and are painted with the large red sun in the background. Last but not least, the oceans are teaming with life and offer fishermen some very challenging sport.

The creature shook itself from the daydream and concentrated on the Wizard. He was finishing his story and thinking about what he had written about the jade- green crystal skull at the same time. The crystal skull was resting on the creature's neck in front of him. It was ringing alarm bells in the Wizard's head. The intensity of the two beams of light that Sam described, which poured out of those lifeless crystal eyes and penetrated the clouds above, was beginning to sound like a design feature the more the Wizard thought about it. The crystal skull was equal in power to the other twelve skulls, but like the other twelve skulls it had a different function. The crystal skulls were designed to work together on a variety of different mission scenarios.

In a couple more minutes the Wizard had finished his story. The men had enjoyed the tale and looked forward to meeting with Gerta when they returned home but for now they returned to their posts. The crew's sailing skills were sharpened by experience to a perfection. They had got away with the unthinkable and the ship was continuing at a respectable clip on a stable course.

Helmut walked over to the helm where he recorded their position. Much to his delight they were further north than he had previously estimated. They must have sailed past Morocco the home to some of the world's most ancient cities. Helmut recorded the longitude and latitude on a piece of papyrus then walked back to Sam and handed it to him.

"Thank you Helmut." Sam looked down at the papyrus and their recorded position in Helmut's neat handwriting.

"We have sailed past Morocco east of us, and will get home sooner than we thought. Congratulations everyone!" Sam shouted.

This received a happy round of applause from the crew.

Sam looked back at the Wizard who was now clutching the crystal skull; a sign he was leaving the ship.

"Sam I have enjoyed our meeting but I have to return to the island now. There are some notes of mine I need to consult and I promised Amy we'd be home in time for lunch." The Wizard said anxiously.

"Thank you Wizard. We understand." Sam replied.

He stood aside giving the creature a clear path to teleport. In the next second the Wizard and the creature disappeared from their spot on the main deck and reappeared on the portside of the ship one hundred yards from the ship and twenty feet above the ocean. The creature's wings immediately unfolded and they shot forward into the sky where an electrified circle of energy awaited fifty yards away. The creature flew directly for it and from Sam's angle he could see the creature's head, neck, and body with the Wizard riding on top clutching the skull, disappear until the last part of the creature that Sam saw was the end of its tail and that's when the electrified circle vanished. The Wizard would be home in two minutes.

The Wizard had enjoyed a great meeting with the men and was happy to be reunited with the jade-green crystal skull. However, he had neglected to speak about the creature's idea's concerning the eventual control of the earth. He had neglected to speak about the creature's thoughts concerning his hypnotic experiments which Heather had gone through. The creature believed this might have been responsible for the changes Heather has experienced. The creature suggested this might work for Gerta and that the Wizard should continue to monitor Heather.

If Lee's surveillance had caught everything said and done over the last three days he would have told Heather to steal the helmet and screen. It would have alerted the Wizard and he would build another but not before Heather had produced an army of immortals to overpower the Empire forcing its surrender. Unfortunately, his alien artificial intelligence would prioritize its time and skip over stories and information it had recorded before. Lee had no way of knowing that the Wizard and Amy were considering this technology for Gerta.

***

The Wizard's screen showed an eleven and a half year old Sally finally landing her swordfish which was almost as large as Sally. Mitch had been by her side to coach and help her with the last ten minutes of fighting this stubborn monster. Sally was smiling happily. Heather had set her timer again and she was amazed at how accurate the brains internal timer was. Lee had called this the suprachiasmatic nucleus and he said the helmet had mysteriously enhanced this part of the brain. Suddenly, Sally turned and seemed to face Heather watching her on the screen. Heather was surprised wondering if it meant Sally was aware of the experiment, which seemed impossible, or if this was coincidence and her overworked imagination getting the better of her. On the screen, Sally closed her eyes and Heather moved her head to peak around the screen as Sally began to regain consciousness in the real world. Sally immediately started undoing the straps to remove the helmet.

"How do you feel?" Heather asked in a whisper.

"I feel great." Sally whispered her reply.

"Could you hand me the helmet so I can put it away and then remove the needlepoint chair from the door behind you?" Heather whispered.

Sally stood up and handed Heather the helmet. Heather checked the setting and replaced it back in the Wizard's drawer where she had found it. Sally turned around, walked over to the office door and removed the needlepoint chair which was jammed under the door knob.

"Sally, climb back into the flying machine. I'll be right with you. I have to put something away." Heather whispered.

She walked past Sally and checked the love seat to be sure there were no loose fibres that may have fallen from Sally's clothing which would give away the intrusion.

Sally walked up to the office window and extended her right leg out the window and into the front passenger seat when suddenly the craft was pushed aside and the Dragon Queen appeared. Her wings moved up and down to hold her in position while she glared angrily at Sally. Sally's right leg was four feet away from the flying craft which was hovering at an angle so she pulled her leg in just before the Dragon Queen could catch it with the iron grip of her left hand.

Sally saw a chance to kick the Dragon Queen and did so with all the force she could muster and all the expertise that Ming had taught her while training in martial arts. She landed a lightning fast kick to the Dragon Queen's throat. This would have caused a human adversary to double over in pain and would have crushed the larynx, but the Dragon Queen had super human strength and Sally's well placed kick only forced her head back.

Heather had been ready to put the crystal skull away when she heard the commotion. She looked up from her loose fiber inspection of the Wizard's carpet in time to see Sally kick the Dragon Queen in the throat. She managed to restrain her anger for a few seconds. She confirmed that Sally was safe and Lana still in the back seat of the flying craft but looking very surprised at the sudden and unexpected visit. The Dragon Queen should be recovering from all those drugs they pumped into her or in her cave out of the bright sunlight.

"Maria!!" Heather yelled. Heather was red faced with anger at being discovered, after taking so many precautions to avoid this.

The Dragon Queen drew closer to the office window and peered inside the dark office. Her eyes were keen and she saw the dark blue crystal skull sitting on the Wizard's desk.

"So you came here to steal the crystal skull!" The Dragon Queen yelled back.

Heather realized the Dragon Queen didn't know that they had been using the helmet for the last two hours and decided to reinforce the Dragon Queen's accusation. She was also certain that the Dragon Queen didn't know of her new ability. Heather pulled her timer up from around her neck to show the Dragon Queen.

"Maria! I came back to recover my timer that I lost here! The crystal skull was already on the desk when I got here!" Heather yelled back defensively.

"You're here to steal the crystal skull!! Don't expect me to believe you'd break in to the office just for the timer!! The Wizard wouldn't leave the crystal skull out on his desk!! The Dragon Queen yelled.

Her face was contorted in anger; her features seemed chiseled on from the stress flowing through her and her eyes were unusually bloodshot from exposure to the sun.

Heather had been advancing slowly while the Dragon Queen was raging, almost foaming at the mouth with anger. Heather was within three feet of her when she decided to strike.

The white border that only Heather could see appeared around the Dragon Queen and when it enveloped her wings Heather moved in fast. The Dragon Queen's wings were slowing down fighting against the force that was pinning them to her green back. Her expression turned from anger to one of panic. She struggled to keep her wings moving and maintain her position in mid-air. The Dragon Queen would have dropped to the ground below but Heather had caught her by wrapping the rest of the white border around her lower half. She pushed the Dragon Queen out further in mid-air and ten feet away from them.

Lana had watched the entire scene unfold, never doubting her best friend's ability to handle the unexpected. She moved into the pilot's seat and waited for Sally' and ¡Heather,

Sally had been standing beside Heather at the office window while the Dragon Queen was yelling at Heather. She carefully nudged past her sister, after the Dragon Queen had been contained, and passed into the front passenger seat then climbed around into the rear seat.

Heather realized once she took her eyes off the Dragon Queen that the white border would disappear and the Dragon Queen would stubbornly pursue them. To give herself some lead time to get away she must send the Dragon Queen tumbling across the backyard. Heather started to spin the Dragon Queen in mid- air. The Dragon Queen began yelling again and screaming unintelligibly as she turned counter-clockwise so fast she looked like a spinning top.

Heather heard someone outside in the hall, banging on the door for the Wizard's office. Then she heard that familiar voice and knew that her time had run out.

"Who is in there!! Open the door immediately!! The Wizard shouted.

The Wizard had just arrived home and after leaving the Dheginian creature in the outside courtyard he had wandered into the reception room on his way to his office upstairs. That is when he heard all the screaming. The Wizard was alarmed and took the stairs two at a time. It was when he reached his office door that he realized he had left the key for his locked office hanging on a hook in the kitchen cupboard downstairs.

Heather had to get out of the office so she flung the Dragon Queen, still spinning, to the end of the backyard. The Dragon Queen landed in a heap on the exact spot the flying craft had started to cross from. Then Heather hopped through the window and into the passenger seat. Lana closed the hatch while Sally and Heather buckled themselves into their seats.

"Here she comes!" Sally yelled from the back seat.

Heather turned to see the Dragon Queen getting up, her powerful leathery white wings flapping frantically as she rose into the air and flew after the flying craft. Lana moved the flying craft forward and upwards on a sixty-degree angle, accelerating rapidly. Amazingly the Dragon Queen got close enough to the back window for Sally to see her blood-shot eyes angrily peering in and green face twisted in anger shouting out threats before the flying craft left her behind.

The Dragon Queen gave up the chase when Lana's flying craft disappeared into a bank of gray clouds. She flew back to the Wizard's open office window to be sure the crystal skull was still in the office and was relieved when she saw it still resting on the desk. She heard the banging and yelling on the other side of the office door and recognized a familiar voice that she had not heard for some time.

"I'll open the door in a minute Wizard!" The Dragon Queen shouted out from the open window.

The Dragon Queen hovered in place while she opened the other half of the window and spread the floor length curtains out of her way. She was able to climb in within thirty seconds and opened the office door to a Wizard so angry, his face was a darker shade of gray.

"What did they steal Maria!?" The Wizard asked while panting like a tired dog from all the exertion and excitement.

"I caught Heather inside your office beside the crystal skull on the desk. I assumed she was stealing the crystal skull and confronted her with the accusation. In her defense, she showed me a mechanical wind up timer which hung on a rope around her neck. She claimed she had dropped it here last time she was in your office. At the time I had pushed Lana's flying craft away from the window so that I could confront the burglars. I was surprised to see that Sally was with her and I tried to grab her. Lana was still in her flying craft but in a state of shock from my sudden arrival. However, before I could ask more questions or take these thieves prisoner, Heather had trapped me in an invisible force which stopped my wings and pinned them to my back. I began to fall but Heather caught me somehow and raised me up. Then Heather sent me ten feet away from the craft and somehow caused me to spin counter clockwise, in mid air at an incredible speed. Then she tossed me to the rear corner of the backyard. By the time I gathered my wits and stood up to spread my wings, Heather and Sally had entered the flying craft and were getting away. I tried to catch them, almost reaching the rear of the craft, but they sped away at an incredible speed." The Dragon Queen finished.

"Maria thank you. You've done more than I could ask after all those drugs they filled you with while you were captive in Azorka. When did you wake up?" The Wizard asked.

"I woke up in the laboratory on the gurney you were somehow able to place underneath me, to voices and footsteps coming from above me in your office. Apparently, my hearing didn't suffer while I was being held prisoner." The Dragon Queen answered.

Suddenly the Dragon Queen's attention was drawn to the open window. The Wizard turned around in time to see the Dheginian creature fly past the window heading in the direction of Lana's flying craft; this information read from the mind of the Dragon Queen.

"What is that!?" A shocked Dragon Queen asked.

"That is what put you on the gurney and the creature that rescued you from Azorka in broad daylight." The Wizard answered.

The creature had figured, the white haired lady piloting the flying craft, would accelerate to three hundred miles per hour which meant that the three ladies would be five miles away from the castle in another twenty seconds. The creature conjured the electrified circle fifty yards in front of its flight path. The spectacle of this fiery circle appeared within the eye shot of a surprised Dragon Queen looking up from the office window. The creature flew through the circle and vanished from sight. Before she could turn to the Wizard for an explanation the electrified circle of energy disappeared.

The creature arrived in mid-air, five miles from the castle and when it looked down through the parting clouds it saw the flying craft approaching about five hundred yards away. Looking about frantically for cover, the creature spotted a drifting gray cloud to hide in while its powerful wings kept it hovering in place. Watching through the cover of the gray cloud, the creature got ready to fly in front of the approaching flying craft, surprising the white haired lady before she could react.

Lana was smiling confidently about escaping and Heather sitting beside her was lost in thought about her new ability. She could manipulate two objects at the same time now. Behind her, Sally was dreaming about receiving her new ability in two weeks' time as Lee had calculated. All three ladies were relaxed and happy about the mission now accomplished like some weight had been removed from their shoulders. It was a beautiful day for flying and they would be in time for Tamara's lunch if they continued at the leisurely pace of three hundred miles per hour.

The creature watched as the ladies approached and when they were within two hundred yards the creature flew out in front of the flying craft.

Heather casually looked to her left and was shocked when she saw the creature leave the small gray cloud it was able to drift with undetected from a distance.

"Lana, look out!!" Heather yelled.

By the time Lana looked up from the instrument panel, the creature was only one hundred yards away from them and approaching fast. The creature opened its mouth and released a sonic boom powerful enough to shake the craft and slow it down. The sonic waves caused the nose of the flying craft to jump up and down erratically. The ladies heard a pounding noise with each sonic wave that hit the flying craft. Lana checked her speed. The flying craft had already dropped down to one hundred and eighty miles per hour and was still slowing.

Lana was thinking that the sonic waves as Heather calls them, must have stalled the flying craft. Suddenly there was a loud thud above her and the flying craft shook. Lana was distracted from restarting the motor and looked up at the creature which had landed on the glass roof of the flying craft. Its powerful arms were wrapped around both sides of the flying craft holding it securely. The creature began to pump its black leathery wings wildly as it started to carry the flying craft and its occupants downward.

"The creature is probably going to take us back down to the Wizard's backyard!" Heather shouted.

"Remember what Lee told us about the creature. It can read our minds. Try not to make eye contact. When we have landed open the hatch and let me out while you restart the flying craft. I'll hold the creature the way I did with the Dragon Queen then when I'm back inside the flying craft we'll take off at top speed and enter outer space where it can't follow." Heather instructed.

The unearthly feeling of falling backwards was shared by Lana and Heather but Sally had a front row seat facing the direction they were travelling. She could see that they were heading into what looked like a fiery circle in mid air.

"Hey, what's that?!" Sally shouted.

Both Lana and Heather turned around to see what Sally was talking about.

"Heather! Is that monster going to burn us up?! Lana yelled.

"We're not in danger! The Wizard would want us back to answer for the break and enter of his office." Heather reassured Lana and Sally.

The ladies held their breath, not knowing what to expect.

Lana, Sally and Heather watched in silence as the creature carried the flying craft into the fiery circle and into total darkness. They noticed a very faint humming noise. Fortunately, they were in an air tight flying craft and escaped the nauseous odor that Gerta had experienced which was like a fowl atmosphere throughout the tunnel of darkness.

Heather looked up in the darkness and could make out the form of the creature. In about five seconds, the darkness gave way to a tiny pin prick of light. The light grew rapidly in size and the familiar sight of the Wizard's backyard under his office window rushed up at them. The tunnel opened to its full ninety-foot circumference and the creature dropped the flying craft down gently on the Wizard's backyard as both the Dragon Queen and the Wizard watched from the office window.

The Dragon Queen was impressed with the creature and very grateful for her rescue. She wanted to help the creature deal with the intruding thieves but the Wizard sensed her temptation and turned to the Dragon Queen to put a stop to that ambition.

"Maria! I order you not to get involved!" The Wizard said firmly.

The Dragon Queen knew he wanted her to regain her complete strength before risking injury fighting Heather.

"I know the creature will understand. I think that the creature is conducting its own experiment to learn more about Heather's abilities. We need to find out how to fight against telekinesis." The Wizard said.

The Dragon Queen turned away from the Wizard and looked below to watch the scene unfold.

Heather looked behind her at the creature waiting for her to emerge from the flying craft. She didn't see the Dragon Queen on the lawn and looked up to see if she was in the office. The Dragon Queen was standing at the office window beside the Wizard. Both sides of the office window were open and her two enemies peering down at her, reminding her of a King and Queen preparing to be entertained from the excitement of two battling gladiators. Their expressions were calm and they were silent.

"Lana, I need you to open the hatch so I can get out and deal with the creature. Try and keep your head down while your doing this and restarting the flying craft's motor. Sally! Look away from the creature!" Heather whispered.

Sally immediately turned to look at the view of the rest of the Wizard's yard which over looked the ocean. Heather crawled out through the hatch and walked around to the back of the flying craft to face the creature.

The creature's black scales glistened in the bright sunlight. It sat on its rear legs. looking at Heather. The creature was trying to read the minds of both Heather and Sally but their minds were occupied with thoughts of combat and escape. The creature couldn't see Lana, the person with the most information concerning the flying craft's abilities. The creature's tusks sparkled in the sunlight as it opened its mouth and began creeping closer to Heather.

Heather knew she had mere moments to respond before the sonic waves hit her. She raised her left hand, pointed it at the creature's open mouth and wrapped it shut with the white border only she could see. Heather watched as the creature struggled, moving its head side to side frantically in an effort to shake off its invisible bindings so it could attack Heather with its sonic force. Then Heather did something she had thought about trying earlier in the day. She tied a knot with the white border and cut it. She watched with satisfaction as the frustrated creature tried to open its mouth with its own claws. Now Heather's hand was free and ready in case the Dragon Queen decided to join the fight.

Heather quickly gazed up at the Wizard who had a look of amazement on his face and the Dragon Queen who looked down at Heather with burning hatred. Heather took some satisfaction from their obvious disappointment. She focused her attention back on the creature who had decided to charge Heather resorting to brute force in order to defeat her. Heather was quick to act and sent another white border which enveloped the creature's entire body. She raised the monster five feet in the air and tightened the white border which pinned the creature's black leathery wings to its back and locked its scaly six-foot long muscular legs together. Heather sent a mental command for the white border to turn around continuously, counter clock wise. She watched as the bound creature began to turn around from head to foot in mid air then commanded the white border to spin faster.

Heather was careful to keep her eyes on the spinning creature so that the white border would not disappear. Backing up slowly, she made her way around to the front of the flying craft's open hatch and climbed back in. Heather was kneeling on the front seat and looking through the flying craft's rear glass at the spinning creature. Heather sent the spinning creature crashing into a tree in the backyard fifty yards away from the flying craft. The creature fell into a heap under the tree while the flying craft rose into the sky and took off accelerating at full throttle.

The creature had guessed that the white haired lady would ascend at sixty degrees, past the clouds in the troposphere where ninety-nine percent of the water vapour in the atmosphere is found and where the creature was waiting to ambush the flying craft on their last encounter. After clearing this lowest level of the atmosphere which extends for ten kilometers, the flying craft would enter the stratosphere which extends to fifty kilometers above the ground. This layer contains ozone molecules which absorb ultra violet light from the sun and converts the UV energy into heat. The white haired lady would travel towards Azorka in the stratosphere for at least fifty miles then re-enter the troposphere and travel on a level path till they reached Azorka. In the mind of the white haired lady, she would be travelling over the waiting creature and avoiding confrontation and capture. She would realize now that the creature could travel faster than she could using its teleportation abilities. The white haired lady would devise a different strategy to out fox the hunter.

In a few short moments the creature's guess work had proved correct. The flying craft appeared eight hundred yards below and five hundred yards ahead of the creature's position. The creature was about to fly forward into the flying crafts path and blast it with sonic waves when something incredible happened.

"Wait! Stop! Let them go! We'll take care of it!" A familiar telepathic command entered the creatures mind.

Heather happened to be looking out her side of the flying craft's glass when she saw the creature about one hundred yards above them and five hundred yards away to her left. She realized that she would be the only one that could see the creature and decided to keep its proximity to the craft to herself when she witnessed the creature holding off on an attack. The creature had begun to fly forward into the flying craft's flight path but suddenly stopped and returned to hovering after it had flown forty yards in their direction. Lana was looking down at her instruments and Sally was looking to her left in the back seat as the flying craft sped past the hovering creature only four-hundred and sixty yards away. What had caused the creature to stop suddenly? Could the Dragon Queen or Wizard somehow have communicated with it and called off the attack?

Lana was watching her instruments now that she had entered the mesosphere. This level of the atmosphere is quite cold. At the lowest level of the mesosphere, the temperature is 5 degrees Celsius and the highest level of the mesosphere the temperature falls to negative eighty degrees Celsius. The creature would not follow them into this level of the atmosphere because of the temperature and inadequate levels of oxygen. Lana's instruments caught the changes in atmosphere and the flying craft's internal heaters came on protecting all of the moving components from freezing as well as the passengers. The flying craft's main motor automatically shut off and the crystal powered motor came on leaving a small trail of flame behind the craft that Sally could see from the back seat. After converting to crystal power they were speeding to the end of the mesosphere at eight hundred and fifty miles per hour. Heather could faintly hear the sonic boom outside when they exceeded the speed of sound. The oxygen gauge was active and the vents opened to let in new air and recirculate old air. After a short while the craft cleared the mesosphere and entered the thermosphere where X-ray and UV radiation from the sun is absorbed. The air in this layer of atmosphere is extremely thin and sun activity affects the temperature and height of the top of this layer. This layer of the earth's atmosphere is where the Northern lights and Southern lights as well as the aurora occur.

"Hey! We're entering outer space!" Sally shouted from the back seat.

Sally was looking down at her belt which wrapped around her robe and tied into a knot at waist level. The belt was half an inch thick and two inches wide, the same color as her robe and made of cloth.

The gray belt ends were floating in mid-air above her legs. Sally was so fascinated with the spectacle that she forgot her companions had remained silent.

"Heather? Lana?" Sally said.

199

CHAPTER NINE

Sally relaxed the tension on the straps enough that she could turn around in her seat. That is when she got the surprise of her life. Both Heather and Lana were silent. Heather's mechanical timer had somehow squeezed out of her pocket and was floating in mid-air in front of her but she didn't notice or care. All three ladies had their eyes fixed on a gigantic metallic disc which was slowly approaching the flying craft.

"What's that!" Sally shouted. Then in a whisper, "This could be the alien craft Lee told us was heading our way." Sally tapped Heather on the shoulder when she didn't answer.

"Sorry Sally, I'm just a little shocked at what we are seeing." Heather replied. "You're telling me!" Lana answered beside her.

Sally immediately snapped into her leadership role, out of necessity and concern that her companion's thoughts were overcome with the unknown.

"This is a ship of unknown origin. We know nothing about it. The crew and its mission is not known to us. Lee did! talk about the alien craft. We have a responsibility to show the visitors that we are a peaceful people and should offer our welcome of friendship. We should give some indication of our willingness to meet. Lana slow down the flying craft so that we will appear to be requesting permission to meet." Sally instructed.

"I will deal with the diplomacy by introducing myself as leader of this welcoming committee for the planet earth. Heather don't use your ability unless we are threatened. When we get inside the ship use your enhanced eye sight to obtain whatever information may be useful to us. Look for a layout of the ship's rooms and pilot area." Sally said in a whisper Lana slowed down the craft and the three ladies waited for a response from the disc. They were creeping forward slowly at ten miles per hour,

Heather was thinking about the creature and what could have persuaded the creature to abandon the pursuit. Perhaps it knew the disc was here and was afraid of it.

As the silver colored disc came closer, Sally saw how enormous it was. The disc must have had a circumference of at least one thousand feet. The height of the disc's outer rim was six times higher than the height of Lana's flying craft. Its upper body rose gradually to its center where a metallic bubble with an estimated circumference of one hundred feet suggested that this was the command center where the disc's pilot would be seated along with the commander of the disc and other crew members. As if to confirm that suspicion, a large curved panel on the command center slid open and light poured out from this window onto the disc's upper body. Before Sally could get a better look the outer rim of the disc loomed larger and Sally's view point disappeared.

Another flash of light caught Sally's eye and she returned her gaze to the outer rim in front of them where a square orange light appeared about the size of the Wizard's office window. The orange light began flashing and oscillating on an invisible track along the outer rim of the disc. Another square of light, the same size but green in color, appeared on Lana's side. It flashed and began oscillating in the opposite direction. Sally thought this was to warn approaching craft that the docking procedure was underway and looked through the flying craft's glass in every direction but all she could see was the darkness of space and more stars. She couldn't see any smaller alien craft waiting to dock.

Heather felt nervous about entering an alien craft without knowing anything about the disc's inhabitants. She decided to turn on the heat seeking scanner they had used earlier to find the Wizard's sentry. Heather reached over and flipped the switch which was close to Lana.

"That's a great idea Heather." Lana and Sally whispered in unison.

The round green screen came on and immediately started beeping every five seconds signaling that it had located a lifeform in the silver disc in front of them. The ladies stared in silence and horror when they saw the hideous black image of a Dheginian rider facing the screen. They had been warned about the appearance of the rider by Lee last night and knew that the rider would be close to ten feet tall with a lower half similar to the Dragon Queen's hideous legs and feet. They knew that the rider was completely covered by black scales. They knew that the head, with its protruding lower jaw and six inch fangs, was unusually large with an elongated cranium. The rider's upper half was slimmer, looking out of proportion with its hips and legs. Those long slim arms didn't look powerful but Lee warned the ladies that the rider was incredibly strong.

"Alright now we know that the disc belongs to the creature's world and an ally of the Wizard from everything Lee has told us. It's to late to run so we'll deliver a message. We must convince our adversaries that we will not tolerate disruption of our planet. Heather we will rely on your abilities to escape the ship after I've tactfully delivered that message." Sally quietly instructed.

"I can overcome them physically in the disc. I can hold their position in space with my ability after we've left the disc." Heather replied in a whisper. Suddenly both squares of light touched together and stopped oscillating directly in front of Lana's flying craft. The square orange and green lights continued to flash until part of the rounded outer rim collapsed inwards and an opening appeared on the lower half of the disc's rim. This doorway enlarged enough to accommodate Lana's flying craft and the two square lights above the opening disappeared. Bright yellow light poured out of the doorway illuminating Lana's flying craft which was almost at an idle as the disc approached. Sally, Lana and Heather slowly entered the disc and the docking area.

Lana wasn't experiencing the jittery anticipation of meeting Dheginian aliens; the enemy. She was more concerned with memorizing the disc's features than the fight ahead of them. Lana assumed that the outside of the disc was made of metal which must have been manufactured with a special finish making it impervious to the effects of friction and extremely strong. The metal on the outside of the disc gleamed like freshly polished silver. As Lana's flying craft slowly made its way into the docking area the metal walls on each side rose up to the top of the doorway which must have been twenty feet in height and twenty feet in width. There were no lighting fixtures for the square green and orange lights above the entrance which had stopped flashing and automatically shut off, disappearing from sight after oscillating in opposite directions along the disc's outer rim. Lana guessed that they were concealed by sliding metal panels. As the flying craft crossed the threshold Lana noticed that even the floor was made of the same metal as the exterior.

Lana brought the flying craft to a stop twenty feet past the docking area's doorway. Inside the disc, bright yellow light poured down on them from above. Lana saw that there were two other flying craft, so she assumed, parked thirty feet in front of them. It was a large docking area about the size of an auditorium with a forty-foot high ceiling covered completely in glass panels where the bright yellow lighting originated from. The other two identical alien craft were a flat black color and rectangular. They looked to be about twenty feet long and ten feet wide. Lana wished she could see the front of the alien craft which looked large enough to carry six ten foot riders comfortably.

Left of the alien craft, and at the front of the docking area, Heather noticed that there was a square gold colored frame fifteen feet tall and twenty feet wide. The frame supported five panels, about twelve feet by twelve feet, and detailed with what looked like alien symbols, planets and stars. Each twelve by twelve panel was hung from a thin round pole which joined to the sides of the frame. They were lined up one in front of the other and Heather thought they must be a map of different star systems so she decided to memorize them.

She knew that her intelligence level had been enhanced and that she would be able to reproduce the map back in Azorka after this mission. However, something was scratching at Heather's memory ever since she had seen the Dheginian rider on the heat seeking scanner. She felt a sense of urgency but so far was unable to remember.

Sally looked to the far left from her position in the back seat, at a large circular black and white screen which hung on the metallic wall. The screen was divided into various sections or rooms within the circle by white lines. On its left side, two rows of gold colored alien symbols which looked a lot like the rune alphabet, ran up and down, arranged in columns on the silver wall beside the screen. Each one of these symbols had a raised round red button beside it. She assumed that the button had a specific function. Sally looked back at the circular screen when she detected a small tear-drop shaped white light moving. Sally watched this white light leave a triangular shaped room. It entered into a long and winding hallway which ran past other compartments of various shapes and terminated in the largest room which was the square docking area they were in now. The ladies were represented as three smaller tear-drop shaped white lights grouped together in the docking area on the screen. Sally saw other tear-drop shaped white lights in other parts of the circular screen, some moving, others stationary and assumed this to be a map of the ship with its crew. Possibly the light making its way through the round hallway, was the ship's commander or ambassador coming to meet them.

Heather's mechanical timer was still floating in mid-air and Sally's belt ends moved aimlessly above her knees.

"We have to remember that this Dheginian rider will speak to us telepathically. The rider can't read our minds so we will have to respond vocally. There will be a chance of a Dheginian creature appearing in an attempt to read our minds and that is when we will have to do our best to block this effort by shielding our thoughts. If this fails, we'll probably have to escape from the ship before they decide to take us prisoner." Heather whispered.

Sally was facing the same direction as Lana and Heather. She had released most of the tension on her seat belt to do so.

"Lana get back to the flying craft and start it up if it looks like we have a fight on our hands. Heather and I will hold off the Dheginians then we'll try to throw the ship into chaos by pressing, what we are assuming to be, operational buttons beside that screen in the hopes that this will create an emergency." Sally instructed.

Sally watched the tear-drop shaped white light on the screen as it moved along the hallway. It came to a stop on the circular screen and the doorway behind Lana's flying craft closed, which caused the mechanical timer to drop into Heather's lap while Sally's belt ends fell back into place hanging loosely around her waist. The white light began moving again resuming its journey towards the docking area.

"Look! That symbol on the wall beside the circular screen, the third symbol in the second row, the round red button beside it just lit up! I can use my laser derringer to trip it after we all get back in the flying craft to escape and I'll bet the door opens." Lana said excitedly.

"That's a bit of guess work we'll try out if we get into that situation. You have a laser derringer with you?" Heather asked.

"I always keep one in the flying craft. It's in my pocket now. It's a precaution always take should I find myself in these situations. It may not be a big help for self-defense against Dheginians that can heal as quickly as Lee said they could but it will cause the button to depress if it's been designed to do so." Lana answered in a whisper.

Lana, Heather and Sally looked back at the circular screen, which they assumed was the layout of the disc. The moving white light, representing a friendly host they hoped, was almost at the docking area. All three ladies were experiencing trepidation and 'butterflies' in their stomachs.

"I think we can get out of the flying craft now without floating away. The Dheginians require oxygen as we do so the docking area has probably been acclimatized." Sally said.

Lana reached over and released the latch on the flying crafts exit. The glass popped up and Heather climbed out with Sally following. Lana reached under the dash of the instrument panel in front of her and pulled out her laser derringer, tucking it into the pocket of her dark blue jacket. She climbed out and joined Heather and Sally who were standing on the shiny silver floor five feet in front of the flying craft. The floor was so smooth it was almost slippery and there was a faint hum that she could hear which must be coming from the ship.

Both Heather and Sally were anxiously looking at the empty hallway to their left at the front of the room, waiting for the host to arrive. They wondered if a doorway sealed the docking area from the hall. From their position in the room they couldn't see a door that the rider would have to open in order to enter the docking area.

Lana was more interested in the two flat black colored rectangular alien flying craft. She craned her neck to get a better view and was able to make out the cone shaped front of the two craft and part of a windshield or view port from the alien craft on the left. She wondered about their capabilities.

Lana was standing beside Heather and Sally was standing to the left of Heather's position. They heard a peculiar whoosh sound coming from down the hallway and assumed this to be a door sliding open to give access to the docking area. Sally was the first to see the shadow of the rider appear against the shiny silver wall which wound into the docking area. She nudged Heather and all three ladies watched as the shadow of two long arms and four clawed fingers projected against the wall and crept around the bend until their attention froze on the ten- foot figure who had come to a stop in front of them.

"Welcome to our ship. My name would be difficult for you to pronounce so I will simply introduce myself as a senior officer." The Dheginian rider said telepathically.

All three ladies heard the voice, which sounded like a male voice, in their minds. It was an eerie experience because the voice sounded like it was right beside them when in fact the rider must have been twenty yards in front of them.

"My name is Sally and my companions to my right are Heather and Lana. We are pleased to meet you and come in peace to welcome you as visitors to our planet." Sally spoke loudly because of the distance between them and without any tremor in her voice.

"I thank you for your welcome." Our planet received a distress signal from your planet about six days ago and we have just arrived, about two hours ago, from our journey here to respond to this request for help." The Dheginian rider replied. The ladies manners were impeccable and even though they found their host's appearance frightening they weren't about to let him know it. Instead they moved forward closing the distance between them so that shouting wouldn't be necessary. They moved close enough to shake his hand, which looked more like a reptilian claw. The rider towered over Heather, Lana and Sally as they looked up at his elongated head, which curved back slightly past the shoulders. It was covered in small shiny black scales and they noticed that his dark orange almond shaped eyes had reptilian pupils. Those six-inch fangs on his lower jaw looked lethal and covered some of his upper lip which was a small flat black strip no larger than the lower lip. In the center of his head, the rider had two thumb-sized round nostrils on either side of a slightly raised ridge of scaly flesh which must have been the nose. His black scaly lower body was larger than the upper body like the Dragon Queen's. His feet, almost twenty-four inches long, had three hideous long toes with long claws and they made a clicking sound whenever he shuffled about on the metal floor. Despite his appearance, the ladies looked up at him and were able to mask their reaction with a smile.

"That is a curious thing, sir. I can assure you we did not send a distress signal into deep space and the population on this planet is not advanced enough to send out a distress signal that would reach a distant star system." Sally offered.

"Yes, I understand that. There is only one signal like that in the universe. The distress signal came from a crystal skull which was crafted by our friend and ally, the Wizard. I believe you have made his acquaintance." The rider replied.

Heather received another mental scratch when the rider mentioned crystal skull. She was beginning to sense an urgency that she still couldn't define.

"We have been the Wizard's neighbors but he is in opposition to our civilization." Sally answered.

"What do you mean by being in opposition to your civilization?" The rider asked. "We have tried to explain to the Wizard that the outside world, as we call the world's various societies, should have the freedom to develop their own values. They need time to accept and work with the diversity of the planet's population. We believe the world community will eventually choose the path of peace and non aggression. If we force the outside world to adopt our way of thinking and living, there could be dissent from some of the world's communities. This dissent could lead to revolution and the ostracizing of the advanced society that has forced the world communities to adapt. Those war like groups may even decide to attack our advanced civilization in order to steal technology so they could swiftly win against their opponents. In other words, we would be at war with the outside world; something we strive to prevent by remaining hidden and secretive. We keep a close eye on the outside world and act secretly when it is necessary to prevent bloodshed. This has been an effective means of keeping the threat of war in check. To give you an example, we may find it necessary to surreptitiously relocate a trouble maker to another part of the world when there is a danger of this individual starting trouble." Sally explained.

"What if they become technologically more advanced in the future and possess the power to destroy the planet through war? Shouldn't they be guided away from this path while it is still easy to do so? Don't you think they could be more difficult to deal with in the future? Right now, they present themselves to the universe as immature and dangerous humans that may destroy the planet. The Wizard's plan wouldn't allow them to develop destructive technology." The rider said.

The rider was polite and his telepathic voice was not threatening nor was it to shrill or to deep but mid-range, almost pleasant. He was silent and motionless standing in front of the ladies perfectly straight, his posture military perfect.

Lana was listening to the conversation while closely observing the rider. She noticed that he was wearing tight shiny black pants and a tight fitting black vest which covered his skinny chest. He was barefoot which suggested the use of those lethal looking claws in combat. His facial expression never changed, in fact it seemed motionless while he spoke to them telepathically.

"Your argument is logical sir but we feel that the Wizard's solutions will result in forced slavery and we can't agree to that. We already have a problem with the outside world taking advantage of societies which seem primitive to them. The unfortunate members of these peace loving and welcoming societies are forced into slavery as a result. And this is a practice we cannot tolerate because human beings are meant to be free to choose to develop or not develop their individual society. We only require a peaceful and agreeable planet in order to balance the effects of diversity. The outside world is inviting revolution and war by adopting slavery and control in order to meet its needs." Sally answered.

The rider stopped talking and seemed to be thinking. Sally assumed he had to think of a rebuttal for her answer that would legitimize the Wizard's plan. An uncomfortable silence set in and Sally waited patiently for the rider to speak. Heather had time to think and she had come to the conclusion that the disc's occupants were able to communicate with the creature and call off its attack. The creature was obviously allied with the rider. This suggested that the disc's commander would eventually attempt to capture them in order to learn of their plans, past and future. Maybe Heather's abilities had made her over confident but this possibility didn't worry her. She was certain, although she didn't know why, that the rider's abilities would not stop her from escaping this fate.

The rider shuffled about on the metal floor, his claws making annoying clicking sounds as he moved his feet. He began speaking to Sally, Heather and Lana.

"There is an organized effort called the "Alliance of Peaceful Worlds" that seeks to create peace in the universe through mutual agreements. There has always been a shortage of resource rich uninhabited planets in the universe. We rely on these planets for our resources and survival as do other races from different star systems. Thousands of years ago we signed a treaty with the Alliance that assured them of our cooperation while your planet was under consideration. Your planet is extremely resource rich and everyone wants a share but it was agreed by this. treaty, to allow Earth and other resource rich inhabited planets to develop without outside influence. These inhabited planets would mature and eventually trade with us for mutual benefit. But if they continued to remain violent and primitive than a gentle coercion would be applied through outside influence. The agreement was for a set period of time and this treaty will conclude at the end of the Earth's twentieth century. There are many signatories from other star systems that hope the humans become civilized and there are just as many signatories that are prepared to invade Earth if this is not accomplished. The treaty is a benefit for all signatories because of the large pool of resources shared in order to search for the resource rich planets we all so desperately need for our survival. So for now we hold off on what you would call an invasion and what we would call a necessary precaution in order to preserve the natural resources of your planet." The rider finished.

Although Heather suspected their capture and containment aboard the disc on behalf of the Wizard was the rider's plan, she also believed that both parties would benefit from the exchange of information. It was a calculated gamble that the three of them had taken in order to learn more about the visitors and this knowledge would hopefully result in more effective strategies to defend Earth from invasion.

Heather believed the rider was getting close to the end of his speech and diplomacy so it was time to formulate their escape. The rider would find out that Heather could not be controlled and may decide not to follow her back down to the planet when they escape. The Dheginian's were still bound by the treaty so they shouldn't enter Earth's atmosphere for any reason. However, Heather would have to watch out for her companions who had not fully transitioned. The rider would send out his assault, which would freeze their movements, without realizing that Heather wouldn't be affected. She would use this to her advantage. When the enemy wasn't looking she would lash out and bind the rider and any reinforcements he might send to capture the three of them. Heather would threaten them until they agreed to release Lana and Sally. They would leave peacefully without any possibility of being pursued.

Heather heard a mechanical whoosh and squeaking sound that interrupted her thoughts. The sound seemed to have come from behind the rider. She looked at the blank shiny silver wall behind the rider. The wall had a few interesting panels and controls mounted five feet above the floor with the same symbols and red buttons that were used for the round screen which showed the ships rooms and movements of the crew. Heather payed close attention to the rider, pretending that she wasn't aware of the sound. She didn't have to check to see if Sally and Lana were distracted by the sound because only her enhanced hearing could have picked up the sound.

Sally was in a stew of her own thoughts and perceptions. She knew the conversation with the rider would only result in the same conflicting arguments as they had with the Wizard in the past. However, she would continue with her diplomacy and point of view act until it was no longer necessary. Sally turned her head to stretch a kink out of her neck. She noticed another white light on the round screen and in the docking area with them directly behind the rider that wasn't there last time she had seen the screen. Could this be reinforcements for the rider who had introduced himself as a senior officer? Sally felt the potential threat from a hidden observer but remained silent. For now, that was all she could do while in the company of the rider, playing the part of peaceful diplomat.

The rider shuffled along the metallic floor, his feet making those annoying clicking sounds, and stood in front of Lana. Those dark orange, expressionless eyes regarded the ladies as he prepared to launch into his next telepathic speech. Lana didn't flinch, wasn't intimidated and thanks to her overly self-confident nature, didn't care.

"A mission to Earth was launched by several brave members of our exploration team twelve thousand years ago. They travelled here on a disc much smaller than the disc you are on now. This ship did not have the technology to locate secondary portals, so it took some time to arrive. The mission was launched to see if we could locate the Wizard and Amy as well as a routine observation of your planet's progress. We lost contact with this disc shortly after it arrived in Earth's atmosphere, so we assumed that the mission had met with disaster like the Wizard's mission thousands of years before this. We would have attempted a rescue but a new war and our space travel capabilities prevented this. Today we can travel to Earth much quicker. The new power source and technology allow us to travel here in seven of your days. The discovery of a crystal from a distant star system will allow us to travel at half the speed of light. Advanced instrumentation can detect more portals, what we call secondary portals, by magnetic field and energy particle measurement. A space portal is like an intergalactic fold in space providing a significant short-cut to different galaxies and planets. There are at least two portals in Earth's magnetic field. Secondary portals are invisible and elusive and would have been dangerous to use in the past. They can open and close without warning. Now we can predict when this instability will strike and use the portal. Our new technology paid off handsomely today. I'm delighted to announce we have found the only surviving member of that ill-fated mission, a Dheginian creature who has also found the Wizard." The rider finished. The ladies were silent. He assumed they understood so carried on.

"We travelled here from forty-six light years away. Your scientist would say this is impossible in seven days. Our scientist believe portals are a result of the deformity caused by the gravity of a massive object like Earth. To make this easier to understand, try to think of space as an invisible grid with evenly separated horizontal and vertical lines. These lines distort, appearing curved and deformed from the gravity of a massive object like the Earth or the Sun.

Travel in the universe can be complicated. Galaxies orbit in our universe so these portals disappear making it necessary to locate new portals, often secondary portals which requires more advanced technology." The rider explained.

"Lana, I have noticed that you have rectangular pupils. My first reaction, if I didn't know you, would be that you're a visitor from another star system. Of course this isn't true. But what about Heather? She has the eyes of a Yetz. Sally is the only one here with eyes that our records show is normal for a human." The rider said. Lana didn't have a reply so she shrugged her shoulders as if to say so what.

"I assume that you ladies are not in military dress. Sally and Heather, sisters and guardians of your civilization, are dressed casually in gray and Lana is in a dark blue outfit. So why does Lana have a laser pistol in her pocket for our peaceful meeting?" The rider asked.

Heather was thinking that the nice talk is over, Sally knew they were facing trouble, but Lana pulled out her laser derringer and aimed it at the rider's head.

"The meeting is over! We are going to get back in our flying craft and leave!" Lana snarled.

The rider yelled out, telepathically, drop that weapon! The laser pistol fell to the floor and Lana was frozen to the spot, with her trigger finger, which had been swiftly forced from its curled position, pointing at the rider.

"Ladies, I think we can safely assume, that if you misbehave that you'll become motionless like Lana. Don't worry she's alive and well, just unable to move until release her. Now there is someone here that would like to join our meeting. I'd like you to say hello again to a member of our star system that you met earlier." The rider said sarcastically.

The rider moved closer to the rectangular flying craft, his ship's reconnaissance craft, so that Heather, Lana and Sally could see clearly that special someone who wanted to join the meeting. A panel in the metallic wall in front of them began to slide to the right, disappearing into the recess in the wall and revealing the glass behind it. There behind the glass was the creature, their pursuing adversary glaring down at Heather with those malevolent dark orange eyes.

Heather knew the creature could read her mind and immediately raised her right arm and hand sending an invisible white band one-foot tall and three feet long to wrap around the top of the creature's head. This was a lucky guess on Heather's part as it shut off the creature's ability to read her mind and communicate telepathically with the rider. The rider didn't attempt to hold Heather so that she would be motionless, either out of fear or curiosity. The creature reacted with frustration and began to frantically feel around the top of its head with both of its hands. It stopped this futile exercise and looked at Heather from behind the glass, then ducked down out of view. The rider watched Heather and the creature with great interest, realizing that she had somehow cut off the creature's ability to communicate.

While the rider was distracted, Heather took the opportunity to look at Lana. The rider had used his ability to freeze her movements and even her eyes were unblinking. Lana stood as still as a statue, pointing at a spot where the rider had stood only three minutes ago. She wondered if Lana's thoughts were frozen as well. Heather welcomed that possibility because it meant the creature may not be able to read Lana's thoughts. again.

The rider was still confused by the creature's disappearing act, which was assurance for Heather. He was looking at the back wall with its glass window. The rider had peculiar looking ears halfway down his elongated head that looked like round holes with a thin layer of black skin surrounding them and curling inwards. He turned his head from side to side possibly to listen for any moaning or squealing sounds that might be an indication that the creature is injured. However, the creature remained silent and all that could be heard was the low mechanical hum from the ship.

Heather had successfully cut off the telepathic communication between the two which is probably the reason the rider hadn't thought to freeze her movements. The rider, not knowing what to do yet, watched to see if the creature would reappear behind the glass.

Heather was looking at the laser derringer on the floor. It had fallen out of Lana's hand and landed closer to Heather's position. She could raise it off the floor if the rider became distracted, but would only have a few minutes before the rider noticed it missing.

Sally was looking at the laser derringer and thinking that she stood a chance of wounding the immortal rider. If she dived for the pistol and shot the rider in the head from her position on the floor, it might be the best way to neutralize his ability.

Heather tapped Sally on her right shoulder with her left hand just before Sally was about to put her plan into action. The rider had started to move towards the back wall and glass window to look inside for the creature. Heather knew she only had about thirty seconds or less before the creature's mental binding disappeared. The rider couldn't communicate so he was looking inside the room to be sure the creature was conscious. His back was to the ladies so Heather reached out with her ability surrounding the laser derringer with an inch-wide white band. She raised it off the floor and brought it around to Sally dropping it in her gray robe's pocket. The rider began speaking to them telepathically again. There had been about two minutes of silence. Heather's bindings would remain effective for this amount of time after she had taken her eyes off her subject. Standing beside the glass, having confirmed the creature wasn't injured from Heather's attack, the rider turned around and faced the ladies now thirty yards further away from him.

"The creature has confirmed that Heather's ability to restrain her adversaries will eventually wear off after a short period of time and for that reason the creature will remain out of view, but speak through me." The rider said.

"Heather what were you doing in the Wizard's office with Sally when Maria caught you?" The rider repeated the creature's question again to emphasize its importance.

"I had come back to the office in order to recover my mechanical timer that I had lost last time I was with the Wizard. The mechanical timer has sentimental value." Heather answered. The creature couldn't read her mind without seeing her and the rider couldn't read minds. The rider could only send the Dheginian creatures and other riders' telepathic messages.

"Why did you have the Wizard's dark blue crystal skull out on his desk?" The rider asked on behalf of the creature.

"I used my ability to remove it from the shelf and brought it to the desk. I was thinking of stealing it but it came to life by glowing a lighter and brighter blue when I touched it and this scared me not knowing what might happen next." Heather answered.

"Heather the crystal skulls can be dangerous in the wrong hands. There are thirteen of them crafted. One of the thirteen is capable of taking the user forward or backward in time. This skull is the same size and silver color as two others. These three represent humanoids from three different star systems. Three of the crystal skulls are quite a bit larger than the rest, representing different humanoids that would be considered giants standing twelve feet tall. Two more of the missing crystal skulls are noticeably alien because of their elongated shape. There is a crystal skull representing the Yetz star system and a crystal skull representing the Dheginian star system. There is a crystal skull for humans on earth representing this star system. When we find all thirteen they are placed in a pyramid and arranged into a half-moon and triangle formation, they will reveal the location of the uninhabited resource rich worlds we so desperately seek for our survival." The rider said on behalf of the creature.

"Today the Wizard was reunited with a jade green skull so we are still missing eleven crystal skulls. Join us and help us find the missing eleven skulls." The rider finished for the creature.

"We will not help you! You have missed our earlier conversation with this senior officer. We are to far apart with our solutions concerning Earth's development. Humans must have free will and can't be used as slaves. When they find the peaceful solutions for living together and using their diversity advantageously, then they will progress enough to be seen as acceptable to the signatories of your treaty." Heather answered.

The creature had its answer and remained crouched down on the floor on the other side of the glass. It was time for the creature to pass the diplomatic speech making back into the hands of the senior officer.

"There is someone else who has just arrived I'd like you to meet. Our highest- ranking scientist is my wife. The females of my race are entirely covered in beautiful white scales and have the ability to shape shift, but lack the offensive mental capabilities of the male." The rider said.

He pointed at the left-hand wall and about three feet down from the round screen. The borders for a six-foot high ten-foot long panel, previously invisible, suddenly appeared. The panel began to move to the right, neatly disappearing into a recess cut in the wall. Behind the panel was a glass of identical dimensions and a beautiful female Dheginian rider. Both Sally and Heather were taken by surprise because of her radiant beauty. Her features were similar to the male rider except that they were very petite and feminine. She was covered entirely in bright white scales and her petite, almond shaped light-yellow eyes, glowed with an intensity of their own. Her arms were slender but the hands had slightly longer claws than the male rider. Heather thought she was an estimated foot shorter than her husband. Sally had noticed that her mouth did not have the protruding lower jaw with the six-inch fangs. The ivory colored lower lip and upper lip were about the same size. The nose on her elongated skull, as though perfectly sculpted, rose gently, almost looking human, some might even think, that it lent her some character. The Dheginian scientist looked over at Heather and Sally but didn't greet them telepathically.

Lana was missing this demonstration of alien glamor but Sally and Heather had been captivated by the introduction. Much to their surprise, the white scaled beauty began to change right before their eyes. Suddenly the top of her head began moving downwards as though it was shrinking and the female riders face was becoming more oval in shape with a gentle chin and round cheeks. Her complexion changed in color to that of human flesh and her eyes changed from yellow to a deep green. The rider's wife now had blonde hair instead of no hair at all and she had lost at least three feet in height. Her arms were human. The hands had lost those lethal looking claws and now had thumbs. She reached back and pulled a strand of hair over her shoulder to cover her naked breasts. She smiled over at Heather and Sally with ruby red lips. The transformation had taken about thirty seconds.

"One of those rectangular reconnaissance craft will leave tonight. My wife will escort the Wizard back to our ship." The rider said.

The rider moved forward from his position beside the glassed wall, the claws on his feet causing that annoying clicking sound on the metallic floor.

Sally and Heather saw what was coming next and with their most innocent expressions looked up at the rider as he approached. They were both trying to think of a way to distract his attention away from the missing laser derringer. "Sir, I am curious about something." Sally began.

"Could you tell me which room on the round screen is the room your wife is in now?" Sally asked.

The rider knew he left the laser weapon on the floor but he quickly answered before checking to see if it was still there.

"My wife is in the first room beside the round screen. The rider answered. The rider thought this was a peculiar question. The white borders for three rooms appeared on the screen. Could Sally have thought that the first room was on the left side of the screen? He wondered some more then he saw that the other two rooms were now occupied. A round white light had showed up in room two and room three which were closest to the ship's entrance into the docking area. It was possible that the commander had sent the security back up out of concern for the safety of his crew.

There were no more questions from Sally or Heather so the rider looked to his left for that spot on the metallic floor where the laser weapon should be and saw that it was missing. This caused a surge of anger to boil over as the rider's blood rushed through those reptilian blood vessels. He turned his ugly elongated black scaly head to see if the creature had come out of hiding but saw that the creature still preferred to remain hidden. He couldn't rely on the creature's mind reading skill, which caused him to lose his composure and show Sally and Heather the more threatening side of his personality.

"Where is the laser weapon!!" The rider yelled telepathically with so much force that both Sally and Heather winced from an indescribable pain that centered around the top of their heads.

Sally saw that her distraction plan hadn't worked and was desperately thinking up another possibility which would buy them some time.

The rider was only twenty feet away from them. Sally saw that expressionless face those dark orange reptilian eyes of hatred looking down on them. She had finally thought up an answer for the rider's question. Sally pointed at the first rectangular craft, about to say that the weapon had slid under it when the rider froze her in that position. Her frozen body had a side view of Lana's frozen body, the arm and trigger finger still pointing at that spot the rider previously occupied. Heather was facing the rider and pretending to be frozen. She was grateful her hunch had been correct about the rider's ability not affecting her. But Heather's anger was building. The rider was on the offensive and had attacked them with his ability and she had finally found all the pieces to the puzzle nagging her at the back of her mind. Heather remembered her nightmare. All this talk about the crystal skulls had brought back the hideous image of a rider about to attack Indie who was holding a crystal skull. This had created storm waves of anxiety within Heather and she knew it was her responsibility to get her companions out of this disc and to arrange protection for Indie.

The rider was moving about in front of them, frantically looking around the docking area for the missing laser weapon.

Heather couldn't hear his telepathic grumbling or if he was communicating with his wife, but out of the corner of her eye, she saw the two round lights in the rooms beside his wife's room moving. The senior officer must have requested assistance.

The creature had raised its head after Sally and Heather had been immobilized from the rider's assault. The creature was hoping that this would stop Heather and wanted to see for itself.

Heather could see it was just a matter of moments before the creature discovered her act so she decided to launch her plan for their escape.

Heather sent the creature that same invisible white band that would cut off the creature's telepathic communication with the rider and watched with satisfaction as her foe struggled. The creature's arms and claws were a blur of motion as it tried to remove the invisible band that it could not even feel. It finally gave up and looked up at Heather just in time to receive another binding which wrapped around its mouth; cutting off the creature's punishing sonic waves. The creature was moving around in the room, probably looking for the exit. It was willing to risk more injury in order to help the rider subdue their enemy.

The rider had been amazed by Heather's deception and her ability to resist his mental assault. He charged Heather hoping she wouldn't be able to react quickly enough to hold off the attack. Just a few quick steps are all he needed and then a sharp blow to her head would leave her unconscious.

Heather bound his legs together wrapping them from top to bottom in an invisible white band that left the frustrated rider looking like a partially unraveled Egyptian mummy. He crashed to the floor.

Before Heather could deal with the rider, she heard a rush of heavy footfalls and the annoying clicking sounds which told her more riders were coming from the curved hallway for the ship's entrance into the docking area.

Heather sent a net of invisible white bands that attached to the front metallic wall, where the creature was still stocking about, and the metallic left-hand wall beside the last room down from the rider's wife. She had created an invisible net. In the next ten seconds four riders appeared and came rushing into the room only to get tangled up in the bands of the invisible net.

It was a strange sight that caught the attention of the rider's wife, who looked on in shock. She was still in her human form and those green eyes were wide with surprise.

Heather turned back to the senior officer.

"Release both of my companions immediately!!" She yelled at the rider.

The rider looked up from his position on the floor. He was defiantly silent laying there squirming on the floor. The rider looked up at Heather but did nothing to free her friends.

Heather's anger was building and her patience thinning. She raised her arm and pointing with a trembling finger sent a white band to wrap around the rider's neck. He immediately felt his oxygen being cut off and started choking, reaching up with those horrible hands to try and remove a white band he couldn't see or feel.

The rider's wife silently shifted back to her natural Dheginian form while Heather kept her concentration on the senior officer. She pressed a red button on her side of the room and a perfectly straight line appeared on the glass in front of her. The line began running down the metal wall until it reached the floor where it stopped. There was a three-foot wide, ten-foot long door for the rider's wife to walk through and into the docking area where Heather tormented her husband.

She quietly opened the door and stepped out. Heather was turned away from her unaware of the impending danger, as the nine-foot tall Dheginian scientist crept closer.

"Give it up! Mister you had better release my friends or I'll choke you until your last breath!!" Heather barked.

She tightened that invisible white band and the rider squirmed some more, his hands desperately clawing at his neck,

Suddenly Heather felt the incredible force of the rider's wife as she flew through the air hitting Heather right between the shoulder blades with those hideous clawed feet. Heather went flying into the side of the first reconnaissance craft and crumbled to the floor below. She wasn't knocked unconscious from the attack, and she got to her feet, wondering in the back of her mind where she got this super strength from, and charged at her enemy using the same combat tactic.

The rider's wife was bent over her husband wondering how to help him when she detected a flurry of motion out of the corner of her eye and looked up just in time to see Heather's feet fly into her chest. She was knocked off her feet and fell to the floor ten feet away from her oxygen starved husband.

Heather moved in quickly to bind her feet and legs the same way as her husband had been bound. Now there were two Dheginian riders laying on the floor looking like half wrapped Egyptian mummies. Heather looked at the senior officer with a very impatient and threatening expression. The rider was amazed at how Heather defeated his wife and had become intimidated enough to release both her companions. Heather removed the band from his neck and the rider gasped for air.

"What... what happened? We're still here?" Lana asked.

Lana choked out a dry cough. Heather thought it sounded like she was clearing her throat of dust.

"Lana get back to the flying craft and start it up. Be prepared to leave in four minutes." Heather calmly instructed.

Lana ran back to the flying craft and climbed through the open hatch.

Sally had silently woken up looking around the disc's docking area before speaking. She felt the laser pistol in the right pocket of her robe.

"Heather what happened?" Sally asked.

"I'll explain later. For now, I need you to get into the flying craft, take the seat directly behind Lana and buckle up." Heather called out while keeping her eyes on both of the riders.

Heather looked around to see the open door for the room the rider's wife had occupied and realized that the same option might be available for the creature's room: She looked past the rectangular craft to the creature's room. The annoyed creature couldn't teleport through glass. It saw the open door from which the rider's wife had entered into the docking area and had fumbled around until it had found the button on its side of the room which would create a door way into the docking area, a new technology it wasn't familiar with.

The creature pressed the button and a line appeared on the glass in front of it. The line began running down the metal wall until it reached the floor. The creature had a door way five-feet wide and ten-feet tall to squeeze through. Heather tossed two invisible white bands, each six-feet wide. The first one stuck to the top of the door and wall, the second stuck to the door and wall at floor level. The creature was on its hind legs and reached out with its left arm and pushed with its horrible clawed hand expecting the door to swing open. It couldn't see Heather's first invisible white band which was in front of its head, so it continued to push and then it ran at the door but it still wouldn't open. Finally, it looked up and saw Heather smirking, adding to the frustration it already felt about being unable to teleport through the glass.

Heather continued with the final detail of her plan and bound the two riders together with another band around their legs and tied the excess band length to the invisible net where the four security riders still struggled to get free.

She ran back to the flying craft and climbed in beside Lana. Now it was just a matter of finding the correct button to push in order to open the back door. Heather tossed a two-foot long white band at the first column of symbols and red buttons beside the round screen, eight red lights flashed after the white band struck but the door still didn't open. Sirens were sounding around the docking area which told Heather she had started to cause some trouble for the Dheginians. Hopefully this would send the crew into confusion while they escaped. Heather took another shot with a four-foot white band at the second column of symbols and red buttons beside the round screen and the back door started to open. She breathed a sigh of relief, keeping her eyes on those captives caught up in her white invisible bands.

"Good shot Heather!!" Lana yelled excitedly.

Lana had warmed up the flying craft while checking all systems and noticed that the crystal had eighty percent stored energy remaining for her to use. She could afford to take the craft over one thousand miles per hour reaching maximum speed. For re-entry, the Aryan engineers had installed specially treated steel, which had been case hardened for her automatic heat shields. This would permit a swifter re-entry. Lana remembered the suggested speed for safely descending through the thermosphere and mesosphere.

The disc's exit door had finished opening. Sally was securely buckled into the seat behind Lana, facing the bright stars of space and the glowing blue Earth below, thinking what a welcome sight.

Lana reversed out of the docking area which was now in a state of chaos. Heather kept her eyes on the crew she had trapped in her invisible bands. She wasn't sure if she could trigger the device for an airlock which would prevent the loss of air and change of pressure in the docking area. She had assumed that a second door, likely durable glass, had been lowered for their arrival to prevent what was happening now. The hanging maps were still and hanging vertically when they arrived. Now the five hanging maps of star systems that Heather had memorized, were floating upwards as though trying to escape from their metallic anchors. The senior officer and his wife began to slide along the floor as the door had opened but were secured by the band that tied them to the invisible net where the four security officers were tangled together. The creature was the only crew member that had escaped the sudden change in the docking area. The white bands kept the room air tight.

"As soon as your clear Lana, give it full speed. We have two minutes to get as far from this disc as possible. I think I made an enemy today. I'm almost certain the rider's wife will try to follow us. She might even take a pot shot at us if the reconnaissance craft are weaponized. I'm going to swing around and sit beside Sally. I want to be facing the enemy in case I'm correct about my hunch." Heather said.

Heather maneuvered around until she was sitting beside Sally and buckled her self in securely.

"We've got more energy stored in that crystal than I had originally thought. If she takes any pot shots at us I'm going to loop around and fire on her!" Lana barked. The flying craft was still missing a rear laser weapon.

Good for you Lana Heather thought. That's how I feel about the Dheginians after todays experience.

"I know how you feel Lana but first let's see if she sets out after us before we make our diplomatic decision to fire on the Dheginians." Heather said.

Sally was watching the back door on this enormous spaceship close after Lana had reversed out and turned their flying craft around to leave. Lana gave the flying craft full throttle and it accelerated much quicker than she had expected. Just before they were almost to far away to see the disc, Sally caught the smaller reconnaissance craft leaving the disc.

"Heather was correct about a pursuit!! I'll bet the lady scientist just left the disc alone, and is headed in our direction." Sally yelled.

Lana turned on a monitor on the dashboard in front of her. It came to life illuminated by green light and she watched as the alien craft gained speed rapidly closing the distance between them. Lana looked down at her crafts speed monitor which read two thousand miles per hour. She knew that their craft would have to move skillfully in a dog fight with a superior flying craft.

Heather looked closely at the craft with her enhanced sight. When, it was two hundred yards away, she saw the rider's wife piloting the craft through the narrow view port above the craft's triangular nose. It was dark inside the alien craft but enough light created by the pilot's monitor must be what had shown Heather her enemy. The scientist's bright yellow eyes had a new expression; they burned with hatred and anger.

Heather thought it would be best to some how diffuse the situation. She wasn't sure about the limits for Dheginian telepathy but tried communicating to see if the scientist would answer.

"Why are you following us! You already know I can defeat you! You're in a far more vulnerable situation and endangering your life!" Heather called out firmly.

Lana and Sally were surprised by Heather's sudden attempt to communicate with the enemy. They knew Heather's confidence was a result of the power her new abilities provided and looked forward to their own transitions.

Much to Heather's surprise the Dheginian scientist answered back.

"You brought a weapon to a peaceful meeting! You bound our senior officer and tormented him by strangulation!!" The angry scientist yelled telepathically.

Heather flinched from that same pain that the senior officer had unknowingly inflicted when he noticed the laser weapon missing. The pain concentrated at the top of Heather's head and she tried not to show her discomfort.

"Your senior officer's sarcastic speech and accusation intimidated Lana enough that she was concerned that our peaceful intentions were misunderstood. I'm sure many other civilizations in the universe would carry defensive weapons to meetings. It seemed more of an excuse to imprison a well-meaning delegation of three from Earth who were prepared to welcome you to our planet!!" Heather fired back angrily.

The Dheginian scientist didn't have a reply and what followed was a nerve wracking silence.

As a precaution, Heather willed a giant white band behind Lana's craft to act as a shield against the possibility of an attack. The giant white band was twenty yards wide and twenty yards in length. It was attached mid-way on the sides of Lana's craft by two bands three feet wide and twenty feet in length which attached to the rear of the shield on each side. The shield was fifteen feet away from the rear window and invisible to Sally and Lana. Only Heather could watch it ride along behind them, without creating any physical drag as though it didn't exist. However, she couldn't see through it and simply waited to see if the scientist would use violence as a means of persuasion.

Sally was the first to see the laser charge coming their way.

"Heather! Watch out! That alien craft has just fired at us! Sally screamed.

"Under control! Watch me catch it fifteen feet away from us!" Heather yelled back confidently.

The laser charge streaked towards them then suddenly stopped, caught by the shield, precisely where she said it would. Heather couldn't see the charge because it had stopped on the other side of the shield, but Sally could see the dazzling round charge of destructive energy, which held its position behind them and seemed to be turning counter clockwise, unable to move forward.

Heather thought the rider's wife, this intellectual scientist from another star system, had been driven to attack them by her primitive emotions. She had struck out of revenge for Heather's attack on her husband, who even now was still massaging a bruised throat. Unfortunately, the scientist didn't take into account the fact that they were trying to escape from the hostile actions of the Dheginians.

Lana had caught the drama in her rear view monitor and let out the breath she had been holding while watching a laser charge with considerable force approaching the rear of her craft. She had watched this destructive charge unexplainably stopped and remaining fifteen feet behind their craft which was still travelling at two thousand miles per hour. It was such a strange sight or display of paranormal power that even the Dheginian scientist couldn't explain how this was possible.

"Turn back! Return to your ship!" Heather commanded.

The rider's wife didn't respond. Instead she accelerated towards them on an upward angle, planning to fly above them and possibly fire again from a different position the shield might not cover.

Heather wasn't going to let this happen and immediately surrounded the alien craft with her invisible white border and pulled the craft back down until it was directly behind them. She kept her eyes on the alien craft and decided that she would tow it behind them until the scientist came to her senses.

"Alright! I'll just tow you until you see things my way!" Heather shouted.

The rider's wife was stubborn, fighting the invisible force that wouldn't let her move up or down and had confined her ship to travel at the snail pace of two thousand miles per hour. The alien crafts propulsion system whined helplessly as the Dheginian increased the power uselessly unable to break free. Those white scaly hands were clenched tight around the steering mechanism, which was a two-foot wide bar thick enough to withstand the squeezing pressure the frustrated and obstinate scientist applied to a control that could not respond. The first laser charge had eventually fizzled out from trying to break through Heather's shield and turning counter clockwise. The rider's wife decided to set the Dheginian laser cannon on maximum charge. She fired three more charges at Lana's craft. Each of the maximum charged laser shots made a peculiar mechanical whining noise as they left the alien craft and a descending in pitch whistling sound, that only Heather heard, as they accelerated towards the rear of Lana's flying craft.

"That crazy scientist just fired three more times from her laser cannon!" Sally shouted. She was feeling a little nervous about their enemy and her obsessive desire to destroy them.

All three of the maximum powered laser charges were caught in Heathers shield and turned uselessly in a counter clockwise motion like the silent or medium powered laser charge had before its energy ran out.

The Dheginian scientist paused a moment to think of another way to break through what must be an invisible shield. She thought about blasting all three laser charges where they were caught and turning fifteen-feet away from the rear of the enemy craft. This would logically make use of the energy trapped and cause it to explode and hopefully destroy the shield. The white scaled reptilian scientist fired and another mechanical whining noise sounded in and outside her craft. The maximum laser charge hit the other three as they turned in Heather's shield and a huge explosion of laser energy sent a blinding star burst pattern of sparks and the blinding light of spent energy in all directions behind Lana's craft. Lana's craft. remained unharmed. The rider's wife cursed and fired wildly four more times before giving up.

Sally and Lana had seen what was coming and had both instinctively closed their eyes before the explosion occurred. They both opened their eyes as four more charges were caught and now spinning in Heather's shield. "Nice light shows crazy ladyli" Lana shouted triumphantly.

"Do you think she'll give it up Heather?" Sally whispered in the back.

"I hope so. It is a waste of time, accomplishes nothing and I'm getting tired of the game! I'm liable to do something more drastic!!" Heather yelled. Hoping the rider's wife was paying attention.

"Wait a moment! I think I've got a good idea! Why don't we re-enter with the rider's wife in tow? We could present her to the other guardians as a violent threat to humanity and let them deal with this Dheginian scientist. Maybe she would like to feel what it is like to be imprisoned." Lana suggested.

"That's a great plan Lana!!" Sally called out from behind her.

"We could bind her in chains and there is nothing she could do to stop us!" Heather joined in enthusiastically.

"Wait!!" The rider's wife yelled so loud that Heather's pain returned. Heather was the only person who had heard this telepathic message, and she was grateful for that because of the pain it would have caused her companions.

"I will accept your offer of freedom and promise that while we are in orbit above you, my people will not interfere with Earth's affairs. I will return tonight to the Empire's island to pick up the Wizard and bring him back to the disc. You will see some bright orbs above his island in a half-moon and triangle formation as a signal to him that we will arrive shortly. Then the disc will leave for the Dheginian Star System." The rider's wife finished. She had sent this message to Heather in a calmer telepathic tone which Heather appreciated.

While the rider's wife waited for Heather's reply, she reached over with her left hand and those four, three-inch claws, hovered above the toggle switch to turn off her directional microphone which she had been using to hear the conversation in Lana's flying craft.

"I accept your peaceful retreat and shall allow the visit to the Wizard to proceed without interruption from Azorka." Heather answered out loud while Sally and Lana listened.

Heather removed her invisible white border around the alien craft. The Dheginian toggle switch returned to the off position and the rider's wife turned her craft around and flew back to the Dheginian disc.

"Sally could you let me know when the laser charges fizzle out?" Heather asked.

Sally looked out at the four laser charges, trapped in Heather's shield. They were still shining bright, full of energy.

"Alright Heather but I think it will be another five minutes at least, because they look just as strong as when they arrived." Sally answered.

"Great as soon as they dissipate we can re-enter Earth's atmosphere and home for a late lunch. I'm starving right now and I know Tamara has some left over chocolate cake in the fridge that I'm dying to get at." Heather said.

"Lana was beginning to salivate thinking about her own experience with Tamara's extra rich homemade chocolate cake.

"Better put me down for a couple of slices!!" Lana yelled excitedly.

"Sorry Sally but the chocolate cake is now virtually gone and devoured. Would you settle for a banana?" Heather asked knowing she was teasing her sister.

"Very funny Heather but I happen to know where the marzipan is hidden." Sally answered.

Sally looked out through the rear glass and saw the beautiful view of the Earth below.

"Where do you think we'll descend to when we re-enter? How far off course are we?" Sally asked.

"We are travelling eastward at two thousand miles per hour. We spent some time with the Dheginians and I don't know how fast their disc was travelling. Your guess is as good as mine." Lana answered.

Heather had dropped out of the conversation and had found herself thinking about her enhanced strength and how she was able to fight the rider's wife. She was also wondering about Lana's and Sally's coming transition. Being aware of the changes they would go through and how it might affect them made Heather determined to be there to help them. Heather knew it was time to move Lana into the guardian's castle. That is what Lana is now, an immortal guardian. Lana looked down at the remaining energy for the crystal powering the engine and saw that they still had sixty per cent left. They could get home quicker travelling at two thousand miles per hour,

"Heather, the laser charges look like they are beginning to dwindle." Sally said. "Sally, let me know when the laser charges are no longer visible" Heather asked. In another five minutes Sally answered. "They are gone, Vanished!" Sally shouted.

"Finally, we can re-enter earths atmosphere." Lana said.

"I have to take the craft up to top speed of twenty-thousand miles per hour. Hopefully this will not cost to much of our remaining energy in the crystal." She informed her passengers preparing them for the increase in speed.

After reaching top speed Lana re-entered earth's atmosphere and flipped a switch on her dashboard for the shields below them. They dropped down from the left and right side. They had been folded up and tucked into the recessed sides of Lana's craft and were designed to unfold automatically while the craft was in operation. Each specially treated panel began to unfold and stretch towards the middle of the bottom of Lana's craft, until the final left side and right side panels joined and locked together in the middle. Now the flying craft and its occupants were protected from the effects of re-entry.

Lana watched on her dashboard main screen where the process was illustrated in green. When the final panels had joined at the center below her she pushed a green button to lock the mechanized shields.

Lana positioned the nose of her craft slightly downward for the descent. She would gradually slow the crystal powered engine down to ten thousand miles per hour during the re-entry. A successful re-entry always tested the skills of the pilot. Lana was well versed in all of the techniques she would employ to re-enter Earth's atmosphere effortlessly. The Aryans took for granted the high power density of their crystal energy. In the future, they would wonder why re-entry maneuvers would seem so difficult for the outside world. Lana would consistently slow her speed down as she re-entered Earth's layers of atmosphere. She would aero- brake periodically as required by raising the nose of her craft which exposes more of the crafts surface area to the flow of air and therefore increases drag helping to slow the speed of descent. The shields could protect against four thousand degrees Fahrenheit. The re-entry would take one hour.

Sparks flew up around the craft as expected. Lana recorded the sparks overlapping the shields, guessing a two-foot overlap all around the craft. Some design adjustments were needed and more testing to eliminate the overlap.

There was complete silence inside the craft except for the high pitch of the laser powered engine which was barely audible. Heather and Sally were lost in thought and Lana was busy punching in her records on the dash keyboard with the results appearing on a black and white screen to her right.

Sally enjoyed watching the phantom tendrils of wispy clouds rushing up to greet them as they got closer to Earth while Heather was wrestling with her nightmare and ideas on how to best protect Indie from the Dheginians.

Back on the Empire's island, the Dragon Queen and Wizard were still in the Wizard's office, pouring over his notes on the crystal skulls, recorded on papyrus thousands of years ago. They had discovered that the jade-green crystal skull that Leif and Sam had recovered, could be used as a beacon to the Dheginian Star System. It was intended as a signal requesting assistance and could be activated by a reptilian eye looking into the eye of the crystal skull. It was thought that the python mentioned in Sam's story had unknowingly set the beacon off. The Voodoo King must have been waving the skull in front of the snake.

The Wizard thought it would be answered and was expecting a Dheginian space cruiser to arrive. Although he wasn't sure when. He made a mental note to tell Amy of the recent events and to prepare to govern the island in his anticipated absence.

While he read over more of his notes, the Dragon Queen was reading about a special crystal skull in his collection. She sat on the loveseat in front of the Wizard. who she could barely see for all the paper clutter on his desk.

"I find this small crystal skull, the shape of a human skull and silver in color, to be the most interesting of all. This skull will turn gold in color when activated by the touch of a Dheginian or Yetz humanoid. Then the skull will take the user back or forward in time." The Dragon Queen said.

"That is one of the most dangerous crystal skulls in my collection. It could change history! The participant's arrival and actions could accidentally alter history when going backward in time." The Wizard answered.

"I agree that could be dangerous. It says in order to return to the participant's original time that three words have to be whispered into the skulls left ear. What words have to be said?" the Dragon Queen asked.

"When the crystal skull takes the time traveler forward or backward in time, it shrinks in size and changes into a piece of jewelry when arriving at the desired destination. If the destination is not specified it will take the traveler to a destination it considers relevant to the traveler's needs. The skull will wrap itself around the wrist of the traveler and appear as a golden skull laying on its side. The gold band it is attached to is one-inch-wide and a quarter inch thick. If the traveler wishes to return to their original destination, the three words, "earth, ice, fire" must be spoken. The Wizard recalled.

The Dragon Queen turned to the next page of the Wizard's notes and saw that the left side of the papyrus paper was stained slightly from the long ago sweat that must have come from the Wizard's trembling hand. This was a picture and notes of the largest crystal skull which had a deep red color. This was the crystal skull that the Dheginian or Yetz high priest would talk directly to for their request. This crystal skull was positioned in the middle of the half-moon formation in the pyramid and faced the other crystal skulls below in the triangle formation.

Both the Dragon Queen and Wizard continued to study the notes on the crystal skulls while the Zapatsaurs finished their meeting in the Elder's cave on Zapatsaur Mountain.

The Zapatsaurs received the alarming details by reading the minds of the ladies before they left on their morning mission. The elders had arranged a meeting and were discussing the Yetz satellite orbiting above Earth. They were delighted that the Alliance were aware of matters unfolding in their part of the universe. Heather, Sally and Lana were the next topic of the telepathically communicated meeting. The next few centuries were going to be a challenge, however with the three new super-human guardians opposing intruders' things might go a little easier.

The Minister of Defence had returned to the inner world where the majority of the Zapatsaurs lived and gave orders to refurbish and prepare the flying discs for military purposes. The idea of a disc above, them from an unknown star system had a nerve-wracking effect not knowing if this situation had potential for violence. The Minister of Human and Zapatsaur Affairs had sent three Zapatsaurs to a northern beach on Azorka where they prepared a message for the Yetz satellite. The remaining Ministers in attendance continued with their daily duties on a beautiful sunny day at Zapatsaur Mountain.

Lana's flying craft had effortlessly reached the stratosphere in fifty minutes thanks to Lana's piloting skills. Regular engine thrust and aero-braking made the re-entry safe and simple. Lana switched over the engines in her hybrid flying craft and cruised at a comfortable five hundred miles per hour.

Remarkably, Lana's energy storage gauge for the crystal showed fifty per cent energy left and its screen was illuminated in an orange color instead of green, a feature designed to grab the attention of the pilot.

Lana decided to ask Heather and Sally what they thought about travelling home at full speed.

"Are you two interested in getting home soon?" Lana asked.

"We are starved and have already missed lunch." Sally said.

"I'd like to get home, shower, get into some fresh clothes and have dinner. We need some time after to explain some more ofour stories. I need to tactfully mention to Indie that we must assign a special security squadron to protect her because of the Dheginian threat." Heather said.

"Why is she a target for the Dheginian threat?" Sally asked.

"I haven't told you two about the dream concerning Indie that I had while I was suffering from nightmares because I had forgot it until today. It came flooding back in pieces when we met up with the Dheginian's today. The memory of the details began to assemble piece by piece in my mind. Indie was holding a crystal skull in my dream then a Dheginian rider approached her and I tried to warn her but she couldn't hear me. You've both probably had a nightmare before with that special effect, it's just in this case the circumstances suggest mine might be a psychic warning of what is to come, if I let my guard down." Heather explained. "Alright I get the idea. We need to get home soon. Would you both agree to flying at two-thousand miles per hour? If so its only ninety minutes to that yummy chocolate cake!" Lana said.

Both Heather and Sally agreed so Lana went ahead and switched back to the crystal powered engine and they began accelerating until they were flying past icebergs and over water at top speed. Heather and Lana were enjoying the sensation of speed. They thought that two thousand miles per hour over land was more exhilarating when compared to the same speed in space.

Lana piloted the flying craft expertly and occasionally tested it for agility at top speed by suddenly pulling upwards at sharp angles or diving sharply. Sally didn't complain, though the effects on her body were challenging her restraint while seated in the back of the flying craft.

They flew over the Davis strait which was the northern part of the Labrador Sea between Baffin Island and mid-western Greenland. Lana decided on some more tests in this area or aerial acrobatics as Sally had begun to think of the maneuvers. They continued flying over the Labrador Sea. It was around the Labrador Peninsula that Greenland really showed off its stunning scenery. Beautiful forests with mountains in the background nestled on the untouched coastline of Greenland. Eventually the lush scenery gave way to a rolling ocean that sparkled like diamonds from the reflection of the mid-afternoon sun.

While Azorka's three super-heroes flew home the Dragon Queen and Wizard had continued to study the notes on the crystal skulls. The Dragon Queen had commented on the Wizard's thumb print visible on the papyrus scroll for the large red crystal skull. She wanted to find out if the red crystal skull was powerful enough to cause this much anxiety for the Wizard. She had also read that the skull was hinged at the jaw and wondered if it spoke back to the person requesting its help. First the Wizard wanted to see the thumb print. When the scroll was handed to him across his now thoroughly cluttered desk, his facial features froze when he realized it wasn't his thumb print.

"This thumb print is human and much larger than my thumb print would be. Possibly this thumb print belongs to the thief that stole my crystal skulls!" The Wizard growled.

A flicker of light from outside the Wizard's office window caught the Dragon Queen's attention. She got up from the love seat arranged in front of the Wizard's desk, and walked over to the window to investigate. In the afternoon sky she could see a half-moon formation of bright round lights over a triangle formation of similar lights, hanging motionless above the Empire's island.

The Wizard wanted to see what the Dragon Queen was looking at so he joined her at the window.

"There here!!" The Wizard shouted.

He had hoped the Dheginians would arrive. The Wizard knew they could be of assistance with some of his problems and he looked forward to his reunion with his allies after all these thousands of years.

The Dragon Queen looked surprised from his dramatic reaction. However, she quickly returned her attention to the spectacle the motionless lights provided hanging in the afternoon sky.

The Wizard returned to his desk to roll up some of the papyrus scrolls that he was finished reading over. He sat back down in his comfortable chair and looked at the clutter on the desk top trying to decide where to begin.

"Those are drone orbs. They are a form of artificial intelligence the Dheginians use for signals. Tonight, I would expect a female representative from their disc shaped starship to arrive. The formation you see in the sky is the same formation that the crystal skulls are placed in during the ceremony in the pyramid. This is the signal we agreed to thousands of years ago before I arrived here on Earth. The female Dheginian riders are shape shifters and will take human form while visiting Earth. Quite often they are scientists or doctors and the intellectuals of the Dheginian Star System." The Wizard said.

The Wizard saw that the orbs had captured Maria's fascination. He swung around in his chair, reached across the pile of papyrus scrolls that had heaped up on his desk to retrieve his gray cone shaped hat. He put it on then got up to join Maria. "While the creature was here I had considered asking for its help. I was going to travel to our firestone, now that I had the location, and plan to retrieve it. I would use my blue crystal skull to travel in my astral body and if all was well I could arrange for the creature to teleport down to pick it up providing there was no significant physical harm caused by the ocean pressures it would have to withstand." The Wizard continued.

"That plan will have to wait. I suspect I shall be leaving tonight. I had better warn Amy to expect a guest for dinner tonight. Maria, I want you to dine with us and meet our guest. You can stay anywhere in the castle so Amy can monitor your recovery from that awful incarceration. I also want you and Amy to rule the Empire while I'm absent." The Wizard finished.

"I'll give Amy all the assistance she requires." The Dragon Queen answered.

"Thank you, Maria. There could be challenges from the Azorkans while I'm gone." The Wizard cautioned.

"I'm certain there will be future attempts on this room which I shall dutifully occupy while you're with the Dheginians." The Dragon Queen said.

The Wizard thanked the Dragon Queen again then turned from his position at the window and left the office to tell Amy about his dinner guest and probable departure. The Wizard was confident about Maria's ability to defend the Empire and he took comfort from her vigilance. He thought that today's intrusion would not be attempted again. But on this matter, he was wrong.

***

It was a quiet flight travelling three-hundred feet above the ocean at two- thousand miles per hour. Lana had flown over some large and small ships of various origins, noticing the occasional crew member looking up at them as they flew overhead. She imagined the vast majority of sailors wouldn't report the sighting for fear of being accused of intoxication. Heather and Sally were lost in their thoughts and relaxing from the challenges of the day. Lana was day dreaming about having more power in the flying craft. She wanted to be able to travel at forty-thousand miles per hour in space and she would need the flying craft engineered to withstand high speed and dense radiation environments that surround this planet thousands of miles from its surface. Lana sat back in her seat as she dreamt about the improvements.

After a quiet hour, they flew over the Azores island chain. In about two and a quarter minutes, Lana could see Azorka on her monitor twenty miles ahead. The ocean had become calm and the sun was in the west waiting to sink below the horizon. Lana switched over to the other engine and recorded thirty-five per cent energy remaining in the crystal. She slowed the craft down to one-hundred miles per hour as they approached the northern shores of Azorka.

The Guardians castle reminded Lana of a white arrow poking up through the old growth forest. From a distance it was easily mistaken for a rocky face of a small hill surrounded by trees. Lana slowed the craft down to twenty miles per hour and looked over at Heather. Heather was looking down at some scrawling in the sand on a lonely beach they flew over but couldn't make any sense of it. In the back seat, Sally was looking down at the beach and had just enough time to read the message which was legible from her view. It was printed with three-foot long letters gouged in the sand with a large stick. It read, "Dedicated to The Alliance of Peaceful Worlds". She decided not to mention it, although there was something familiar about it. Sally was tired and hungry wanting nothing more than to just relax at home.

The flying craft slowly made its way toward the Guardian castle's backyard.

Heather decided to interrupt the silence of the weary. "I do think we all need to sit down together when we decide to tell our story of today's events." "What do you think Lana and Sally?" Heather asked.

"That is a point that I agree with. It will be enough for Mitch and Tamara to digest another super-hero daughter and all the problems they might have during my transition." Sally answered.

"I've become the transitioning addition to the family and that will represent a few extra concerns for everyone, although I can spend some time in my Aryan village until things settle down. But I agree with your suggestion Heather. When we begin to relate today's events, I'd recommend we all be present so there will be no doubt about the accuracy and believability of our stories." Lana suggested.

With that settled Heather returned to her thoughts.

The flying craft felt like it was floating at twenty miles per hour. Sally looked down at the forest from one hundred yards above. She recognized this area and knew she was drawing near the Guardian castle's backyard. Sally released her seat buckle and swung around on the back seat so she could look through the front glass. They flew over a clearing and Lana dropped the craft down to thirty feet above the ground, flying forward slowly until they reached the beginning of the backyard.

Indie looked up at Lana's flying craft from her comfortable chair on the backyard patio. Heather, Lana and Sally waved down to her and she waved back then got up from her chair and called through the open window for the kitchen where Tamara was preparing dinner.

"Our three test pilots have returned from their mission!" Indie shouted sarcastically.

Indie looked up with a big smile on her face and relief in her heart as the flying craft flew over and into the front yard. She had been worrying because of their late arrival.

Heather looked down at Indie dressed like royalty in a colorful full-length red, gold and black robe. She thought both Indie and the General should have permanent living accommodations at the Guardian's castle until she could advise on the best defence strategy against the Dheginian threat.

They flew over the multi-level castle with its white and light gray roof, made to look like marble; (but in actual fact was the same material as the domed homes of Azorka). Lana dropped the craft down slowly past the many recessed windows at the front of the castle and into her favorite parking spot on the lawn in front of the living room. She released the glass hatch and Heather then Sally climbed out with her following behind. They began stretching beside Lana's craft, getting their travel cramps ironed out when Tamara opened the castles front door. As the castle's beautiful ornate wood carved front door slid into its recess, Tamara looked out at the three ladies relieved to see that they had arrived home safely. She stood there in the open space wearing a full-length white robe, her dark hair tied in a pony tail and still holding a large fork in her left hand which she was using for cooking in the kitchen.

"Well, I'm glad to see you're all home in time for dinner. We're having a delicious forty-pound turkey with Zen and Indie. They'll be staying over another night." Tamara called out.

This was the situation that Heather had hoped for because they would need time to explain their stories and Indie would be safe tonight.

"We have to get showered and changed, Tamara. Lana will stay the night again. I was wondering, could you lend her some clothing while we wash her clothing?" Sally asked.

"Of course, I will. My brown cardigan is a snug fit for me and I have baggy black pants that Lana could tie up well enough without them falling off." Tamara replied.

Heather, Lana and Sally giggled at Tamara's good sense of humor. They walked up to the front door and Tamara led them up the gold gilded staircase to the bedrooms where they could change. She collected their dirty laundry in a pile and carried it down to the wash area, then returned to the kitchen to finish the dinner preparations.

While the ladies cleaned up and changed into clean clothing, Mitch and Zen were in the library down the hall. They had spent the afternoon researching the crystal skulls in village "8". There wasn't very much information in the university library but they did find one scroll that directed them to Azorka's Ancient Hall of Records. They left the university where their Zapatsaurs had enjoyed a late morning breakfast in the university gardens and flew west to the edge of the village's boundary.

There was no sign to identify the Hall of Ancient Records for the sake of secrecy and it was a small non-descript, fieldstone and rectangular building. It had been built to hide two levels below ground where hundreds of ancient scrolls containing sensitive and highly secretive information were stored. The top floor was an eight-hundred square foot area filled in with book shelves and a small twelve-foot by sixteen-foot office at the back where an elderly attendant was available to help those seeking information on various topics.

Mitch and Zen had knocked on the door then entered the small back office where the attendant was gazing out the window and enjoying the view of Azorka's west coast on a beautiful day. He was dressed in a dark red long sleeve shirt tucked into a pair of dark blue pants that were scuffed up from his early morning gardening of the grounds. The elderly attendant turned from the window and ran a weathered old hand through his thick white hair and smiling up at Zen and Mitch he motioned for them to sit down on the two chairs in front of his wooden desk.

"Welcome gentlemen! My name is Arthur. How can I help you?" He said.

"I'm General Zen and I'm sure you recognize Mitch from the Guardian's castle." Zen answered.

Arthur paused a moment then reached into the left drawer of his desk and pulled out a small pair of glasses which he put on. His posture was already slightly stooped from old age but his back hunched up even more as he leaned forward to look at his visitors.

"Oh yes! I'm sorry! Well I'm honored to have you visit me. I don't get many visitors you know. Your both dressed in the black pants and boots of the military and I should have recognized our seven-foot Guardian Mitch, but as you can see my eyesight has deteriorated." Arthur said.

"That's quite alright sir. Zen and I are looking for information left behind by a Guardian who was alive before the war broke out. The scroll we found in the university library, records his name as Omar and he was working undercover before the war spying on the Wizard." Mitch said.

"His family had covered for his disappearance from the castle saying that he was in Africa and on a secret mission. Omar was clever disguising himself as a house servant working close-by to the Wizard." Zen added.

Arthur scratched his clean shaven chin then like a light bulb going on inside his head he stood up and snapped his fingers.

"I know where we have information on him! The second floor below. You'll both need to walk back to the entrance and turn right at the book shelf against the wall, go to the end and pull back the book on the middle shelf with a gold spine that says "Azorka's Best" and a small section of the shelf will move slowly towards you giving you access to a circular stair case that leads to the first and second floors below. You need the bottom floor, which is not much larger than this office and the shelf that is marked "Azorka's Guardians" where you'll find the scroll for Omar. The scrolls are arranged in alphabetical order and when you find it you may take it home and return it when you're finished. If you need further assistance, I'll be outside finishing my gardening." Arthur said.

Arthur grinned and shook hands with both Mitch and Zen before they all left the office together. Arthur sauntered to the door in the windowless wall. The elderly attendant, now doubling as a gardener walked through the door closing it behind him as Mitch and Zen located the circular staircase and descended below.

Zen led the way while behind him the steps squeaked in protest with every step Mitch took. The metal rail they hung onto as they went, had accumulated years of dust which was picked up by the sleeve on Zen's green shirt. When they reached the lower second floor, Mitch brushed off dust that clung to his red shirt sleeve and Zen took time to do the same.

Mitch reached ahead in the dim light drifting down from an undercharged crystal mounted at the top of the stairs and found the light switch for the small eight- hundred square foot room. The second floor's crystal light barely provided enough light for them to see in this dusty room crowded with shelves storing years of ancient Azorka's history.

They searched for a further ten minutes until they reached a scroll marked "Guardian Omar" with a date revealing that this scroll was about ten-thousand years old. Zen found two more scrolls with the ancient Guardian's name marked on the outside while Mitch searched further until they determined that these were the only three they needed for their research.

Mitch and Zen made their way back up the staircase and exited the Hall of Ancient Records to return to the Guardians castle. After a short flight, they entered the castle and jogged up the gold gilded staircase with its red gold carpet runner that ran down the long hallway to the library at the end. Zen was carrying the three scrolls and in his haste he almost knocked over a porcelain figurine sitting on a half-moon teak table that Tamara proudly displayed against the mahogany wainscot and white marble wall. Mitch opened the door and cleared a space on the long library table which sat in the middle of the room cluttered with books and scrolls. Zen placed the scrolls on the cleared space and opened all three. They both began reading from the scroll with the oldest date and what they learned in that hour before the ladies had returned from their mission was astonishing.

The first scroll began with the usual salutation; "To the Guardian-Top Secret" then paragraphs of information followed describing the mission of that ancient time. Omar had gone into great detail to describe his undercover role and his friends Gabriel and Yurem who had risked their lives to help him. The next paragraph revealed Omar's discovery concerning the Wizard and Amy's origins. The Wizard had accidentally left his diary open out on his desk while away at a meeting in the city. Omar had posed as a cleaner hired to tidy the temporary apartment where the Wizard and Amy stayed. At the time, many of those living in the south thought that Amy, who had accompanied the Wizard to the meeting, was his wife rather than fellow scientist.

Omar recorded his discovery about half way down the first scroll.

"I had found the Wizard's diary open on his desk while he was attending a special meeting with Amy. The diary had made mention of banishment from Yetz-an for their illegal dealings with the Dheginian Star System. The Wizard and Amy had hoped to one-day return and conquer their home planet ridding it of the influence that was reluctant to make a peace agreement with the Dheginian Star System and eager to banish those politically opposed to their views."

A few more paragraphs followed which were a description of their journey to Earth, then the Wizard recorded his concern for Amy's health and well-being. It was important for their society to see Amy as human and the Wizard's middle-age appearance was easily disguised with lab gloves and his own gray beard. She was able to pass as a human with light brown contact lenses which disguised her dark eyes and flesh tone make-up which she covered her gray skin with. The Wizard was concerned that her skin would have a negative reaction to the make-up and that her eyesight would be affected by inferior contact lenses and he vowed to find a solution for both problems. They were immortal and unable to leave Earth so he would have to find a solution.

The Guardian had said that the Wizard's hybrid experiments with animals of various types and creatures that should be extinct had caused some concern amongst the ruling class. It became necessary to organize a covert mission in order to access the threat this presented to Azorka after the Wizard's creatures got loose on one occasion and slaughtered a number of innocent people in the research and development district. We didn't want to have the problems with large dangerous animals of the past, returned to us.

About sixteen hundred years ago we had suffered loss of life and property from the woolly mammoth, sabre toothed tiger, and some large lizards that had managed to survive meteors from space, floods and volcanic eruptions. The genocide initiated thousands of years ago, had not done a complete job. The remaining large animals began migrating as the climate changed. They threatened the balance of nature and mankind. Arguments arose against acting, but in the end, hunting parties were approved and sent out to assist our trading partners in other parts of the world.

Mitch stopped reading from the scroll and turned to Zen in order to review what Omar had written down in the scroll.

"During the ice age, both Azorka and Atlantis were situated in areas of the globe that weren't covered in ice thanks to warm Atlantic water flowing into the Nordic seas. When the ice age ended in 11,600 BC, large animals began migrating more frequently. Azorka's trading partners were having trouble with the death and destruction they left behind. We didn't have large animals like our trading partners had, although we saw large tortoises appear on our shores. However, we had to free the world from the threat of these monsters so we set out to different regions of the world in several groups of hunting parties to help our trading partners free their communities from these horrific creatures. The sabre-toothed tiger and the woolly mammoth were the most difficult to put down and there was talk of some bipedal lizards that had survived. We discovered large caves that tunneled deep downwards into the Earth and figured that some of the large lizards had disappeared into the inner Earth where it would be much warmer than the icy surface. Siberia, where Tamara's family lived, has one of these entrances. Later we found other entrances in South America, Antarctica and the Arctic. We didn't investigate the inner Earth but kept a guard near the entrances to be sure dangerous animals wouldn't enter our world on the surface." Mitch said.

"I thank you for the ancient history lesson. I wasn't aware of some of the challenges of the past." Zen replied.

They began reading the second scroll which was a description of the mission's difficulties and accomplishments, then Mitch and Zen unraveled the third scroll. Omar talked about the crystal skulls and what he had learned about them from the Wizard's diary. The diary had been especially informative about the crystal skull used to navigate the time lines both in past and future time. It was amongst crystal skulls of similar color and size and only the Wizard knew which one it was. Omar had used Gabriel's talents to steal the crystal skulls when the war broke out and when Gabriel returned to northern Azorka to deliver the skulls, it took a long time to sort out the individual locations where they would be hidden from the Wizard. Some of the crystal skulls were delivered to the Mayans, some went to Haiti, some to Europe and some to India. Omar had finally found that special individual with the ability to point out the dangerous time travelling crystal skull. This was a slight man no taller than five feet in height and a popular council member for the last thirty years, named Aleko.

He pointed out the skull while Gabriel was with him. Then he asked Gabriel to leave him so that he could perform a special test, that required absolute silence. Gabriel agreed and when he looked in half an hour later Aleko had disappeared with the crystal skull.

Omar was pacing back and forth in the Guardian's castle for the next week wondering where Aleko was and hoping the popular councilor was safe. Two. more days went by and finally Aleko turned up on the steps of a government facility in village "A" exhausted from his unusual journey. He had the crystal skull with him wrapped up in a linen sheet.

Omar was relieved and decided to celebrate Aleko's return. He invited him to the castle for dinner the next night.

Aleko told Omar about his journey into the future and what he had discovered. The Middle East was part of Aleko's journey including Egypt.

Aleko followed a tribe for a while as it journeyed through the desert. In another two weeks Aleko had used the crystal skull to travel further into the future to see what became of this tribe. They had settled in a land previously occupied by giants and Aleko wondered how they had conquered this land from such formidable opponents.

He was as popular with these people as he was here at home and soon they inundated him with their knowledge.

Aleko told Omar that he could have stayed a further year and still return, in what would be a ten-day absence from Azorka, because of the mysterious nature of time travel.

The information that Aleko had found had been what he'd been looking for to complete his mission. However, the information about the Great Flood lasting a little over a year was something he would warn Omar about. With Omar's help Aleko recorded all that he had learned, then disappeared.

While Zen and Mitch read from the third scroll, fifty feet down the hall from them Sally was struggling to find a green blouse that would match the same shade of green that her pants were. She had already selected a warm knee length brown robe, placing the laser derringer inside the robe's pocket and making a mental note to give it back to Lana before dinner. Lana and Heather had gone downstairs to help Tamara with dinner preparations.

Finally, Sally found the right blouse and put it on. She tucked it in around her waist and slid her feet into a pair of black shoes with ankle protection and the same action tread the military used. Sally walked over to the far wall of her eight hundred square foot bedroom and plucked the brown robe from the bottom half of her bed. She put it on then looked around her bedroom to be sure everything was put away. Sally had preferred a light tan color for her walls and dark brown furniture with her pictures framed in walnut. Nothing was out of place except for her desk drawer which she had left open in her haste and frustration with color coordination. Sally walked back across the bedroom floor pushing her desk drawer closed and turning off the square crystal lamp framed in walnut and mounted on the ceiling in the middle of the room.

Sally closed her bedroom door and walked down the hallway to the landing at the top of the staircase. Before she could leap down the steps two at a time, Heather appeared asking her to go back and tell Mitch and Zen that the before dinner appetizers they had been preparing were ready. Tell them to come down to the kitchen..

Sally walked down the long hallway again and knocked on the library door before entering. She walked in and saw all the papers and papyrus scrolls out on the library's long dark mahogany table. Mitch and Zen were both standing half way down the tables length, stooped over and reading a papyrus scroll. A silver colored crystal skull was on the other end of the table close to the library wall safe where Mitch had removed it five minutes ago.

"Gentlemen! The dinner party is about to begin and the other hungry Guardians are requesting your attendance." Sally said with a chuckle.

Zen broke his concentration from the scroll and looked up at Sally.

"Thank you for your cheery announcement. We shall be along shortly." Zen said.

"What are you two reading that has claimed all of your attention?" Sally asked. Mitch looked up from his reading while Zen returned to where he had left off. "I'm sorry Sally but we have found some very interesting history which might help us to understand the crystal skulls and the Wizard's motivations. We will be another five minutes then I promise you we will be coming down to join everyone." Mitch answered.

He smiled down at Sally looking apologetic for any inconvenience they might have caused.

Sally didn't respond or turn to leave the room to notify the family of the minor delay. Instead she moved forward and read from the scroll Mitch had temporarily abandoned to answer her. Mitch didn't object. Sally was a Guardian and had a right to educate herself with the latest facts.

She looked up from the papyrus with a look of amazement on her face. Sally could understand why Mitch and Zen were so absorbed in the scroll. She looked down at the crystal skull Mitch had removed from the safe for examination. It sat there like a work of art on the end of the table. For some reason, after quickly reading one paragraph of information about the crystal skulls, Sally thought it looked more alive than just a work of art. She walked down to look at it while Mitch returned to his reading.

"Heather told us she had a dream about Indie holding that crystal skull under a tree in her favorite outdoor area for meditation. Heather finally remembered her nightmare and became very anxious about those memories on our way home." Sally said.

Zen looked up from the scroll but Mitch continued reading. Mitch remembered Heather's nightmares and her state of mind. He didn't consider her nightmares to be an ominous portent.

"Are you sure that this is the exact crystal skull in Heather's dream?" Zen asked. "I think that only Heather could tell us that." Sally said.

"Of course. Why don't we confirm that after dinner?" Zen said.

Sally didn't answer. She walked over to get a closer look at the crystal skull.

Sally looked down at the crystal skull. She thought it was smaller than a normal human skull would be. So this must be one of the skulls the Wizard made to represent an alien race and possibly member of the "Alliance of Peaceful Worlds" information that the Dheginians revealed to them. A light of recognition flashed through her mind. Sally remembered now that she had seen this organizational title gouged into the soft sand of the beach they had flown over about forty minutes ago but didn't say anything because her mind seemed to be cluttered with other thoughts. Who was responsible for writing "Dedicated to the Alliance of Peaceful Worlds"? Sally decided to put that question on the back burner for now.

Sally reached down and picked up the crystal skull carefully with both hands clasping each side of its quartz head just below where the ears would be situated. Suddenly she felt the skull bonding itself to her hands. It was an unusual sensation as though her hands had been glued to each of its two surfaces. Then the skull turned to a gold color right before her eyes and she was beginning to feel dizzy. Sally had just enough time to gasp from the shock of feeling her body changing and after a few seconds she couldn't feel anything but could still see Zen and Mitch who had looked up when she gasped.

Mitch and Zen's expressions had changed from happy and relaxed to extreme alarm. They both dashed over to Sally. Zen couldn't resist the temptation to reach forward with his hands in a vain attempt to somehow free Sally. Fortunately, Mitch caught this and brushed away the Generals hands.

Sally's head peered out from a peculiar gray gaseous atmosphere contained within a five-foot radius. It was hanging in mid-air four feet from the floor and rapidly rotating, resembling an amoeba that was mostly circular but constantly changing its shape by extending small projections of its gaseous consistency. Below her head, Mitch and Zen could see the crystal skull, now a blinding gold color, and her hands attached to it but they couldn't see the rest of her body. Sally's lips were moving but Mitch couldn't hear what she was trying to communicate.

Right at that moment Heather had entered the library without knocking and when she saw her sister incased in this gaseous prison she froze. She had hurried up the staircase and down the hall to find out what was taking these people so long.

Heather began walking towards Sally. Mitch and Zen were on both sides of the amoeba-like prison floating in mid-air at the end of the table, looking at Sally and wondering how to free her.

Sally was somehow coping with the eerie feeling of disconnection from her body. She couldn't feel her body yet she was sure her head was still attached and she could see her hands clasping the crystal skull with those penetrating golden eyes that glanced up at her. Those strange, piercing eyes seemed alive and communicated confidence. They were somehow reassuring where her own personal safety was concerned. The skull had a mission for her and she would be safe from harm.

Heather saw her sister's eyes turn her way as she approached and could read her lips when she called out her name but Heather couldn't hear Sally's voice. Sally seemed in control as she always did when confronted with a challenge or danger. Her eyes were wide and alert. Heather was about six feet away from her when suddenly the golden light from the crystal glowed brighter, expanding and covering Sally's face. In the next five seconds Sally and the crystal skull, which had seemed to glue itself to Sally's hands, blinked out of existence. Mitch Zen and Heather were speechless. Two minutes had gone by from when Sally grasped the skull, to the moment that she had disappeared.

Sally was experiencing the sensation of falling in a long dark tunnel.

The crystal skull had stopped glowing but retained its gold color and it was the only thing Sally could see. She felt as though her body had become part of the amoeba-like cell she was contained in. Perhaps she was changing to another state like liquid or gas, she wasn't sure. There was complete silence while she continued falling in the tunnel but Sally wasn't going to panic; she was immortal now and nothing would be able to kill her. She would investigate this experience and then find a way back to her family.

After thirty seconds of falling through the tunnel, Sally landed gently in a field of tall grass. It was night time and she felt the chill of late autumn. Thankfully her body had been restored, clothed as before and she wasn't injured or hurt in any way from her fall. She heard explosions off in the distance and raised herself up out of the grass to survey her surroundings. The faint lights of a small town across a barren field were visible about one mile ahead. Sally was wondering where she was but before she could get to her feet and investigate, she heard the barking of a dog about one hundred yards away. She quickly crouched back down behind the cover of the tall grass, then she heard the deep booming voice of the dog's master speaking in a foreign language she didn't recognize. She had almost twisted her left wrist crouching back down and as a result of that mishap, had become aware of an object wrapped around it. She looked down at a bracelet and saw it glitter in the faint moonlight and knew it was gold. On top of the bracelet was half of a golden skull. It's left side was exposed, one eye staring west and it was so meticulously fashioned that it looked alive. Sally heard the sound of the dog running through the tall grass, so she reached into her pocket and pulled out the laser derringer. She was breaking out in a cold sweat as the dog's barking grew louder. Above her a dark cloud rolled by cutting off the light from the moon briefly. The wind was blowing against her back and Sally knew the dog had picked up her scent. The grass was rustling twenty feet in front of her and she heard a menacing growl. A dark outline of the dog behind the grass appeared ten feet in front of her then she could see the dogs head poking through in front of her. A vicious looking German shepherd showed its fangs then crouched down and leaped up in the air to attack her while Sally trained her laser derringer on it and fired.

After Sally's startling disappearance, Mitch, Tamara, Indie and Lana remained in a state of shock for about one hour. Heather was more preoccupied with finding a way to rescue Sally from the time in the future or past that the crystal skull had selected. A great deal more research was needed on this crystal skull and perhaps Lee could help. This was definitely going to require an emergency meeting. Lee had said to leave a note in her bedroom, on her dresser top and that would be picked up by the satellite. Heather anxiously wondered how long it would be before a meeting could be arranged.

They talked amongst themselves; Heather Zen and Mitch gave their account of the events as they unfolded in the library before Sally was taken. Mitch comforted Tamara although she was a tower of strength and like Heather didn't shed a tear out of concern for Sally's safety, but was confident in Sally's ability to survive.

It took a couple of hours before their moods lightened up enough to have something to eat. The appetizers were served and everyone got a healthy slice of Tamara's turkey which was cooked to perfection. Tamara didn't bother cooking anything else and replaced the vegetable plates in the fridge for the next day. A light snack in the comfort of the family room sufficed, while Heather and Lana explained the events of their day as they unfolded and the decisions they had to make.

Lana and Heather explained their meeting with Lee and why they went to the Wizard's castle. Once the experiment was completed it was Heather's theory that a sufficient amount of Yetz influence was already present in Sally and that was responsible for her sister being accepted by the time-traveling skull. It was now understood that in order to access the magic of the crystal skulls the participant had to be either Dheginian or Yetz. That is why humans could freely move them about without the skulls lighting up and coming to life. Heather had an enhanced memory and she remembered, while she was the Wizard's prisoner, that the Wizard had handled the blue crystal skull above the ears and perhaps that is why it didn't come to life. Sally had gripped the skull below the ears and in the Wizard's office Heather had touched the blue skull in the same area then swiftly removed her hand from the skull.

Lana explained their decision to approach the Dheginian disc. It was a common sense and unanimous decision not to run. The disc had advanced technology beyond their own and could easily capture them if they did run, which would be a negative portrayal of their character. It was best to masquerade as representatives from Earth's welcoming committee, then learn all they could about the visitors. Sally had played the part of diplomat brilliantly and in the end Heather had demonstrated superiority with her ability and compassion by not taking the lives of their adversaries after escaping.

The next day, still recovering from the shock of Sally's sudden disappearance, the remaining Guardians set about to find a way of rescuing Sally. Heather had left her request for a meeting with Lee on her dresser top. They were all thirsting for more knowledge on the subject of this time travelling crystal skull. Stealing information from the Wizard's library of scrolls and books would be a logical start so they began organizing a covert mission to do so.

When a week had gone by, Heather had grown stronger as had Lana who now had dark blue eyes like Heather and was transitioning rapidly. In another week Lana would receive her special ability which would be different from Heather's and Sally's. Lee had a quick meeting with Heather and scheduled another meeting in two weeks' time so that he could work out a method for contacting Sally.

Mitch and Zen had returned the scrolls to Azorka's hall of records. Omar's mission was heralded as a great success and he went down in Azorka's history as one of this civilization's great Guardians during the year 8,312 BC.

Aleko was never seen or heard of again, despite the efforts of search parties arranged by Omar. Aleko's manuscript was published almost immediately. What this extremely popular councilor had learned in the Middle East was available to all the people of Azorka and was included in the school curriculum.

Sally had not read enough of Omar's scroll to know that the golden the skull was waiting for three special words to be spoken before the portal could open up and return Sally to 1688.

We will learn more about Sally's experience in the next "Adventure in Ancient Azorka".

About the Author

I enjoyed a career in the Plastics Industry for twenty-two years, believing that I was saving trees, by producing vinyl siding for homes. During the time I worked for this large multi-national organization I was offered the opportunity to attend college, fully paid for by my employer. I successfully completed my courses in Marketing, Business Psychology, Sales, Management in Industry. Unfortunately, by 1995, the protective layers of our atmosphere were breaking down and plastic designed to weather and maintain its color outdoors was fading from more intense UV rays from the sun. Today our trees, the most precious resource on this planet, are facing extinction from climate change.

I developed more respect for our environmentalists fighting for change.

In 2017, I was concerned about the conflict between Russia and Ukraine. If we had a neutral committee organizing meetings and proposing solutions, perhaps the conflict would never have boiled over into the horrific consequences of war.

I believe that as a civilization, we need to have more respect for God, our planet and ourselves.

I hope to appeal to a younger generation, with my creation of two advanced societies fighting for dominance, in order to solve the problems of a world developing a lust and passion for war.

9 781961 117570